# BRANDED

The Dragon's Game
BOOK II

## H. N. Henry

Presse Dragon Libre
Free Dragon's Press

Trois-Rivières, QC, Canada

**FREE DRAGON'S PRESS**
**Huard, Norman Henry**
**220 B Farmer**
**Trois-Rivières, Québec, Canada, G9A 3E6**
**www.hnhenry.com**

Publisher's Note: This is a work of fiction. Names, characters, places, and incidents are a product of the author's imagination, except for his use of the Cree language in Roman orthography to number and title chapters and as one of the languages spoken by certain characters; and also for his use of certain Tai Chi exercise names. Locales and public names are sometimes used for atmospheric purposes. Any resemblance to actual people, living or dead, or to businesses, companies, events, institutions, or locales is completely coincidental.

Book Layout © 2014 BookDesignTemplates.com

**BRANDED The Dragon's Game BOOK II by H. N. Henry**—1st edition

ISBN 978-0-9958367-4-7

Dedication

To my son, Lennon.

*There is no witness so terrible and no accuser so powerful as conscience which dwells within us.*

—SOPHOCLES

# CHAPTERS

From BANISHED
Book I
The Dragon's Game

*Legend tells us dragons fly so high they can see the future.*

*Reason tells us that to know the future is a curse.*

*Our hearts tell us the seeds of hope are sown in the reality of the present.*

— † —

# Taken
## *Kâcitinew*

— † —

*Reality tells us that to lose hope is to welcome death.*

— † —

Back then, dragons no longer flew over the sad Land of the Danu, but the one that hoped to fly in those skies again watched over Nagora with pride. Almost a year earlier, Nagora, as lone wolf-warrior Edana, had brought hope to the people of the Land of the Dragon. In doing so, Nagora rekindled that dragon's hope for freedom.

On the shore of Sandy Hook Bay, the young maiden, Nagora, close to her eighteenth birthday, looked more like a young man tarring the stitched seams of one of the small leather boats she built with her uncle, Dangor.

...

"Tar piss!" Nagora waved her left hand to cool the liquid tar that had run onto her fingers. She could have jabbed them into the sand, but years of spreading tar on curragh seams had taught her it was a waste of time. She would have to clean the sand from her fingers. The tar would go cold. Her uncle, Dangor, would have to reheat his special tar mix on the fire. No. Better I endure the burning sensation, wipe my fingers on my work shirt, and keep at it. Besides, I'm almost done.

The wind had picked up, turned cold, and rain clouds were building, thus the urgency to work with hotter tar than usual and finish the job. Not the ideal conditions for tarring, but do-able, although the risk of tar burns was greater. I can take it.

Nagora stuck her wooden spoon into the copper pot of hot tar and pulled it out, careful to scrape the bottom of it along the lip of the pot. She repositioned her knees on the sand and set the curragh's edge on her thighs. As she leaned over the last seam, she blew on the molten tar. She watched the tiny dark brown waves in the spoon, and when they changed to the proper shape, she poured the tar in a line along the seam. At the right temperature the tar flowed on fast, keeping its initial bulge for a moment before its outer edges spread and sank into the surrounding cow hide to create a strong flexible bond across the seam. Perfect. Done.

Nagora dropped the spoon back into the big shell that rested on the sand at her side. She leaned back on both hands, closed her eyes, and slowly rotated her head to ease the dull pain in her neck muscles.

"Nice work, Nagora. Couldn't have done it better myself." Dangor's compliment made her open her eyes and look over at him. His smile was warm on his tired face. Her uncle too had worked hard.

"Thanks. You look how I feel. We've been at this since the ice left the bay, building all those frames, hauling and hanging hides in the hut, then stretching and sewing them to the frames." Nagora pushed herself forward, slapped the drum tight skin of the curragh, and lifted it off her thighs before turning back to her uncle. "We've delivered most of them. These are the last three. What's with all this work? Are you trying to make up for my not helping you last summer? We've never made this many in a spring season."

Dangor's smile turned into a crooked grin and a wink. He dropped his gaze as he spilled forest tea leaves into the cooking pot on the fire. "Some tea?"

"No, no, Dangor." Nagora had taken to calling her uncle by his name when she wanted to get information out of him. It seemed to work most times. Would it now? "If I didn't know better I'd say we're building a fleet of war ships for the Cause. But I don't see the fishers we've sold them to do battle in them. You seem to be on a schedule of some kind. You haven't pushed me to go train with the other warriors in Cairnmase. As a matter of fact, you haven't been there as an instructor since early spring. Something's up with the Cause."

Dangor's eyes shot up to hers then back to the pot he stirred.

"That's it, isn't it? Finally! Something's in the works, and you won't tell me what!" Nagora shook her head and rolled her eyes.

Dangor smiled wide as he looked back at her and kept stirring.

There's that twinkle in his eyes. I'm getting close. "I'm not stupid, you know. I had plenty of time last year on my way back to look at that chain with all the coded numbers the eleven smithies stamped on their links. Many a night I spent by the fire turning it over in my hands and examining each link. It only makes sense that the code is about the number of rebels in those cells and the number and kinds of weapons they have. I'm right, aren't I?"

"You're not stupid. You're right about the coded information. As to the exact numbers from each cell, well, if you have that figured out, I'd have to say you're in Geirador's head." The smile left his face as he tilted his head and stared at her.

Does he want me to give him numbers? I've worked out possibilities based on what I've seen going on in Cairnmase, but they're only guesses. "I won't give you a number, but I will say that if each cell has trained fighters for the Cause, then we," here she paused to stress the next word, "might be able to mount a credible attack on Queen Raganora's force and her mercenaries." Nagora raised a finger, "But it'll have to be very well planned."

Dangor leaned his head to the other side and did not change his expression.

Keep digging. "Since I returned the chain last year, every time we go to Cairnmase, you spend your time alone with Geirador. And you two always have these solemn looks on your faces when you come back into Geirador's lodge and sit at the table. Those looks only change when Pare sets food on the table. Something is about to happen soon. The uprising is coming, isn't it?" Was that a nod or a sign of resignation that what I spoke holds truth?

Dangor licked his upper lip and poured tea into the two bowls next to his knee on the sand. When his eyes came back to hers he spoke. "I'll not deny revolt is on the wind. It's close, but other details remain to be looked into. Until they are, I can't say a word. Trust me. You'll know soon." Dangor leaned forward and handed her a bowl of tea.

Nagora held the bowl with both hands, letting its warmth seep into her palms and fingers as she brought it to her lips to blow on it. Dangor did likewise and kept his eyes on hers. That's all the information I'll get today. Uncle and Geirador must've been in contact with the rightful king. They surely know what the plan is. Soon. He said I'd know soon. I can wait. She took a sip of the hot tea and stared past her uncle to the growing waves splashing onto her beach.

This had been a place where she played as she grew up, where she trained with Dangor, and where she worked with him. Last year she had missed most of the summer here. Nagora had been banished for a hundred days for actions against the Cause, but, thanks to her skills, she was entrusted with a mission for the Cause. Could I ever have imagined the events of those hundred days? No. Though, now, I swear I was destined to follow that path. What path will I be set on? Will it be with the revolt? Will I play a part in it? Will I have a choice?

Nagora's right hand reached for the amulet that hung from her neck.

Dangor was still watching her.

No, Uncle. I won't pester you about the amulet. In almost six years I haven't. What you told me I believe is true. Yes, it has powers. What they are exactly, I don't know. I think one is a gift of a language strange to me yet that I understand when it speaks in my mind as if I've always known it. It started by calling me by a name, *Ka Peyakot Mahihkan*, Lone Wolf. Why does that voice call me Lone Wolf?

It makes me feel good. I feel stronger when I think of myself as Lone Wolf in that language. Stronger, but not as in control as when I think of myself as Nagora in our Danuian language. When I speak those strange words they're familiar in my mouth, like the words of a song, like the ones I sing to Storm. "*Tastapiw sohkapiskaw kaskitewastim*, my 'strong, swift, dark horse.'" I love the sound of those words. They don't come out awkward like when I speak the Coastal Trader's tongue and I struggle to get by with the help of a few hand signs.

As *Ka Peyakot Mahihkan* I feel I'm at the service of that strange voice I hear. Is that why I feel my path has been drawn for me?

Dangor emptied his bowl and stood. "Finish your tea. We'll move the curragh alongside the other."

Together, Nagora and her uncle carried the leather-skinned vessel above the high water mark and set it down hull-side up next to its twin so the seams could dry in the sun. Dangor looked to the sky. "No sun until midday tomorrow when this blows over. It'll rain most of the night. Can you pull the curragh you tested this morning higher up on the beach and make sure the anchor's set? I'll douse the fire and put away the pots and spoons."

"Sure."

Nagora hauled on the curragh's anchor rode to bring the small craft away from the growing waves climbing onto the beach. She set one of the four shovel-like prongs of the killick into the damp sand a stride from the high water mark.

Dangor preferred to make these small anchors from two hardwood planks, four fingers in width and the length of half an arm. Each had four holes near their middles. Through these he threaded long thumb-thick roots so the planks crossed to form a platform for a rock, and the four root stems formed a cage to hold that rock in place. The rock gave the anchor its weight. Simple and efficient. The waves won't take it away.

Nagora carried the oars to the hut before joining her uncle at the base of the cliff trail.

Dangor placed a hand on Nagora's shoulder as they began their climb up the path to the meadow at the top of the cliffs. "We put in a good day's work. Tomorrow will be a good change of pace. Cormack will load bags of coal in our wagon for Geirador. While I do that you can shop for a gift for Paruline at the market. There should be plenty of traveling merchants hawking their wares."

Nagora smiled at the prospect of the party. "Pare's birthday. She's going to be twenty-five. I hope I can find something special. That weaver who came to market two years ago might be back. His linen was so fine and the choice of colors from his spun threads was beyond belief. I'd never seen such variety. If he's there, I know what I'll get Pare. Oh! And he had pots and pots of nacre buttons in all sizes. I'll get her some of those too."

Before her uncle took the lead up the steepest part of the path he stopped. "We'll do our best to get to Yhorgal early tomorrow. You're right. That weaver comes every two years. He stays until his wagon is empty of wares. You'll want to get the best choice. Then we'll be off to Cairnmase for Paruline's party."

Nagora grabbed Dangor's sleeve. "Will we stay the night? Please. Can we?"

He smiled. "That's the plan. Wear a dress tomorrow and bring a change of clothes so you two can go riding the day after."

"Can we bring Storm?"

Dangor shook his head. "No. Geirador'll let you ride any one of his horses. You've trained on most of them and haven't ridden them in a while. They're probably jealous of your Storm. Besides, you know what it's like for any riders going into Yhorgal. Soon as you cross the bridge, you'd have to leave Storm at that horse line with soldiers from the prince's fortress."

Nagora spit. "True. I won't risk having Storm disappear now that we have our own stable. We've heard too many of those stories since the prince's arrival. Do I have to wear a dress?"

Dangor pointed a finger to his head. "Think. You don't look like a man, but you don't want to give those soldiers a reason to search you for weapons because you're dressed like one. Remember what happened the last two times. Lucky I was with you. Tomorrow you'll be shopping on your own if we're to make it to the party on time."

Visits to Yhorgal had changed since the prince's arrival to take up residence at the rebuilt fortress at Yhorgal Cliffs. The armed soldiers posted throughout the town seemed to always be on the lookout for an excuse to pull someone over for questioning.

Carrying an unstrung bow and quiver on one's back is now out of the question. No swords or knives either. Uncle was right last year when he said evil would make its way to our part of the land. It had come with the prince and was manifesting itself.

The next morning, as Nagora took the steps down from the weaver's wagon, she was happy her uncle had kept his word to bring her early to the market in Yhorgal. Now there was a line of women waiting for their turn in the wagon. The colorful flags of fabric hanging from the open shutters of the wide caravan allowed them to sample what they would find inside.

The weaver had assured her he sold, "... only the finest quality linen made from stream-retted, sun-dried, sun-combed, and yes, lass, even sun-spun flax." Nagora chose the palest bolt of linen in the wagon, set it on the cutting table near the open door of the weaver's wagon, and asked him to cut a piece long enough for a thigh-length shirt and a headscarf. To add to that, while the weaver cut her length from the bolt, she found skeins of embroidery thread: six of green, three of yellow, and three of blue.

"You'll want buttons," said the little baldheaded man as he spilt oval-shaped nacre buttons onto her piece of cloth next to her chosen skeins. "New this year, this shape and only in this size, and mind you, lass," he pointed to two of them, "each one is the same size, and not a chipped one among them. Smooth edge all around each one. Perfect for a lady's shirt. Their iridescent colors will complement the embroidery skeins you chose." He was right. Nagora chose a dozen oval buttons. Pare will be happy.

Not knowing what to pay, she dropped the four coins she had been holding in her palm onto the table. To her it represented a month's pay her uncle gave her. With a grand smile the weaver swept them up, dropped them into the purse at his waist, and set to wrapping the skeins and buttons inside her length of cloth. He folded it into a neat, compact package which he pinned closed with two stiff, shiny, bronze needles. With fingers on the needles and a smile on his face, the weaver pushed the packet toward her and said, "A wee gift to remind you of my return in two years."

"Thank you." Nagora returned his smile. I'll have to ask Uncle if the price was fair. No matter. It's worth it for Pare.

Nagora was happy with her purchase and how the weaver had wrapped it, but not happy with forgetting to wear her scrip. It seemed to happen every time she wore her dress. The scrip, because of what it contained, was always a part of her other outfit. No need of flint, fire starter, spare bowstring, or a whetstone today.

Nagora held her package in one strong, tar-stained hand as she looked down at her simple, flax-colored linen dress. Now where can I put Pare's gift? Her other hand ran up along the buttons of her forest green, woven, woolen tunic. Maybe I can stick it in the bodice for now. Tar piss! Just carry it. Don't drop it and mind where you step so you don't cover your feet in mud.

The sun had come out and warmed the damp air. Nagora untied the knot of her white headscarf at the back of her neck and lifted it away from her wavy, black hair which she had gathered and tied earlier with a fine, leather lanyard. Nagora held her parcel with her teeth as she folded her scarf in two and draped it over her shoulders.

Nagora picked and danced her way through the crowd along the wooden planks that stretched over the mud in front of the vendors' stalls and wagons. Her leather slippers were already damp from doing that as water, squeezed from the mud beneath the boards, puddled onto the tops of them.

Nagora headed toward the sound of the music on the other side of the square, hoping to capture a new tune she could commit to memory to play on her flute at Pare's party. Dangor was supposed to find her on that side of the square.

Nagora joined the other eager onlookers near the wooden platform of the musicians. The lute player was strumming unaccompanied. His smiling eyes had followed Nagora to the stone she now stood on. But as soon as the lute player's eyes looked past Nagora, he lost his smile. Trouble had approached. Before she could react, it was upon her. A soldier grasped her left arm and spun her around. His grip was like a large belt being buckled tight around her arm.

Then his companion clamped onto her right arm. Her hand held tight the packet she carried. She struggled to free herself. "Let go of me!" Tar piss! What's going on? They held her tighter and reached for her wrists. She kicked out at them, twisted and turned to bite them. "Let me go! What do you want of me?" Her scarf fell from her shoulders, now lost to the mud.

They dragged Nagora along, fending off her kicks with their raised boots. Her flailing legs and feet flew over the ground. As she strained against their hold, she searched the faces of the crowd around her for her uncle.

Tar piss! What do they want with me? The tiny voice she hated, taunted. You let your guard down. You said you never would. Never again. To shut it up she twisted and turned one way and then the other and kicked out. Damn dress! I shouldn't have worn it. Can't land a decent kick!

"We've got a live one here," one guard said as they brought her to the line-up before their commander. They held her off the ground as she jerked her whole body and kicked at them.

"Let go of me!"

One soldier stung the back of her head with a vicious slap. "Settle down or the next one'll put you out."

Nagora obeyed and took her place in the line-up with the other girls. Her eyes blinked away tears as she searched the gathering crowd. Her chest heaved with her incoming breaths through her clenched teeth as she contracted her arm muscles. The guards did not loosen their grip on her, and she did not loosen her grip on her small bundle.

The commander spoke the same question to each girl. "Are you a virgin?" All people within earshot in the Yhorgal town square could hear. When one girl hesitated, the commander slapped her face with the back of his gloved hand and repeat-ed the question so loud everyone in the square must've heard. She cried out, "Yes!"

"We'll see about that soon enough," growled the com-mander. Some of his men laughed.

...

Before the commander could get to Nagora, Dangor cleared his throat loudly. Nagora let her muscles relax. He must've pushed his way through the crowd. She looked right, then left, and saw him next to the guard who held her left arm.

There you are. Now what?

Dangor stepped forward and spoke to the commander. "Pardon me, sir. What business do you have with these young girls?"

She had kept her eyes on her uncle, but he had not acknowledged her. He did, however, make a subtle hand signal, which she read—Bide your time.

I can do that.

The commander gave Dangor a quick look up and down. "Hold him. Tie his hands and bring him along."

Oh! No! Not Uncle too!

He remained calm and offered no resistance.

The commander continued his questioning of the other girls. They all answered yes. And so did Nagora.

Twelve of us. Is the prince still searching for a virgin bride? Is that what this is about? Now our prince of a pig will want to take his pick from among us.

The prince's men had come prepared with twelve pairs of shackles attached to a single length of chain. The two soldiers who held her did not let go until they had locked her wrists in.

Virgin brides? No, we're a herd of heifers.

The commander and his men marched them out of the square through the narrow village street, which led to the road of the prince's fortress. None in the square dared to complain.

Instead, they cowered and grumbled amongst themselves. What else could they do but submit?

*Is this to be my end? Will the prince recognize me somehow? If I'd had a clear shot that day at the docks in Windhaven, he would never have showed up here last winter.*

Nagora pieced together what she had learned. So it was true. Queen Raganora hadn't been able to find a bride for her son among the daughters of her allies. And evidently she had had enough of his cruel monthly death game with the virgins at the Temple of Fire. So she had sent him and her witch, Hag, here, far from her. *Why send Hag too?*

For years, the people in this far part of the land had lived, mostly away from the evils that camped in many of the bigger towns of the land. Almost a year ago, she had seen it in those towns, over and over again—the unjust tributes demanded of the farmers, tradespeople, and merchants.

And the forced carrying out of the queen's decrees to deface and remove all traces of dragon images and sculptures.

And the prince's cruel, unjust murder of Maton and Ilma. Maton was her age; his sister, just turned twelve. Both were forced into an empty wine barrel. Hungry people driving nails into the barrel for a food reward. The barrel rolling down the streets from the castle to the harbor wharf. Bile rose in her throat. The image of their bloodied bodies torn from the barrel shook her. Nagora spit.

*Tar piss! Now it's our turn to suffer the prince's evil ways.* When her son was four, Queen Raganora had begun to build the timber fortress upon the ruins of the ancient stone castle at Yhorgal Cliffs. Rumors were that she wanted him out of her sight, even then. Somehow, he had stayed put in the castle at Windhaven.

Perhaps this was because his mother spent most of each year in her fortress on the Isle of Smoke, off limits to her own son. And she only wintered in Windhaven. What had Queen Raganora said to Prince Acindor? "If you wish to rule this country someday, go rule your domain. Find a bride. Produce a male heir."

Nagora spit on the ground. You don't rule with terror. You don't find a bride with terror. If I ever have a hand in this, you'll never produce an heir.

Most of the girls ahead of her were in tears. Why did their parents submit to the prince's wishes? They're powerless. They can do nothing and will do nothing for their daughters. The only thing they can do is hope she'll be chosen by the prince to be his bride. Then maybe they can, in some small way, benefit from the prince's kindness.

Ha! No! Not his kindness. His cruelty. Yes, count on it. If only your parents knew, would they stand up to this tyrant? Sorry, girls, I have nothing to say to comfort you.

Uncle, do you expect me to submit? You know I won't.

She had escaped the evil prince's hunt last summer, just. Today, his snare held her.

As they left the last of the onlookers behind them, an old woman said, "Pity the poor man who goes to intercede on behalf of his daughter. May he live to see the outside of the fortress again and not go to the stars."

Uncle, if there's one thing you taught me, it's to be strong. I know you are. I'll try to be.

With the town behind them, the chain of virgins entered the woodland road that would bring them to the prince's fortress on Yhorgal Cliffs. The commander yelled an order to his men to pick up the pace. The condition of the road, which was still wet from the long night of rain, didn't help matters. Shackled as they were to the chain, the girls in their slippered feet had no traction in the mud. Their efforts to walk faster only brought on slipping and sliding and loss of balance. It wouldn't be long before one took a fall.

A girl ahead of Nagora stumbled and fell, bringing two others with her. In the time they took to get to their feet, the chain went slack.

Nagora reached for her amulet and held it for a moment. Tars appeared in her mind. He brought her comfort. Last year Dangor had given her a task, had asked if she could take on the appearance of a boy and act like one. She had chosen to become Tars. She had succeeded in that task. Would Tars help her today? She just had to ask.

Tars, what does the prince have in store for us today? Eyewitnesses had testified that the rebel, known as Edana, had been killed. They had her bow and quiver as proof. But that dead body in the river gorge wasn't mine. Was it, Tars? We made it home. Gone a hundred days. We brought the chain back for the Cause. Task done. Me as you. Back home and no one the wiser. Prince Acindor can't pin anything on me.

But she would most likely face Hag. Remember, Tars, when I met her on the Twin Rivers Bridge? I thought she saw me as who I truly was and not as you. Tars, will she recognize me today? She'll be looking at a young woman, not a young man, like on the bridge. Maybe if she has her magic staff with the amber stone and the silver snakes that hold it. She didn't have it on the bridge though. So I think I'll be good.

Well tars, I'm not headed to Cairnmase with the gift I bought for Paruline. This won't be the party I was expecting, aye, Tars? Is this to be my star story? Her stomach churned.

The line was moving again, even slower now. The commander, in exasperation, had left his men behind with the virgins. The stretch of road, lined with tall spruce that closed out the rays of the midday sun, seemed to have pulled a sullen veil of quiet over the girls. What frightening thoughts are they lost in? Are the rumors about the prince's hunt for a virgin bride true? We'll find out soon enough.

The forest on each side of the road thinned to bushes and shrubs as the fortress, with its open gate, stood to greet the guarded virgins. A boulder-strewn field of short, coarse grass lay as an ugly carpet at the edge of the fortress wall.

The remaining ancient stone ruins of Yhorgal Castle had been converted into a timber fortress with lumber from giant trees logged on the Isle of Smoke. From Nagora's spot in the line, the last standing corner the castle's stone wall seemed to cling to the new timber walls like an old torn flag.

The fortress seems to sit on the edge of the sky. How high must that cliff be, Tars?

As they reached the gate, the whimpers and cries of a few of the girls returned. Others looked back, eyes wide with fear. Tars, they must be wondering, like me, if they'll ever see the outside again. Stay with me, Tars.

In the fortress courtyard, with his gloved hands on hips, the commander stood on worn cobblestones. He pointed to the water troughs near the hitching posts next to the nearby wall.

"Unshackle the girls. Bring them to the troughs. Have them rinse the muck away. The ones with muddied dresses go first, from one trough to the next. Then stand them barefoot near the stairs, their cleaned slippers in hand."

Guards on the wall lowered the timber gate as those escorting the virgins released them from their cuffs on the chain and lined them up at the end of the first trough.

The commander pointed to Dangor. "Bring him here."

The guards had tied Dangor's hands behind his back. They shoved him forward. Dangor remained passive, bowed to the captain, and kept his eyes lowered.

"What's your name?"

"Dangor, sir."

"Is your daughter among these girls?"

Nagora dared to glance at her uncle and bend her ear to his answers.

"No, sir." True. I'm his niece, like a daughter to him. He raised me as his own.

He doesn't want to draw any more attention to me than I already have.

The captain took a step closer to Dangor. "Then what is your concern for my business with these girls?"

"Begging your pardon, sir, none. I did once serve under the king many years ago in the battles against the invading Outlanders. Among the captured Outlanders were many women and children. Our king, sir, had ordered us to treat them with the utmost respect."

The captain leaned his head to one side. "Why was that?"

"'To better be able to make them honest citizens of our fair land,' was what the king said, sir."

"How is this related to your concern today?"

"It's the question of respect of the prince's subjects, sir. I once volunteered my life for my king when our country was in need because he respected his subjects. To my knowledge, so does my prince, the dead king's son. The way your men were treating these young women, sir, made me wonder."

The captain raised his chin and looked down his nose at Dangor. "How do you earn your living now that you're no longer in the forces?"

"Sir." Dangor turned to show his tar-stained hands and callused fingers. "With these hands I make coracles and curraghs used by the fishermen in these parts and far along the coast to catch fish for my prince and for his subjects."

The captain raised an eyebrow as he examined and flexed the fingers of his gloved hands. "You will have another job, Dangor, maker of curraghs. You will be briefed on how Prince Acindor's search for a virgin bride here is going. After they've been questioned by the prince, you'll go back to the villagers and report to them what has become of their so-called virgin daughters. In the meantime," the captain looked to his men and pointed, "put him in irons and chain him to that wall."

"Sir." Dangor bowed, and the guards led him to one of the iron rings on the wall of the fortress.

Again, Nagora caught the bide-your-time signal. *Uncle, I don't like this.*

By the time Nagora had had her turn in the troughs and, with wet slippers in hand, joined the other girls, guards from inside the fortress had come down the stairs to surround them. Nagora had tucked Paruline's gift inside the bodice of her tunic. She had been careful not to let it fall in the troughs. Some of the girls held their sides and shivered. Others fought back their tears. One of the guards walked down the line and handed each girl a clean rag. "Dry your feet and slippers."

While the commander watched them, he pulled at the tight leather fingers of his gloves until they were free of his hands. He held them in a fist behind his back. When the girls finished putting their slippers on, he slapped his gloves against his thigh. "Bring the virgins inside."

The fortress guards led the girls, some still in tears, down a hall into a large room with five armed guards, two at each of its doors and one, standing in the middle, who greeted them.

The greeter pointed. "You'll find water at those tables. Combs and brushes near the mirrors on that wall. Get ready. The prince will call for you soon." The soldier pointed to Nagora. "You will go first."

Nagora stood motionless as she took in his words. First to the slaughter? Don't think that way. The faces of the girls who looked at her showed a brief sign of relief as they moved past her to the wash basins and mirrors.

Nagora took a deep breath and stepped in the direction of the bench. She pulled Paruline's gift from her tunic, and unpinned one of the embroidery needles from the folded packet. For the moment, she pinned it to the inside of her tunic, leaving the gift on the bench. Three girls younger than her occupied the other end of the long seat, two rocking with hands pressed between their knees, the third biting a thumb nail.

Pare, perhaps your gift will be here when I come back. If I come back. I've got a feeling I'll miss your party.

...

Nagora crossed to a mirror on the wall and squeezed into a space next to a few of the other girls. Her face was clean, her hands not, so she went to a basin at the narrow table on the adjacent wall to wash them. She shared the piece of soap with another girl who kept wiping her runny nose on her sleeve. As Nagora dried her callused hands on a cloth, their tar stains stared back at her. At least you are clean stains.

Nagora returned to the mirror, untied the fine leather lanyard that held her hair, picked up a brush, and pulled it through her hair so it fell below her shoulders. Two girls next to her were busy brushing each other's hair. They must be friends. They can support each other. She leaned to the right and made a tight braid, bringing it up, over, and under at the back of her neck where she tied the end of the braid with the leather lace. She then concealed the needle in the knot just behind her ear.

Without my blades, Tars, I won't be able to put up a decent fight. She only had a needle and her dagger strapped to the inside of her thigh.

Tars, had I been wearing my leggings instead of this dress and tunic, I might've been able to land a good kick and break free from those guards. I'm to bide my time to wait for what, an occasion to escape? To be released from questioning?

None of the girls in the room were familiar. Most were younger than her. Some, most likely, had not seen their own first blood. Would the prince choose her? If he did, she would make him regret it. Lesser men desired something else. Pug had taught her that. Would the prince want her virgin blood? Probably part of your disgusting games with virgins.

Prince Acindor didn't keep Nagora waiting.

A skinny, one-eyed woman dressed in black, who barely looked at her, accompanied the soldier who came to get her.

They led her out the door opposite the one she had come in.

As the door closed behind them, the soldier pointed Nagora down the long hallway. A simpleton limped ahead of them, paused near a guarded door, and turned to look at Nagora for a moment. The sentry at the door shoved him on his way. The door of the chamber opened, and the guard stepped aside.

A tall man dressed in black with a trimmed mustache and beard and shoulder-length black hair stepped into the hallway and paused in front of her. With one hand resting on the pommel of his silver handled sword, his cold, dark eyes looked into hers as he reached for her chin with a gentle hand.

Its touch helped convince Nagora she was right not to strike him.

On his hand he wore a human-hand-bone bracelet. Her eyes focused on the bones spread over the back of the man's own fingers, hand, and wrist as he turned her face to the left and then to the right. Silver wire loops held them together and attached them to all the silver rings he wore on each of his fingers and thumb, and to the silver bracelet on his wrist. All the pale bones of the skeletal hand flexed with each movement of the man's hand.

Moreena's story about what Hag had done to her mother flashed in Nagora's mind.

The man's black eyes were like the lifeless holes in a skull. The smell of death rose from the bones on his hand. Let those bones not be the ones I fear they might be.

He let go of her chin and looked back into the room. "Acindor, I envy you in your task of finding a virgin bride. I would truly enjoy watching, but I must be on my way. The smoke of the candles works its magic and soon there will be a throne at play. Then we'll meet another day." He bowed and turned to leave down the hall.

One-eye waited. Words Nagora did not understand came from beyond the doorway. It must've been a command. One-eye led her into the prince's chamber.

She pushed Nagora to the center of the room. The woman closed the door before standing back to it with arms crossed, her hands hidden in her sleeves. Nagora followed the gaze of the woman's single eye. It led her to the prince. His back was to her as he looked out the window. Nagora's eyes went to the bed on the adjacent wall. It was bigger than any she had ever imagined.

Hag was sitting in a chair near the wall on the other side of the bed. Tar piss! A chill drop of sweat crept down her back. Hag's beady eyes in her wrinkled face stared at Nagora from behind wisps of white hair. The bony fingers of her two ancient hands clutched a wooden staff, inlaid with the pattern of three intertwining silver snakes climbing to the staff's top where their open mouths met to hold an egg-shaped amber stone. She pulled herself up with the help of her staff. Hag wore a garment of black save for the red silk scarf, which wrapped around the palms of her hands and disappeared into the sleeves of her cloak to reappear wrapped three times around her neck.

Hag tapped her staff on the stone floor. "Call in the guards."

One-eye opened the door.

As Hag approached, she locked eyes with Nagora.

The guards came in and stood just behind Nagora, to the right and left of her.

Hag leaned her staff in toward Nagora. "Hold her."

The guards gripped her forearms and held them tight behind her back.

The prince turned from the window. As he approached, his gaze took her in from head to foot.

Nagora's breathing increased. Easy now. Don't lose it. You're not in position to strike at him, not matter how much you want to punish him for all his evil you witnessed in Windhaven.

His fat belly seemed to lead him to her.

To slit you open would be too sweet a vengeance for my friends.

Did his close-set, frog-like eyes want to jump out, or would they just fall out of their sockets if she hit him hard enough?

No, I wouldn't hit you. My blade could carve one out first so the other could watch in terror at what was to come.

His long, thin-beaked nose kept his eyes separated.

I could hack that off so it wouldn't get in the way.

He had more hair in his black bushy eyebrows, mustache, and beard than on his head.

He pursed his lips over buck teeth, which stuck out like a gable roof peak. His lower teeth leaned out like shovel blades.

I'd have you guess what I'd hack off and stuff into your mouth.

Without leaving Nagora's gaze, the prince spoke to his witch. "Is she the one?"

When he spoke, his lips moved over his teeth, opening and closing like a fish, causing him to speak through his nose. After those few words, the tip of his tongue snuck out from behind his lips to wet them with spittle while he breathed in through his nose.

Hag stepped closer, and the prince stepped aside. She lowered her staff. Its amber head, seen from head on, looked like an eye. Hag directed it between Nagora's legs. "She is armed. Strip her."

In no time the guards stripped off Nagora's tunic, dress, and simple linen shift. Now she stood naked with her amulet around her neck and her knife sheath strapped to her inner left thigh. This is what happens when I bide my time, Tars.

The prince pulled the knife from its sheath and pressed the tip to her thigh, letting it linger for a moment before dragging it up her hip bone and across to her navel, and holding it there as he looked her in the eye.

Nagora held her breath.

Then he dragged the tip of the blade up her abdomen, barely scratching her skin to stop pointed between her breasts. The amulet rested on one side of the blade where a tiny drop of blood beaded crimson on her skin.

"Do not harm her, Acindor." Hag's command came from the back of her throat.

"Why, Hag? She obviously has come with the intent to do me harm."

"She did not come here of her free will. She is one of many you had the captain of your guard fetch for you. See the amulet she wears. She has power and if she dies at your hand, you will suffer endless days of misery."

"Am I to let her go so she may live to try again to harm me?"

"Acindor, do as I say or suffer the consequences." Each word was heavy with warning.

Prince Acindor leaned back. "What power does she have?" Before Hag could answer, he leaned closer. "What power do you have, fair maiden?" He grabbed the knot of hair behind her ear. "SHIT!" He jerked his hand away.

The prince held his hand before his face. His eyes crossed as they stared at the needle protruding from the side of his thumb. "FUCK!" He struck Nagora with all his might across her mouth with the back of his other hand. "You little bitch!"

In a momentary flash of stars, Hag's white-haired profile transform into a black-haired beauty as she reached for the prince's hand with a red silk-wrapped hand and yelled at him, "Acindor! No! Stop! You've done enough!" In the time Nagora blinked away her tears, Hag's pale bony thumb and finger had reached for the prince's hand, grabbed the needle, and pulled it from his thumb.

And in that same moment, in her mind, the expression, *kiskwehkan iskwew*, "witch," echoed as it had almost a year ago when it had given her warning of Hag's approach on that bridge. Are you warning me again?

"SHIT!" Prince Acindor put his thumb to his mouth and sucked at the blood drops of his wound. "You bitch! You little bitch!" He spit the insults at her between sucks on his thumb. "You will die for this."

Hag pushed the prince back with her staff "Not by your hand. She has the power to do you great harm."

Nagora licked at the blood trickling from the side of her lower lip. She kept her eyes on the prince, glaring at him. Count your days! I'll do more than great harm to you. She took a deep breath. "I know not of what power this old woman speaks."

Hag reached for the prince's arm. "She wears the amulet that bears the power of the dragon. Look, but do not touch it."

*Kanawisimowin,* "amulet," another strange yet familiar word entered her mind.

Prince Acindor bent his face closer to her chest, ogling her breasts more than the amulet. Still sucking his thumb, he backed away. "What if I cut it from her neck and throw it away?" The way you say that tells me you'd just as soon cut my neck and throw me away.

Hag shook her head. "You risk certain death."

The prince glared at Nagora. "Why then, Hag, can I not kill her?"

Hag ignored his question and turned to Nagora. "How long have you had the amulet?"

"For as long as I can remember." That was true.

"Since you were a young child?"

"Since I was born I've been told." That also was true.

"Are your parents alive?"

"My mum died giving birth to me." True. "My da died at sea." A lie. Good as true since I've never known him.

Would one truth hide one falsehood?

Hag's face came closer. "You are a lone wolf."

*Ka Peyakot Mahihkan.* Yes, Lone Wolf is my name. How Nagora was certain about this was beyond her comprehension. Last year she had asked herself if her mother had given her that name before dying. That thought had comforted her just as it did now, and, for a moment, it made her brave.

Hag backed away and held the amber stone of her staff above Nagora's head. "Only the pure of heart can have and hold this amulet. She is so pure she knows not of its power yet. Today, she will discover the responsibility that comes with bearing the power of the dragon."

The word, *isihtwawin*, came to Nagora. I am "gifted?" Then, *ayi nikcikaw paskwaskisiw*, "the distant shadow shoots fire." The shadow's shape—a dragon! Their meanings were clear as she spoke them in her mind, as if she had always known them and they were part of her.

Why are all these words coming into my mind? On that bridge, Hag, you read my future with your rune tiles. You whispered in my ear, "Child, a dragon awaits you." Is that why you fear me?

"What is this dragon power?" The prince turned to the window, placing his thumb in his mouth.

"Powers secret and unimaginable. Upon your father's death, the queen imprisoned the last dragon and its master rider in the vent hole beneath her fortress on the Isle of Smoke. On that day, the dragon's wings were bound as it was forced into a cage and lowered in the vent hole, to be confined to the cave below with its rider."

*Wacikâpahkitek.* Nagora spoke this word too in her mind, "exploding mountain." It was so familiar, just like the first time it had come to her a year ago. Voice, are you trying to tell me something?

"On that day, fire and smoke spit from the Isle of Smoke. With the ash, molten stones containing blood tears of the dragon were cast forth. The Dragon Master's friends collected those stones. They formed a secret society sworn to free the dragon. Its members wear amulets like this one, bestowed with powers that allow them to manipulate fire to their own ends."

Tar piss! Not that I'm aware of. The word, *kiyaskiwin*, "a myth," came to mind. Certain of its meaning, Nagora tried to make sense of how the words connected to her. My amulet holds a dragon's tear? Can that be? It gives me power? What power other than this strange language I hear in my mind?

The prince returned, pulled his thumb from his mouth, bared his teeth, and feigned to strike Nagora. She and the guards who held her cringed. "I'm not done with you, bitch!"

Then he turned to Hag with a smirk on his face and his clenched fist resting in the palm of his other hand. "My dear Hag, I thought all this was the stuff of legends I learned in my childhood. And anyway, since then my dear mother, Queen Raganora, in her great wisdom, has decreed we are never to speak of dragons again in this land, nor to hold statues or images of dragons of any kind."

"Hold your sarcasm for someone else. That is so and it is one legend you would do well to heed."

"Then how do we deal with this dragon damsel bitch?" yelled the prince, both his hands pointing at Nagora.

Hag pulled on his sleeve, turning him away. "How do we fight fire?"

Prince Acindor rolled his eyes upward. "With water?"

Hag shook her staff. "The sea will take care of her, for no well or lake is deep enough to forever put out the power of fire she potentially bears."

I bear the power of fire?

The prince pointed to the window. "Do we just throw her into the sea?" His tone was mocking.

Hag ignored it. "No. We must let the sea drown her. We cannot do it ourselves. I have a plan. I'll tell you later. Not in her presence."

Nagora swallowed. Her mouth was dry. I'm gifted with a death sentence from this witch because of my amulet. Could there be truth in what Hag spoke?

Hag pointed to the guards with her staff. "Remove her belt and knife sheath. Give her back her shift. Don't touch the amulet. Get rope. Have her hold her wrists so." Hag showed how by holding her opposite forearms with each hand.

"Then tie her wrists together and take her to the coast tower dungeon. Allow her a cup of water and a piece of bread. Tell the jailor no harm is to come to her. He is not to lay a finger on her and when he does, it will be to my exact orders."

The guards obeyed. While one kept a hold on her arm, the other let go, unfastened the leather strips from the knife sheath that crisscrossed around her thigh, and unfastened the belt. He dropped them onto her dress and tunic, and then picked up her light linen garment and tossed it to her.

Nagora caught it with a trembling hand as the other guard let go of her arm. Her whole body shuddered as she fumbled to pull the shift over her head. She succeeded just as the first guard was leaving with her belongings.

Prince Acindor now stood next to Hag and sneered at Nagora. "What did I tell you, bitch?"

*I know, Tars.* She clenched her fist and held it against her stomach as the second guard grasped her other arm, but her hand still shook. *The witch didn't recognize me, but she's just handed me a death sentence.*

*Could it be true my amulet can give me power? The power of the dragon? The power of fire? Is that what the voice of these strange words is telling me? Is the amulet speaking to me, Ka Peyakot Mahihkan, Lone Wolf? Why are those words so familiar? Isihtwawin—I am gifted, kanawisimowin—* amulet, *ayi nikcikaw paskwaskisiw—*the dragon, *wacikâpahkitek—*exploding mountain, *kiskwehkan iskwew—* witch.

As she spoke them to herself, the shaking in Nagora's legs eased, and she relaxed her fist against her belly. Speaking those words in that language brought her strength. *Yes, I am Ka Peyakot Mahihkan, Lone Wolf. Could what Hag said be true, or just myth, "kiyaskiwin," like the voice said? If she lived to see her uncle again, she would bring up all these new questions about her amulet.*

He had been her patient yet firm teacher all these years. He had taught her to be strong, given her the tools and the knowledge to survive in the wilderness. He had also taught her to defend herself as a warrior from an enemy. *Did I fail the test today?*

*Uncle didn't give me the amulet and he didn't teach me these words. I want answers!*

The guard, who had gone for rope, motioned to her to hold her forearms as Hag had directed. He pulled the sleeves of her shift clear of her wrists and tied them with the rope.

Nagora tensed her arm and hand muscles, hoping that doing so would cause slack in the rope when she relaxed her muscles, but the coarse hemp rope bit into her skin.

I wasn't able to defend myself when the prince's men grabbed me. Then Uncle appeared and signaled me. I've bided my time. I don't see a way out of here. My situation has gotten worse. I'm still a virgin. Looks like I'll die a virgin. Uncle is in chains. Who'll help Lone Wolf, *Ka Peyakot Mahihkan*?

Nagora stared down at her amulet as the guards led her out of the prince's chamber. Give me strength.

# Dungeon
## *Kipahitokamik*

The guard pulled Nagora down the hall by the rope tied to her wrists. A younger guard followed behind her. As they passed the last window, she craned her neck and tried to see outside, but couldn't. The wooden steps at the end of the hall led down to a stone landing and a torch lit stone corridor. We must be in the old part of the castle.

They came to a door. It opened onto a stone staircase. As soon as Nagora started down it, a rank mixture of smoke, sweat, stale bread, ale, seaweed, and piss invaded her nostrils. The foul odors seemed to cling to her in the cold damp air. Waxed tapers, set in wrought iron holders at regular intervals, lit the steps that curved along the circular stone wall of what had to be the remains of the coastal tower of ancient Yhorgal Castle, its dungeon. She swallowed.

"Worsham! You old whoreson. Get up," said the older guard, as soon as his feet touched the stone floor. His voice echoed in this part of the deep, vaulted, underground chamber.

"I'm up. I'm up." The jailor was sitting on his cot, which rested against the wall, not far from one of the three dungeon cell doors. His legs spread wide with his paunch hanging between them. He was leaning forward and trying to push himself up with one hand, while his other held the remains of a half-eaten chicken.

"You eating in bed? Worsham, you're ever the pig. All you ever do is eat, drink, piss, shit, 'n fuck."

The jailor was on his feet scratching himself and licking his lips as he stared at Nagora. "Such is my terrible life, lads. Wishing you were in my boots will do you no good. What have you brought me today? Fresh meat?"

"You wish. Hag says you're not to lay a finger on her. When you do, it'll be to her exact orders."

The jailor looked Nagora up and down.

Tar piss! Nagora's eyes darted about. Nowhere to run to down here. To her right beyond the jailor a big fireplace stood recessed in the wall and past it the high vaulted wall of the dungeon fell to a tunnel with a much lower vaulted ceiling that ran off into damp darkness. Perhaps to the sea?

"That so?" The jailor bit into the chicken and walked over to the table, dropping the rest of it onto a plate. He took a sip from the pitcher and returned it to the table. He burped, wiped his hand on his shirt, and walked over to her. "We'll see about that."

"Better mind Hag's orders." The guard shook a finger at the jailor. "Even she seems to be afraid of this one. She's supposed to have some kind of dragon power. Don't ever say I told you though. Just be warned."

...

The jailor was standing close to Nagora, his paunch almost touching her breasts. He towered over her and the two guards. As he eyed her, he licked his lips and then wiped them with the back of his hand which he let come to rest on his chin as if considering the warning.

She tried not to breathe in the stench of his sweat and the chicken fat mixed with ale on his breath.

He took a step back to look her up and down.

His stink lingered close to her.

The jailor brought his hand to his crotch, leaned toward her as he scratched himself. "Well, how would you like to play with my dragon?" He laughed loud and looked at the two guards. "Don't ever say I said that." He winked at the older guard. "Bring her over here."

Tar piss! I better get ready to fight this giant. But how?

"Worsham, we've warned you. You know we'll have to report you. No harm is to come to her."

"Don't worry. I'm just going to remove dragon lassie's slippers."

The jailor moved the plate and jug of ale to the other end of the table. He patted the thick table top with his left hand. "Sit yourself here, lassie." Then he pulled a small footstool from under the table and left it in position for Nagora to step up on. He moved back and motioned to the guards to bring her over to the table.

She stepped up onto the stool and turned to sit herself on the sturdy table. Each corner of the well worn tabletop had two holes in it. It was no ordinary table. It surely had other purposes.

A guard stood on each side of the table. The older one still held the rope tied to her wrists. They watched as the jailor came forward, bent, and held out his hands, waiting for her to lift a foot into them.

Nagora lifted her left foot. He smiled at her as he held it in his big hands. He moved the fingers of his left hand over the soft crisscrossed leather strips on her calf, pausing on the bare skin between each crossing strip.

When he reached her knee, he untied the knot and let the strips fall back. He placed his left hand under the back of her calf while he unraveled the strips with his right hand, pulling the crimped-edged leather slipper off her foot. He brought her bare foot up to his crotch.

Nagora tried to pull her foot away from his arousal, but he held it there and grinned at her. All the muscles in her back tensed. *Should I kick him?*

Then the jailor let go of her calf, placed the slipper on the stool, and held out his hands for her other foot.

She placed it in the jailor's hand.

"You see, lads. No harm done. I think she likes me already." He laughed and patted her knee before proceeding to unfasten the leather strips of her other slipper.

*If I stood the slightest chance, you wouldn't be laughing.*

This time he did not pull her foot to his crotch.


The jailor picked up the other slipper, tied them together, and walked over to hang them on a hook on the wall above the head of his cot. *Tar piss! How many others like mine hang from that hook? Dozens!* Nagora's mouth went dry. A metal ring, with a single key on it, hung from the next hook. A coat and a felt hat hung from the third.

The jailor grabbed the metal ring with the key and walked over to one of the cell doors. He pulled it open and motioned her in. The guard who held the rope tied to Nagora's wrists led her to the open door.

Nagora had to squeeze past the jailor to get into the cell. As she did, he caressed her hair. The cobblestone floor in the cell, like the dungeon floor, was cold and damp.

At the far end of the dim cell she found a pile of damp, piss-soaked straw. She breathed out of her nose to keep from gagging.

As she turned back toward the door, it slammed shut. The cell's floor, walls, and ceiling were all of stone except for the heavy wooden door with a square wrought iron framed window holding five vertical iron bars.

The jailor smiled at her from the other side. "Welcome home, dragon lassie." The key turning in the lock turned in her heart. At the same time Nagora's legs shook. She pressed them together and squeezed her arms to her sides and her tied wrists to her belly.

"Worsham, she's allowed a cup of water and a piece of bread."

"Well, she's out of luck. No more water in the bucket. No more bread on the plate. When you go back up, have water and bread sent down. If Hag's idiot is there, have him bring them down. Make sure he also brings a pitcher of ale."

"Will do. Behave yourself, Worsham. Oh. By the way, do you think you could save us a piece a tail for when we get off duty? The young lad here doesn't fancy goin' to the old widow in Yhorgal. We'd pay in coin."

The jailor laughed. "For some coins and a flask of mead, I just might be able to do that."

Nagora pushed the pile of straw into the back corner of the cell with her feet, trying to separate the damp from the dry. She sat on the small dry pile with her back in the corner and gnawed on the end knot in the rope. She pushed away the pain in her jaw and ignored the loose tooth on that side. Get the first knot undone. One at a time. If I can free my hands, I might stand a chance.

She froze at the sound of a key in a lock. She stared at the door of her cell. A door opened. It was the cell next to hers. A scream, and then crying.

Nagora stood up and stepped to the door's window. On tiptoes she could just see past the iron bars into the dungeon. She had a partial view of the staircase and a full view of the table she had sat on. The edge of the open cell door next to hers slowly swung into view.

The voice cried out again. A girl's! The voice whimpered and begged in a language she did not understand. And then the girl cried out of control.

The jailor emerged from the cell carrying on his hip, as a mother would an infant, a naked young girl, not a day older than twelve. He caressed her hair and cooed to her. He seemed to soothe her.

Bruises covered the side of the girl's face, arm, and leg. What had they done to her?

"Now, now. Calm down. I'm going to feed you. I've some chicken here on the table. You've been a good girl. I know you're hungry. Here's your chance to eat." He sat the crying child on the table, reached for the plate, and placed it on the girl's knees.

The poor child tried to choke back her sobs as she reached out to hold the plate with both hands. Her whole body heaved in a continuous wave with the effort to calm herself.

The jailor pulled out the bench that was against the wall next to the table. He sat and leaned his back against the wall.

The girl could finally control herself enough to pick up what remained of the chicken and bite into it. She was obviously starving. She bit into every available morsel of meat on the bones and barely chewed what she bit off.

When there was no more to bite off, she broke apart the bones to suck and lick any traces of meat or fat. All the while, she focused on her meal and ignored the jailor. He sat silent, watching her.

When she finished, she wiped her mouth with the back of her hand as she looked around the table.

The jailor pointed to the pitcher. "There's ale in the pitcher. You can drink it all."

The girl hesitated.

He waved her toward the pitcher. "Go on. Go get it. It's yours." He watched her as she set the plate down and turned to crawl on her hands and knees to the pitcher at the other end of the table.

She sat cross-legged with her back to the jailor. She reached for the pitcher, looked inside, and glanced back.

When the jailor motioned, she brought the pitcher to her lips, tilted her head back, and drank until there was no more. She set the pitcher down and burped.

The jailor laughed.

The girl turned away, frightened, and sat back on her heels, covering her tiny breasts with her hands.

The jailor stood, walked over to his cot, picked up a blanket from it, and brought it over to the girl. He draped it over her shoulders, lifted her up, brought her over to his cot, and laid her down.

Then the jailor went over to the fireplace and put a few sticks of kindling and two logs on the iron dogs before setting them on fire with a taper from the wall. He pulled a low stool over to the front of the fireplace, reached for the poker, sat on the stool, and poked at the logs, adjusting them to best take advantage of the flames from the kindling.

The heavy door at the top of the dungeon stairs opened.

Tar piss! Now what?

"Good! It's you, Chive, my fine idiot friend!" the jailor's voice boomed. "Been expecting you. If you come bearing food and ale, then you're most welcome here. Mind you don't spill anything."

The poor simpleton hobbled down the stairs carrying a tray of food. In his other hand, he held on to a wooden bucket of sloshing water.

"You, sir, are a welcome sight. Let me help you with that, Chive." The jailor met the simpleton at the bottom of the stairs and reached for the tray. It held a big pitcher, bowls, and plates with bread and ham hocks. He took it over to the table and set it down.

Nagora couldn't make out what the simpleton was saying. He followed alongside the jailor, pointing to the bread and then to the water in the bucket. Looking for the person for whom it was destined?

"Yes. Yes. I think I know what you mean. Bread and water for dragon lassie, right? Right?"

Chive was nodding and seemed pleased he had made himself understood.

"Count on me, she'll get her due. The guard already told me Hag's orders. If it was you delivered the orders, I'd've never understood your jabbering. How Hag understands you I don't know. That's good for you she does, otherwise you'd not be here, would you?"

From what Nagora gathered, Chive seemed to insist that the orders be carried out right away as he had set the water bucket down, reached for a bowl, and scooped it full of water. Then he grabbed a piece of bread and made his way toward the cot where the young girl lay.

"No. No. Okay. Okay. She's not dragon lassie. Not her. The one you want is in the cell over there."

Chive limped toward the cells.

"Hold on. I'll get the key. You're stubborn and as single-minded as a fly on a fresh turd."

Nagora backed away from the door and waited for it to open.

When it did, the jailor held Chive back. "You wait here. You don't want dragon lassie to set you on fire, do you?

You," he said pointing to Nagora, "move back against the wall at the end."

She obeyed.

The jailor pointed to the corner near the door. "Set them down here."

Chive did and then the jailor pushed him back and closed the door.

Whatever Chive spoke next, neither Nagora nor the jailor understood.

"Yes. Yes. Okay. Okay. What you say is okay with me."

The sound of Chive's limping steps travelled back up the stairs as Nagora knelt next to the bread and water. First, she took care to find the bowl and stick her fingers into it, then pinch its outside with her thumb so she could lift it to drink as she raised her arms. She was thirsty. The water was cool.

It mixed with the blood from the wound in her mouth. She swished the water around to wash out the blood. She set the bowl down and turned away from the corner to spit this first mouthful on to the rope that bound her wrists, hoping the wet knots would be easier to untie.

Again, she took up the bowl and drank another mouthful to ease her thirst. She bent to set the bowl down. She found the piece of bread, bit into it, and remained on her knees savoring the dark rye, all the while listening for sounds from the other side of the door.

Chive had chosen a big piece, and it wasn't stale. I won't eat it all now.

Nagora stood and had a quick look through the window. The girl was still on the cot. The jailor was adding another log to the fire.

She returned to her pile of straw, sat down, placed the piece of bread in her lap, and went back to work on the knot in the rope, ignoring the pain in her mouth.

It was not long before the sound of Chive's shuffling was on the stairs again.

How will the jailor react this time?

"You again? What do you want?"

Nagora couldn't make out what Chive said, so she went to the window to see. She was just in time to see Chive drop sheaves of straw from the staircase onto the dungeon floor. Six of them. With sweeping gestures and pointing to the straw and then to the cells, it was obvious Chive wanted to clean out the cells and put in some fresh straw.

"Hag sent you to do this?" asked the jailor.

Chive nodded and headed for the wooden rake in the corner near the cell closest to the jailor's cot. It hung from two pegs next to a broom, which was made of young birch branches wrapped and tied around the stout end of a bigger birch limb.

The jailor shook his head, threw up his hands, and sighed as he headed for the hook to retrieve the key. He started for the cell doors, then stopped in his tracks. Pointing to his own head, he turned and headed for his cot.

He reached under it and pulled out a wooden box. From the box, he took two thick leather straps. They were wide at one end, tapering into a longer, narrower strip at the other end. There were slits in the wide ends of the straps.

He went over to the table and moved the tray of food from the table to the bench.

The jailor returned to the cells.

...

Nagora stepped away from the door. The key turned in the lock.

If only my hands weren't tied, I could surprise him and push past him to make a run for it. Where to? Tied this way, there's no way I can grab onto something to use as a weapon to fight my way out.

"Back against the wall." The jailor watched through the window.

When she had complied, he opened the door.

"Keep your back against the wall. Hold your arms up." The jailor approached and slipped the leather strap over the coiled rope on Nagora's wrists. He threaded the narrow end through the slit and pulled it all the way through until it was taut.

Holding onto the leather strap, he pulled Nagora along with him over to the table.

He had her sit on the table as before. "Now lay down. Put your arms over your head."

She obeyed as the jailor moved to the other end of the table.

Reaching for her wrists, he pulled her back on the table top and tied the leather strap to one of the table legs, all the while staring down at her face.

I don't like the way he's smiling at me. Will he obey Hag's order?

As the jailor moved to the other end of the table, he let the tips of his fingers trail over her skin and light garment, from her arm all the way down her side to her foot. She arched her back and tensed the muscles in her legs. I'm afraid. Will he rape me?

"Easy, lassie." He held her foot, lifted it, and looked down the length of her leg as he placed the leather strap around her ankle, threading the narrow end through the slit at the wide end. He lowered her leg and tied the leather strap to the table leg.

Nagora swallowed and closed her watering eyes. Don't cry now.

Chive raked out the straw from the three cells. He jabbered away all the while he worked.

The jailor returned to his stool in front of the fireplace, his back to Nagora.

Chive kept up his incessant jabbering. He came in her direction as he pushed a pile of dirty straw with the wooden rake.

Through her teary eyes, Nagora caught him wink at her as he went by and, for the first time, she recognized a word that made sense to her, the only understandable one he had uttered so far.

Fid! Did he say "fid"?

In her mind the expression, *awîyak ka wiyasihkamaket*, "trickster," dropped like a nail on a stone floor.

Chive pushed and raked the straw down the stone steps. He struck the water repeatedly. To make the straw sink in the sea water below the steps? On his way back as he came alongside her, jabbering as ever, he again distinctly said, "fid."

Could it be? If it is so, there's hope for me yet.

"Are you done, Chive?" asked the jailor.

Whatever Chive answered, he followed it with rapid sweeping of the birch broom. He swept along the remaining debris of straw toward the sea cave steps.

Again as he passed Nagora, he winked at her. There was no mistaking what he said for a third time, and he added two more words that were a command—"Swim free."

Will I find a fid in the clean straw in my cell? Let it be so. I could undo the knots. Use it as a weapon. Swim free? Is that even possible? If I find the fid, that'll mean I stand a chance. Chive, who are you? You're no idiot. Are you a trickster?

Chive hobbled back and forth from the cells to spread the sheaves of straw. Her heart beat faster with the hope Chive gave her. Even so she swallowed again as she strained against the leather straps.

Chive had finished his work and was now after the jailor to release her and bring her back to her cell. In fact, Chive headed her way and started to untie the leather strap which held her ankle.

"All right! All right! We'll lock her up again. You're right, Chive. I wouldn't want her to set me on fire. You know what I mean." This time the jailor winked at her as he bent to untie the leather strap from the table leg.

Chive had undone his end and was pulling the strap from her ankle. He gave her heel two intentional squeezes before letting it go.

"Up you get, lassie." The jailor lifted her into a sitting position. He touched her hair before putting his left hand at the base of her back to push her along the tabletop to its edge.

Chive held out the leather strap for the jailor to take. As he reached for it, Nagora let herself down from the table and waited to be led back to her cell. This time, she was happy to be returning there.

As soon as the jailor locked the door behind her, Nagora set about searching the straw with her feet. The fid would be like the one she used when building curraghs. Her toes wouldn't mistake it if they found it in the dark. The pointy hardwood stick helped her thread and pull tight the brine soaked leather lanyards when stitching cow hides together and lashing them to the ash frames of the small boats she built with her uncle. The tool she used was about the length of her open hand.

She pushed and spread and patted the straw. She kept in mind the cobblestone floor of the cell as she pressed her toes between the stones, feeling for a fid of any size.

Where is it? Perhaps there isn't one. I've imagined this. He's an idiot after all.

Okay. Don't panic. Wait. Breathe. Think. If I were him, where would I put it? Somewhere you'd find it. Now where would that be? Where would I put it?

Nagora pictured herself bringing straw into the cell. She would have the fid concealed on her. Once in the cell, she would place the fid where it would be found.

Of course! With the bread and water.

She turned to head for the door of the cell. She went to her knees and found the water bowl, the piece of bread, and a bigger, heavier crusted piece of bread. A small loaf! The backs of her fingers marched along the floor stones to the edge of the wall. Certain there was no fid there, she moved the water and bread to that spot.

Then she searched the floor right into the corner. Her heart stopped beating when her fingers caused the fid to fall on the cobblestones. Being so close to where it fell, the noise it made sounded deafening, even though it was the same size as the one she used at the beach hut. It had been standing in the corner on its pointy end.

Nagora picked up the tool and hurried to the other end of the cell. She stood the fid in the corner there, and then she got up and pushed the fresh straw into a pile in that corner. Her heart was beating faster.

Chive, I don't know who you are, but you're no idiot. I owe you. Someday, I hope I can thank you. Now I can undo the knots, and then I can use the fid as a weapon.

A jab to an eye or to the neck just might slow the jailor down.

Chive, you told me to swim free. How do you even know I can swim, let alone that I stand a chance to swim out of the sea cave?

Hold on. Oh! No! You almost had me, Trickster. What did Hag say? Let the sea kill me. They can't do it directly. So! Hag! This is your plan!

Trust no one but yourself. Thank you, Uncle. Your wise words of advice come to help me once again. Okay, now what?

Nagora moved to the corner, knelt on the straw, bent down, and retrieved the fid. She turned to sit with her back in the corner and drew up her knees. As she rested her forearms on them, she reached for her amulet, *kanawisimowin*, and placed her lips against it. Somehow it brought her comfort and allowed her to focus her thoughts. Perhaps that's another power it has—it protects me.

Moments later, she lifted her head and set to work with the fid.

Her plan was to untie the half-dozen knots that held the two ends of the rope together, and then she would loosen the four hitches that bound her wrists to each other, enough to allow her to slip the fid in between her wrists so she could then pull it out with one hand and pull her other hand free of the rope hitches. Retying the six knots would be a little more challenging, but doable.

She paused now and then in her work to listen. All seemed quiet on the other side of the door.

When finished, she tested her work and found she could push each wrist toward its opposite elbow with the fid concealed beneath the rope between her wrists. The hitches of rope were tight enough on her and would not give away what she had accomplished unless inspected.

Now I have to bide my time and wait for an opportunity. To do what? I wish I had a plan. What if Chive is on my side?

Nagora stood and went to the cell door window. She stood on tiptoes. The jailor was asleep on his cot. The young girl was curled into a ball apparently asleep on the floor before the fireplace. She had wrapped herself in the blanket the jailor had given her.

Nagora listened. The jailor snored. She tried to hear sounds from the sea cave beyond the steps leading down to it.

How long have I been down here? It was late morning in the square.

I'm hungry. It must be close to the evening meal.

Would she hear the surging sea as it filled the sea cave? If she could, the tide might tell her the time like it did at the beach hut when working on curraghs with her uncle.

Eat. It'll help me think. Yes! The crusted bread Chive had left. Nagora went to her knees and removed the fid so handling the bread would be easier. It was heavier than any such loaf she had ever picked up. Her fingers explored the crust and found it was slit on one side. Aha! She pried it open.

The unmistakable sharp smell of cheese struck her nose. Oh! Chive! If only I could trust you. She reached in with her fingers and found not only cheese, but a hunk of honeycomb.

Is this part of Hag's plan? To make me trust you further so I swim to my death in the sea cave? Well, if this is to be my last meal, so be it. I can't give up. There has to be a way out.

Nagora pulled the honeycomb out and deposited it in the bowl of water.

Then she bit off a thumb-size piece of cheese and chewed it before tearing off a mouthful of bread with her teeth. Her sore jaw forced her to take her time and savor each bite, even though it went down with some difficulty into her unsettled stomach.

She paused now and then to sip water between bites.

When Nagora finished eating the cheese, she managed to place the fid and what remained of the crusted bread in a fold of her smock. With her other hand she picked up the bowl. She brought these to her pile of straw at the other end of the cell.

Kneeling, Nagora placed the bowl on the floor, took the chunk of honeycomb, and sat on the straw with her shoulder against the wall. She took a bite of the honeycomb and chewed its sweetness until all that remained in her mouth was the wax.

Then she bent over, found the bowl, and dropped the wax into it. She took another bite of the honeycomb and while she chewed it, she reached for her amulet.

Does my amulet truly hold the fire power of the dragon?

The black stone, encased in tightly woven cat's sinew, had hung from a fine leather lanyard around her neck for as long as she could remember, almost eighteen summers now. The stone contained a blood-red crystal visible from two of the stone's sides. When held up to the sunlight, a pale pink filament seemed to float as a prisoner within the red crystal. It had always fascinated her.

On her seventh birthday, Nagora had asked Dangor: "What is this stone? What does it mean?"

"When the time is right," was all he had answered.

From that day on, at least once every ten days, she had asked the same questions and made the same accusation— "You don't trust me. Why? Tell me."

Dangor would shake his head and find something to do or somewhere to go.

His words to her on her twelfth birthday, after she had stopped yelling her accusations, came back to her as if he had spoken them the day before. "I'll tell you this, child. There's power in the stone. If I tell you what it is, you'll not believe me. Trust me on what I tell you. You'll only discover its power when you have complete trust in yourself. How you go about finding that, I can't say. That's when you'll learn its true power, all on your own. I won't be the one to reveal it to you. It'll reveal itself. Stop asking me."

...

Is it revealing its power today? Are you *kanawisimowin*? Had her amulet been doing so since last summer when the strange words began to come into her mind?

On that day, six years ago, Nagora had stopped questioning her uncle about her amulet. She had withdrawn and become Lone Wolf, one of the names fellow warrior trainees called her.

Today I know I am *Ka Peyakot Mahihkan*, and I've never been so alone.

Back then as Lone Wolf, Nagora had focused.

She focused on her daily exercises: ward off, rollback, press, push, pull, elbow strike, shoulder strike, advance, retreat, look left, gaze right, center balance. She repeated them a hundred times and did them each morning with a different weapon in hand, outside near the cliffs no matter the weather, at times deliberately slow, at times blindingly fast.

She brought the same focus when training with the others. After paired combat training, they all wore the bruises and the scars from the inner storm she would unleashed on them from behind her outward calm, which so confounded them.

It's been almost a year now since I last trained with them.

Will I ever even see them again?

And Nagora had brought her focus to her work, building curraghs at the beach hut with her uncle.

Will I ever see my beach again and build another curragh with Uncle? Tears filled her eyes.

When she took time for herself, it was to be alone to swim in the sea, play her flute on the beach, or sit on a high cliff looking off to the sea's horizon, hoping to spot the sail of a ship that would bring her father home from his voyage of exploration at sea. And recently to ride her horse, Storm.

The da I've always wished and dreamed to know. Da, will I ever see you? Doesn't look like it. Storm, will I ever ride you again? She couldn't hold back her tears.

Some summer nights, she would play her flute on the sod roof of their stone lodge. Or she would retell to herself the star stories Dangor had told her so often when putting her to sleep: *The Dragon Tamer*, *The Twins*, and *The Woman Waiting*, lying on her side with one knee bent, resting on her elbow to see out her window. She imagined the woman waiting in the stars to be her mother.

Will I ever see home again? At least, Mum, you're up there somewhere with all our ancestors, looking down, watching, and tallying my good deeds and bad, to hold in the balance and weigh to decide if I've earned a bright spot next to you when my time comes. Someday I'll meet you, Mum.

Often that thought had brought her sleep.

Now Nagora's shoulders shook as she tried to soak up her tears with the rope that bound her wrists.

Will I live to sleep another night? Perhaps, Mum, we'll meet sooner than I ever thought.

Nagora's jaw locked open as she tried to catch her breath through her open mouth as she cried. She let herself cry in silence until the shaking inside subsided and no more tears would come.

Burn straw! Burn! If only I could do that. Ha!

If only I truly knew how to use the power of the dragon, perhaps I could get out of here.

There must be something to it for Hag to fear it. But what?

Something at the back of her mind wasn't showing itself, something that bothered her, a connection she wasn't making that might give the answer.

She held her amulet and brought it to her lips. Just when the answer was about to reveal itself, a ruckus broke out on the other side of the door.

# Torture
## *Awîyak ka wîsakahpinet*

Nagora rushed to the cell door window. Prince Acindor had two girls by the hair. One, he pulled along on her backside behind him. The other, he marched down the staircase ahead of him. Both girls were screaming and crying. "Shut the fuck up! You little bitches! I said shut the fuck up! Your asses are going to pay for this right now. I told you I mean it and now I'm going to fucking well show you how much I mean it."

Tar piss! Am I going to witness him in action?

The girls didn't shut up, and neither did the prince who kept yelling his threats.

The jailor was on his feet, heading for the staircase. "Prince Acindor. What's going on?"

"Worsham, don't you fucking 'Prince' me. Grab this little whore and lock her in a fucking cell. I'm going to tie this one to the fucking table and teach her a fucking lesson or two about how she should behave."

The prince was livid as he dragged the girl across the floor to the cot and pulled out the wooden box that contained the leather straps. "Oh! You fucking little bitch! You're going to regret you are alive today." He dragged the girl and the box over to the table. Tar piss! This is no prince. He's a pervert!

The jailor marched the other girl to the cell on Nagora's right and locked her in.

The prince saw the little girl wrapped in the blanket cowering next to the fireplace. "What the fuck are you doing out of your cell? Worsham, will you fucking get her back in her cell right now? Have you been fucking her?"

"No. No. Pri ... Acindor, I only fed her and let her sleep by the fire. No. That's all. She's all yours."

"Well get her the fuck to her cell, right the fuck now."

"I will. I will. I mean I am. I am." The jailor went to pick her up. The poor child's eyes froze wide with terror as the jailor brought her into the cell.

Tar piss! What kind of sick mind he must have to do this!

The jailor locked her cell door and returned the key to its hook. "Acindor, why don't you have some ale while I take care of the girl?"

"Worsham, why don't you have some ale, while I fucking beat the shit out of the girl?"

A pervert and a damn bully! I hate your guts even more.

The jailor bent to the wooden box and pulled out four of the leather straps.

In the meantime the prince had pulled the girl up onto her feet. She had fight left in her and struck out at the prince with her small fists and feet, yelling, "You fat pig! Let go of me!" She almost got away from him, but he caught her by the back of her dress, which tore open, allowing him to bring her down. He also went down on his knees and ended up crawling over to her. He fell onto her back and bit the back of her neck.

"You bitch!" He bit into her neck again and spit on her. "Bitch! You're going to pay!"

Tar piss! He's mad. He's not right in his mind. That poor girl. She doesn't stand a chance.

The jailor reached down to the prince. "Here, Acindor, let me help you up."

"You hold the bitch. I'll get up." When he was on his feet, he kicked the girl in the ribs twice before the jailor picked her up and placed her on his shoulder out of the prince's reach.

Nagora bit her lower lip and squeezed her elbows to her sides. If I get out of here alive, I'll be more than a witness to your cruel abuse. I'll make you pay!

"Acindor! Get a hold on yourself. Come sit on the bench and have some ale." The jailor went over to the table. He lifted the tray of food from the bench, set it on the table, and pushed it closer to where the prince sat.

"I'll lock her in the cell for a while so you can calm down. You'll better deal with her then. Okay?"

The prince bit on his thumb, kicked at the bench, and sat down. He waved the jailor away without looking at him.

The jailor carried the girl on his shoulder as he went to get the key. He locked her in the cell with the other girl the prince had marched down. He stuck his face to their cell window. "If you two know what's good for you, you'll be quiet."

When the jailor went back to the table, he poured ale into a bowl and set it before the prince. He poured ale into a bowl for himself. He took his time to reach for the stool under the table and set it near the corner of the table opposite the prince.

The jailor sat his towering height down on the stool, placing himself beneath the prince's gaze.

The jailor's eyes went from the prince's outstretched boot, which pumped at the air, over to his other bent knee, which bounced up and down as the prince's clenched fist pounded it. He seemed to be waiting for signs the prince was regaining control.

When the prince's pounding fist opened and his hand grasped the bouncing knee, the jailor raised his bowl to the prince in a toast, "To finding a worthy bride."

Tar piss! I can't believe what I'm hearing. You two aren't worthy to be called men!

Prince Acindor reached for his bowl and raised it. "Yes. To a worthy bride." He drank his bowl empty.

Worthy bride? Worthy? What does that even mean to you? You idiot! You pig! She turned from the window for a moment and kicked at the straw.

The jailor finished his drink, stood, and took his time refilling the bowls.

By the time the jailor sat down again, the prince had his temper under control.

The jailor raised his bowl again to the prince and took a sip. "Tell me, Acindor, what's the story on the dragon lassie?"

Nagora swallowed and pressed closer to the window.

"Where'd she come from? Word is Hag is afraid of her. Is that so?"

The prince raised a clenched fist. "That fucking bitch! The captain of my guard brought in a dozen supposed fucking virgins from town this morning. She's the first one I got to see. Hag says she's armed. We strip her. She's got a knife strapped to her leg."

Tar piss! I should've fought for my knife.

"I take the knife. Hag warns me about the amulet she's wearing. It's supposed to give her the powers of the dragon, whatever the fuck that is. I grab her hair to ask her about the amulet. She's got a needle in there, sticks right into my thumb!" The prince held up his thumb. "I want to make her pay, kill her, but Hag says no because if I do," his voice took on a mocking tone, "I'll suffer for it. We can't just kill her outright. We got to let the sea take her life."

The jailor grinned. "That so? Well, she hasn't breathed fire or farted so much as a spark down here. At least not until now. What's Hag got planned to get rid of her?"

So now I'll know. Nagora took a deep breath.

"Worsham, that's where you come in. Tomorrow at low tide," the prince pointed to the dungeon ceiling. "Hag wants you to set the noose end of the hanging rope through the iron ring in the sea cave above the stone pillar."

I can't see the noose from here. It must be up higher above the level of the stairs.

"Tie the other end to the ring near the bottom of the steps from the dungeon. Then you're to stand dragon virgin on the pillar. Leave her wrists bound. Adjust the rope so the knot in the noose hangs down in front of her face." Acindor drew his spread fingers down and across his face to reveal his sinister smile.

The jailor leaned his head to one side, holding an imaginary noose. "Okay, but why not put the noose around her neck?"

The prince waved a finger. "That's the thing with this dragon girl. We can't have a hand in killing her directly. You see," he pointed at Nagora's cell, "she'll have a choice. She can stand on the pillar as the cold sea water rises to toss her around the sea cave, shredding her to bits so the sea creatures can eat her remains. Or she can stick her head through the noose, hanging herself to end her misery." He slapped his palm on the table.

Okay, Tars. Let's not panic. We're not there yet. We've got a fid.

"Why not set her out there now to get it over with?" The jailor pointed in the direction of the sea cave. "The water's probably reached the top step at the pillar. I could set up the rope in no time and stand her on the pillar."

The prince shook his head. "No. Not today. Hag says tomorrow because tomorrow night will be the highest of the high tides. That way whatever she chooses to do, she's sure to be torn to bits and washed out to sea."

The jailor was nodding. "Hag's got a point. Sea surge will be booming in there tomorrow night. Some water will splash up on the floor here. I don't want to be sweeping body parts back into the cave. There won't be much of anything left of her the day after, that's for sure." The jailor raised his bowl. "Here's to the dragon lassie's disappearance."

The prince raised his bowl. "Yes, to her fucking disappearance forever."

Nagora turned from the window, let her back slide down the door's surface until she was sitting on the floor with her knees pulled up to her chest, held in place by her bound wrists. She rested her cheek on her knees and touched her lips to her amulet. She was like a tight leather ball with no place to roll, no place to bounce, no one to play with. Her fate was sealed.

My disappearance. Unless Chive is right and I can swim free of the sea cave. Perhaps I can do it.

The motion of the sea as it comes into the dungeon sea cave! Think. Stay calm. Look for the solution.

What do I know about how that works? What would I do if I'd come into such a cave to explore it and found myself caught inside by the rising tide?

I would have looked for the safe spots on my way in. That's the problem. I'll be going out one way blind. It's all timing. I must make the force of the water work for me. Dive into the incoming sea surge, swim strong, and hope the back-wash pulls me out with it.

Problem is—what's the distance? Will I be able to hold my breath until I surface? Do I swim down to the bottom then aim for the surface when I can't hold it anymore? The moon'll be full. If it's over the water, I might see it and aim for it. It would probably be best to stay to one side to take advantage of the backwash that'll push me along the shore past the cave entrance. It's a shore of cliffs. Is there even a possible safe landing spot? I'll see that when I get there, if I get there. No sense in panicking. Is there another way?

Okay, if I don't go that way, what are my chances of fighting my way out? No way. I've trained to fight one-on-one with a weapon or to give support to a group attack with bow and arrow. And I've trained to run from danger and hide. Fight to defend myself as a last resort?

Uncle always says to know my weapon, know my skill, know my opponent, and to pick my fights based on that. Right now I have a fid. If lucky, I might land one good hit with it. Then what?

I can swim. Like a fish, Uncle says. Chive, you better be right. Either way, I'll have to swim. Will I be able to keep my wits about me? I hope so.

The sound of the key in the lock of the next cell brought Nagora to her feet.

The jailor pulled the door open, entered, and then came out with the girl wearing the torn dress. He pushed the door closed with his foot and locked it. His big hand held the girl's forearm twisted up behind her back in such a way she had no choice but to follow along on tiptoe. He slipped the key ring onto its hook and then brought her to the table.

The jailor pushed her face down onto the table top and pinned her upper arms flat. At the same time he pushed his legs between the girl's and forced them spread wide.

The prince pulled off the girl's slippers, set them on the stool under the table, and then bound each ankle to a table leg with a leather strap. After, he tied the straps from the girl's wrists to the table legs at the opposite end of the table.

When the prince finished, the jailor moved away, leaving the girl bound with her hips hanging over the table's edge.

The prince hadn't said a word so far, but, as he undressed, he bent and looked into the girl's face.

His breathing came faster, and anger flooded his face, readying him to release more words of abuse on the girl.

The girl hadn't said a word. Would she try to match the prince's verbal abuse in the position she now found herself? Either way, girl, you're in trouble.

"Strip her."

Bastard!

The jailor obeyed by finishing the tear down the back of the girl's dress. He reached for the knife he wore in a sheath at his side, cut the sleeves from the girl's arms, and cut away her undergarment.

The girl cried.

The prince leaned over on his end of the table on one hand and slapped her with his other.

Nagora flinched.

"Shut up! Bitch!" He hit her again and got blood on his hand. He reached over and wiped his hand on her shoulder and then in her hair.

You cruel bastard!

"Her slippers."

The jailor bent to get the girl's slippers from the stool.

The prince reached for them with both hands and brought them to his face and inhaled their insides. He inhaled deeper and deeper, each time with his eyes closed. He kept one at his nose and brought the other to his crotch and stroked himself with it as he came around the table and stood between the girl's legs.

Am I actually seeing him do that?

He set her slippers down on the table and leaned over the girl to grab her hair and pull her head back.

The girl cried out and sobbed in a strangled voice.

Tar piss! I swear, if ever I get out of here, you'll pay for this.


Nagora ran to the back of her cell, crouched down on her knees and pushed an ear against a stone on the wall, bringing the back of her wrist up to cover her other ear.

I don't have to witness this, Tars. My body can't escape this cell, but I can escape to a memory. It was her own abuse a year ago at the hands of Pug and his cronies—the side of her face pressed into the pine needles of the forest floor where they'd ambushed her. Again, she let her eye take in the detail of each needle, comparing the color to the ones next to it, and counting the ones that lay across each other as Pug tried to plow into her backside.

The door to Nagora's cell opened. The invading light caused her to turn and bring her arms down. In the backlit doorway, the jailor's naked silhouette held the foot of the unconscious girl he dragged along the cobblestones into the cell. He let the foot slip from his hand until he only held the girl's big toe. He let the leg fall and turned to step past the body, out of the cell.

He returned with a bucket of water and the girl's torn clothes. He threw the clothes on top of the girl and set the bucket down. "Clean her up. Take care of her."

Nagora had to unclench her jaw to speak. "My wrists are bound. It's dark in here. I can't see what I'm doing."

"I'll bring you light. Stay where you are."

She listened. She couldn't hear the girl breathe.

The jailor returned with two tapers. One was lit and the other was not. The unlit taper was in an iron holder, which he put in place so it held from the outside edge of the window bars. He lit the taper, then closed and locked the door. The taper pointed into the cell and provided just enough light for her to see.

The jailor looked down at her through the window. The light from the taper cast the shadows of two of the cell window bars on his face. He looked evil.

"What about my wrists?"

"Make do." He left.

His voice sounded different. Maybe he was drunk.

Nagora knelt beside the girl and bent to look at her face. She was barely breathing. Did she dare touch the girl's bruised and bloodied face? She sorted through the girl's clothes. The dress would be a blanket. She kept the long linen undergarment to clean and cover the girl's wounds. She tore strips with her teeth, as best as she could, and set them on the other side of the girl.

She pushed straw alongside the girl and brought the bucket of seawater to her other side.

Gently, Nagora rolled the girl away from her onto her side to look at the wounds on her back. Bite marks covered the girl's neck and shoulders. Bruises and welts covered her back, probably from being hit with a fist and struck with a belt or leather strap. A stick had most likely inflicted the cuts and welts on her buttocks. Blood covered the back and insides of her legs.

Will this be my fate also?

Nagora soaked one of the bigger pieces of linen in the seawater and patted and wiped the wounds on the girl's neck and shoulders, and then the cuts on the girl's buttocks. She took another big dry piece and covered those wounds. She washed away the blood on the girl's legs.

She reached over, pulled straw over to the girl, and eased her onto the straw.

She soaked another piece of cloth and cleaned the girl's face. The salt water in the wounds around her lips and nose must've stung. The girl groaned when Nagora pried the girl's lips and teeth further apart to see the condition inside her mouth. Two front teeth were missing. Blood oozed from her mouth. Her eyes had swelled shut. Tar piss! They won't open for days. Her right ear had bled.

Nagora fetched her bowl of water, soaked a smaller piece of cloth in it, and brought it to the girl's lips. She squeezed the cloth to dribble water past her lips to see if she would drink. The girl coughed up a clot of blood and then swallowed. Nagora dribbled more water. The girl swallowed, coughed, and tried to lick her lips.

Nagora placed her palm the girl's forehead. "You're going to be all right. Can you hear me? If you can, tell me your name."

She got no response.

Bite marks covered the young girl's breasts.

The prince's teeth had done this, like all the other bites.

Would the girl lose one of her nipples? After cleaning the wound with saltwater, she found the remaining honeycomb in her bowl. She bit off several cells and squeezed the honey onto the open wound. She pressed a folded piece of linen over the girl's breast and held it there until the bleeding stopped.

Skin on the girl's hipbones was raw and worn away where it had chafed against the table.

Blood still seeped from between her legs.

They tore you. This is terrible.

She made a pad of linen and placed it between the girl's legs. She cleaned the skin wounds at the hips, applied honey there also, and left them uncovered.

She washed away the blood on the front of the girl's legs. Her ankles, like her wrists, were raw from struggling against the leather straps. She placed the girl's arms at her sides and covered her with her torn dress.

She placed more straw under the girl's head. Would she survive? What else can I do? Damn it! She needs more help than I can provide.

Nagora's teeth clenched as her breath came quicker through her nose. This was so much more than the abuse she had suffered. The revenge she had exacted on Pug helped to ease the pain of that memory. These girls, however, would never be in a position to seek redress let alone revenge for their suffering.

She reached for the unconscious girl's hand and brought it to her lips, kissed the palm, and touched her forehead to it.

If I make it out of here alive, I will be your justice. I will be your vengeance. I will make them pay for the evil they've done to you. Don't lose hope. I'll be back. I'll do all in my power to get you out of here. You have my word.

She kissed the back of the girl's hand and set it back at her side.

Then Nagora let herself fall on her side. She took the girl's hand in hers. She curled up in a ball next to the girl and cried. If only I could do more for you. Why are men so cruel? Animals don't do such things. How can I ask you not to lose hope when I am?

I'm your only hope. I'm my only hope.

She wiped her tears on her upper arm sleeves, took a deep breath, and forced herself to her knees, and then to stand.

Why was it so quiet?

Nagora stood on tiptoe and peeked through the cell door window. The prince was naked. He was sitting on the bench at the table with his head resting on one forearm. The hand of that arm rested in a plate and held a ham hock bone. He appeared to be asleep as his other hand, on its outstretched arm, seemed to have slipped from the handle of one of the four pitchers of ale and now rested on its side.

Someone must've brought them. Maybe the jailor had gone for them.

Where was he? His cot was empty. A fire raged in the fireplace. Splashing in the distance shifted her gaze. The jailor's head appeared as he climbed the stairs from the sea cave, naked and wet from head to foot. He carried two buckets of seawater which he brought to the table and set on the floor opposite the prince.

"Acindor. Are you asleep? You should go for a dip before the tide fills the cave. It'll refresh you. It'll get you ready for the next virgin." The jailor laughed as he reached for a pitcher. He drank from it, burped, and set it down, reaching over to shake the prince's arm.

The prince shook himself awake and seemed to nod at the suggestion.

The jailor went to his cot for a rag. He sauntered over to the fireplace, stood in front of it, and wiped his face and his hair. He looked over his shoulder at the prince. "Got a good fire going to dry you off. Feels good."

The prince stood and staggered over to the sea cave steps.

...

The jailor watched him take the steps one at a time.

The splashing didn't last long.

The prince danced up the steps and along the cobblestone floor to the fireplace. "Water's fucking cold." He held his sides in front of the fire.

The jailor handed him the rag.

The prince wiped his face, head, shoulders, and arms. He gave the rag back to the jailor who hung it from a peg next to the fireplace.

The jailor moved his stool over for the prince and went to get another from under the table. He set it on the table, placed a bowl on it, filled it with ale, and then filled another bowl. He offered the prince the bowl on the stool and then set the stool down. Once he sat, he raised his bowl to the prince.

"To virgins."

"Yes. To virgins. May I someday actually fuck one."

The jailor lowered his voice. "Acindor, can I level with you?"

"About?" The prince took a swig from his bowl.

"About ... Well, it's about your problem with keeping it up when you try to fuck. You're thinking about it too much. What I mean is, on one hand you're set on giving a girl a correction, and on the other, you're set on having your pleasure with her. One takes over and shuts the other down. You go soft and end up hitting and biting. That's what you have to shut down. Just think about your pleasure. Get your pleasure first."

"You think so?" The prince stared at the jailor.

"Unless there's something else on your mind. That stuff with Hag you told me about last time?" said the jailor.

The prince shook his head. "No! No. Forget that. I was beyond drunk when I spoke that nonsense."

"Well she's on you to find a bride, isn't she?"

The prince nodded. "Yes, Hag and my mother, both! They want the bride with child by my seed. And a male, no less! And as soon as fucking possible! Shit, you know how much I tried in Windhaven. I wasn't able to get with child even one of those older virgins chosen from the Temple of Fire."

"Oh, aye, so what … why's that become so pressing?" asked the jailor.

"Fucked if I know. They want me on the throne, but only once I've fathered an heir. Produce the male heir and the throne is mine. My mother will step down and act as adviser to the crown."

"What of Hag? She's advised the queen all these years."

The prince smiled. "They have an agreement. When I'm on the throne with a son of my own, Hag gets what she's been wanting all these years—the death of the last dragon. Don't ask me why. Then Hag takes her leave. We'll never see her again. What I was told."

*Kiskwehkan iskwew asotamowin*, "Witch promise." A chill went through Nagora. Last year, Moreena had told her the story of Queen Raganora's promise to Hag. This was confirmation. Why kill the last dragon? What was in it for Hag?

The jailor had taken a long swig from his bowl and was setting it down. "Is that something you look forward to?"

"Being king?" said the prince.

The jailor scratched his neck. "Yes, that, and having a son, and being rid of Hag. Acindor, you can barely fuckin' fart without her approval."

The prince held up a finger and licked his lips. "Then it'll be my mother."

The jailor held up a finger. "But you'll be king."

"That, Worsham, is the fucking truth. And my first gift to my adviser will be this fortress as her new and only residence in the realm. And I'll see to it she advises me from here while I rule from the throne in Windhaven."

"And then her Isle of Smoke fortress ... "

"Will become my throne's seat in summer."

"I see you've given this serious thought, Acindor. You miss Windhaven, don't you?"

The prince looked up and closed his eyes briefly. "Miss it is not the word, Worsham. We had a good time with the virgins there, didn't we? With the little ones it wasn't much of problem. They were afraid of me. That's all I think about."

The prince wagged his finger. "Mind you, I've got my sources. They glean the information I need. We'll be back there once I get the details worked out."

The jailor's face lit up with a big smile. "Well, there you go. You have a lot on your mind and a lot of pressure to produce an heir. No wonder your performance with these virgins suffers. In Windhaven it was never this bad." The jailor stood and went to the table.

Was what she was hearing fact? How was it she was hearing it at all? They must be sure I won't live to breathe a word of this to anyone.

Here she was, the one who had raised Prince Acindor's ire in Windhaven almost a year ago, the one the prince had hunted down, and who the bounty hunters had supposedly killed. But not before she had woken up a kingdom when she had promised Edana would return and that dragons would once again fly over Windhaven.

Tar piss! How'd the people at the Temple understand what I said? Next thing, I became Edana and my name was spreading hope like a rising tide throughout the land.

It had given new urgency to the Cause she had been training for in secret all these years. I can't complain about that. Will I live to see that come about?

Here she was, looking at the enemy, the future tyrant without honorable claim to the throne. She had already sworn an oath to one of his victims to make him pay.

Yes, I'll make you pay. That is my cause. If I get out of here alive, I'll stand in your way to the crown and fight to return it to the rightful heir.

The jailor brought a pitcher back with him and filled the prince's bowl and his own before setting it on the floor.

Nagora went to her knees to check on the girl. She held the girl's hand, placed two fingers in her palm, and closed the girl's fingers over her own.

"Can you hear me? My name is Nagora. I'm trying to help you. If you can hear me, squeeze my fingers."

The girl did not react. Nagora touched her forehead.

Fever was setting in.

The sound of a key turning in a lock brought her eyes up. The neighboring cell door opened.

The jailor must've been surprised, for he called out to the prince. "Look at this one, Acindor."

...

Nagora peeked from the corner of the window of the cell door. The jailor backed away from the open door, stood aside, and waved the naked young girl over to the prince.

She walked into the prince's open arms. The jailor followed behind her.

"I lied. I'm not a virgin. I've fucked many boys. My brothers also. I know how to please a man. You can have your way with me. I'll do my best to please you." She leaned back on the table, pushed herself up onto it, lay back, and spread her legs.

*Tapwew* slipped into her mind, "She tells the truth."

The girl watched the two men approach.

The jailor was already ready.

The prince was looking from the girl to the jailor and stroking himself.

The girl smiled at them.

You just might avoid a beating. You must've watched what happened to the other girl. You're a brazen one. Don't say something stupid.

"Worsham, you go first."

Nagora turned away from the window to check on the other girl. Would she be able to make her drink? Nagora dribbled water on the girl's lips, but they did not part. She bent close to the girl's face and found she was barely breathing. How long would she hold on?

The prince yelled, "Fuck! Shit! Piss!" Was he also slapping that girl? Nagora stood to go see.

...

"You!" The prince smacked the jailor's shoulder with the back of his hand. "Fuck her! Fuck her!"

The jailor obeyed.

"Harder! Harder!" The prince was pounding on the jailor's back. "Fuck her harder!"

When the jailor finished, the prince grabbed his clothes and climbed the stairs. "Damn bitches! Damn virgins! Damn them all!"

After the door at the top of the stairs had slammed shut, the jailor sang out, "Better luck in bed with Hag. Prince, I wouldn't trade places with you for fucking anything. Ha! Ha!"

The girl giggled, slipped off the table to go fetch the rag from the peg next to the fireplace. She returned, smiling at the jailor as she soaked the rag in a bucket to clean herself off.

The jailor watched.

He was obviously quite taken with the girl.

Her rinsing the rag and cleaning the jailor off in turn seemed to seal her unspoken pact with him. She rinsed the rag a final time and went to hang it from the peg. While she was there, she added two logs to the fire.

Girl, you know how to win favors.

When the girl returned, the jailor said, "Go put something on."

She skipped to the cell.

The jailor went to the cot to put on his shirt and pants. When the girl returned wearing a light garment like Nagora's, he offered her some ale and a ham hock.

...

Nagora leaned her back against the door and tried to listen beyond the conversation at the table. Was that the booming of the rising tide in the sea cave? It sounded like it.

Tomorrow'll be my turn. I better try to sleep. I hope I get another piece of bread tomorrow. She went to her knees to check on the girl. Still no response. The fever hadn't increased. Nagora moved to the other side of the girl and lay down next to her. She brought her amulet to her lips and closed her eyes.

Nagora's eyes opened to the darkness of her cell and the sound of gulls. She had slept curled in a tight ball on the floor. Now she listened without moving, daring to believe she was not dreaming.

How long have I slept? The taper was out. Those were gulls. Unless her mind was playing tricks on her.

She stretched out and the side of her foot and calf slid into a puddle of wetness. She brought her leg back up, pushed herself onto her knees, and twisted to touch her calf. It was wet and sticky. Her nose confirmed it was blood.

She reached out to touch the girl. The arm was cool. She bent over the girl's face and couldn't detect the slightest breath. Her fingers touched her neck and could not find a heartbeat.

She's dead.

Nagora clenched her teeth. Her face and ears swelled with the flush of her own blood. Her oath of vengeance seared itself in her heart. She stood and stepped to the other side of the girl's body to the bucket to rinse her hand.

...

Then Nagora tiptoed to the door to peek through the window. The only light in the dungeon came from the two remaining tapers that lit the staircase. The neighboring cell door was still open. She could make out the jailor's cot. He and the girl were sound asleep on it. He held her in his arms. A blanket half covered them.

As she stood on tiptoe, the gulls called in the distance. Is that ...? It is! Daylight appeared at the head of the sea cave steps.

The sun rises on this coast. The light would be brighter here. It must be morning after sunrise, and it must be low tide. If I can hear the gulls, it means there's an opening to the cave above the water right now. I could swim out of the cave on the surface of the water. Maybe I stand a chance. Maybe Chive is right.

Nagora was hungry. She bent to find her last piece of bread, not much of a meal. She returned to the other side of the girl to find her bowl and the last piece of honeycomb it held.

She put it in her mouth, leaned against the door, and chewed it until all the sweetness faded and only the wax remained, all the while seeing the bowl at home where she and her uncle would spit the wax, keeping it to make a candle or two whenever they had saved enough.

Uncle, where are you now? Are you still chained to the wall? Did you spend the night there? I hope not. You won't believe what I've been witness to.

The sound of the gulls seemed louder. It made her stop chewing. She spit the wax into the bowl, turned to the window, and peered over at the cot. She raised her bowl to the bars and tapped it against them, hoping to get the girl's attention.

Come on, wake up, girl. Wake up. Wake up. I need your help. Wake up.

She kept tapping and trying to will the girl awake.

She tapped some more.

If only I knew your name.

She tried to change the sound by dragging the bowl up and down against the bars. The girl stirred. She nestled closer to the jailor. Nagora alternated the tapping and the dragging.

Then she tried calling out. "Lassie. Lassie. Wake up, lass."

The girl opened her eyes, looked up, and then closed them again.

"Lassie. Wake up, girl. Wake up, lass."

Again the girl looked up. She searched where the calls had come from.

Nagora stuck a hand through the bars and waved it. "Over here, lassie. Over here. Get up. Come here. Please."

The girl was up on one elbow, looking at the cell door.

"Please girl. Come here. I need your help."

The girl lifted the jailor's arm from her hip and placed it on his. She pulled her legs out from under the blanket, brought them over the cot's side, and pushed herself into a sitting position. She sat still and looked back at the jailor before standing and tiptoeing to Nagora's cell.

...

When the girl arrived, she looked back at the jailor. She stood so she could keep an eye on him. I bet she wasn't even asleep.

"My name is Nagora. What is your name?"

The girl glanced up at Nagora's eyes then back to the jailor.

"Don't be afraid. Please, tell me your name."

"Vonna."

"Hello, Vonna. You're a brave girl. To do what you did last night takes courage. Vonna, will you help me? Please?"

Vonna glanced up, brushed a strand of hair from her face, and bit her lip as she looked back to the jailor.

"What do you want?" Vonna's words were less than a whisper.

"I need you to help me to escape."

"I can't." She stepped away from the door.

"Wait. Vonna. Please, wait. At least listen to what I have to say."

Vonna stepped back to the door.

"Do you know the name of the other girl who was with you yesterday?"

"No."

"Vonna. She's dead. Did you see what happened to her?"

Vonna mouthed, "Yes."

"I only need you to do one thing for me. Are you listening?"

Vonna nodded.

"Please, Vonna, can you unlock this door for me?"

"No. He'll know and I'll be good as dead. I don't want to die." She turned away.

"Wait. Okay. I understand. Can I ask you a question?"

Vonna waited.

"Vonna, can you swim?"

"No."

Nagora's mind raced, looking for options.

"Vonna, do you see the hook with all the slippers hanging from it?"

Vonna looked at it.

"Your slippers aren't there. You left them in your cell. What do you think happened to the other girls who wore those slippers?"

"I'm not stupid. I don't want to end up like them. Can you blame me for wanting to stay alive?"

"No. You're right. I have a favor to ask you."

Vonna waited.

"I promise it won't ruin your chances of staying alive."

She waited, her eyes always on the jailor.

"When you get back in the cot, can you wake the jailor and tell him you heard noise coming from my cell? Can you do that for me? Please?"

Vonna nodded and walked back to the cot.


Nagora came down from tiptoes to let her feet rest.

When the jailor wakes up, I'll get his attention. Tell him the girl is dead. He'll come to check on her, and I'll try to surprise him with one good hit with the fid and then escape to the sea cave and swim out. Once I'm out of the cave, I'll figure out what to do next.

...

Nagora let her back slide down the door. She sat on the stone floor and worked the fid out from the rope between her wrists, her ear cocked to hear the jailor stir.

"Nagora! Nagora!"
It was Vonna.

Nagora scrambled to her feet. Vonna's terrified face was in the window. Two big hands held Vonna there by her throat, and Vonna held on to the jailor's wrists.

"Dragon lassie, I want you to watch what I would do to you if Hag hadn't ordered otherwise." The jailor brought his face next to Vonna's and grinned at Nagora as he kissed Vonna's cheek and then bit into her ear until she screamed. "Keep your eyes at the window and watch because if you don't, I won't obey orders, and both of you will die."

Nagora swallowed hard.

The jailor turned to walk away. Four paces away, he paused and spun around twice, holding Vonna out from his extended arms as he did. They were both naked. The jailor had an erection.

Nagora screamed, "Leave her alone! Put her down! Come and take me! You know you want to. You've had her already. Come and get me! Come get some fresh meat!"

"Oh! Dragon lassie, you've taken a liking to me. Don't be jealous. You just might get your turn to taste my dragon." He rubbed Vonna against himself and laughed as he brought her to the table.

"You're afraid of me! You fear the power I have! You'd rather rape a girl than risk fighting me. You're such a fucking coward! Always picking on those weaker than you. Even with my hands bound, you're scared. You know I'd scratch your eyes out. I'd tear your balls off! You don't dare let me out of this cell, do you? Coward! There's no way you can get your prick close to me."

The jailor held Vonna down on the table with one hand as he reached into the wooden box to retrieve the leather straps.

Vonna did not resist.

The jailor bound her wrists to the table legs facing Nagora. He placed the straps around Vonna's ankles, but did not tie them to the table legs at the other end. He pulled Vonna down to him. Then he pivoted the table. "Look to the dragon lassie in the window. We're going to show her a few things, aren't we?"

Nagora kept her face at the window, but her eyes went beyond to the sea cave entrance where her mind escaped. It ran along the shoreline to her beach, then up the cliff path past her home, across the fields, into the forest, and down the woodland path to the spot where Pug and his gang had ambushed her.

In the woods, again, she stared at the pine needles on the forest floor, taking in their detail, searching for the individuality of each needle as she clenched the muscles of her own legs and buttocks, waiting for Pug to finish his attempted penetration of her and planning her revenge.

Now, with her mind in that distant place, she planned her revenge on this jailor, his prince, and the prince's witch.

How long she had kept her mind on those pine needles, counting each one and comparing it to the next in color, texture, length, and shape, she did not know.

In her mind she had been able to escape, but in truth her eyes had not. Instead, they had taken in each brutal horror and sealed it in a tiny room in her memory to keep it locked away forever. If only.

Vonna's scream of "Nagora!" pulled her back into the moment. It was to be the last word to leave Vonna's lips. Through silent tears, Nagora's eyes witnessed the jailor's hands crush Vonna's windpipe and twist her neck.

Then the jailor came around the table to remove the leather straps from her wrists. He looked over at Nagora as he pulled Vonna off the table and unto his right hip.

Vonna's head lolled back, her lifeless eyes staring upside down at Nagora.

The jailor turned away to walk to the sea cave entrance.

Vonna's bloodied legs hung down from her limp back.

The jailor went down two steps, lifted his right knee as he grabbed Vonna's elbow with one hand and her knee with his other. He swung Vonna's body back once and then flung her into the water.

Numbness pushed Nagora's back against the door, forced her to her knees, but it did not stop her from crying. Her whole body shook as her tears choked her. All her strength drained from her as she gave up any hope of escape. She fell onto her side in a ball and cried as her body convulsed.

...

The splash of sea water struck Nagora. She rolled over and raised her arms. "Move to the back of the cell." Two guards stood in the doorway. One held an empty bucket, the other a rake.

She did as ordered. Tar piss! I didn't hear the door unlock. When did the guards arrive in the dungeon?

"Sit. Hands above your head."

When she had complied, the guards came in empty handed. One of them threw the dress against the wall and then they each took an arm and a leg of the dead girl. They carried her out of the cell. The jailor closed the door behind them, locked it, and peered in at Nagora. He grinned at her.

When he left, Nagora went to the window. The guards threw the body into the water of the sea cave.

She could no longer hear the gulls.

The tide must have risen. Whatever is left of their bodies will go out when the tide does. Then it'll be my turn tonight.

The jailor was dressed. He was over at the sea cave steps with the guards. She could not hear their conversation. A big tray of food and ale sat on the table.

Nagora waited for them to return. When they did, she called out, "Some food and drink, please."

The jailor waved a guard over to Nagora's cell with a piece of bread and a bucket. When the guard arrived, he looked in.

Nagora stood at the back of the cell. The guard unlocked the door, found Nagora's bowl, scooped water from the bucket into it, and placed it back in the corner along with a chunk of bread.

She was wet and cold. She found the girl's torn dress on the floor. Most of it was dry. She put it over her shoulders and went to the bread.

She took a deep breath.

It's not over yet. I need to eat.

She sat with her back against the door, taking her time to eat before bringing her amulet to her lips.

# Execution
## *Onipahtâkêw*

Tars, it's good to see you again. Those were our days of adventure. We took care of ourselves. If you would've shown up yesterday, I wouldn't be here, would I? I know. It's not your fault. I'll tell you what, Tars. If I ever make it out of here, it'll never happen again. Yes, Tars will have his weapons, always.

Were you there when I got my blades? That's right. It was just after Uncle finished painting the map on the hide side of my vest. You were there.

If I had my blades on me now, Tars, I'd take those three out there in no time. But I don't. They're on my bed up in the loft.

Tars, we're going to make it out of here, aren't we? When we do and we get our blades, we'll have scores to settle.

Nagora finished her piece of bread and sipped from the bowl. She put it down, leaned back against the door, closed her eyes, focused on her breathing, and let her mind escape to that place where she found hope, her beach.

It was where she built curraghs for fishers with her uncle. One had to have hope to be a fisher and return to the sea day after day to try to catch enough for the family and have extra to sell. The little leather boats the curragh builders made were the vessels of hope that carried those fishers out to sea each day. If those small craft weren't there to tell the fishers the catch would be better tomorrow, would they even try their luck again?

Soon, I'll go to sea. Hope is all I have.

The pounding on the door and the key turning in the lock brought Nagora to her feet. She stepped to the back of the cell, turned to lean against the stone wall, and waited.

The jailor opened the door. "Dragon lassie, it's your turn."

Her eyes stared straight ahead, past the jailor. Her legs carried her out of the cell and kept her moving toward the sea cave steps. "Hold on, lassie."

She stopped and waited, her eyes on the sea cave entrance. Do I want to live or do I want to die?

The jailor stood behind her with a hand on her right shoulder. He turned her to face the soldiers. "These men are here to witness you do not set me on fire, and that I follow orders."

Her eyes, as if no longer part of her, stared at the table where the two guards sat looking up at her. They relayed information back to her. Had the jailor interrupted their game? They were sitting on opposite sides of a small circular shield on which three game pieces and a set of dice rested.

Next to them on the table was a big coil of hemp rope with a noose on one end.

"Lassie, you seem to know what's in store for you. Have you any questions?" asked the jailor.

Her legs turned her toward the sea cave entrance. In her mind she did her ritual exercises in a slow cadence with only her small blades as weapons to keep her heartbeat calm.

The soldiers got up from the benches.

Ward off, rollback.

Once the jailor had reached for the coil of rope and slipped it over his head to rest it on his shoulder, he gave her a gentle push. "Let's get on with it then."

Press, push, pull.

Her legs brought her to the sea cave entrance where she waited on the top step.

The jailor stood next to her, kissed her cheek, bit on her ear, and fondled her breasts with one hand while he raised her shift with the other. "Now lads, isn't that a sight to behold. That'd keep your pricks warm in a cold bed, wouldn't it?" He slapped her ass and laughed.

Elbow strike, shoulder strike.

She remained silent and motionless. I want to live.

"Worsham, you know Hag's orders," a soldier said.

"Oh! Yes!" He spread his legs each side of Nagora's leg, holding a breast in one hand and a buttock in the other while he bent his knees to rub himself against her thigh. "I'm not to lay a finger on her. They're all on her!" He licked her ear and laughed.

Advance, retreat.

She didn't move though in her mind her blades were busy at work on the jailor. Tar piss! Yes! I want to live! I swear I'll make you pay!

"Okay, okay, lads. Just playing with dragon lassie. No flames. No sparks. No problem."

Look left, gaze right.

"Get on with your duties, Worsham."

"Down we go, lassie. I'm right behind you. Head over to the pillar. Water shouldn't be no more than above your waist. Wait at the steps."

Center balance.


No sound of gulls and no more daylight.

Except for the light from the big taper on the wall of the cave next to the bottom of the entrance, the cave was in the dark. The tide had come in. The cave ceiling was like an over-turned bowl with water rising all around its edge.

Nagora waited at the pillar steps.

The jailor climbed to the top step. He had brought a long stick with him. It had a two-pronged fork end. He removed several coils of the rope from his shoulder and placed the noose in the fork of the stick. It allowed him to lift the knot and thread it through the iron ring hanging from a big eye bolt that was screwed into the rock of the cave ceiling.

When he came back down, he motioned Nagora up the steps. He followed her. She stopped on the top step. From there, the top of the pillar was level with her belly.

"I've got to lay my fingers on her to help her up."

The jailor placed one hand under her left arm and the other just below her right buttock.

"Lift your leg, lassie. On three up you go."

His count was quick, and he held her on top of the pillar, one hand on her left thigh just above her knee and the other on her right calf. "Steady, lassie. There's not much room here. I'm going to let go."

The jailor's left hand slid down her leg and came to rest on the top of her foot. His right hand went to the top of her right foot. They lingered on her feet. "You know what your choices are, lassie. I bet you'll hang yourself."

She closed her eyes and breathed in as the jailor left the pillar.

"Almost done, lads. We'll come and check on dragon lassie before the tide fills the entrance."

When Nagora opened her eyes, the noose hung before her face, waiting for her to hang herself.

I won't even consider putting my head through this noose.

Her eyes followed the rope up to the big iron ring. She had heard stories about ancient Yhorgal Castle, supposedly cursed since it was built, and the terrible fate that awaited those sent to its dungeon. Death by drowning in an iron cage was supposed to have been a lenient death as the victim's bones were returned to the family, if the victim had one.

This ring would surely have supported such a cage.

Has Hag cursed me?

Her eyes moved along the rope over to the iron ring on the cave wall near the steps where the jailor had tied it, just below the big taper.

A guard sat on a step watching her. An arrow and a strung bow leaned against the wall next to him on the step.

Has there been a change of plan?

Nagora's eyes surveyed the edge of the cave and the movement of the water. From where she stood, she faced the entrance. The wave action of the sea outside reflected itself in the cave as rippling wavelets on the surface. They would grow into chaotic splashing waves bouncing around the cave walls.

She bent forward, pushing the noose away so she could look down at her feet on the pillar. She had a little bit of room to maneuver. The surface was rough enough for her to keep her foothold. She stood straight, widened her stance on the pillar, bent her knees slightly, and spread her toes.

A first chill went through her body. Neither her wet smock in the cool air of the cave nor her almost-empty stomach helped fight off the succeeding chills. Soon as seawater covered her feet, it would only get worse. She would focus and wait until the time was right to take advantage of the strongest rebound of the tidal backwash. Would it help carry her clear of the cave?

Yes, I want to live.

In her mind she pictured the steps she would take to swim to freedom. Taking her time to lay them out before her, she reordered certain ones, removed one, and reviewed them. Satisfied, she put them to memory and let them play out in her mind in order, over and over. Doing so comforted her.

Thank you, Uncle, for teaching me this.

By now, the cold seawater gripped her ankles.

Tars, let me take you to another place where you'll find comfort, warmth, and freedom. Back to my beach. I call it Sandy Hook. It's a sandy spit of land which pokes into the sea. It was once my playground down and away from the headland cliffs. From the base of the cliff to the tip of the spit, the beach ranges in a long gentle curve into the bay. Its tip isn't visible in the distance from the beach hut where I worked with Uncle.

There, where the sand was warm, even hot, Nagora now walked in her mind. She walked to soothe her cold feet as she had done many times after a swim in the sea. Sometimes, if the wind was blowing from offshore, she would find a dip in the sandy dune and lie naked on the sand, letting the sun and the warm sand bring her chilled body to a sweat. Sometimes she even slept, having hugged warm sand around her, free and at peace.

The ice cold water had become an agitated chop in the cave and it reached above Nagora's knees and splashed the hem of her linen shift, but her toes still did their job.

"Dragon lassie."

She turned her head to see the jailor. He was alone, sitting on a step, with both feet on the seawater-submerged step just below. He pulled open the crotch piece of his pants and relieved himself. His left elbow supported him on the step above the one on which he sat while he shook himself with his right hand. He let his eyes travel along her body. His unwanted gaze lingered and his eyes met hers, dark and cold as the water that was swallowing her up. He was stroking himself.

If only you had been allowed to have your way with me as you had with the others, I wouldn't be standing here. You think I won't be here for much longer. You're right. Count the days till we meet again because, believe me, your days are numbered.

The next pulse of the ocean washed into the cave, foaming up to Nagora's neck. It filled the entrance at the base of the stairwell where the jailor had stood before he turned to climb the steps. It had drowned the taper's flame, leaving her in the dark except for the dull glow of light in the water near the steps.

Relax. Breathe. Think of the sun-warmed sand on the beach.

She slipped the fid from between her wrists and slipped her hands free of the rope, just in time.

The water in the cave surged, rising to her shoulders, splashing in a roar on the cave walls surrounding her, covering her head in foam as it rebounded and splashed about her.

Hold on. Focus. The shock of the surge rocked Nagora as her cramped frozen toes did their best to hold onto the rock. With her arms free she could keep her balance. She bent her knees and rode the swell as the surge withdrew. She located the noose and then pulled her smock up over her head and kept it draped over her shoulders.

With the next surge, she could tread water and keep contact with the noose to relax the ache in her foot, calf, and thigh muscles.

Now I have to make my move.


Nagora placed a foot in the noose and hoisted herself up to the rusty iron ring. She threaded her smock through the iron ring so it hung there.

Then, with both hands, she grabbed the ring and hung from it for a moment before bringing her feet to the cave ceiling. She placed one on each side of the ring and pulled herself into a crouched position, ready to push off into the pulse of the sea as it again invaded the cave. Her amulet hung down over her chin and rested on her lips as she inhaled deeply through her nostrils, set to dive to her freedom.

She kissed the stone and let go of the ring as she pushed off the cave ceiling into the foaming surge. For a dozen powerful strokes, she fought her way into the darkness of the icy sea current.

Then the current changed as the backwash pulled her through with it. Now she kept her hands open in front of her, prepared to brace against and pull away from any obstacle. She continued to kick with her legs as her lungs burned for air. She let air bubbles escape from her lips. Her hands contacted the rock of the cave wall she judged to be in front and above her. She continued to kick with her legs and pull with her arms and fingers as she found handholds in the rock. The bubbles she had released raced ahead of her and up with the backwash current.

Then there was light in the liquid night.

The moon?

Yes! The surface is near!

Nagora broke to the surface and gasped for air as she pushed away from the rocks with her feet and swam with the remaining backwash before another roller came breaking in. It was coming. She would have to go back under and swim into it so as not to be brought back onto the rocks.

She dove and when she resurfaced with the backwash current, she turned to get her bearings in the moonlight. The jagged, rock-strewn cliffs of that part of the coast stood like unwelcoming giants guarding the shore.

No beach in sight, Tars. We must make it to shore on the rocks. What are our chances? My whole body is turning numb. Will I have the strength? How much time?

Not much.

At least I'll not have died in that cave.

...

Nagora grasped the stone that hung from her neck and closed her eyes.

I'll get to you in another lifetime. Come creatures of the sea. Take me. Give me peace.

With those words, the last ounce of strength left her. The icy cold seawater seemed to have grasped her by the skull. A feeble kick of her legs kept her face at the surface of the water. To breathe then hold her breath was all she could do as the slow surge of the next incoming roller approached.

Light shimmered in the dark. A voice, distant and unfamiliar, beckoned to her. Splashes, distant and familiar, echoed with the voice. Her own blue silhouette walked into the light, dripping seawater as it raised a hand toward the voice.

And then an eye appeared like no other she had ever seen. It looked deep inside her and spoke a message she did not understand.

The light faded.

# Resurrection
## *Âpisisinowin*

Stifling heat woke Nagora. Her eyes opened. She pushed aside the sheepskin and sweater that she found covering part of her belly and legs. As her eyes adjusted to the dim, brown, translucent light, they confirmed her last memory.

Earlier, she had awoken under another overturned curragh and her first reaction had been to flee, despite recognizing its trademark handiwork, one she had made days previous with her uncle on her beach. They had set it upside down above the high water mark to let the stitched hides and tarred seams dry in the sun.

She had feared for her safety and her instinct was to flee, even though she didn't have the strength to flee far on foot.

Nagora had propped up the edge of the craft with a stick and spied another leather boat, a forearm's length away. She had spread the sheepskin fur-side down on the sand between the curraghs before clutching the sweater to her to roll over onto the sheepskin and release the prop stick.

Then she propped up the edge of the next curragh and rolled off the sheepskin under that leather skiff, pulling the sheepskin in with her before freeing the prop stick. She hoped the sheepskin wouldn't leave a trace on the sand to where she had escaped.

Nagora had fallen asleep, exhausted from her effort.

Now she was in an oven. Her mouth parched, she listened for any sounds. Only the sound of the gentle surf on the beach and gulls in the distance came to her.

Nagora propped up the side of the leather skiff and smelled soup—soup just like the one she often made for her uncle and herself when they worked at the beach hut.

Again, using the sheepskin, she rolled over to the first curragh, propped it up on its edge and discovered Dangor's cooking pot and a waterskin laying next to it. She reached over to the pot. It was warm to the touch. She dragged herself closer and, when she raised herself on an elbow, she found a knife in its sheath resting on the cover next to two eggs that sat in a nest of leather strips. She picked up one of the eggs. By its heft and slight warmth, it had to be hard-boiled.

She smiled at the heart on the egg.

A message from my savior?

She set the egg back in its nest and reached for the waterskin. Nagora pulled the plug, brought the lip of the bag to her lips, and drank deeply. She licked her lips and, replacing the plug, she set the bag on the sand.

Nagora lifted the cover off the pot, set it on the sand, and fished for an open clam shell. She ate the clam and used the shell to eat some soup. She licked her lips. It was just like the one she had often cooked.

Was this what freedom tasted like? She called it shore soup. Her uncle called it egg-drop soup. The recollection of their little ongoing argument about what to call it filled her eyes with tears. I'm lucky to be eating this again.

The salty dulse gave the pieces of flounder a delicate flavor. All that was missing was a piece of freshly baked stone bread. This is the best soup I've ever eaten. Someone has taken good care of me. Could it be Uncle? He was arrested also.

Already, the soup warmed her insides. It was bringing her strength back. I could eat the whole thing. I better take my time. Only eat my fill.

Resting on her elbow, she looked at the egg. Who'd drawn the heart on it?

Uncle? Was he still being held? Was he safe? The Watcher? I haven't seen him in days. He just watches and always from afar. Why? Uncle says I'll meet him when the time is right.

Nagora returned the egg with the heart to its nest and took the other, which she cracked. The shell peeled away in two pieces. She took a bite of the egg and dropped the rest into the soup. Okay, Uncle, you win. We'll call it egg-drop soup. She wiped away a tear.

As she looked inside the empty shell, her ordeal in the sea cave flooded back.

Well, Tars, we made it after all. Chive was right. And someone else helped. Do you know who, Tars?

Nagora reached for her amulet. It wasn't there. Now she was truly naked. She let herself fall back on the sand.

Did I lose it swimming in the sea, Tars? Was it taken from me by the one who saved me? By the one who made this soup to feed me? Was it Uncle who saved me? Probably not, otherwise he would be with me now. Is he safe? Is he alive? When will I know the answers to these questions? We have to find out, Tars.

Nagora leaned up on an elbow and pulled the knife from its sheath. It was like hers and Dangor's—a burnished steel blade the length of her middle finger with an oiled, cherry-wood handle, bearing the same carved rune symbol, Raidho, which would touch the palm of the hand of whoever held it. The blade was sharp. Its oiled leather sheath kept it rust free. Whoever owned this knife knew how to use it and care for it. Like hers, it would throw well. She could make it find its mark.

The jailor. A knife to his heart would be too kind.

The knife sheath needed a belt. Nagora rummaged through the pile of leather strips and lanyards to find a suitable piece. She threaded the strip of leather through the knife sheath loop. She had enough length to tie it around her waist. She slipped the woolen shirt over her head, pulled the sleeves over her arms, and rolled them up to bare her forearms. Nagora tied the strip around her waist and slid the knife sheath to the middle of her back.

Time to go, Tars. Let's see how strong I am. Then we'll decide what to do next. It must be nearing midday. How long has it been since I was taken by the prince's guards? I'm guessing three days, Tars.

...

Nagora peeked out from the underside of the curragh, looking down the beach and along the water's edge as far as she could see while letting her eyes adjust to the bright light.

All clear in that direction.

Then Nagora propped up the curragh and rolled out from the other side, to bring herself next to the other curragh beneath which she'd awoken. She scanned the cliffs above her and then the path leading up to and past the cliffs.

No one in sight.

She peered towards the beach hut.

Still no one in sight.

Nagora lifted the side of the curragh and reached for the leather strips and the waterskin, pulling them out on the sheepskin. She placed the cooking pot on the skin also, and then dragged it out next to her feet. She slung the waterskin's strap over her shoulder, picked up the rest, and headed for the hut not fifty strides away. That's when she staggered after a dozen steps and had to slow down. She bent to one knee. She was not yet her usual lithe self. Her body was still weak and cold inside.

She looked to the curragh at the water's edge. Its small killick anchor was dug into the sand on the beach, but not in the place she had set it. She touched her tender ribs. Someone had gotten her into the small leather boat. Someone brought me here in that, Tars.

Inside the hut, Nagora threw the sheepskin onto the cot and set the pot's handle on the hook over the fire pit where the soup had most likely been made. A pouch and a fishing spear lay close by along with scraps of dulse, fish scales, and egg shells. She put the spear back on its pegs above the hut entrance.

Not like Uncle to not put things back in their place.

More soup should help, aye, Tars? She scooped the last pieces of flounder from the pot, swallowed a last piece of hard-boiled egg, and drank from the waterskin. My stomach needed that. My legs too. She reached for her amulet to think about her next move. Damn it! Where is it?

She had made a vow to a dying girl and to Vonna. If she were to keep her promise, she would need help. So finding her uncle came first. If he were still a prisoner, she would need more help. Uncle's best friend, Geirador, would help. It meant going to Cairnmase. If anyone can help us, Tars, it's Geirador.

Nagora walked out into the sunlight and once again scanned the beach, the cliffs, and the path. She stretched her arms above her head and stood on tiptoes before returning to the hut to gather the hemp pouch; into it she placed the remaining boiled egg and the waterskin.

First, she would head for home.

Barefoot, Nagora made her way up the cliff path. Their mule, Patches, was not in the pasture above the cliff nor was Dangor's cart. She headed for their small stone hut, less than a brisk walk of three counts away. A day's work was twenty-four counts and a day was three times that. She would run the distance in half that time to test her strength.

...

The stone chimney, poking up above the sod roof, stood like a welcome beacon for Nagora, yet today a weight in the pit of her stomach gnawed at her. Would it stop if her uncle were there?

Now she could see the whole sod roof that flowed onto the rocky outcrop at the edge of the forest clearing. Soon she would see the hut's two walls of stacked, slate stones and the wooden door and single window.

The run had tired her, but she picked up the pace. The corral came into view. Patches, their mule, was nowhere in sight nor her horse, Storm. Could Storm be in the stable? Not likely. She walked the rest of the way to catch her breath. Uncle, I hope you're free as well.

As Nagora approached the stable, she called out to Storm. Her horse didn't answer. She walked through the open doors and stopped. Storm's stall was empty. Not in the corral and not here. Who'd taken Storm? She bent to examine the footprints and hoofprints.

The Watcher! Did he save me? His appearances have been more frequent in the past year. Who is he? Where'd he go from here? Didn't he have a horse of his own? Or did he borrow a horse from Geirador? That's strange. Storm, I'll worry about you when I get to Geirador's.

Nagora rushed over to their lodge, pulled open the door, and stepped over the threshold. All seemed to be as they had left it a few days earlier. She set the pouch on the table and climbed the short ladder to the loft.

...

Nagora pulled aside her blankets and reached for the big blade, pulling it from its sheath.

I'll never be without you again! I swear!

She pushed it back into its sheath and flicked the latch over the crossguard to hold it in place. Next, she checked if the two small throwing knives on each of the sheath's straps were tight in their holsters. She set her blades aside.

Nagora opened the wooden trunk at the foot of her bed and took linen undergarments, wool socks, a pair of doe-skin leather leggings, a hooded linen shirt, her sheepskin vest, and an embossed leather belt she had been working on. The belt had a brass buckle attached; only some embossing on the leather remained to be done. I'll get to that later.

She closed the lid of the trunk and reached under the bed for her boots. When she had them in hand, she froze for a moment. Her slippers were on the hook in the dungeon with all the others. Did that pig of a jailor collect them? Count your days, Worsham, you pig!

Nagora threw the boots on her bed with her other things and reached for the empty leather pouch that hung near the head of the bed. She laid it on the bed and opened its flap. Except for her sheepskin vest, the embossed leather belt, and her blades, she folded the items lying next to the pouch and placed them inside it.

She untied the leather strip at her waist, removed the knife sheath, threaded it onto her leather belt, buckling it over her sweater at her waist. She slipped her blades on and then the vest.

...

Nagora climbed onto the bed and reached up above her head to find one of her unstrung bows. It was among the other pieces of ash wood, resting on the two wooden crossbeams. which spanned the curved ceiling. Her fingers found it.

She ran her fingers over the bow and its string. No cracks. No frays. Good. Reaching overhead once more, she grabbed one of the two small spears, slid it ahead, then pulled it back and down. It was as long as she was tall.

Nagora stepped from her bed to the floor, moved to the edge of the loft floor, and let the spear drop, tip first, to stick in the earth floor below. She returned to the bed, picked up the pouch. Pulling its strap over her head, she brought it onto her left shoulder so the pouch rested on her right hip. With her bow in hand, she climbed back down the loft ladder.

Once on the dirt floor, Nagora walked over to their weapons cabinet to retrieve her quiver full of arrows. She tied her bow to the quiver and set them on the table.

Nagora went to the cold box at the back of the hut and found a last piece of cheese and a wrapped, hand-sized piece of last summer's honeycomb. She brought the food to the table and laid them alongside the hemp pouch before returning to the cupboard to fetch two earthenware jars and two square pieces of cloth. These as well she set on the table.

Next, she took a handful of shelled hazelnuts from one of the jars and a handful of dried currants from the other. From the linen pouch, Nagora retrieved the hard-boiled egg and wrapped it, along with the nuts and currants, in one piece of cloth. She wrapped the pieces of cheese and honeycomb in the other piece of cloth. She tucked these food packets into the leather pouch on her right hip.

She slipped her quiver over her right shoulder, pulled the spear from the floor, and headed for the door.

Outside, Nagora walked around the rocky outcrop against which the back of the hut sat until she came to the stream. She emptied her waterskin and refilled it before following the water downstream until she came to that place in the brook where she usually bathed. She stripped.

Nagora stepped into the water up to her mid-thigh and sat on her bathing rock, facing the oncoming current. The water came up to her chest. She leaned back in the curve-like depression of the rock and let the water wash over her.

The cool, rushing water flooded her mind with images of her swim to freedom. They made her shiver. She sat up and let them run their course as she scrubbed her face, arms, and the rest of her body to remove the sticky salt residue of the sea. Even so, the cries and screams of the two young girls lingered.

She scrubbed harder where the jailor had touched her. Satisfied she hadn't missed a spot, she lay back again and let the stream take care of washing the beach sand and sea salt from her hair. She tried to calm her desire for vengeance. How do I get Geirador to help me free Uncle?

Nagora ran her fingers through her hair a few times. When it felt clean to her, she let the current lay her back and comb her hair for her. What was to be a refreshing pause left her with an ache inside. It was close to fear, the unknown, the unpredictability of the events to come, and the need to have a plan to try to deal with them.

She reached for her absent amulet. What happened to it? She sat up, examined the bruises on her ribs, and stood up to let the excess water drip from her hair.

Nagora stepped out of the streambed onto the shore. While waiting for the dripping to stop, she cracked the shell of the hard-boiled gull egg, salvaging the charcoal-drawn heart before biting into the white flesh.

How would she ever thank the one who had saved her? With the heart resting in the palm of her left hand, she gingerly ate away the white flesh of the egg until she held the solid orange sphere of yolk between the thumb and pointer finger of her right hand. She inhaled its distinctive odor and popped the sphere into her mouth to let her tongue play with it before crushing it to the roof of her mouth to savor its rich flavor.

Nagora's left hand reached out over the stream and let the piece of shell fall into the water where it sank, tripped, and tumbled among the rocks on the streambed, until it came to rest on a stone that held it still enough for the current to begin to wash away the charcoal outline. The heart's outline faded as she made a single braid with her damp hair.

Was love like that? Would she ever be able to love a man?

She had no answer.

Nagora unwrapped the piece of cheese and set the whole thing into her mouth and chewed through the sharp taste as the pieces crumbled between her teeth. This was a treat when she was hungry like this. The best was yet to come. She bit a chunk out of the honeycomb to meld its sweetness to the sharpness of the cheese, one of her favorite tastes. Tars, I'm lucky to be alive.

As she sucked the sweetness from the chambers of the honeycomb, she slipped on her undergarments, pulling the drawstring tight and tying it snug with a bow knot. Next, she pulled on her wool socks and her leather leggings. She tied these to the drawstring visible at the hips of her undergarments before putting on her boots and lacing them around her calves.

Working the waxed residue of the honeycomb with her teeth and tongue to extract the last of its sweetness, she donned her sweater, belt, and blades. She slipped on her hooded shirt and her vest over that. Her pouch went on one shoulder and her quiver on the other.

Tars, if we make good time, we should be there for the evening meal.

# Revelations
## *Kîkway ka wihtamihk*

Instead of continuing on the wagon road that went from Yhorgal and wound its way to Cairnmase, Nagora took the woodland trail shortcut to Geirador's. Why wasn't she surprised to see Storm's hoofprints on the trail? Storm, I'm sure I'll find you.

As Nagora came down the path through the trees just past Cairnmase, she stepped onto the approach road, which brought visitors to the blacksmith's forge from the main road. Her heart beat faster. Patches was in the corral next to the stable adjoining the smithy. Let it be so. Uncle must be here.

Nagora hurried along the road to the wooden doors to Geirador's shop. They were open, and no one was inside.

Nagora doubled back into the stable. Storm! She ran to the stall and hugged him. She scratched his nose and patted his neck. Her saddle sat on the wooden rail next to the stall.

...

Nagora headed for Geirador's hut, almost three hundred strides away, set among the trees against a high cliff wall. She paused for a moment. Tar piss! Pare's gift! She'll understand, won't she Tars?

She paused at the door.

Do I knock or just go in?

She smelled bread baking and heard voices. She opened the door and stepped in.

The conversation stopped as those at the table turned to watch as Nagora leaned her spear against the wall and removed her weapons and her pouch to hang them on a free peg next to the door.

"Nagora! My sweet Nagora! You're alive!" Dangor was up from his chair in no time to hold her in his arm. "You're alive! You're alive! He told me. I needed to see for myself. We knew you'd come."

"Uncle! You're safe! I'm so happy!" Her breathing almost stopped as she held on to him.

"Oh! Child! Let me see you." He held her by the shoulders and looked her up and down. Relief covered his face.

"Uncle, who told you? Told you what? How did you get away from the prince's fortress?"

Dangor put an arm around her shoulders and pointed to the Watcher. "The man who saved you."

So it was him! Truly?

Geirador and Paruline stood and were approaching. Only the Watcher remained seated, calmly staring at her. It was the first time she had ever seen him so close. He wore his usual green hooded shirt and black headband that kept his shoulder-length hair behind his ears.

Nagora finally spoke. "He saved me?" How did he know?

"Aye, he did. You'll find out how soon enough."

Geirador stepped forward to embrace her. "Nagora, if you'd stepped in here with a shield and a sword, I could say you're armed to the teeth. You look like you've come ready for a fight." His big arms pulled her gently to his barrel-sized chest, and for a moment he rested a bearded-cheek on top of her head.

She smiled at Geirador and tried to focus on the next question she would ask her uncle. "Well, for a while, I thought I might need your help in a fight."


Paruline, wearing her knee-length linen apron, put her arms around Nagora and held her close. "Oh! Nagora! I'm so glad to see you're safe. We've just heard what happened. Not everything, of course. You must have much to tell us."

Nagora's eyes watered as she hugged her dear friend. "Oh! Pare! I'm happy to see you too. For a while, I thought I'd never see any of you again. Aye, there's much to tell, and I have questions. I guess we'll all have some talking to do to help put order into what I've been through." She pulled Paruline closer. I don't want to let you go, Pare. You smell of your cooking, and it's so comforting to me.

Dangor's eyes locked onto hers. "All in good time Nagora. You'll have answers to your questions and you'll surely have more questions. There's much to be told and understood. First, introductions of sort need to take place, and then we'll talk."

She nodded. Her questions would have to wait.

The Watcher stood and approached. He was slightly taller than Dangor and shorter than Geirador and of a much smaller frame. He spoke first, before her uncle could. "Finally, we meet face-to-face, and both of us are conscious today. Nagora, Dangor tells me you've known me as 'the Watcher,' especially these past few months because that's all you've ever seen me do—watch you from afar. You'll want to know why. You'll learn why soon.

"First, let me introduce myself. My name is Raynhard and I also go by several other names. Those you'll also learn today. I'm pleased to tell you that the last time we met, I didn't just watch. I had the good fortune to put myself in the right place, at the right time, to save you. How that came to be is another thing you're about to find out.

"Right now, Nagora, believe me, I'm most happy to see you're alive and, from all appearances, well."

She looked from Raynhard to Dangor and back. "I don't know what to say. I owe you my life."

"Two simple words will do."

"Thank you. Thank you, Raynhard, for saving my life. How will I ever repay you?" *What am I not seeing?*

Raynhard smiled at her.

Geirador filled the moment of silence that followed Nagora's question. "The makings of a good stew are in the pot on the fire right now and bread in another. And I have cool ale to wet our tongues while we talk."

"Thank you, Geirador. You're always the generous host," said Raynhard.

Then Raynhard turned back to Nagora. "Moments ago, Geirador said you looked like you were ready for a fight. You answered that you thought you might need his help in a fight. What did you mean?"

She took a moment to frame her reply.

"Listen, Uncle and I were taken prisoners to the prince's fortress. While I was in the dungeon, I saw the terrible rape and abuse and senseless killing of two young girls. They also had been rounded up like me." She pointed to herself as her fingers balled into a fist.

"The prince and his jailor have to be stopped, and that old witch, Hag. She wanted me to die in the dungeon sea cave, but I escaped thanks to the person of Chive in the fortress. And you saved me when I lost consciousness after swimming out of the cave.

"Those other girls who were rounded up also have to be saved!" She clenched her fist in front of her.

"When I left the beach, I went home to see if Uncle was there. Then I thought I'd come to Geirador to seek help to free Uncle and the girls. Uncle, you're free too. Those girls aren't! I don't see freeing them without a fight. That's the fight I meant."

Raynhard pointed to Dangor. "Nagora, your uncle and I thought you'd say as much. That fight will come.

"First, I'll let Dangor fill us in on recent events. I'll jump in to tell you what I know from my perspective. Then I expect you'll have your turn to tell your side of the events."

Her mind searched and came up empty, no matter how hard she willed it to remember something, even the slightest detail of her rescue. That wasn't important. Freeing those girls was.

Raynhard put his palms together and brought his fingers to his chin. "Nagora, I beg you to listen carefully to all you'll be told, because much of what you learn will come as a great surprise to you. You'll come to realize that now you are about to become involved in events of greater importance than any you can imagine. You'll surely have questions. You can ask them when you wish. We'll do our best to answer them for you."

Is this a dream? No, this is now. This is real. I escaped from the dungeon cave. Why can't I remember the rescue? Did I die? No, I'm told the Watcher rescued me. I am alive. Or have I come back from death?

The memory of the shimmering light in the distance flashed in her mind, and then that of the eye, the one that looked into her and spoke to her. I'm not myself, Tars.

Dangor must've seen Nagora's puzzled look and so he spoke, "Allow me to reintroduce you two." He cleared his throat. "Raynhard is not one to stand on formalities, but for your sake, you should be introduced formally, the sooner the better.

"My king, permit me another face-to-face introduction to my niece, Nagora.

"Nagora, this is our king, Raynhard, the rightful king of this land, the Land of the Danu as it is known to us; the Land of the Dragon as our allies once knew it."

Am I in a dream? Nagora took the hand Raynhard held out. It was real. She was holding it. Why do I feel like I'm not here? Am I a ghost?

Paruline mouthed the words "My king" and motioned that she bow.

"My king." Nagora bowed awkwardly. She looked at her feet, then to Paruline and Geirador. They were smiling. As was Dangor. Raynhard's face was solemn.

"That's unnecessary, Nagora." He smiled. "Please, call me Raynhard, as the others do, and as I introduced myself to you. Paruline, that goes for you as well."

The Watcher is the rightful king of this land? Well, Tars, what do you think? Is this truly happening? Is this the truth or am I in a dream?

Paruline's hand on Nagora's back took her away from her questions for a moment as they moved to sit at the table, but Nagora remained standing, holding the back of the chair, trying to grasp at something that would make this real to her.

Nagora's eyes focused on the big table before her. It could seat six and with two more around it, they would be tight. Just like everything else fashioned by Geirador's hands in his home, it had a story.

I know that story.

Lightning had split this huge piece of wood from the side of a big tree. Several of the tree's branches had remained attached to that piece when it fell to the ground. Geirador had found it and figured if he cut the branches, skinned away all the bark, and sawed off the ends of the fallen slab, he would have the makings of a sturdy table to stand before his fireplace.

Sarah, his wife, had been reluctant because of the rough surface. To please her Geirador had smoothed the top with his adze and a plane until it was to her liking.

The reflections of the light of the lamps on the tiny dips left by Geirador's adze were like the tiny wavelets on the surface of the water of Nagora's bay at sunset.

She had as many questions as the glints of light before her eyes. *If I were a ghost, would I still know that story? Maybe I did survive and this isn't a dream.*

*So the Watcher is the rightful heir to the throne. We've been training to fight for him. The rightful king's been here all along. I've seen him now and then over the years. More often recently. Why did they keep this from me? For my own protection?*

*My king brought me to the beach last night? He carried me from the boat and placed me under the new curragh above the high water mark. Why not in the hut?*

*How did he get me into the curragh in the first place? My bruises?*

She touched her ribs with her hand. They were still sore.

She looked at her hand resting on the chair's back. The raw marks left by the rope on her wrist brought back the awful images from the dungeon.

The urgency to act to free the girls prodded Nagora back into the moment. She had to get busy doing something. "Pare, can I help?"

"No, Nagora. You sit at the table and I'll join you as soon as I'm done."

Geirador set mugs of ale on the table for everyone and a dish of salt.

Raynhard raised his mug. "To Nagora's safe return."

All raised their mugs as she took a sip of ale and licked her lips, her face wincing. Her jaw was still sore and swollen. She looked to her uncle, eager for the talk to begin. Let's do this so we can save the girls.

All eyes were on Dangor as he recounted the events up to his being chained to the wall in the prince's fortress yard, where he saw Nagora being brought inside.

Geirador's features became stern as Dangor spoke. Obviously, he didn't like what he was hearing one bit.

"Nagora, continue from there," said Dangor.

Nagora recounted her meeting with Prince Acindor and Hag.

She forced herself to recount the ordeal and deaths of the two young women in the dungeon sea cave. "Geirador! Raynhard! Uncle told you how we were treated in the square. We have to save those other girls! Surely, they'll all suffer the same cruelties. The prince and his jailor have to be punished! If I had my way, they'd get no mercy from me."

"Nor I," said Geirador.

Raynhard had been tight-lipped during their recounting of events. Now he looked Nagora in the eye, raised his hands, fingers spread, just above the tabletop, and took a breath before speaking.

I read uneasiness in your gestures.

"You're right, Nagora. We have to save the girls and we have to serve justice on Acindor and his jailor. In time, that will happen."

In time! Damn it! We have to do it now! Why can't we act now?

"We cannot just run to the fortress and do that. Nagora, my answer must be painful to you, but soon you'll understand why. First we need to hear the rest of your own ordeal."

Nagora clenched her teeth and pressed the knuckles of her fists against the tabletop as she tried to understand and accept Raynhard's words, her king's words.

Dangor placed a hand on her shoulder. She looked at him. His look was one of reassurance, yet it did not reassure her. She took a deep breath and continued to relate what the jailor had done to her right until the rising water had blocked the dungeon entrance.

"If Hag hadn't ordered I not be touched, I wouldn't be here right now." Her voice wavered.

Get a hold on yourself. With a shaking hand, she dropped a pinch of salt into her mug, took a sip, and licked her upper lip. Almost like the taste of the cold sea that night.

Geirador was shaking his head. Paruline reached across to take her hand. Raynhard and Dangor stared into their mugs.

Nagora told of her swim from the sea cave, of seeing moonlight at the surface of the sea above her and swimming up toward it, of trying to get her bearings at the surface, and of finally giving up to the icy cold water.

Do I tell about the strange eye that spoke to me? No, they'll not believe me. They'll think I've lost my mind. I have trouble believing it myself.

She looked around the table. Silence sat with them.

Raynhard spoke up. "Dangor, Nagora, if you let me, I'll speak. Today, Nagora, Dangor introduced me to you as Raynhard, the true king of this land. Until that moment, you had known me from afar as 'the Watcher' so to speak. Your uncle went along with that and assured you I meant you no harm. To your uncle, Geirador, and Paruline, I have another identity."

What's he trying to tell me?

Raynhard stood up, walked to the fireplace and stood with his back to them. He untied his headband, released his shoulder length hair. He moved his head from side to side, shook his shoulders, and then his legs, until he let his right foot fall out at its ankle so his knee twisted inward, causing his whole posture to change. He turned around to face them with the deformed face and body of Chive.

"You!" Nagora pushed her chair back to stand.

Barely understandable in Chive's stutter, Raynhard said, "You recognized Chive, Nagora, but you didn't see the Watcher at the fortress, did you?"

Could she trust what her eyes were seeing?

Raynhard turned back to the fireplace and reversed his transformation. Then he returned to the table.

"Please, Nagora. Sit.

Raynhard brought the tips of his fingers to his chest. "Being Hag's idiot scrounger of roots and plants for her potions, and someone who's barely understood when he speaks but by her alone, gives me access to many conversations that normally wouldn't take place in front of an unsuspecting third party.

"Sometimes, Hag's idiot gets to speak a word that might cause her to change her decision. You were to go on the night tide of the same day they took you from the square. Hag was in her chamber with the prince, discussing her plan to let the sea ... dispose of you.

"As I huddled in the corner, sorting roots I'd collected, I kept repeating, 'Full moon; high, high tide.' Acindor couldn't understand what I was stuttering, but Hag did, and picked up on it, and decided to wait for the highest tide, which would occur late the following night.

"That gave me time to get into position to help you since, as Chive, I get to come and go as I wish with my collection bag and basket, sometimes for days at a time.

"Nagora, having observed your swimming abilities, I knew that if anyone had a chance of making it out of the sea cave, it would be you. What I had to do was make it to the sea cave entrance below the cliffs to watch for you to come up to the surface. I almost lost hope. You surfaced for a moment and then went back under."

"I wouldn't have made it that far without the fid you brought to me."

"I swam to you and brought you back up to the surface and dumped you into the curragh."

The bruises on my ribs ...

"You were blue with cold when I got you out of the water, unconscious. Then it was a long row back to the beach, where I covered you with warm sand under the curragh. Then I hunted the ingredients to make soup to feed you."

"I owe you a great debt." How can I ever repay him?

Raynhard smiled and shook his head. "That you're alive and here with us now is payment enough, believe me."

Tars, he's revealed who he is. Perhaps he knows something about my da. "Raynhard, when will my da return?"

He looked to the others around the table before answering. Obviously, he hadn't been expecting her question. "Nagora, like you, we're waiting for him to return. All I can tell is we've heard news."

So he does know something!

"Once we get confirmation, then we'll be able to tell when he'll most likely return."

"Can you share that news with me now?"

Raynhard took a deep breath. Again he looked around the table at the others, and then back at her. "Not yet Nagora, but soon. There are things that have to be kept secret to protect our cause ... and to protect you. I think Dangor has explained this to you in the past."

The less I know about the Cause, the less I'll reveal under interrogation. I don't intend to ever be taken captive again.

Her mouth became dry. "I don't understand. This is about my da. I've been waiting for his return all these years. Surely there's something you can tell me?"

"When we tell you, you'll understand why we aren't giving you any information today."

"It's because he's dead! Is that it?"

Raynhard held up a hand and shook his head. "Nagora, please. There are things you'll learn today that will most likely make you angry as you've never been. Some of that anger might be directed toward me, your uncle Dangor, Geirador, and even your father." Raynhard paused. "And toward your mother as well."

"My mum? Why should I be angry with her? She died at my birth."

"Nagora, your mother is alive and well and fighting for our cause," said Raynhard.

She moved her mouth, but not a sound came out; her eyes went to her uncle, then Geirador and Paruline for confirmation. Their hands reached out to hers to confirm Raynhard's words.

Nagora pulled her hands away and stood. Her whole body was shaking. She kicked back her chair as she left the table and headed for the door. She pushed the door open and her vision blurred as the tears of anger and deception welled up into her eyes.

As Nagora took her first step outside, she sobbed and tried to catch her breath at the same time. She almost choked on the great gob of tears and phlegm she coughed up from her throat, out of her mouth and through her nose.

She wiped it from her mouth and chin with the back of a forearm while the heel of her other hand pushed away the tears from her eyes.

Nagora screamed as she ran past the big oak to the cold shade of the stone cliff face that towered above her.

Nagora leaned there, against the wall of rock, her cheek against its cold surface, her hands spread to each side trying to cling to its rough surface. The deception and confusion she felt were too much to bear. Her sobs shook her until her legs could no longer hold her. Her knees gave way. The fingers of her hands failed to hold her up.

She was on her knees, crumpled over, her hands and arms clutching her sobbing sides, her forehead wedged against the cliff when Dangor got to her.

Dangor went to his knees next to Nagora and placed a hand on her back, above her heart.

She looked up at her uncle's face. Could he read all the conflicting emotions her face could not hide as they ran through her now—deception, confusion, disbelief, and sadness?

Those ever patient eyes of his stared back, filled with concern and compassion. Still, she couldn't understand why they had kept this from her.

"Soon you'll be reunited with your mum."

His words brought Nagora up on her knees. She turned toward him with clenched fists and her face twisted as her eyes blinked tears from them. She struck out at him as she sobbed even more.

He turned his face from her weak, shaky blows and let them fall on his chest as he opened his arms and brought her into them, encircling her. Her sobs shook her ever more until she let herself melt into Dangor's strong embrace.

With the back of her head resting in the palm of his hand, he said, "And you'll be reunited with your sister too."

Nagora snapped her head around and blinked away tears as she looked at him. I don't believe this. She coughed to clear her throat before croaking, "I have a sister?"

"Aye, a twin sister, identical in appearance to you."

She couldn't take her eyes away from her uncle's.

"My mum's alive and I have a sister. What's her name?" She leaned her cheek into the palm of Dangor's big hand, expecting to find relief in the answer he would give her.

"Sagora."

"Sagora." She repeated it. "And my mum's name is Tagnyoriva."

"Aye, those close to her call her 'Tagnya.'"

"Why? Why have you kept all this from me? Why have you kept me away from my mum and sister? What is this all about?"

"It's about our cause and the role you'll be playing in it, and your mother and sister. It's about circumstances that brought about terrible decisions."

Nagora pushed away from him and lurched to her feet. "I have a sister and my mum is alive! You tell me this today! Today? After all these years of training to fight for some noble and just cause I still hardly know anything about? And you expect me to believe this? Don't you think I would've trained that much harder had I known what you're telling me today? Who do you think I am? A puppet? Well, I'm not!"

The tears and sobs welled up once again inside her as she turned to run back to the hut.

Nagora pushed past Paruline, pulled open the door and, in a flash, stepped in, grabbed her pouch and quiver, and left.

She ran, her tears and sobs blinding her. I don't believe this. They've betrayed me, lied to me. Why? Mum, is it true? Are you alive?

Well past the smithy, Nagora left the road and cut across a field of young barley toward a forested hillside. Her face was wet with tears. Her throat burned, and her sides ached as the uncontrollable sobs tore at her insides, shaking her and choking her.

Just as Nagora fell to her knees between two oak trees, Raynhard reached her. He went to his knees at her side and placed his hands on her shoulders. They shook as she cried louder and twisted away from his hands. She struggled forward on her knees and struck out at him with a weak blow from her hand.

She turned toward him and wailed, "Leave me alone with your lies! Lies! Lies! It's all lies! Why should I sit around and listen to these lies when the girls in the prince's fortress are being raped by the jailor and by the prince himself? We could do something about that!"

Raynhard reached out to her. "Do you think I don't want to do anything about that and all the other injustices I know go on unpunished in my land? I can't do it by myself. You can't do it by yourself. Five or a dozen of us can't do it! But a credible force of warriors can, and if you want to be part of that force, you can be."

Nagora fell back on her heels and slumped forward at the waist. As she brought her hands to her face, she cried more and moaned, "Why? Why? Why me?"

Raynhard brought himself down on his side next to her and he turned so he lay on his back with his head next to her knee. When her crying subsided a little, he spoke. "I'll tell you if you're willing to listen. I had thought the best way to tell you was to do so in the order that the events happened. Now I realize, perhaps, there is no right way. When you're ready, I'll tell you why and then backtrack so you'll understand why."

Nagora regained control of her breathing as she wiped away her tears on one of her sweater's unraveled sleeves. She glanced at Raynhard, who was staring at the canopy of leaves above, waiting for her reply.

Why me? Why should I believe you? Why did you save me? Why have you watched me all those times? Okay Raynhard, I'll listen.

She took a deep breath, placed her hands on one knee, and brought her cheek to rest on top of them. "Tell me."

Raynhard turned his head and brought his gaze to her face. Their faces were fingers apart and their eyes met. Raynhard's were clear and truthful. "Because the laws of a land chose you, Nagora. At your birth, your mother had a terrible choice to make in the land where she now lives.

"Being the second-born of twins, according to the law in that land, you were to die or be banished to live away from that land. Your mother chose for you to live, even if it broke her heart and you would be away from her. Her only consolation was that she could see your face in the face of your sister and know that you would live in the safety and good care of your uncle Dangor."

Banished at birth. Banished for a hundred days. Twice banished. It must be in my star story.

Nagora blinked more tears from her eyes. "That's not a choice. No mother should have to do that. I think about the mothers of those girls rounded up and brought to the prince's fortress. I can only try to imagine what they're feeling."

Raynhard brought his right knee up, clutched it with both hands, and pulled himself up into a sitting position.

Nagora pushed herself up from her knees so she sat on her heels. She wiped her tears with the sleeve of her sweater.

Raynhard was nodding. "The mothers of those girls, like your mother, must not be having an easy time of it either."

Raynhard reached inside his shirt and pulled Nagora's amulet from around his neck up over his head. "Here, this belongs to you," he said, as he handed it to her. "It has saved your life once and it may do so again. I took it from you to give me the strength to bring you to the safety of your beach.

My intention was to replace it before you knew it was missing, but you had disappeared before I could do so."

Nagora held the fine leather lace that was fastened to her amulet. She looked from it back to Raynhard. "Does it truly have the fire powers of the dragon?"

Raynhard shrugged. "I wish I could say it does. Those of us sworn to free the dragon spread such stories about stones containing the blood tears of the dragon. I know for a fact that your amulet once belonged to your father, and that he gave it to your mother for her to give to his daughter, or son, at birth. Your mother placed it around your neck when she handed you over to your uncle to bring you here."

Nagora held the black stone up, trying to see the red crystal and the pale pink filament held prisoner inside it. "Uncle says it has power that will reveal itself."

Raynhard shrugged. "It very well could. I guess your mother could tell you more about it."

He pointed at the stone. "Right now, that amulet is the closest you'll get to your father until we get confirmation of the news we've heard. Join our force and help us free the dragon. I won't ask you to make that choice now, but I will ask you to hear us out so you'll know what you're getting into, if you join our cause."

Raynhard stood and held out his hand to her. When she grasped it, he pulled her to her feet. "Allow me to walk you back to Geirador's hut so you can hear the rest."

Nagora placed her amulet around her neck and as soon as it touched her skin under her sweater, the strange eye appeared.

In her mind, every action Raynhard had performed while wearing her amulet flashed in rapid sequence, slowing only for the words he spoke. Everything he had done for her overwhelmed her as did the words he had spoken aloud, for she was witnessing his actions and words as if they were all happening before her eyes at this moment.

Her legs became weak. Her eyes burned. Her insides ached. She wanted to be left alone to try to comprehend all that raced through her mind; yet she needed to be held. She looked into Raynhard's eyes for a moment and then reached out to him.

He put his arms around her and held her close. She rested the side of her face against his chest and let the strength of his arms envelop her.

Why me? Why is this happening to me? Am I dreaming? Did this truly happen? Did he truly say that? Should I tell what I have just seen and heard?

"Are you well, Nagora?"

She looked up into Raynhard's eyes. "Yes, I'm just tired and hungry. The events I lived through, and this news about my family—it's making my mind race off in all directions to try to make sense of it all. There's so much to consider."

"I'll make sure you get something to eat as soon as we get back."

"I can wait like the others."

"It'll be no trouble. We all need something in our stomachs. Paruline's meal will soon be ready."

They crossed the field of barley together, arm in arm. Nagora leaned on Raynhard as his right hand at her waist held her. When they reached the road, she slipped from Raynhard's hold and continued to walk by his side.

Dangor, Geirador, and Paruline met them at the door. Nagora reached out to her uncle. "I'm sorry for my words spoken in anger." She embraced him. He held her and patted her back. He forgave her.

When he released her, Paruline took her by the arm. "Come, you'll feel better after you've washed your face."

Nagora followed Paruline inside and sat on a chair at the table. "I'll get a cloth and some water."

"Okay." Paruline who had shared so many secrets with her and taught her so many things, had kept this one from her. To protect me? To protect the Cause? There must be more they're not telling me.

Paruline set a big bowl of water on the table, dipped a cloth in it, and wrung it out. "The water's cold. It'll soothe your burning face. Close your eyes. Let me wash you." Paruline's gentle hands went to work. One held the back of her head. The other patted the cloth over Nagora's eyes, cheeks, nose, and around her mouth and chin. Paruline soaked the cloth once more and washed her forehead, the sides of her face, and her neck.

Then Paruline patted her face and neck with a dry cloth.

What to say to Pare? Is she afraid I might confront her about keeping the secret from me?

Paruline stood behind her and rubbed the back of her neck. Then she kissed her ear. "In time, Nagora, you'll forgive us. Once you understand. Trust me."

She stood up and reached for Paruline. "Hold me." Nagora held onto her dear friend, taking comfort in her closeness and in her words. "I trust you, Pare."

"I'll get the others," said Paruline, when Nagora let go of her.

When they had all once again sat at the table, Nagora stood. "Today you've revealed many things to me. This news, as you've seen, has overwhelmed me and I must admit there is much I don't understand about this cause and my role in it. I need to learn more about it. I'll try to listen now. First, please tell me about my parents." Nagora sat.

Raynhard looked at her and the others at the table before speaking. "Your parents were rebels, much like you became last year, but not quite with the reputation you gained as Edana. Raganora chased them also, and put bounties on their heads. Your father left on a boat to seek help in countries beyond those Raganora had trading agreements with."

Paruline was nodding as she stepped over to the counter and motioned Raynhard to continue.

"Since your mother was pregnant, she didn't want to chance such a journey."

Raynhard looked to Paruline's father. "Geirador had an idea. Go ahead and tell it."

Paruline set a plate with bread and pieces of cheese on the table before them. She leaned close to Nagora and said in a voice the others surely heard. "Help yourself. I can tell you're hungry. As are these other wolves."

...

Geirador smiled, pulled his chair closer to the table, reached for a piece of cheese, then sat straight. "In hindsight, I almost regret having voiced that idea. Though for Tagnya's safety, in her condition, it seemed like the best solution. I suggested your mum go to the Land of Skulls. No one would follow her there. Its reputation was more dreadful than the place itself. I knew this since I had safe passage through their land. At the time this was news to your da and Dangor.

"I explained to them how, the previous fall, while hunting a splendid stag to shore up our winter provisions, my hunt had brought me further and further into the forest following the stag, hoping for a clear shot with my bow. I was so intent to have my prize I didn't realize how far I had traveled until I came upon a surprising scene."

Geirador looked at the piece of cheese he held, then at Nagora.

"A boy was fighting off a bear with a stout stick. The bear had already dispatched his companion who lay lifeless on the ground nearby. And, from the looks of it, the bear had also clawed the boy's leg and was standing, about to finish him off. I let fly my arrow. The arrow struck true between the bear's shoulders, and it fell backward onto its back. I came forward and shot a second arrow into the bear's heart.

"The young lad looked at me, not knowing if he were to fall next from the third arrow I'd drawn.

"Satisfied that the bear was dead, I put my bow and arrow down and made signs to the boy that I would attend to his bleeding wound. He waved me away and pointed to his companion.

"My examination of the man confirmed my thinking. The bear had struck a fatal blow to the right side of his head and his unstrung bow confirmed he hadn't been expecting the attack."

Geirador waved his hand. "Anyway, I cleaned the lad's wounds, and with some unraveled thread from my spare bowstring and the needle I always carry in my scrip I stitched them up. After, with a few words of the Traders' tongue and some signs, I was able to bring him back to his father who turned out to be King Godomor the Terrible, King of the Land of Skulls.

"We became friends, he and I. I left with a talisman that gave me safe passage to his home in Skull Bay. We still meet occasionally at his hunting lodge near the border to trade casks of our own homemade mead, among other things. He's still grateful that I saved Gabe's life. Gabyndor's a grown man now."

Geirador's eyebrows rose. "Your father didn't hesitate to send your mother there with Dangor and the safe-passage talisman."

Geirador looked over at Raynhard. "Raynhard told you the rest." He popped the piece of cheese into his mouth.

Nagora looked to Raynhard. "Why hasn't she returned? Is she a captive there?"

"Far from it, Nagora. She's been working for our cause and, like us, waiting for conditions to be right." Raynhard smiled at her.

"Well, are they right?"

"Thanks to you, Edana, they are," Raynhard said, giving her the dragon chord salute. "Edana's reputation has traveled beyond the borders of our land. Thanks to it, your mother has struck an agreement with Godomor, on my behalf. It needs to be approved by his vassals. He's now willing to send his Hundred Best to fight for our cause.

"If you join our cause, your mother has plans for Edana, the Dragon Warrior Princess, who will come to free the dragon. If you join us as Edana, all those loyal to our cause, as tallied on the chain you brought back last year, will follow. As will all the slings of the Stone Standers. As will The Guard. As will every countryman and woman who can swing an axe, a shovel, or a rake. Such is the hope you've given our cause."

So hope is still alive as the old woman of the Guard and the elders of the Stone Standers had said it would be. All because of my actions. I only wanted to help friends. Can I wear the mantle of Edana's reputation for the Cause? That's another matter altogether. For my promise to the girls, I will.

"If I join, will we move to free the girls in the prince's fortress?"

"As soon as you return with the Hundred Best." Raynhard held her gaze.

"Nagora, I know the evil you've seen inside the fortress. Hag embodies that evil. There's no denying that. We will put an end to it."

"It won't be soon enough for me." She had questions, but didn't dare speak them out loud to embarrass her king. Why haven't you already acted to stop Hag? You've surely had opportunities. Is she that powerful? Is it a question of the time being right? Or are you gathering information for the revolt? If so, is the harm done to those girls worth it?

Raynhard continued. "It means traveling to the Land of Skulls with your uncle. You'll be bearing gifts for Godomor and his Hundred Best. He wants to see what Edana is made of since she will lead his Hundred Best. And you'll be bringing medicine to your mother. She's a respected healer in the Land of Skulls. Godomor is ill. She hopes to cure him."

"And if I don't live up to his expectations?"

"It's a formality, Nagora. I'm sure you will."

"And if Godomor dies of his illness before?"

"His son, Gabyndor, supports his father's decision." You seem so sure of this. Is your certainty based on the information my mum has provided?

Paruline approached the table with bowls and spoons. "The stew's ready. I think you're hungry, Nagora?"

"Aye, I am. I'm sure I've eaten more than my share of bread and cheese from the plate."

Paruline set a pot holder down, along with the bowls and spoons, and placed a hand on Nagora's shoulder. "You can come and cut more to refill the plate while I bring the stew.

"Da, pass the spoons around the table."

Geirador took the mug of spoons Paruline had set on the table.

"Dangor, move the keg over to make room for my pot."

He was already standing and lifting the keg to set it to his left between him and Raynhard.

"Raynhard, refill the mugs."

He motioned for Dangor to pass Nagora's mug to him.

If Pare can order these three around, can Edana lead a hundred, just with her reputation? Right now, I don't know if I can do that. I'm not a leader.

...

Nagora brought the plate over to the counter, found the knife, and cut the rest of the loaf into pieces.

Paruline paused next to her to set another loaf on the counter. She held a ladle. "You know who will truly run this country when it's back in our hands?"

Nagora frowned as she looked at Paruline.

To answer her own question, Paruline pointed the ladle at Nagora and then back at herself, winked, and smiled. "Cut up all the cheese as well. They're hungry."

When Nagora returned to the table with the bread and cheese, Geirador handed Paruline a bowl. She filled it and Geirador passed it on to Raynhard, who in turn passed the steaming bowl to Dangor. "No ceremonies here," said Raynhard. "I'll wait my turn. This should be Nagora's."

Dangor set it before her.

When Paruline had filled all the bowls, she took her place.

Raynhard had refilled the mugs.

Geirador raised his mug. "To Raynhard. Our thanks to you for saving our Nagora."

Raynhard raised his mug as he smiled at Nagora.

She smiled back, set her mug on the table, and held up a hand.

The others looked at her, waiting for her to speak.

"Again, I want to thank Raynhard, my king, for saving me. I wish I had some memory of those moments. My last memory is swimming up to the moonlight, hoping to reach the surface because my lungs were screaming for air. I could've drowned."

Nagora paused and looked around at them again. "Now I'm here with all of you, learning about my family. More information will come." She cleared her throat. "Yet right now, inside of me, this all feels like a bad dream. I'm not the warrior you say I am. I'm not Edana. I'm a frightened little girl."

Tears welled up inside her. She took a deep breath. "And I'm as hungry as a wolf, and knowing Uncle, so is he. So let's do justice to Pare's stew."

"And so am I," said Raynhard.

Dangor was the first to empty his spoon. "Paruline, if there's any of your stew or bread left over after this meal, it won't be from my not trying to empty the pot. Your stew is most tasty."

"Dangor, you always say that."

"Well, it's true. Right, Geirador?"

"I won't argue with you on that," Geirador managed between spoonfuls.

Nagora welcomed the hot stew in her stomach. She couldn't recall enjoying the aroma and flavor of stew so much before. Have all my tears done something to my nose and my mouth? Was that why the smell and taste of everything was so distinct? Or was it the day's events?

She paused between spoonfuls. Only one piece of bread was left on the plate. She stood and left the table with the plate to go cut some more. As she cut the bread, the spoons seemed to be speaking to the bowls. Hunger was feasting at their table.

What were those captive girls eating?

After they finished the chores of the evening meal, Paruline held Nagora's shoulders. "It's been a long day for you. You must be tired. You'll stay the night. Besides, the men have much to discuss in the morning. We'll have the cots in the loft. The men will sleep down here."

Nagora hugged her friend. "Thanks, Pare. I wonder if I'll sleep. I missed your birthday. I should've said it sooner. Happy Birthday. Your gift ..."

Paruline put a finger on Nagora's lips and shook her head. "That you're alive and here with us now is the best gift I could ever dream of." She held Nagora close.

Before going to bed, Nagora stepped out into the night to gaze at the stars. She looked to the sky and found *The Twins* and *The Woman Waiting*, the latter lying on her side with one knee bent, resting on her elbow to see out her window.

The star stories Dangor had told and retold all those years, the same stories he had her retell ever since she could remember; now, these too made sense. She held her amulet to her lips.

Da, which is your favorite star? I hope to learn your answer someday.

Mum, Sagora, are you looking at the stars right now? Do you know the same star stories as I? Do you spend counts upon counts staring at them like I do? I'll ask you these questions someday. If I have the answers to these questions, I'll feel connected to you and perhaps, I'll never lose that connection.

Right now, I don't feel a connection to you.

Now that I know you exist and are alive, I still doubt it because I've lived without you all these years. To me you're just stories. You're not real. At this very moment, I live in fear of you because I don't know how I'll deal with you.

I'm still trying to accept what they've told me, to understand why they've kept you from me, why they've hidden the truth from me all these years. Why tell me now? Why do I have this doubt in me? Why do I doubt myself and who I am? Why am I not in control of who I am and what I am to do?

I'm told I have a role to play in a cause that involves you, my family, a family I thought I never had. It strikes fear in my heart since I feel I'm alone. I'm not the warrior they say I am. And this cause seems beyond my abilities. I feel so weak and insignificant. I want to run away and hide, yet I want to believe you exist. I want to run to you to get some strength from you. I must be exhausted from my ordeal in the dungeon.

Perhaps, my feelings will change when I see you face-to-face, speak to you, listen to you speak, touch you, and hold you. Perhaps then you will be stories come true. Yet I fear such moments. I won't know what to say or how to act when I meet you. Why do I fear you when, instead, I should long for you?

Tears covered Nagora's cheeks. She looked down from the sky to the road before her. She walked to Geirador's forge, wiping the tears from her face before ambling back on the star-lit road toward the light from the hut window.

When Nagora arrived, Dangor was leaning against the door frame.

"How are you feeling?"

"Uncle, I'm trying to overcome my disbelief of Mum being alive and having a sister. And why you've kept this from me all these years. It makes me sad.

"And the Cause and my role in it. It seems beyond my abilities. I feel so weak and helpless and confused."

Dangor reached out and took her in his arms. "Nagora, don't think it was easy for us to follow your mother's wishes that her existence should be kept secret from you. Soon, you'll understand. I hope you'll forgive her and us."

He rubber her back, then stepped back, keeping his hands on her shoulders. "As for your feelings about the Cause, I know it well. It won't be the last time you feel this way in your lifetime. Remember, last year you had similar feelings. It's what I call 'the feeling of war.' I've felt it many times. It's the feeling of not being in control of all these events going on about you." He's right. That's what I felt then, and now even more.

Dangor pointed a thumb at his chest. "How do I deal with it? I don't, because I don't have control over those events, but I have control over some things. I focus on those things. In my case, it's one of my weapons. I make sure my bow and all my arrows are in perfect working condition; or that my blades are perfectly sharpened. I focus on my task, not the big picture. I let the leaders worry about that. You did that last year. You completed your task, and much more. Do that until you're called upon to lead."

I did, but things happened …

Her uncle took her hand. "Nagora, I don't know if Raynhard told you or not. The knife you wear at your belt is your da's. He gave it to Raynhard when they last saw each other, when he promised to return with help for the Cause. It was Yogari's way of showing his loyalty to the Cause. He told Raynhard if he didn't return, he was to give the knife to his child, who he hoped would also be loyal to the Cause."

Nagora reached for the knife at her back, pulled the sheath along her belt to her side, and rested her hand on the handle.

"Perhaps, if you focus on that, you'll have a good night's sleep." Dangor turned to hold the door open for her. "Good night, Nagora."

"Thank you, Uncle. Good night." She stepped inside, tiptoed to the loft ladder, climbed it, and found the cot near the open window where she lay down. Paruline's breathing told Nagora she was asleep.

She unbuckled her belt and pulled the knife sheath from it. She turned to pull the blanket over her and lay on her side, holding the knife in its sheath in one hand and her amulet in the other, crossed at her heart. Nagora took a last peek at the stars before closing her eyes.

# Decision
## *Kese isihcikewin*

When Nagora awoke, every muscle in her body ached. Each arm and leg weighed as much as her body. Would she be able to stand? Her hand still clutched her father's knife sheath to her chest, her fingers' grip frozen on it. Waking up had never been this difficult.

She closed her eyes and let herself relax on the cot. Would she fall asleep again? Paruline's humming came from below, her knife chopping and scraping on a cutting board. Her wooden spoon tapped on the edge of a bowl.

No sound of the men.

Fresh bread baking and a hint of smoke from the fireplace.

Nagora's eyelids pushed against the parcels of her dream, trying not to be pulled back to sleep. She forced her eyes open. A few of the pieces reappeared—the huge eye staring into hers, smoke, fire, the ground shaking under her feet.

She blinked again and turned her head toward the open window. It must be well past sunrise.

She propped herself up on her left elbow.

*Did I sleep under an ancient pile of cairn stones?*

She shook her head to force herself awake. Her full bladder took over the task, driving her to swing her legs over the cot's edge and look for the night-water bucket, as Paruline called it. Her eyes found it across the loft floor, just to the right of the small winter fireplace.

Nagora hobbled over to it, untying the knot in the drawstring of her undergarments as she went. She removed the bucket cover, pulled down her drawers, and sat on the bucket just in time.

Paruline whistled and laughed. "Is that a warrior waterfall I hear up there, or is that Nagora filling the bucket with foaming ale?"

She smiled at Paruline's comments as the last drops trickled into the bucket. "I woke up under a pile of stones. Good thing you keep a bucket up here. I couldn't have made it down the ladder without causing a flood."

She retied the drawstring, stood on her tiptoes, and stretched her arms above her head. "Have the others eaten?"

"Yes."

"Is there anything left for me?"

"Of course. You sound hungry."

Nagora dressed. A headache threatened from a distance behind her still-sleepy eyes. She attached the bucket to its rope and lowered it to the floor below. She took her time coming down the loft ladder, like it was the first time she had ever climbed down a ladder.

"How'd you sleep?"

"Soundly. My head's not awake yet. Still lost in the fog of sleep and dreams. I'll go empty this, then wash up. That should help me wake up."

"It should. Hold on. I'll get you a cloth to dry yourself. Are you washing your hair?"

"No."

"Here." Paruline handed Nagora the cloth. "I'll comb your hair for you when you come back."

Nagora made her way out, past the side of the hut, and along the cliff wall to the latrine where she emptied the cedar bucket. She brought it with her to the small bathing hut that straddled the stream. Before stepping into the hut, she gave the bucket a quick rinse and left it a third full so its bottom and sides remained tight against the iron hoops that held it together.

She hadn't done her exercises since the guards took her in the square. I can't do a series of a hundred fast. A hundred slow would take too long. A quarter as many slow, my hands as weapons. These she could control and would bring a little relief to her stiff, sore muscles. And they would help her confirm the decision she would make about joining the Cause.

After repeating twenty-five repetitions of ward off, roll-back, press, push, pull, elbow strike, shoulder strike, advance, retreat, look left, gaze right, and center balance exercises, Nagora stepped into the bath hut, awake and aware of how she would deal with the day ahead and the future. To join the Cause will be the only way for me to keep the promises I made in the dungeon.

The bathing hut was another of Geirador's marvels. If only her uncle would make one for their stream. The single wall of the hut curved into itself like a broken circle leaving a single open entrance to its private inner space. Fifteen vertical cedar posts, planted on the shores and in the stream itself, formed the supports through and around which Geirador had woven young sapling branches to form the hut's airy wall. A simple cone of thatch gave the hut its roof.

Nagora undressed, hung her clothes from the sapling branch pegs, then coiled her braid and wrapped it in the linen cloth on top of her head. She stepped into the water and sat on the bottom step of cedar planks that straddled the stream. Up to her chest in the brook, she scrubbed the sleep from her face and splashed water on the back of her neck and shoulders.

Edana's neck and shoulders? Are they strong enough to carry all that responsibility?

She stood and climbed onto the bottom step to sit on the middle step just below the water's surface. She scrubbed the rest of her body. The cool water had the desired effect—her head cleared. She scrubbed her face a final time before climbing to sit on the top, dry step to let the excess water drip away.

Edana's a symbol. She's not the one planning all the moves. I'll just have to play the role. Do what they tell me.

She removed the linen cloth that held her hair and dried her face. She stood and rubbed the rest of her body dry. Her muscles still ached, but she was awake, alive, and hungry. That's better. One day at a time. Focus on what I can control. Edana needs to eat.

Nagora was already stuffing small red raspberries into her mouth as she pulled her chair closer to the table. Paruline set a plate of scrambled eggs with chopped chives and carrots before her and leaned close to give her a hug. Next to the bowl of berries sat a plate with a hunk of goat cheese, butter, and a chunk of honeycomb. A warm round loaf of dark rye bread, smelling of caraway, sat on the table to her right.

"Little sister, you're not hungry. You're starved!"

"Pare, this is so good. You're right, I'm starved."

As she tore another piece of bread off the loaf, Paruline busied herself unraveling Nagora's braid and spreading it evenly over the back of her chair. She ate. Paruline brushed. When she drank her buttermilk, Paruline stopped brushing.

"I'm going to braid now, so take a break."

She stuffed another piece of cheese in her mouth and sat back to let Paruline do her work.

Nagora swallowed and licked her upper lip. "Pare, I can't believe I'll have a sister who'll be brushing and braiding my hair for me. I hope Sagora will do it as well as you do."

"You'll have to do hers. Lucky you've had me to practice on."

"Do I do it well?" Nagora twisted her neck to look at Paruline.

"Have I complained?" Paruline grinned.

"No."

"Your sister will though." Paruline bent over to peek at her.

"Why's that?" Nagora's brow furrowed.

"That's what sisters do. You'll complain too. You'll see."

The painful memory of Pug sawing through her braid a year ago flashed before her eyes. "I've endured more pain than she'll ever dare to do."

144 · H. N. HENRY

Paruline was halfway into her tight braid. She paused to bend and kiss Nagora's cheek. "I know. It'll be another year and half before your braid reaches the length it was."

Nagora sighed and reached for the bowl of berries. That's another promise I'll keep someday, Pug. I'll off your prick and make you swallow it.

Paruline gave a little tug on her braid.

"Ouch! Hey! Pare! You've always been like a big sister. You don't have to act like one and pull my hair." She laughed.

Paruline reached for Nagora's chin with her free hand and turned her head. She smiled. "Stop complaining and eat."

Nagora poured the remaining berries from the bowl into her mouth as her friend tied off her braid with several hitches of a small leather lanyard.

Paruline brought the tip of Nagora's braid under her own nose and then rested her cheek against Nagora's. She wiggled the braid tip so it tickled Nagora's nose. "Little sister, your braid is done."

Nagora reached up to hold Paruline's head closer to hers and kiss her on the cheek. "Thanks Pare, for the braid and for this breakfast. You've spoiled me. You'll always be my favorite big sister."

Paruline smiled, moved to the opposite side of the table, and sat before Nagora. She looked her in the eye. "From your mood, you seem to have come to terms with what lies ahead for you."

Nagora finished her mouthful. "I can't say I truly have because, if I think about it, I still find myself overwhelmed by it all, the role I'll be playing as Edana. Uncle gave me some advice last night. I think it has helped me. It let me sleep soundly. I've chosen to be part of this. I'm going to take it one day at a time and focus on those things I have control of. That's what I decided. So far, it's working."

"That's good, Nagora. Take it one day at a time."

At that moment, Raynhard entered, followed by Dangor and Geirador.

Nagora and Paruline stood.

Paruline beckoned them to sit at the table. "Will you have some tea? Something to eat?"

Raynhard smiled at Paruline. "Yes, please, some of your forest tea would be good."

"Good morning, Nagora." His smile brightened slightly.

"Good morning, Raynhard, Geirador, Uncle."

Dangor approached and touched her arm. "How'd you sleep?"

"Soundly, thanks to your advice. But I'm stiff and sore all over. I had trouble waking up and getting out of bed this morning."

"That's to be expected after what you've been through. Your body used a lot of energy. I see you're giving it the fuel it needs. In a few days your aches and pains will go away." He gave Nagora a hug. "I'm just happy you're alive."

"Today, Uncle, I am happy to be alive. I'll take it one day at a time from now on." She hugged her uncle back and smiled at him.

Raynhard sat at the opposite end of the table.

Paruline set a plate with pieces of bread, cheese, honey-comb, and shelled hazelnuts in the center of the table. "That's for all of us. Nagora still has some of her breakfast to finish. I'm warning you though, with her appetite this morning, she just might reach for this plate as well. Tea will be ready soon."

Nagora held up her spoon, pretending to menace Paruline with it.

Raynhard smiled at Nagora. "Go ahead, Nagora. Eat your breakfast. If you're still hungry, we'll share our plate with you."

Nagora smiled back as she sat and tore another piece from her loaf, crushed a piece of honeycomb with her spoon, soaked up the honey with the bread, and spread a piece of goat cheese on it.

Geirador gave Paruline the mugs, and she poured the tea.

Raynhard spoke when everyone was seated. "Nagora, you seem to have slept well. Do you have any questions on what you learned yesterday?"

She nodded with her mouth full, but took the time to finish chewing before answering. She stood. "All my many questions will be answered in good time. Today, I don't have a question, but I have something to say."

Nagora took her father's knife from its sheath at her hip and placed it near the plate at the center of the table. "If my father and mother were rebels, fighting for this cause, then I choose to be one also if you guide me in my role in it." She sat.

Dangor stood, took his knife, and placed its blade on the blade of his brother's knife. "Nagora, count on me to help you."

Geirador did the same. "Count on me, Nagora."

"I'm also with you, Nagora." Paruline placed her knife's blade on her father's.

Raynhard stood, took his knife and placed its blade on the others. "We are with you in this, Nagora." He pointed to the rune symbol that marked the handle of each knife. "Raidho— the journey. Our journey to the dragon's freedom begins."

Raynhard sat and bid the others to do so. Then his face took on a dark mood. "Nagora, early this morning we received news from a messenger. Acindor has sent out search parties along the coast to look for anyone with information about a young maiden who may have survived drowning in the sea, or to see if anyone has seen or heard of a dead body of a young woman being washed ashore. Before search parties come snooping inland and your whereabouts becomes known, we've decided that you'll be leaving for the Land of Skulls tomorrow."

Nagora was about to take another bite, but stopped. His words stood in front of her like a wall of stones around which she tried to see. At any moment she expected to see her mum and sister appear and make the wall vanish. How would she react if that happened?

Why am I so frightened? Why do I want to cry?

Would they be tears of joy or tears of longing? One day at a time.

Nagora took a deep breath and looked to the others at the table waiting for her speak. She blinked away her tears. "Okay, tomorrow. Uncle, how long will it take to be reunited with Mum and Sagora?"

"We'll prepare today. We'll have our horses and four mules loaded with gifts of weapons, our own gear, and equipment. The going'll be slow."

Dangor held up his thumb. "Tomorrow, we leave at first light. We'll make camp near the border of the Land of Skulls and cross into that land the following day."

A finger went up next to his thumb. "We'll go as far as Godomor the Terrible's hunting lodge and wait for the regular border patrol to arrive. They'll provide an escort to ensure our safe passage to Tagnyoriva.

"If we're lucky, before the day's end, the patrol will arrive and we'll leave the next day at first light." Another finger went up.

"We'll camp for a night, move on, camp for another night," two fingers joined the others, "and, by the next day, we should share an evening meal with your mum and sister, and possibly Godomor the Terrible."

Dangor wagged the spread fingers of his hand. "If we're lucky, five or six days of travel. We'll have a cask of mead for Godomor and," he pointed at Nagora, "you, my dear, for your mum and sister."

"I'll actually see my mum and sister. It's hard to believe. Will my arrival be a surprise?"

Raynhard spoke up. "Yes and no, Nagora. On the day you were taken captive in the prince's fortress, I dispatched a message to your mother, informing her of your situation and that, if we freed you, we'd tell you about her and Sagora, and that she should expect your arrival soon."

Raynhard looked to Geirador and Dangor and then back to Nagora. "We had planned to tell you of all this, but your being taken caused a change in our plans. As a result, you are learning it ten days before planned."

Nagora shook her head. "I still don't know what's involved in the role I'll play as Edana, the Dragon Warrior Princess."

"That, your mother will tell you since it will also involve your sister, and since it's your mother's idea. You must be eager to meet your mother."

She took a breath. "To be honest, I'm afraid to meet her. I won't know how to act or what to say when I meet her."

Raynhard gave Nagora a reassuring smile. "Try to imagine how your mother feels. Just be yourself. The moment will take care of your words and actions."

He's right. I've been so taken by my own feelings that I've not considered how Mum must still feel all these years after giving up her own child. She's just come back into my life, and we've yet to meet.

Raynhard stood. "Thank you for the tea, Paruline.

"Nagora, finish your meal. I've certain details to discuss with your uncle and Geirador back at the forge. I'll need to speak to you before I leave. I'll send for you when I'm ready."

Dangor stood to leave. "Nagora, will you take care of preparing trail rations for our journey to the Land of Skulls?"

"I'll take care of it, Uncle."

"You should find most of what you need in our stores in Geirador's larder. I'll be riding to our home for our saddlebags, bedrolls and the clothes we'll need. Is there something you want me to bring back for you?"

"No, you know what's essential. I'll leave that up to you."

"Should you think of something before I leave, let me know." Dangor left.

...

After breakfast, Nagora rounded up dried currants, dried mushrooms, hazelnuts, walnuts, barley, ground oats, flour, honeycomb, and dried meat. She and Paruline prepared the packets of food she would later place in the saddlebags.

Paruline picked a dried currant from Nagora's sweater. "Do you think you'll have enough to eat?"

"Knowing Uncle, he likes to hunt partridge or hare and forage for berries and wild onions when he's on the trail. He won't waste much time doing that on this trip. I'll just have time to unsaddle the horses and set up camp before he comes back from a quick hunt. He doesn't always find something to kill. These rations'll be plenty."

At that moment, Geirador stepped through the doorway. "Nagora, I've saddled Storm for you. Raynhard's waiting for you in the stable; he'll ride with you until he reaches his destination. Then you can return here with his mount."

Nagora frowned and looked from Paruline to Geirador and back. "Looks like I've got to go, Pare." She went to the pegs near the door, slipped on her blades, and slung her quiver and attached bow across her back. "I'll see you later."

Paruline smiled. "Aye, until then."

# Secrets
## *Kimotan*

Nagora set off for the stable and found Raynhard saddling his mount. Without saying a word to him she gave all her attention to Storm. She loved how her stallion's black back melted into the dark brown of his sides.

In the year she had him, she grew to love him. He came into Nagora's life at the right time after she had returned from her banishment, a gift from Dangor. Since then, she had trained him and spent most of her days with him. Not only was he her trusted mount, but her confidant. She shared her secrets and fears with Storm. He always seemed to sense her moods. Riding him today would be good for her.

Nagora looked into his big eyes. His short ears twitched as he came to her and touched her first. She caressed his broad nose and forehead as he rested his strong neck on her shoulder. She wrapped her arms around it, grabbed a fistful of his long shaggy mane, and whispered, *"Tastapiw sohkapiskaw kaskitewastim,* my 'strong, swift, dark horse.'" She loved the sound of those words. They would become her private song to Storm.

"I'm so happy to have you take this journey with me. I trust you to take me wherever I want to go." Storm gave her the same respect and trust she had given him since the beginning.

Raynhard interrupted. "I enjoyed my ride here on Storm."

She smiled at Raynhard. "Isn't he the most splendid storm you've ever seen? Together we ride like the wind."

"Aye, I've seen that. I'm sure Storm will give you no problems on your trip."

"I know. He's already told me so."

Raynhard led his horse, Yhoura, out of the stable.

Nagora followed with Storm. Outside, she grabbed onto the saddle and pulled herself up onto his back in one fluid motion, throwing her right leg up and over the saddle. She reached down and patted Storm's neck. Thought I might not be able to do that today.

She looked at Raynhard. "Where to, my king?"

"'Raynhard' will do fine for now, Nagora. Chive has to show up before he'll be missed, so a horse will help. We'll ride to a spot no one else knows about. And I do mean no one. This spot then will be known only to me and, as of today, you. I trust you'll keep the whereabouts of this place secret. Divulge it to no one, not your uncle Dangor, Geirador, your mother, nor your sister unless there is someone who, in your honest judgment, needs a place like this for a very good reason."

"Why must it be kept secret?"

"For your safety and mine, and for the future of my country. It'll be a refuge for either one of us. The others do not want to know about it so they won't tell its whereabouts under the pain of torture. I consider you keeping this place a secret as payment for me saving your life. By knowing about it, someday you may use it to help me, or yourself, or even someone you truly care about."

"I think I know what you mean. Now I'm curious and I want to see this place."

"We've a distance to go yet and more to talk about, so why don't I take the lead and you'll show me what Storm can do." Raynhard kneed Yhoura and away he went.

Storm would have no trouble following. You want to chase Yhoura, don't you? She slapped Storm's reins and pressed her knees into him. Off they went, like the wind over open water.

Storm followed Raynhard's mount through the glen, across streams, and up through mountain meadows at a good pace. Nagora kept Storm a dozen lengths behind Raynhard.

In the high meadow, Raynhard glanced over his shoulder and when he did, Nagora let Storm loose. In no time, they overtook Raynhard.

She slowed Storm to a trot and waited for Raynhard to come alongside.

"Plenty of energy in Storm. You ride well, Nagora. Geirador trained you well."

She smiled. "Yhoura sets a good pace."

"You've ridden her?"

"You know I have."

Raynhard smiled. "We're almost there. Follow me. We'll tie the horses behind the trees ahead and go the rest of the way on foot."

Unless someone had followed them or spied their arrival, no one could see where they tied the horses.

Raynhard led Nagora on a climb up a tree-covered slope and around rocks and boulders.

Nagora searched the slope as she followed. "There's no trail to find if I come back on my own."

"You're right, but when you know what to look for, then you'll realize that as long as you make it to the top of this hill, you'll find your way."

"Hill? You mean 'mountain,' don't you?"

"If you wish. In a little while, we'll be at the top and you'll see."

When they arrived at the top, they were on the mountain's broad ridgeline, with rough edges of rock running through the trees.

"You realize we're on a ridge right now, and the direction it goes?" said Raynhard.

Nagora pointed. "To where the sun sets."

"Right. Now, as we continue, look where we're headed and tell me what stands out."

They continued on for a while along the ridge to where it divide in two. One ridge moved left, and then it turned right again, in what seemed to be a parallel ridgeline to the one ahead.

She pointed. "There, ahead, the ridge divides in two."

"Right," said Raynhard. "Reach the top of the mountain ridge from the high meadow below, then follow it in the direction the sun sets until you come to the divide."

Raynhard kept walking, leading Nagora to the divide, and then on past it to the right-hand ridge. "About three hundred strides along this ridge, stop, turn around, and look back to where the two ridges meet. What do you see?"

"Trees, bushes, and shrubs growing in the valley formed by the two ridges."

"Yes, and ...?"

"I don't see anything. Wait ... Is that a tiny stream flowing out of the rocks?"

"Yes. Let's go see where it comes from." Down they climbed, into the valley, until they met the tiny stream which they followed back to the base of the big clump of bushes.

As Nagora pushed past the bushes with Raynhard to find the stream's source, they came upon a tall narrow opening in the rock which took them inside a dark cave. "Wait a moment." Raynhard bent and scraped his knife blade against a flint, creating sparks to light a pinch of fire starter so he could light the taper that lay on the floor of the cave not far from the stream. Once his taper was lit, he took another from its holder further in the cave, lit it, and handed it to Nagora.

"This cave is a passage to an opening on the left ridge we saw a while ago. It was once an underground river fed by the lake that long ago filled the valley between the ridges. The passage gets narrower and climbs to the middle of the cave, which levels out. We'll come to a high vaulted ceiling and a small lake with an island in its middle."

Nagora took in as many of the details she could see with the light from the taper. Neither spoke as they passed through the lake section. She was careful of her footing on the sometimes narrow path as they skirted the lake. A stout pillar of stone rose from one end of the island in the lake.

They continued on in the draft she had detected upon entering the cave. It became more noticeable, almost a breeze.

The darkness became less heavy as light from the end of the tunnel shone in.

"We're almost at the end," Raynhard said. "Give me your taper and follow me." He placed his taper high in a hole in the cave wall, then he walked on and placed her taper in a similar hole about a dozen paces away on the other side of the cave.

The light from the two tapers and the cave's entrance revealed a chamber equipped with a fire pit, a simple bed made of four logs lashed together, and supplies stored on the natural stone shelves within the chamber.

One shelf held three bows, arrows, knives, and even two swords.

"This is my lair. Now our lair." Raynhard showed a stout, wooden box with a heavy stone on its cover. "Inside, you'll find dried meats, mostly game. Also, dried berries and nuts." He pointed. "Plenty of skins on the bed to keep one warm, even in winter. A store of firewood along that wall. Fires for heating and cooking are best kept for the night. I'll show you why."

Raynhard led Nagora to the mouth of the cave, where the rocky outcrop was like a cracked bowl. She could see it would be a tight fit for one man coming up through the crack.

"A defendable position for one with enough arrows," said Raynhard as he helped her up to the lip of the bowl on the short ladder which led to a platform of lashed branches on one side of the crack.

Once on the platform, Nagora could see over the forest treetops below the bowl down to the Village of Yhorgal and on to the coast where she had been captive, days before, in the prince's fortress.

Rage grew inside her.

Hag, you witch, if my thoughts could set fire to the fortress, you and that pig, Prince Acindor, and his pig of a jailor, Worsham, would all go up in flames with it. If only I had that power!

But I don't. Know that if I have my say, all of you will taste my blade! Your combined screams will equal those of all the young maidens you've abused. And if I can, I will torch your fortress.

She took a long breath before looking away from the fortress.

Coming this way obviously made for a much shorter route for Chive than had he taken the longer coastal road.

"How did you find this place, Raynhard?"

"My father found it a long time ago when hunting in this area. The stag he hunted kept climbing through the forest. My father tracked him, but then it rained. Even though he could no longer see the tracks, my father figured the deer had continued to climb, so he did too. He was about to turn around when he spied the crack in this rock. He climbed to see if there was a cave where he could find shelter from the rain. This is what he found.

"He told me about it when I was a young boy, on my eighth birthday." He held a hand out at his side to indicate how tall he was at the time.

"As Chive, coming to this area, I remembered what my father had told me about this place. On my scavenger hunts for forest plants this past spring, I looked for it. It wasn't easy to find and when I did, I knew no one else besides my father had been here."

"How'd you know that?" Nagora glanced back to the inside of the cave.

"My father left his hunting dagger here and the sheepskin vest he'd been wearing that day. His emblem was on the hide side of his vest. The same emblem was on the knife sheath. He figured, should someone find them here, that person would come looking for him, perhaps to get a reward. No one ever showed up. He told no one, except for me." Raynhard pointed to his chest.

"I found the dagger and the vest, untouched, in the exact place he said he'd left them." He climbed down the short ladder and offered his hand to Nagora.

"Since the snow left, I've been setting it up for myself as a place I can get away to be by myself, to collect my thoughts, a place where I can spend a night or two in peace, without fear of attack, and away from the fortress."

He pointed to the bed, the firepit, and the shelves that held weapons. "As you can see, I'm ready to defend myself from attack. To my knowledge, no one has ever followed me here. I've always been careful about that."

Raynhard led her over to the firepit near the back wall.

"So will I, Raynhard, if ever I need to come here. Your secret is safe with me."

"I know, Nagora. I have something to give you because you've joined our cause." Raynhard turned to reach into a recess at the back of a stone shelf. He brought out what appeared to be a roll of sheepskin.

Could it be his father's vest?

He unrolled the skin with care. As the crest appeared, so did the sheath with the hunting dagger. "These are for you, Nagora. Reminders of your chosen duty to your king. I want you to accept them as a symbol of the trust I have in you."

He held the sheath so she could pull the dagger from it.

Nagora did and examined the gold handle. A dragon's spread wings, body, and tail curled around the handle. The dragon's neck and head completed the handle's pommel, with the dragon's open mouth holding a crown. Its studied workmanship was so fine as to make the handle comfortable to hold.

The dragon's tail formed the crossguard, which looped out on each side of the blade's edges and ended with the tail's tip pointing down on one side of the blade.

"It's beautiful. A gold dragon holding a crown. I can't imagine the value of this dagger. I can't accept this."

"I think it's worth my kingdom. If you return with King Godomor's Hundred Best to help me get it back, I'll owe you so much more. More than I could ever pay you in gold. Please, accept it."

Raynhard's words, from when she had put her amulet back on, rushed into her mind. "Soup fit for a king, and his queen. Let's go see if my queen is awake."

Was my head playing tricks on me? Am I right in my mind? I've heard strange words and understood their meaning. At least I think I do. Am I in the same world as I was before?

Nagora returned the dagger to its sheath. "I owe you my life. I need to repay you."

"No, you've already done so by joining our cause."

She stared at the embroidered royal emblem on the vest. It was the same as the one on the sheath, but much bigger. Two blue and green dragons in profile held a white shield with a gold crown on the top. On the shield was a black bellows at the bottom, its nose pointing up into a flaming red forge. On one side were an anvil, a hammer, and tongs in the flames. On the other side was a table on which rested two items: a long cylinder with a handle on one end and a long black pipe with an orange ball on the end in the flames. Glass blowers tools?

"It's the first time I see this emblem. Will you use this when you become King of Innisfhail?"

Raynhard shook his head. "That is the name Raganora gave our country. I'll never speak that name. Nor will I call her by the title she usurped.

"Years ago, in the good days, there were many emblems—on flags, on gates, on statues, and on buildings. Raganora put an end to that—no more flags, especially royal flags showing the fire arts of those who work with glass."

He pointed to Nagora and himself. "We are the People of the Danu. This is the Land of the Danu. We will give it back its greatness once we free the dragon." Raynhard had spoken his words with determination, and it showed on his face.

"What say you, Nagora?"

"It's a tall and noble order. Right now I want to avenge those girls and free the others the prince holds. If I were to listen to myself, I'd be on my way down there to put Acindor and his jailor under my blade." She held up her hand. "I know, I know. I can't do it on my own. Though that's the way I feel. When I return with the Hundred Best … " Her eyes held Raynhard's.

"I understand your feelings. We'll free those girls and serve justice on those who've abused justice." His face was sincere.

"I'm sure your feelings for revenge and justice are as great as mine, if not greater."

"They are. Believe me. Now, it's time I head back to become Chive again."

Nagora held out the golden dagger and the vest. "I'm honored to accept these, but I'd prefer not to wear them now. They're so beautiful and so valuable. I fear losing them. Perhaps once we've freed the dragon. Can I leave them here until then? Besides," she said as she reached for her father's knife, "Now I have this to remind me of my duty. I want to help my father keep his promise to you."

Raynhard swallowed as he took the knife from her and examined it. "You honor me, Nagora, by honoring Yogari's promise." He returned it to her and took back the royal hunting vest and dagger.

"You're right about these. The risk of losing them in the coming time of war will be great." He wrapped the dagger in the vest and put it back on the shelf. "Promise me you'll wear them once we bring peace to the land."

"I promise, Raynhard."

Raynhard took a taper from its hole in the cave wall and handed it to Nagora. "Let me escort you back through the cave. Will you be able to find your way back to the horses?"

"Not a problem. Our steps are visible to my eye. I'll bring Yhoura back. I know Uncle will have a list of things for me to do for the journey tomorrow."

A dozen paces on when Raynhard paused to retrieve the other taper, Nagora touched his arm. "I don't know when we'll meet again. In a way, you've given me back my mum. Meeting her will be a strange experience. Will it be a rebirth of sorts? And I have a sister who's a living, breathing mirror image of me.

"In five days or so, I'll be living a unique experience. I know I've no choice but to take it one moment at a time and be true to my feelings. My feelings are all mixed up right now."

"Do so Nagora, and all should go well. It will be a time of discovery for the three of you. Tagnyoriva will be most pleased. As for Sagora, if she has adopted your mother's values, then you two should become best friends."

He took her hand. "There's something I should tell you. Like you, your sister has not known of your existence. She will only know of it just before your arrival. It was one of the conditions your mother set when she had to abandon you. She felt that if the two of you ever met again, you would at least be on common footing. Sagora also will be looking forward to news of her father. We hope to have that by the time you return.

"Follow me." He let go of her hand.

Another piece of information to help me rebuild my family. The father piece is not yet complete.

Nagora held the taper high as they made their way back through the cave to the valley entrance.

...

When they reached the ridge, Raynhard stopped. He rested his hands on Nagora's shoulders.

In the silence of the moment her eyes locked onto his. Inside her she wanted to hug Raynhard to her to thank him, and to feel his strength. And she wanted to decipher the look on his face. Was it one of love, one of pride, or a look of foreboding for what awaited her?

Raynhard broke the silence, as if reading her thoughts, and held open his arms, "Remember, Nagora, trust your feelings."

She hugged Raynhard, pressing the side of her face to his chest while her hands reached to his shoulders to pull him closer. He kept his hands on her shoulders and held her close for a moment, returning her hug. He relaxed his hold and touched her hair as he kissed the top of her head.

She looked up, and he kissed her on the forehead, and then held her at arm's length.

"Tagnyoriva, in her wisdom and far-sightedness, felt you should be prepared to take part in these events, rather than watch as they unfold around you. She trusted Dangor to see you gained and mastered the skills necessary to do so. Already you've shown me you are, like your mother, no ordinary woman.

"Meeting you face-to-face these past few days has confirmed that. I don't know when we'll meet again, but I look forward to that day. I also look forward to meeting your mother again, after all these years, and your sister. Tell your mother that for me, please."

"I will. Until we meet again."

...

Nagora ran along the ridge. Was Raynhard still watching her? Most likely he was. She disappeared among the trees.

She found the horses grazing along the line to which she and Raynhard had tethered them. Storm whinnied at her approach. Before returning to Cairnmase, she brought them to a nearby stream to drink.

Well Storm, looks like we're going to be working full time from now on. I know you'll earn your keep. Uncle won't regret what he paid for you. How much, he won't say. All he says is Geirador gave him a good price. He and Pare won't say how much Uncle paid.

Tar piss! Will Uncle remember to bring my map? It'd be best I had it should I ever need to find my pay pouch. Without it I'll never find where Uncle hid it. Storm, home's not far. We'll ride by to check.

"Whoa, Storm!" Two sets of hoofprints followed those of Dangor's mount on the trail leading to their lodge. Nagora dismounted to get a closer look. Two mounts shod military style, not like Kimmo's shoes. Could be trouble. She led Storm and Yhoura into the bush, and tied them. I'll be back soon.

She strung her bow, pulled two arrows from her quiver, and nocked one. She stuck to the trees as she approached their lodge.

...

Two soldiers were in the yard, one of them still mounted and holding a spear. The other had his sword drawn, a coil of rope slung over his other shoulder, and he was in a heated discussion with Dangor. He kept pointing to Kimmo. He obviously wanted her uncle to mount up. Nagora could barely hear Dangor's words. He was obviously trying to keep calm, but the soldier was losing patience. "Get on your damn horse!"

She cawed the crow call once to let her uncle know she was near, and then a second time so he would know she was ready to help.

Dangor signaled he had heard and moved toward Kimmo. The soldier with the sword followed, taking hold of Kimmo's reins as her uncle climbed into the saddle.

The one with the spear held it set to throw.

Dangor signaled: Release on my sign.

Once her uncle was on Kimmo, the soldier stuck the blade of his sword in the ground and slipped the rope from his shoulder.

Nagora had the spearman in her sights, waiting to draw and release.

Dangor signaled.

Nagora drew, let fly her arrow, and nocked the other before the first struck the soldier in the back. He dropped his spear and fell out of his saddle, surprising his horse.

Dangor had kneed Kimmo forward and kicked the soldier holding the reins, who reeled away from the kick without letting go of the reins. Her uncle got Kimmo to buck, but the soldier hung on and was reaching for his sword.

Enough of this. Nagora let fly her arrow and it struck the second soldier in the side of his chest just as he raised his sword to strike at Dangor. He dropped his sword and fell to his knees. One arm came to rest on the arrow as the other made a vain attempt to grab at it.

Nagora had pulled an arrow from her quiver and was running toward her uncle, who jumped down from his saddle. He stood before the soldier, bent to pick up the soldier's sword, and smiled at Nagora. "I'm glad you came along. Go check on the other one."

The spearman lay on his side. His face still showed his surprise at the attack. She knelt and placed her fingers on his neck. "He's dead."

"Good. I'll put this one out of his misery."

She didn't watch, but she heard the stab of the sword and the soldier's last groan. She reached for her arrow. It was broken. "Do I pull my arrow?" Tar piss! I don't want to get blood on my hands.

"No. Leave it."

She stood up. "Now what do we do?"

Dangor spit. "Tie them onto their mounts. Bring them to the beach hut. Fill the saddlebags with rocks. Tie their saddles to them. At dark, we'll row them out to sea. Sink their bodies."

He took a deep breath. "Then, we'll let the horses go. We've got a lot of work to do. We didn't need this added chore. No choice."

She looked at her uncle. "Do we follow the cliff trail to the beach hut?"

"Aye. You came for your map, didn't you?"

"I did."

"It's in my saddlebag. Let's get to work."

Back at Geirador's stable, while Dangor and Geirador prepared the pack saddles, Nagora groomed the mules that would carry the packs they would be bringing to the Land of Skulls.

Dangor had made Nagora agree not to tell Geirador or Paruline what had happened. "Best they not know. I'll tell Geirador we took longer coming back because we had a search party to avoid. Sooner or later such a party'll make it to Cairnmase and start asking questions. When they do, he'll figure it out."

When Dangor and Geirador came to get Nagora, she set the brush on the shelf in the stall. Her uncle patted her on the shoulder. "Plenty of work ahead of us. Since we don't want to leave tracks from here with our loaded mules tomorrow, we'll be making three trips with them, dividing the packs they'll be carrying into three. Each time, we'll take a different way to the spot where we'll unload the packs.

"On the last trip, we'll tether the mules near the packs and leave them with feed and water for the night. When we set out with our mounts tomorrow at first light, we'll go separate ways and meet at the mules, pack them, and be on our way."

"Good plan. When do we start?"

Geirador leaned on the stall gate's frame. "I suggested to Dangor you eat now so you can get back before nightfall."

What excuse will Uncle come up with when we show up late? It'll be pitch dark.

...

The final light of day had melted into night when Nagora and Dangor ferried the bodies out into the bay, towing them in a curragh behind the one they rowed.

By the time they had returned to Geirador's stable it was close to midnight.

Geirador joined Nagora and Dangor as they were brushing down their mounts in the stable. "We were starting to worry. For a while we thought you might've decided to leave without saying goodbye."

Dangor rested an elbow on Kimmo's big hip and looked at Geirador. "Would you believe we got lost in the dark? It's not easy to find a guide star in the forest."

Geirador shook his head, snorted, and spit. "Dangor, you're going to have to get to bed early to dream up a better excuse than that one. You could sleep in the saddle and Kimmo would take you home." He held up his big hand. "Don't tell me. I don't want to know now. Someday you'll tell me. I'm glad both of you are back.

"Paruline'll have food for you when you come in."

When they finished with the horses, they walked to Geirador's hut under a starlit sky. Nagora was tired and hungry. Even with all the work they had done, she hadn't been able to completely put aside her feelings about the soldiers she had taken down with her bow. *I'm a warrior after all. I'm part of the Cause. I did this for my king. I saved Uncle's life.*

...

Inside, the smell of fresh-baked bread greeted them. A plate with slices of roasted venison sat on the table next to the loaf. *I can't believe how hungry I am.*

Paruline stood from her chair at the table. "I'm so happy to see you two. You've had a long day. I've set aside pots of warm water so you can wash up before eating."

Dangor looked at his hands, and then back to Geirador's daughter. "Thank you, Paruline. Much appreciated. I'll better enjoy the food."

"And the ale," said Geirador.

Nagora stepped close to her friend. "You're so thoughtful, Pare. I'd hug you, but you'd probably send me back to the stable."

"Well, I want your hug, so go wash."

The wash in the warm water and the rinse with cool water left Nagora refreshed. She would be ready for bed as soon as she finished eating, but she had a last job to do—repack their saddlebags with the trail rations, their clothes, and their personal belongings.

*I did the right thing not to return with Raynhard's gifts. I won't have to keep them hidden. Should I have even accepted them?* Along with her thoughts about the soldier she had killed, she had struggled with that question and others most of the day. *Had Raynhard given them to her with other intentions? The way he had watched her as she examined the royal hunting dagger. What was he looking at? How was he seeing her? What was that look in his eye?*

...

It was still dark the next morning at breakfast. Nagora had slept perhaps for a dozen counts. The last thought she had before falling asleep was of her mum. No dreams woke her. Paruline did. The candles on the table had been lit again. Nagora stared at one of them as she chewed on a piece of bread.

Everyone was quiet. We're all still waking up. I would've stayed in bed until sunrise.

Her shoulders shook with the chill of the morning. Nagora reached for her mug, held it with both hands, and drank the hot forest tea. It warmed her insides. She focused on the candle flame and tried to imagine the coming events. What plans does Mum have for me and Sagora? What are those strange poles and containers all about? Uncle said I'd learn about them over there, with my sister. One day at a time. One step at a time. Focus on the moment.

She washed down the last of her bread and cooked eggs with a final gulp from her mug. She was the first to stand.

Nagora went to the pegs near the door frame and donned her blades, her sheepskin vest, and her quiver. It held more arrows than when she had hung it on the peg. Now it was full. Must be Uncle, or Geirador. Without a word, Paruline picked up Nagora's saddlebags and watched her friend pick up the wax-coated woolen rain cape that held a bedroll wrapped tight inside. Nagora placed it under her arm, reached for her spear and bow, and headed out the door. Paruline followed with a candle lantern.

...

Inside the stable, Paruline lit another lantern. By the time she had lit the others, Dangor arrived with Geirador. Here too it was quiet, except for the quick brushing then saddling of the horses.

It wasn't like Geirador to be so quiet. Was he worried? Nagora couldn't tell. She placed her forehead against Storm's. Today we set out on our journey. It'll be new territory for us to discover. We'll take care of each other, won't we?

When they were ready, they led their mounts out of the stable.

It was time for goodbyes.

Dangor shook Geirador's hand. "I'll take good care of Kimmo."

"He'll do the same for you."

Nagora hugged Geirador. "Geirador, I've never thanked you enough for all you've taught me and for my blades, and for letting Uncle buy Storm for me."

Geirador kissed her forehead. As he stepped back, she watched him take a deep breath through his nose as he held his lips together in a smile. "Give our greetings to Tagnya. Remind Dangor to give her my package as soon as you arrive at her place."

"I will."

She went to Paruline and hugged her. From behind her back, her friend produced a sheepskin hat with ear flaps joined by a back piece that could be tied up over the top. A wingless dragon, embroidered in moss-green thread, decorated the front flap that balanced the hat. "This will help keep

you warm on cold nights when sleeping under the stars. I
didn't have time to add the wings. Perhaps the next time we
meet."

"How thoughtful of you, Pare. You're so kind. I left the
gift I'd found for you in the prince's fortress. I'll have another
for you next time we meet. You'll always be my big sister."

Nagora put the hat on. Its fit was perfect and its warmth
was immediate. "I'll wear it now."

She hugged Paruline again and kept an arm at her waist a
few moments longer.

Geirador patted Dangor on the back and helped him onto
Kimmo.

Nagora swung up onto Storm's back and patted his neck.

They kneed their mounts and rode off in different directions across the meadow. She took a quick look back.
Geirador and Paruline were still watching as she and Storm
disappeared into the dark, gray, morning mist.

# Journey
## *Ispiciwin*

Nagora arrived first at the spot where they had left the mules. The packs on the natural rock shelf, protected by the overhang of the rocky outcrop above the shelf, were undisturbed. "Good morning. It was a chilly night. Did you sleep well? I'm here to get you ready to work today." She brushed the mules before tying the pack frames in place.

Just as she was placing a pack frame on the back of the first mule, Dangor arrived.

Together, they finished attaching and loading the pack frames.

Dangor did a final check to make sure all was secure. "Slow and steady going from here on. There'll be times when we'll have to walk our horses up and through rocky passes, and down too. I just hope we won't have to unpack and re-pack the mules. I'll lead. It'll be quiet going. Keep your ears and eyes peeled. My hand signals as usual. Bird whistle if you need my attention. Bow and quiver at the ready."

"Aye, I know the drill. Like yesterday, this is for real now. Do you truly expect trouble of any kind?"

"When on the move anywhere, Nagora, I've learned to be prepared for trouble. It's being unprepared that often lets one walk into trouble. Sometimes, like yesterday, trouble walks in on us. Lucky for me you showed up. Your training paid off. You spotted their tracks.

"I've got the front. I trust you'll have the rear. We'll both keep a weather eye."

Her uncle's words made her feel good. I guess I proved I'm as ready as I ever will be. Keep a weather eye like I did yesterday.

Dangor borrowed the term from the fishers. It meant continually keeping a watch on all the surrounding conditions on the water. Fine for them. They're not on horseback leading mules through forest trails and up and down mountain passes.

It meant that her eyes would make a continual slow sweep of the area they traveled. And she would have to listen for sounds. I think I will rely on Storm's ears and neck. He'll hear anything unusual before I do. And I'll have to watch for hand signals from Uncle.

It was a game of survival. Would her uncle test her? Did you see the partridge at such a spot? The eagle in the sky at such a place on the trail? The deer tracks? It meant continual concentration and awareness of her surroundings.

Uncle expects it to become second nature and that I'll stay focused every moment we're on the trail. Like I did yesterday. Maybe I was just lucky.

Okay Mum and big sister, I'm not supposed to think about you. And Raynhard, I'm not supposed to think about you either. Nor the two soldiers at the bottom of the bay. Focus on the moment.

Nagora leaned over to pat Storm's chest. She had trained to shoot from his back, even when galloping. Dangor had designed her bow to allow her to do that—it was not as long as her other bows. Storm was not afraid of the thrum of the bowstring anywhere around his head, and he was comfortable with her hanging from the side of her saddle to do all sorts of things. Will I have to use these skills before meeting Mum?

Dangor chose the base of a high cliff face to set up camp for the night. It was off the trail, screened by the dense growth of trees there, and had a recessed notch that could give them some protection from the rain he said would be coming. Best of all, it left them with only one flank to defend. They would take turns sleeping. While one slept, the other would keep watch.

They unpacked the horses and mules. Dangor went to hunt for supper. Nagora fed and brushed down the animals.

Storm, what more was Raynhard thinking when we were in the stable with him yesterday? Can you tell me? Should I believe what my amulet showed me? What was and what could be? Was Raynhard just dreaming out loud?

She patted Storm and hugged him.

I'm lucky to have you to share my secrets.

Then Nagora collected stones to build a firepit behind the boulder at the mouth of the cliff's notch.

After, she scavenged for firewood nearby.

With enough wood collected to cook with and last the night watch, she set up the bedrolls at the back of the cliff notch, with their waxed woolen capes over them.

As she started the fire, Dangor returned with two partridges and a handful of wild onions.

"You were lucky."

"I have days like that." He handed Nagora a bird.

As she plucked and gutted it, she asked, "Are you going to test me?"

He stopped chopping the wild onions. "About what?"

"You know, things I should've noticed on the trail."

"I don't have to. You weren't always on the trail. At times your mind was in two places at once."

Nagora bit her upper lip and lowered her head. It was as if her uncle had been in her mind while they were on the trail. "How do you know that?"

"I expected as much. After all, you've been through a lot and there's more to come. And you missed a few hand signals. Don't worry about it. Tomorrow, you'll be on your toes."

The birds and onions went into a pot with some sea salt, caraway seeds, and water. She put the pot on the fire.

Dangor stirred the pot and inhale the vapors. Again, he spooned out some broth to taste it. From the look on his face, it was ready.

"I'm hungry too," said Nagora.

"It won't be long." He prepared the dough for the bread, to be spread on the flat stone that sat waiting at the fire's edge.

"Do you think we'll be returning soon with those hundred warriors?"

Dangor shrugged. "That's hard to tell. Tagnya's been working hard to get King Godomor on our side. The definite approval has yet to be made. This is no ordinary trading deal. It's an alliance of sorts. Warriors will risk their lives for our cause."

"Wouldn't it be best if Raynhard himself were to go before this King Godomor the Terrible?"

"Aye, it would." He held up his knife. "That was the plan. Since then, important things have come up that require him to remain here and to maintain his secret identity as Chive. Thanks to your reputation, as Edana, you're the next best thing."

"I'm not Edana."

"True, but you created her, unintentionally, I'll admit. Still, the idea of Edana exists in the minds of many and Edana brings them hope. You can't deny that, Nagora. Can you?"

Uncle is right. Edana exists.

"Your mother, Raynhard, and others planning for the Cause knew a good thing when they saw it. That's why Edana has become a major part of the plan to free the dragon."

Dangor picked up one of the flat breads with the blade of his knife. "Smell this. One of the joys of eating on the trail."

She inhaled the warm singed crust. Her uncle's bread was always delicious, with just the right amount of caraway seeds in it. She held out her bowl so he could drop it there. Then she reached for the spoon in the pot. "Give me your bowl."

Her own helping went into her bowl next to the bread. She would let it soak in the broth of the stew.

As she lifted a grouse leg from her spoon with her fingers, visions of the terrified young girl sucking on the bones of the jailor's chicken carcass flashed before her eyes.

You surely have a name. What is it? Are you still alive? If you are still there, I will free you. I promise.

Nagora tried to push the image of the bruised child from her mind.

She kept the broth in her bowl for the last, soaking it up with pieces of bread so wild onion pieces stuck to them. Twilight turned to darkness, and they watched the fire's embers until they almost died out.

Her uncle took the first watch while she slept.


Dangor woke Nagora for her watch. Had she just closed her eyes? No, she had slept. Such was sleep on the trail. Take it when you can get it and only if you can get it. Somehow, she had found some rest.

The night was peaceful. She put two pieces of wood on the fire and pulled back into the shadows. As she listened, her eyes searched stars through the branches of the trees.

I'm on my way, Mum. I thought I'd have so many questions to ask you. I can't seem to think of one, even though I want to know all about you. I can't imagine what questions you'll ask me. I guess they'll just come when we meet, and we'll ask them. I try to imagine your face.

My sister, Sagora, is supposed to look just like me. Another me. I have trouble imagining how I'll feel when I see another me I can touch and hold. Are you thinking what I'm thinking, Sagora?

An owl called in the distance. For a whole count, Nagora listened and watched the embers in the fire glow before adding another small log on top of them. Counting time at night was not as easy as in the day when she had the sun as reference.

A day's work was twenty-four counts, a full day three times that. Being woken to take a turn on watch meant actually counting time. Dangor wasn't picky about it at night. "A piece of hardwood the size of your arm on the fire lasts about one count. Just count pieces. If you count numbers, you'll fall asleep."

The bark sizzled and smoked before the flames caught and wrapped themselves around the log. The sweet odor of the green birch smoke tickled her nose in the cool night air.

Before long, Dangor awoke for his second turn at watch.

The next morning at the base of the rocky mountain trail, Dangor signaled for a halt. He dismounted and led his horse and the mules off the trail. Nagora did likewise. It was the second stop they had made since their early morning meal and they would be eating again.

After some trail rations, she waited as Dangor set out on foot up the rocky trail, leading the two mules followed by his mount, one behind the other, each tied to a separate line. As agreed, she would allow him a lead of a hundred strides before following.

Each step was slow and deliberate. "Easy, Storm. Be patient. You'll get your turn at the front later." Nagora checked on the progress of her mules. Her horse was eager to climb. "Easy, Storm. You're not carrying a load. Don't push us." She turned to continue her own climb, watching the trail and bending to move aside loose stones the mules might slip on.

Going down the other side of the mountain was even slower than coming up had been. Every step of the way, she not only watched her own footing, but the footing of the pack mule next to her.

The near fall of the mule at her side, as it slipped on the steep patch of rock, had scared Nagora. She had danced alongside and pushed against the laden animal. Luckily, a leveled-out area was just below the steep patch. When the mule had settled, she went back up to guide the second one down, and then Storm.

Dangor was waiting where the mountain trail leveled out near the bottom of the valley. He was wearing the talisman that guaranteed them safe passage into and through the Land of Skulls. "Uncle, is the Blood River far from here?"

"Not far. Our animals will drink there before we cross."

He gave Nagora a thumbs-up salute. "You did good work with the mules. Coming down was difficult." He pointed to the sky. "I'm glad we won't be on that part of the trail with what's coming. We'll need our rain capes."

Nagora walked back to Storm to bring him ahead. She double-checked the lines to her mules, removed her rain cape from the bedroll tied behind her saddle, mounted Storm, and donned her cape.

Dangor did likewise and waited for her to come alongside.

"After the horses and mules drink, next stop will be at Godomor's hunting lodge."

"Is that where messages for Mum are left?"

"Aye. When they find a message for Tagnya, a rider from the patrol leaves with it right away. If the message requires an answer, Tagnya responds as soon as she can, and it gets delivered on the next patrol. The message is in a coded language only Tagnya and a few of us know. Our message carriers have safe passage as far as the hunting lodge."

As Dangor set out, a slow drizzle fell. Nagora followed his mules by a dozen horse lengths.

Before long, she got her first look at the border of the Land of Skulls. The front hooves of their horses stood in the wide, shallow river as they drank.

Across the river, on either side as far as her eyes could see, human skulls sat impaled on stakes driven into the river bank, about twenty strides from each other. The vacant eyes of the skulls stared at her and the skulls with jaws attached seemed to speak a silent yet deadly warning.

The skulls were having their desired effect. Should she cross into the Land of Skulls? Even if they had safe passage, a chill settled on the back of Nagora's neck. She let herself relax and tried to read Storm's reaction. If he noticed the skulls, he didn't seem to mind.

They kneed their horses on, and just as they crossed the stream, the drizzle became a downpour that appeared to not want to let up.

Only when they reached Godomor's camp did they find relief from the rain under a simple framed, single-walled shelter next to the corral. They unsaddled, unpacked, brushed, and fed their animals.

When done, they made their way to Godomor's unguarded hunting lodge. Nagora followed Dangor inside the big circular stone structure. Light from the open door provided a dim view of the fire pit in the center of the lodge. They set their saddlebags and bedrolls on a knee-level platform near the door. Inside, it was cool and damp. The smell of smoke and the roasted fat of animals that hunters had cooked over the fire lingered. Nagora's nose tried to identify the odors.

Venison and boar? Or is that pig? Did they have wild boar here as well? Perhaps they had brought pig from a nearby farm?

Dangor started a fire in the pit beneath the flue hole in the ceiling.

As the fire blazed, her eyes took in the simple stone and timber-framed interior that contained three wooden tables, six benches, and a raised platform that ran around the perimeter of the circular stone structure except for the access to the lodge's entrance.

Two dozen warriors could sleep on the platform and half as many on the floor around the fire pit.

Nagora counted twelve vertical posts of timber around the interior perimeter supporting the ceiling joists, three of which met in the center where the triangular smoke hole was. Three piles of smaller slate stones on the roof at the corners of the flue supported a bigger flat stone that kept out most of the rain.

In the fire pit, she saw an air draft hole at the bottom on one side. It surely ran under the lodge floor, at a downward angle, to emerge outside, below the moss-covered stone wall section of the lodge.

She had seen such an arrangement in a home in Cairnmase. Air from the outside could travel in and up, along this little stone lined tunnel, to the bottom edge of the fire pit. A stone, placed over the mouth of this tunnel, controlled the amount of draft air coming to the fire.

Nagora understood the benefits of this—the lodge door could be shut snug in cold weather without causing the inside of the lodge to smoke up because the fire didn't have enough air. It also helped control the heat of the fire for cooking and heating. And it allowed for circulation of fresh air within the lodge when the fire pit was not in use.

Probably an iron grid at the other end of the tunnel kept bigger animals out. Mice, however, would have the run of this place.

Nagora looked beyond the fire pit at the supply of dry firewood stacked just under the raised perimeter platform.

Practical.

She took in the fire pit again with its four forged-iron posts with hooks that would support iron cooking spits, and the pots and plates hung from them.

Back at the entrance two tripods, cut from the crotch of a tree's trunk where three of its branches met, stood next to each side of the doorway. Pegs had been set in drilled holes near the tops of these tripods.

A series of holes ran down each side of the trunks so the pegs could be adjusted to different heights to support poles set on them.

Nagora found four poles, two caked with smoky tar and two clean, skinned of their bark. Obviously, game was hung from the tarred poles over the fire's smoke to dry and cure the meat. Wet garments were hung from the clean poles near the fire pit to help dry them.

She hauled the tripods near the fire pit and set up a pole to hang their rain capes to dry.

...

"Uncle, do you think we'll see the border patrol show up in this weather?"

Dangor scratched his beard as he looked up at the ceiling, obviously listening to the downpour. "The rain might affect whether they travel and how far. Whatever, we can't go any further without them. They'll show up sooner or later, but most likely, sooner. In the meantime, keep a lookout at the entrance. I'll prepare us something warm to drink. I'll call you when it's ready."

She gave him a thumbs-up and went to stand at the entrance.


As Nagora watched the steady downpour from the slate overhang of the entrance, she imagined the progress of the patrol on horseback in these conditions, wet riders peering down on the ground their mounts would cover, continually assessing the choices their horses would make.

It would be slow going for the safety of the riders and their mounts on the slippery, wet trails. Would they send scouts ahead on foot? Are we being watched already? We haven't tried to hide our presence. Hopefully, whoever's on patrol knows of the possibility of visitors arriving here.

She looked at the skulls that sat on the outer perimeter posts of the lodge and recalled the ones that marked the border.

Not exactly peaceful resting places for the enemies of this land. Their warning seemed obvious—be careful when you cross into this land where your head might end up gathering moss on a pole.

Geirador had said that this land and its people appeared more terrifying than they actually were. Surely a people that put on such a display with human skulls could, if justified, act according to these appearances.

Whatever the situation might be, it would be a while before she would let her guard down.

"Potion's ready." As usual when on a cold, rainy trail, Dangor made his special recipe. He had soaked stone-ground oats in water, poured off the liquid into a pot, added honey and mead, and warmed it on the fire without bringing it to a boil to make a hot, body-warming drink.

He had also mixed the ingredients of his biscuits: a raw egg mixed with flour, sun-dried currants, and honey with the remaining oatmeal paste. He had spooned clumps of the mixture onto a hot skillet to cook.

"Uncle! This is a treat! You're spoiling us!"

"Like Geirador would say, 'When on the trail, treat yourself well. It makes the journey pleasant when you take care of the body's needs.' It's not as smooth as Geirador's winter brew nor does it pack the same punch, but it warms the insides."

Nagora smiled. "Aye, that it does. It's my favorite drink at Geirador's when I stay overnight in the winter. He adds creamy goat's milk. When I sip it in front of the fire, it makes me want to curl up and sleep. Uncle, your biscuits are delicious."

"Enjoy them while they're fresh. Tomorrow, any leftover will be hard as stone. They'll hold us until our evening meal and help warm us from the dampness of the rain."

As Dangor spoke these words, the rain let up. The steady thrumming of the rain on the slate roof overhead receded, and only the occasional fat drops, splashed from the leaves of nearby trees, hit now and again.

She and her uncle walked to the entrance with their drinks in hand.

They stepped outside. The sun was pushing its way through the clouds overhead. The air was warmer, and a slight mist rose from the forest floor around them. A breeze rustled the treetops above them. "Looks like it's going to clear," said Dangor.

Nagora finished her biscuit and her broth. "I think I'll go see if I can hunt something for supper."

"Good idea. I'll check on our animals."

# Welcome
## *Miyoteh ka wisamiht awîyak*

Nagora went back into the lodge for her bow and quiver. When she returned, she took her bearings and headed downwind. She would walk in that direction for about four counts and then circle back upwind to hunt for partridge or rabbit.

By the time she circled back upwind, the sun had made significant breaks in the clouds and was making its warmth felt in the surrounding forest. The mist was lifting, giving way to humid heat and the sound of songbirds reestablishing their territories. Slow and silent, with an arrow nocked at the ready, Nagora made her way around moss covered rocks among the trees, watching for any signs of movement of potential game fit for their pot.

She came to the edge of a small clearing and waited. On the opposite edge, she spotted a hare that hopped once and stopped to nibble.

A clear shot.

Nagora raised her bow, drew her arrow, aimed, and let it fly. The hare pivoted and ran, and the arrow buried itself in the ground.

Tar piss!

She crossed the clearing, retrieved her arrow, cleaned the wet dirt off it, and nocked it on the bowstring again before moving on. She watched for any movement, but she also scanned the forest floor for any places where she might find wild garlic or onions to complete their meal.

Sure enough, as she was crossing a stand of maples, there in the damp dark loam, growing through the carpet of dead leaves, she found wild garlic. She used the blade of her small dagger to uproot four of them and left the rest so other plants would grow from them. These wild garlic bulbs went into her game pouch.

If I can bag a hare, that'll be great.

She continued on her way. The smell of smoke from the hut's flue told her she was not far. That's when she spotted the movement.

A man with a bow ran crouched, away from the direction of the lodge.

Probably a scout with the border patrol, heading back to report that someone was in the hut.

Nagora followed him from a distance and traveled parallel to him.

Soon, Nagora arrived where the patrol was waiting. Eight men sat on horses. One of them held the reins of the scout's mount. He as well was an archer, dressed like his comrade in leggings, shirt, a vest, and black cape.

Nagora snuck as close as she dared to get a good look at them. Seven of the riders wore boiled leather armor. Their forearm and shin protectors bore embossed bones of those body parts they protected. Their thighs were bare, as were their upper arms. Six of them wore black capes that hung from around their shoulders and covered the hindquarters of their horses.

The one to whom the scout spoke wore a green cape.

*Okimaw.* "Leader." Another strange yet so familiar word.

His breastplate, like those of his fellows, bore an embossed skull, with the exception that the skull on his was of burnished metal. The seven also wore leather helmets with a band of metal around the head and bands of metal that crossed on the top of their heads. The band that went from back to front continued down between the wearers' eyes and over their noses.

When one of them yawned, his closed eyelids showed painted black circles, giving the eerie effect of a skull staring. If he grinned with teeth bared and eyes closed just before engaging in a fight, would his opponent be frightened? Her uncle's words echoed: Keep your eye on the weapon when fighting hand-to-hand. Don't listen to the taunts of the face makers.

The seven wore daggers at their belts and their swords were strapped to their backs. In their right hands, they each held a spear that rested in a holder hung from their saddles. In their left hands, they held the reins of their horses. All their horses were beautiful animals, and they reminded her of Storm.

The leader turned in his saddle as he spoke his orders to the others. They seemed to know the drill. They nodded, split into three teams. Two teams of an archer and two riders with spears headed off. Obviously, they would take up flank positions on each side of the hut. The leader, with two riders, would approach from the front.

I'm following right behind you. You better treat Uncle well or there'll be an arrow for at least three of you before you know it.

The leader let his elbow cradle his spear while he rubbed his thigh. Nagora could just make out the lines of the scars on his thigh.

Could this be Gabe the Terrible, son of Godomor, the one Geirador saved from a bear attack? Perhaps so. We'll see.

Nagora followed the three riders toward the lodge. She kept a safe distance, out of sight, yet well within her bow's striking distance. When they arrived within sight of the lodge, the three riders approached abreast of each other.

She could make out the dismounted archers with arrows nocked on their bows, but not drawn, flanking each side of the lodge's entrance. The riders accompanying the archers had dismounted and waited with spears in hand.

When the three remaining riders were within shouting distance, they stopped.

She pulled two arrows from her quiver. One with a big blunt end could sting a horse's hindquarters, causing it to buck and distract its rider. The other had a regular hunting tip. She nocked the blunt tipped arrow.

One rider called out twice. The second time, in the Coastal Trader's tongue: "Who goes there? Show yourselves. We come in peace."

Within moments, Dangor appeared at the entrance. "We come in peace. We are friends of Geirador." He held up the talisman.

"How many are you?" asked the rider who had called out before.

"We are two. I am alone now. My companion is hunting for our meal."

"What is your name?" asked the leader.

"I am Dangor."

"I am Gabe, son of Godomor the Terrible who rules this land. Geirador is a dear friend of mine."

"That same Geirador, who saved you from the bear attack, sends warm greetings to both you and your father; and he has sent both of you some requested goods and, for your father, a cask of his fine mead."

With those words, Gabe dismounted as did the riders accompanying him. The archers returned the arrows to their quivers and approached with Gabe's men. "These are my men. We are the border patrol for this section of our land. Welcome to the Land of Skulls, Dangor. What's your companion's name?"

Nagora stepped into the clear. Dangor saw her and said, as he pointed, "I'll let my companion tell you herself."

Gabe and his men turned to see. "Sagora?" Gabe's face betrayed his confusion.

"That would be my sister. I'm Nagora."

Now Gabe looked perplexed. He looked to his men as if to confirm he was seeing Sagora. He spoke to them in their tongue, mentioned her sister's name, and then the name "Mattay." That warrior came forward, stripped off his left forearm protector, to show a bandaged wound. He spoke something to her. All she understood was "Sagnuska." Does he think it's me who took care of his wound?

"I'm Nagora." She pointed to herself. "Nagora, Sagora's twin sister."

Gabe yelled an order at Mattay. Mattay stopped. Gabe understood what she had said. He must have repeated it to his men, but she wasn't prepared for their reaction.

They drew their swords. The archers pulled arrows from their quivers and nocked them. Gabe's men surrounded her.

"Don't move a finger, Nagora." Dangor approached. "Gabe, we have your father's talisman. It grants us safe passage in the Land of Skulls. We do not come with wrongful intentions. Please restrain your men."

Gabe spoke an order. His men lowered their weapons and looked to him, waiting.

Mattay spoke to Gabe. What did he say?

Dangor came to stand at her side.

Gabe spoke in the Danuian language. "You are Nagora. Not Sagora?"

She stared at him. "Yes, I'm Nagora. I'm not Sagora."

"You do not know my man, Mattay?"

"I know him now. This is the first time I meet him."

"Where were you born?"

"Here, in the Land of Skulls. I was the second born of twins. My mum, Tagnyoriva, obeyed the laws of your land and at birth, I was banished to live away from the Land of Skulls."

"I was not aware Sagora had a sister, let alone a twin sister. You truly are identical to her in appearance."

"Like me, she has only recently been told of my existence. Secrets have also been kept from you."

Gabe spoke to his men, obviously relaying the information.

Two of Gabe's men raised their swords and waved them in front of themselves as they signed with one hand and chanted.

She didn't like their tone. "What are they saying?"

Gabe looked at Nagora and made the signs with one hand, like his men, as he spoke their meaning. "Evil twin, I will see you not," his hand over an eye.

"Hear you not," he said with a hand over an ear.

"Speak you not," with a hand over his mouth.

"Touch you not," with a fist pulled to his chest.

"Remember you not," with fingers spread, back of the hand to his forehead.

"Be away from me and the land I live in," with his open hand pushing away from his forehead.

"Be away, evil twin," he said hammering a fist twice in her direction.

Tar piss! She looked from Gabe to the two who were still signing. Some twin or twins must've done something terrible to instill such behavior.

"Nagora," Gabe spoke her name.

She looked back at him.

"Nagora, for your safety, I'm going to ask you to remove your weapons for now. Dangor, will you please tie her to a tree while I speak to my men? Old ways in our land are slow to change. Twins are still considered to possess evil powers by some, and so they are feared, even by some of our bravest."

She swallowed as she looked to Dangor. "Best do as Gabe asks. I'm certain he'll do his best to set this right."

Anger rose inside Nagora as she removed her bow, quiver, and blades to hand them to her uncle. She walked to the nearest tree, leaned against it and wrapped her arms around it.

Two of Gabe's men said something to him.

Gabe himself tied her hands together with a length of rope one of his men had handed him.

All the while, the other two men kept up the chant until Gabe ordered all of them into the lodge. Dangor went with them.

That's it. Go. Be away from me, ignorant chanters with your stupid beliefs.

If this welcome is a taste of what awaits me, I think I'd rather turn around and head home. So I'm the evil twin. Mum, you'll have to meet me in the Land of the Danu, and you too, Sagora, because it looks like my arrival is going to make things rough for you as well.

I'd like to know the evil done by twins in the past of these people. It must have been so terrible to spawn such fear. Maybe this will, in some way, work to my advantage. One day at a time.

Nagora didn't like the look on Dangor's face when he returned with Gabe and his men. "Uncle, do I have to hug this tree for much longer?"

"It has taken some doing, but I think Gabe has been able to negotiate a solution. It seems to satisfy his men. It doesn't mean you'll be greeted with open arms wherever you go by others in the land."

"Okay. Tell me straight."

Dangor paused, looked her in the eye and took a deep breath. "You're going to be marked."

"Marked?"

"Branded."

"Branded? Do you mean with a hot iron?"

Dangor nodded.

"Oh! No! Wait! I don't have to accept that. That's torture! No one is going to brand me!"

"Nagora, do you want to see your mum and sister?"

"Of course I do, but I don't want to be branded to make that happen!"

"Here's the situation. You can leave now. You won't be branded. But your sister and mother will. And if ever you show up again in the Land of Skulls, and are found to be Sagora's twin sister, and the daughter of Tagnyoriva, the three of you will be put to death."

She shook her head. I don't believe this! How can they do that?

Dangor placed his hand on her shoulder and held her gaze. "There's more. Or you can stay, wear this talisman, be weaponless until you are brought before Godomor the Terrible to be branded by your sister, in front of all present, and then you will be given back your weapons and allowed to come and go in the Land of Skulls … as a marked twin."

She stared at her uncle as he explained these were the choices Gabe had convinced his men to agree to. I don't understand. That's not a choice. After a moment she managed to ask, "Why?"

"To try to understand the choice offered you, based on unfounded fears, will be a waste of time. Simply put, the choice being offered is based on a recent precedent that, so far, seems to have worked to reintegrate a returning twin.

"If you accept, you would be the second attempt. It's one of the slow steps to change old fears. Twins were once killed at birth. Then, second-born twins were once killed at birth. Later, second-born twins were banished away from the land forever. Now, with the precedent, they are to be marked when they return."

Nagora listened to each of Dangor's words and tried to imagine possible scenarios. "What part of me will Sagora brand?"

"Your forehead."

"With what mark?"

"Your choice."

It'll be my first battle scar, earned because of who I am, a twin. I'll be marked, branded to be recognized. Branded by my own blood. Branded to break my mirror image, the source of fear and evil. I survived the icy sea water of the dungeon sea cave. Surely I can survive the burn of a brand.

Nagora swallowed and took a deep breath. "Tiwaz will be my mark. At least, with this mark, those that can read it will know I'm a warrior for what it means—a higher cause. Give me the talisman."

*Kanawisimowin.* "Something to give me protection." Why do I hear these words?

"You are a warrior, my Nagora." Dangor removed the talisman and placed it around her neck.

Nagora glared at Gabe and at each of his men, burning their faces into her memory as she willed her dragon's tear amulet to set them on fire.

If only I had that power.

"Set me free."

"Before he sets you free, I want you to know, unless Gabe orders otherwise, two of his men will be with you at all times. When we arrive in Skull Bay, Gabe and his two men will escort you until you've been marked. If you try anything, you'll be good as dead, as well as your mother and sister—three new skulls to grace Godomor the Terrible's gate."

Dangor looked to Gabe. Gabe nodded, staring.

"I understand." Nagora bared her clenched teeth to stare down Gabe as he approached.

Gabe did not make eye contact as he cut the rope. As soon as she could, she turned her back to him and his men, swung her arms back and forth, rubbed her shoulders, and then rubbed her wrists to help relieve the itch of the rope.

She glanced over her shoulder.

Gabe approached. "Nagora, if you will allow it, I would like to speak to you."

She kept her back to him. "Go ahead, speak. I still have my ears and my tongue. I won't force you to look upon my face."

"Thank you. Please wait just a moment. I'll dismiss my men."

Gabe issued orders.

"They'll take care of their mounts and prepare the evening meal." A gentle hand from behind Nagora touched her shoulder.

She turned to face Gabe. His eyes searched hers. He seemed to be choosing his words.

"Nagora, I don't expect you will forgive this welcome to our land today, but perhaps someday, after you've gotten to know the people of our land, my father, and me, you will. Here, twins hold a certain fear because of the magic it is believed they possess. Magic that can be, at the same time, both good and evil. It is the evil they fear. Old ways and beliefs do not change overnight." I can see that.

"As the son of our leader, in his absence, appreciate that I have to respect and enforce the laws of our land for the good of all the people in our land. Thus, the unfortunate choice put to you as the price for your return to our land."

Nagora lowered her gaze to his breastplate for a moment before looking back into his eyes. "You're right. Forgiveness is far from my heart. My path seems to be drawn for me in ways I have no control over, and no say in. Should forgiveness ever come to my heart, I'll let you know. Understanding and knowledge travel with time and on occasion, carry forgiveness with them."

Gabe had listened intently as she spoke. "You speak wise words, Nagora, like your sister and mother. You have the same look as your sister when she shows her displeasure. It humbles the one who receives it. I've been on its receiving end from her, and now, from you. Forgive me, but I can't get over how identical you are in appearance to Sagora."

His eyes haven't stopped reading my face. Is he comparing me to Sagora? "Well, you confirm I have a sister who looks exactly like me, at least for a little while."

She took a deep breath as she tried her best to control her anger. As a warrior, she had made her choice. Now she would have to live with it. "Who taught you to speak our tongue?"

"Sagora herself and your mother have been my teachers."

"Then you know them well?"

Gabe paused and smiled, his eyes still taking in her face.

You're weighing your words again.

"Yes."

You've paused again.

"Nagora, I noticed Geirador's handiwork in the weapons you were wearing. Am I right?"

And you've changed the topic.

"You have a good eye. They are crafted by Geirador."

"Shall we go to the hut? I'd like to examine them."

She led the way.

Inside, Nagora found Dangor had removed the rain capes from the poles and folded them near their bedrolls, which he had set on the wooden platform further away from the entrance. "Gabe would like to see the blades Geirador made for me."

Dangor turned to Gabe and glanced at the two men assigned to follow her. They had taken up position on each side of the doorway.

Dangor picked up her blades and handed them to Gabe. "If I'm not mistaken, there's a set, just like this one, for you, packed in the goods Geirador has sent."

"Truly? Geirador has spoiled me again. How will I ever be able to repay him, Dangor?"

Dangor smiled. "Knowing Geirador, that you are pleased with his gift will be reward enough for him."

Gabe examined the big blade and the knives. He felt the heft of them and obviously marveled in Geirador's craftsmanship and attention to detail.

Then he looked up at her and said, "I gather you, young woman, know how to use these like a true warrior?"

For the first time, she smiled at Gabe.

He smiled back.

He's blushing. What's he thinking?

Except for the two men who had signed to ward off the evil twin, Gabe's other men entered the lodge with the necessities for the evening's meal, which they set about cooking at the fire pit. They opened a flask of mead and Gabe poured drinks for all around the fire.

Gabe brought a cup to Nagora. She sat near her bedroll on the platform, away from the others. She took the cup, nodded her thanks, and focused on Dangor who was waiting for Gabe to return.

Her uncle sipped from his cup. "Gabe, how long does your patrol of the border last?"

"The patrol of this section usually lasts between seven to ten days, depending on weather and reported incidents that we have to investigate. This is one of my father's hunting lodges. It's his favorite." Gabe glanced up at the ceiling. He seemed to hold an appreciation for the place as well.

"As you probably know, our border with yours has been drawn since my grandfather, King Allyred, and King Bernhard's father, King Kaynhard, finished off the last of a sizable invading Outlander party that had been making incursions into our lands. Their mutual alliance enabled them to crush that larger than normal raiding force in the valley near here, at the river you crossed today."

He looked over at Nagora. Likely he had spoken more for her benefit.

Dangor had told her of the slaughter of the Outlanders on what was to become the Blood River, but not the names of the kings involved in the alliance.

"Allyred suggested that the river become the border of our lands, and that he would mark our side of the river with the skulls of the Outlanders slain that day. Kaynhard agreed on condition they should not fear attack on this mutual flank for as long as they and their rightful heirs ruled the land. On that day, he gave my grandfather the name Allyred the Terrible.

"That agreement suited us fine, so we concentrated our forces on the coasts the Outlanders often invaded.

"Now, however, it looks like Queen Raganora and her son are not the rightful heirs of King Bernhard. As yet she has not made known their intentions toward us.

"Tagnyoriva, on the other hand, has been trying to convince us we must come to help the man who should rightly rule in the Land of the Danu." He gave Nagora a brief smile.

Dangor wore a bit of a frown. "That means border patrols here have been in place since that decisive battle with the Outlander force?"

Gabe was nodding. "Yes, the patrols have been in operation since then. Before that, outposts for guards had been built along this border. Outpost guards would be relieved by passing patrol members. Guarded outposts have since been abandoned, and our patrol on this border stops by at the few farms scattered along the border. They raise sheep and some, pigs."

Gabe pointed about with a wave of his hand. "This hunting lodge was once a border outpost. My father chose to maintain it as a hunting camp. Game in these parts is plentiful, and coming here to hunt gives my father the opportunity to visit subjects in this part of the land."

Dangor looked over at her. "Had your patrols ever reported seeing dragons in the sky?"

Gabe seemed to guess Dangor had asked the question for her benefit, as he turned to Nagora. "To my knowledge, only in two official reports when more than two men saw a dragon in flight with a rider on its back. The existence of dragons in your land had mostly been the stuff of legends to us, and still is, even if those who'd reported the sighting swore it was true."

He paused. He's keeping his eyes on me.

Gabe smiled at Nagora and continued. "I myself have not seen a dragon; however, I believe they exist because Nagora's mother told me stories of them and their importance to the people of the Land of the Danu."

Dangor smiled at her as well. "She must've told you of the dragons with feathered scales that can somehow play with light to make them nearly invisible in their surroundings, especially in the sky." Gabe turned to listen to Dangor. "It takes a practiced eye to catch them in flight. Easier with a rider on the dragon's back."

Gabe nodded. "Yes, and from what Tagnyoriva told me, they also can make themselves frighteningly visible too." He gave Nagora a quick glance.

Dangor grinned. "Nothing like the element of surprise when scaring off an Outlander vessel."

Dangor's conversation with Gabe faded as the scene of Sagora applying the brand to her forehead played over and over in Nagora's mind. It became a living tapestry woven with the threads of fear and worry. She tried to imagine her mum and sister reacting to the news of the welcome that awaited her.

Were they aware of the possibility she would be branded? If they were, how would they prepare for it? How would they try to console her? Would their words have the power to console? Would they even try?

Would it hurt?

Surely.

For how long?

For a moment? For many counts? Many days?

How long would it take to heal?

How do I prepare for the moment? Accept it? Better me, than both of them. It'll be over, and then I'll continue on this path of events I do not control.

I'll be branded in front of a king and a crowd of his people. How will they expect me to react? How did the previous person react? What will my reaction tell them? Will my reaction be what they expect? If not, will I still be considered evil? No matter what my reaction, I'll surely stay the evil twin to some of them.

Maybe, just maybe, I won't disappoint them.


The smell of freshly baked stone bread and a hot bowl of stew, which Gabe placed in her hands, brought Nagora back to the moment and made her realize that he was telling Dangor of his encounter with the bear on the day Geirador had come to his rescue. Where were Gabe's men? Had he dismissed them, or had they left to be away from her? She looked to the entrance. Her two guards were just on the other side of the doorway.

Gabe placed the bear's paw so the claws rested on the scars of his thigh. They were the actual claws that had left scars on him.

He wears his scars with pride. Will I?

He had fashioned the skin of the paw into a small scrip. He wore it on the narrow belt over his shoulder so it rested at his side. "The bear could have torn me to pieces had Geirador not come along."

Then he took a knife from its sheath on the same belt above the scrip. It was one of Geirador's making, like the ones she had learned to throw so well, in great part thanks to Geirador's well, thought-out design and craftsmanship. "I still carry the knife Geirador gave me the following day. It has never left my side, and so I think of him every day."

Nagora could almost feel the Tiwaz, its three lines meeting in a point as an arrow. She would be wearing it for the rest of her life. "You carry the scars of the bear's claws with you since that day. Do you also think of the bear attack every day?"

Gabe didn't hesitate. "I do."

Will I think of the branding every day, or only when I see Sagora? Will I think of her as the one who marked me? She has no choice. I cannot blame her.

"When you see a bear again, how do you feel?"

"Strange as this may sound, Nagora, I've never, since then, seen a living bear again. It's something I cannot explain."

*Maskwa misit kanawisimowin.* If I told you I know "the bear paw protects you," you wouldn't believe me. More strange words I'll keep to myself for now.

"I've seen dead bears killed by others on hunts, but not a living one. For the moment, I cannot tell you how I feel."

Dangor, who had been listening with apparent keen interest, spoke up. "My limp is caused by an arrow that wounded me in battle." He pointed to his lower leg. "It struck my calf.

Every time I watch someone draw a bowstring, I think of the faceless enemy who drew the bowstring and loosed the arrow that struck me. The faces of all those archers flash by as if trying to fit that faceless enemy. Being an archer myself, I wonder if I have caused such feeling in those enemies that survived the wounds my arrows exacted."

"Ah, Dangor! But does one have time for such thoughts in the heat of the battle?" Gabe raised his cup.

"No. How to survive the battle is foremost in one's thoughts, and should be," said Dangor.

Gabe drank and raised his cup again. "May my wits be about me in my next encounter with a bear. Let's eat."

Dangor raised his own cup and responded, "From the battles past we survived, may we bring our strength of body and mind to those we have yet to wage."

I survived the dungeon sea cave, may I bring that same strength to my branding. I'll drink to that. She raised her cup.

Gabe raised his cup once more. "To new friendships. May the bonds we build today become stronger." He smiled at her.

I won't drink to that yet.

"Officially, our people have yet to commit to your cause. When they do, my father will raise his cup to that."

If they do, my brand will be a small price to pay.

Nagora stared at Gabe. "On the day your father raises his cup to our cause, we'll raise ours to thank him and say to our future king: 'Raynhard, your crown is at hand.'"

After their meal, Dangor went to groom the horses. Nagora prepared their bedrolls on the large platform near the fire pit. Gabe did the same, as did a few of his men. Outside, thirty paces from the lodge entrance, two men stacked wood near the fire pit. Probably the first watch getting ready.

Like two of his men, Gabe had washed the black dots off his eyelids. Would those who hadn't continue to patrol this section of the border? Gabe removed his armor, keeping only his bear-paw scrip. He turned to her. "Will you come with me for a short walk? We'll talk in these last moments of the day as the sun sets."

"Aye, I will." *You probably have information to tell me.*

Gabe led the way along the path to a clearing on a rocky outcrop. His two men followed, just out of earshot. The edge of the outcrop dropped off into the tree-lined valley below where the river, with its edge staked with skulls, wound its way. From this vantage point, the orange sky made the forest look like it was on fire.

Gabe pointed to his two men. "Tomorrow, these two men and I will escort you to Skull Bay. You'll be reunited with Tagnyoriva and Sagora. Not soon enough, I can imagine."

Nagora glanced at the two, then set her gaze on Gabe. "That's right. I can't wait to be branded by my sister in front of your father, the king, and all those ignorant onlookers who believe the second born of twins is an evil twin. Can you imagine how I feel about that?"

Gabe lowered his head in thought before speaking. "Ignorance is not easily overcome. It takes time. That our people have come this far in their struggle with superstitious beliefs is, in great part, due to the efforts of your mother. In all these years, living as a healer amongst our people, she has been living and sharing her knowledge … by example."

Gabe turned to Nagora. "The only times she has spoken to share her knowledge has been when we've sought her opinion and counsel. At those times, her words were wise, non-judgmental, and cause for reflection."

He looked Nagora in the eye. "It was her words that saved a twin from being put to death. However, her words could not save him from being marked. Three years later, that seems to have been one more big step away from misguided beliefs about twins. How many years until twins will not be branded? I cannot say. Perhaps your branding will bring us even farther away from this superstition."

Nagora hung her head. "I'm sorry, Gabe. My response to you is forged in ignorance. I can't wait to meet my mum and sister. I keep imagining how I'll behave in their presence. It's difficult for me because, in my heart, I have so many mixed feelings, especially with the coming branding—desire, in-comprehension, love, deception, disbelief, and even fear.

"I see myself trying to behave in a certain way; yet I can-not picture how they will behave, save for my sister, who's identical in appearance to me. That, I imagine, will be like looking into a fantastical mirror in wonderment because, not only will I see myself, but I will touch and hold another me, but only for a short moment, too short a moment."

Gabe stopped walking and turned to her. "Nagora, let the reunion with your mother and sister happen. Listen to your heart. Follow your heart. Trust your heart. They are your blood and you are their blood. With time, your bonds will grow stronger. I wish I had words to prepare you and comfort you for what you will soon face."

She looked into his sincere eyes. "Your words help and give me cause to reflect."

Gabe's smile was just perceptible. "The evening star brings twilight. Let's return to the lodge. An early bed will see us on our way by sunrise tomorrow."

# Reunion
# *Nakiskâtowak*

After a restless night's sleep in the lodge, Nagora was the second to have her bedroll and saddlebags ready. One of Gabe's men was no longer there. Had he been sent ahead to warn of her coming? Most likely, since Sagora has to be prepared for the task.

Let's get on with it.

She was the first to finish her breakfast and the first to leave the lodge in the morning twilight, cutting short the morning meal of her two guards.

They followed Nagora to the latrine.

She glared at them. Do you want to join me? It was enough to warn them. They turned their backs.

When done, Nagora went to groom the mules. She had moved on to Storm by the time Gabe and Dangor arrived. She kept her back to them.

Storm, we'll be on the trail for a good stretch today. Let's take care of each other, okay? I need to feel your strength.

Gabe sent the guards to finish their meal. When he moved to help Dangor pack the mules, she stepped over and in silence motioned Gabe away. He smiled at her and turned to walk away. Dangor didn't say a word and kept his face impassive as he helped her lift and tie on the packs.

It was sunrise when they set off for the day's ride. The going was slow through the rocky trails of the mountain forest. One of Gabe's men took the lead, and another took the rear position. Gabe rode alongside Nagora whenever trail conditions permitted. She tried to ignore his presence at those times.

He's not speaking. He's waiting for me to open up.

After six counts of watching the forest scenery change color as the sun climbed into the sky, Nagora spoke. "Tell me about my sister."

"Like you, Sagora's an archer. Her aim is uncanny. She's a good judge of distance and wind conditions when hurling darts with a throwing lance. Her knife throws are rarely off the mark. She outsmarts stronger opponents with her agility and speed when she fights with a staff. She swims like a fish. She taught me how to swim, but I'm not as comfortable in the water as she."

"Is there something she doesn't do well?"

"I'm still waiting for her to best me with a sword. I've let her win many times, but she knows that. She wants to taste the kill, but hasn't yet." Gabe smiled.

"Then for how long have you been learning our language with my mum and Sagora?"

Gabe leaned his head back for a moment before answering. "Since the year after their arrival in our land. My father said that it was an opportunity for me not to miss. Tagnyoriva was in a state of melancholy. My father figured she needed a task to occupy her, to help bring her out of that state of mind. I became that task. My father brought me to your mother and asked her to teach me your language. He told Tagnyoriva if I proved to be an apt pupil, she could teach me anything else she saw fit I should learn. Anything that would help me as future leader of our people."

He almost makes it sound as if Mum raised him. What about his own mother?

"At the time, I thought she was sad because she was not with her husband. Like my father was sad when my own mother died. Today, I realize that it was more than that. To abandon you at such an early age must've been something your mother deeply regretted."

He turned in his saddle to look at Nagora. "As a young man, I spent most of my days with Tagnyoriva. I watched her nurse your sister. I learned, almost as a child does, hearing your mother repeat the songs and infant talk with Sagora, which she encouraged me to do also. Soon, I'd taken on the role of big brother. I spoke my language to Sagora and the Danuian language with your mother. That way we all learned."

The smile on his face broadened. "I helped carry and care for Sagora, as I ranged the countryside with your mother, searching for and cataloging healing plants. Most of the plants she looked for were based on the ones she'd learned about when she was young and from her travels. To discover new ones, she also reached out to our elders and others who had knowledge of plants and their healing properties."

The trail narrowed, so Gabe fell in behind Nagora's mules.

Will he be seeing Sagora's back as he watches mine? Will he be comparing us? What will he conclude? Dare I ask?

The opportunity to do so did not come, not even when they stopped for their midday meal of trail rations and forest tea. Gabe kept to his men, in discussion all of the time.

Planning on how to deal with my arrival, I suppose.

Nagora stretched her legs, walking into the forest well out of the sight of Gabe and the guards. They paid her no mind.

Dangor busied himself checking the packs on the mules. He must have a lot on his mind. No use in my asking. He'll just say, "All in good time."

The day's ride had been long, and after the evening meal, Nagora was eager to curl up in her bedroll. Though, once there, she had a fitful night of little sleep. Dream scenes of her branding troubled her sleep. One dream woke her up—the smell of her skin burning. She had been burned often with the molten tar mix when working with her uncle to seal the leather seams of the curraghs. That was the odor of tar, not her skin.

She tried to bring up the scent of each of the seared meats she had ever been near. Someone said a person smells like a pig when burned, but she doubted that. Would she be able to tell at the moment of her branding?

Nagora closed her eyes and tried to will herself to sleep. A voice, the one she did not like because it always wanted her to change her mind, told her to run away from all of this. She hated that voice. Her heart wanted to be with her mum and sister.

Raynhard had told her to listen to her heart, to trust it. What would he think and say if he knew of her predicament now?

How will he react when we meet again? If ever we meet again? Will he want a queen with a brand?

Nagora had rested her cheek against Raynhard's chest as he held her in his arms. With that memory, she fell asleep.

Nagora awoke with a start in her bedroll. It was another scene of her branding. This time, everyone in the crowd witnessing it was eyeless, even her mirror sister. All their noses were upturned waiting to smell her burning flesh. But one eye, the strange eye, was the only eyewitness.

Again, it spoke: " ... ka will watch over you." She only understood part of the first word.

In the early light of dawn, Nagora was uneasy as she crawled from her bedroll, as if she was still battling with her dreams. They had stirred anger in her. So much so she wanted to keep to herself. Why do I feel this way? I should be happy to find my mum and sister.

Get busy. Go groom Storm and the mules. As soon as she approached Storm, he turned his neck and kept nuzzling her arm and her hand that held the brush until she stood before him, held his head, and looked into his eyes. Storm pushed forward and rested his head on her shoulder so she had no choice but to put her arms around his neck.

Her body relaxed and her breathing slowed.

Storm, you know how I feel, don't you?

Nagora held onto him and rubbed his neck. Her anger dissipated as she let Storm comfort her. She whispered, *tastapiw sohkapiskaw kaskitewastim*, her private song to Storm—"my strong, swift, dark horse."

Now relaxed, she returned to her task. She patted the horse's neck with one hand and brushed his mane with the other. He nuzzled her neck as he brought his head from her shoulder and allowed her to groom him.

Mum, sister, I hope to find the strength I need in your arms at the end of this journey. Whatever I do or say when we meet will spring from my heart at that moment. They'll not be actions or words I've planned ahead of time.

After having groomed the mules, Nagora joined the others for the morning meal, in silence and in peace with herself, at least for the moment.

Quicker than usual, they broke camp, packed the mules, and saddled the horses. She followed Dangor, who followed Gabe. Two of his men had the rear.

Before long, Nagora smelt the sea breeze. The coastal trail Gabe had spoken of the night before was nearby. The salty air, the seaweed, and the wet sand on the breeze took her back to her beach at Sandy Spit Point where she had so often played and trained while growing up.

Will I ever see it again?

Dragonflies buzzed by and an osprey circled overhead as the coastal water came into view. The sound of waves rolling onto a beach beckoned to Nagora. Although she longed for a swim, today time wouldn't allow that.

Gabe waited for Nagora and Dangor to pull up alongside him. He pointed to the headland in the distance. "On the other side of that bluff is Skull Bay, where my father's Grand Hall sits, and where Tagnyoriva and Sagora live. Our coastal look-outs have most likely spotted us by now and are signaling our arrival. Tonight, you'll share a meal with Tagnyoriva and Sagora."

She looked at Gabe for a moment, and then she gazed to the sea and let the sea breeze caress her face. *Will I be branded before or after supper? Either way, will I feel like eating?*

Nagora kept looking out to sea until the gruff voices of two of Gabe's men interrupted. She turned to see what was happening.

One of Gabe's men appeared to be counting as he pointed up the barren mountainside along the line of forest they had just come through.

In the distance, at least a dozen immobile riders sat in silhouette against the sky.

Nagora looked to Gabe who was staring up at them, as was Dangor.

Gabe didn't seem very concerned. "Vorpinger's men. They've been showing up a lot since Father's become ill. They're like vultures. Difference is vultures wait for their meal to die."

Dangor nodded. "They're posturing. Are they a threat to you, Gabe?"

"No. More like flies on a mule's ass. Not to worry."

His voice was impatient. *If it were up to him, I bet he would've dealt with the problem long ago. Sometimes flies can cause a wound on a mule's ass to fester.*

Gabe signaled for his group to move on. He led them along the rocky shale of the coastal trail, well above the high water mark.

Nagora fell in behind Dangor and kept her eyes on the approaching headland bluffs, searching for the lookouts that were still but tiny specks on the rocky outcrop. As Gabe led them away from the shore on the rising inland trail that would bring them to Skull Bay, he waved, and she caught sight of the distant sentinel who waved back.

The road brought them over a small hill and down its other side to a bridge that crossed a river. Gabe waited for them. "The river's high with all the rain we've had. I don't recall ever seeing it this high."

After crossing the bridge and climbing the hill on the other side, the sentinel came into view again.

The trail wound and climbed among the rocks and boulders and through the scant bushes and vegetation that grew on this rocky land. Yellow cat's ear and violet sheep's bit dotted the occasional green tufts of grass, scattered among the rocks. Further on, the trail straightened out and seemed to rise to the sky in the distance. Nagora spied movement far off ahead.

Gabe stopped, and she and Dangor pulled up beside him. Two riders came into view. Gabe pointed. "That can only be Sagora and Tagnyoriva. No one else rides like they do."

Nagora kneed Storm and rode off up the trail as fast as he could take her. Her heart swelled and her eyes watered. She pressed on and now, one of the approaching riders took the lead down the trail at full speed.

Tears streamed from the corners of her eyes. The approaching rider looked just like her. She also wore her black hair in a braid and was dressed in leather leggings and vest to ride. Nagora screamed Sagora's name, but no sound would come. Is this truly happening? My sister is here before me.

The sisters reared their mounts to a walk and approached, circling each other, examining each other, each trying to decipher the contradictory signals in the mirror mounted on the horse in front of her. Neither spoke.

Their mounts came together, bringing the riders face to face, left knee to left knee. Sagora threw her arms around Nagora almost pulling her off Storm. "Sister!" was the only word Sagora said as Nagora hugged her and cried, "My sister! My sister! My sister!"

This is real! She called me "sister." She has her arms around me.

Through teary eyes, their noses crossed as their cheeks wiped away each other's tears and both cried, "Sister!" They hugged each other even stronger.

Sagora pulled away, wiped her eyes, dismounted, and held her arms up to her. Nagora slipped from her saddle into Sagora's arms. They held each other tight.

Nagora leaned back and with one hand touched Sagora's face, letting her fingers run from the same high cheekbone down to the narrow chin. "My sister, Sagora." Her own face trembled, so Nagora bit her lip to try to stop it. I've never been so happy!

Sagora took a deep breath as she nodded. "Nagora, my sister." Again they hugged each other and held each other's face. Sagora's grey-blue eyes told a story of joyful discovery.

...

As they held onto each other, between their mounts, Nagora had not been oblivious to Tagnyoriva's approach. The tall lean woman had dismounted and led her mount on foot. She was now standing straight. Her proud smile and the tears at the corners of her blue eyes showed she was in complete admiration of her girls.

"Nagora. My Nagora." Tagnyoriva's voice was hoarse with emotion.

Nagora and Sagora stumbled to their mother's open arms. Sagora pushed Nagora into Tagnyoriva's embrace and hugged them from behind.

Tagnyoriva cradled Nagora's face in her hands. They stared into each other's eyes. "My Nagora. My daughter. My child. Oh! How I've awaited this moment." She kissed Nagora's forehead, her cheeks, and looked into her eyes again before pulling her into a strong embrace.

Her uncle had always told Nagora she had a beautiful face. Now she knew who she got it from. She also saw quiet strength and assurance in that face. Was that why she felt immediate trust in this woman?

Dangor called, "Tagnya." Nagora turned to see that he had dismounted and was approaching on foot. Gabe and his two men remained on their mounts, watching from a distance out of earshot.

Her mother held her on one arm and Sagora on the other as she made her way to him. "Oh! Dangor! No one has called me that in ages. Dear brother of my husband and trusted guardian of my daughter. How are you? You haven't changed."

Dangor's happy smile lit up his face. "Nor you, Tagnya. Nagora has kept me young at heart, and busy and sharp."

"Sagora, this is your uncle, Dangor. No finer a bowman nor scout in the land can be found."

Dangor bowed. "At your service, young lady."

Tagnya stepped forward and embraced Dangor. Then she stepped back and looked him in the eye.

Dangor's face became somber as he looked at Tagnya. Sagora reached for Nagora, pulled her close, and kissed her forehead as she held on to her.

Tagnya looked back to Nagora and then to Dangor again. "She knows she'll be marked, doesn't she?"

Dangor nodded. "As the messenger Gabe sent must've told you. She has chosen Tiwaz. Does Sagora know what she will do to her sister?"

"Aye, she does. My Nagora is strong. I wondered if I would truly see her today."

Dangor placed a hand on Tagnya's arm. "She is stronger than she realizes. You'll be proud of her when you hear what she's been through."

Nagora listened to Tagnya and Dangor speak as she held her mirror sister.

Sagora is listening too. Will she be strong? Will I be strong? I have to be.

Tagnya faced her daughters. "Our paths have brought us together, here, today. We come together to join our strength for a higher cause. We could wish we had taken different paths. Often the choice of path is not given to us. From now on, we must focus on our destination together." Tagnya hugged her daughters to her.

...

Gabe approached on horseback and dismounted.

Sagora smiled. "I see Gabe has been your escort."

Nagora nodded. "Aye. He thought I was you playing a trick on him. Some secrets have been kept well in this land. Turns out the trick is on me and you."

"Gabe, thank you for bringing my sister here safely."

Tagnya hugged Nagora closer to her side. "Yes, thank you Gabe. Was there a problem?"

"I don't know what you learned from the messenger I dispatched to my father. I convinced the men of my patrol that Nagora had a right to return. They've agreed to respect the set precedent of marking a returning twin even if Nagora is a woman. Your reputations, Tagnyoriva and Sagora, weighed in Nagora's favor. We'll have no choice but to act upon arriving on my father's steps in Skull Bay. You know all there will come to watch. I wish it were otherwise."

Gabe paused and pointed. "When we go through the gate to Skull Bay, two of my men and I will escort Nagora. I'll lead Nagora and my men will ride at her side. You will follow with Sagora by your side. Dangor and my other men will follow you."

Tagnya listened and nodded as Gabe explained. "We understand. We'll prepare Nagora as we approach. You confirm what Godomor had the messenger tell us."

Tagnya took Nagora's hands in hers. "My daughter, I so wish it were otherwise. We haven't much time. Sagora and I will mount up, and you'll ride between us until the gate. Trust us in what we tell you on the way."

"I will, Mum." The word "Mum" sounded strange as she spoke it to her actual living, breathing mother.

Before pulling herself onto Storm's back, Nagora looked to the sky. Dark clouds would follow them into Skull Bay. For now, Gabe and Dangor led the way. She rode between Sagora and Tagnya. Gabe's men took up the rear with the mules.

Nagora did not have long to wait to hear what Tagnya had to say.

"Three years ago, Lars Marraden, a twin, returned. His branding was the precedent. From what he told us of his experience, the branding itself is not painful. The iron, with the mark, is so hot that, when it's applied, it actually feels cold. The pain comes afterward, but it's bearable. Since then, we've learned from other people who've suffered burns that a thick coat of salve made of clean fat or grease reduces the pain. It keeps the air from touching the burn for a few days.

"After that, Lars said it was a matter of keeping himself from picking at the scab that formed on the wound. We know that is important for, if the wound gets dirty, it can turn bad. If it has to be cleaned, we'll use boiled seawater or mead spirits."

Nagora's dreams prompted her to ask, "Did he say what it smelled like when he was branded?"

Tagnya's eyes widened only for an instant. "No, but I was there and I can say it stinks only for a moment. At least his did. Why do you ask?"

"My dream last night was about that. It woke me."

"I can imagine, my child. Poor you."

"Mum, the sooner this is over, the better."

Nagora turned to her sister. "Sagora, are you ready?"

Sagora didn't hesitate. "Mum says I am. My hand is steady and quick. You mustn't move until I tell you to. I wish I didn't have to do this. I can't believe it when I look at you. I see myself."

Just like me. "Enjoy it while you can, big sister. I know I am, and I also wish you didn't have to do this."

The moment. Focus on the moment. Be strong.

Tagnya reached over to touch her. "Nagora, I have my medical case here." She touched the formed leather scrip tied to the back of her saddle. "I've prepared a salve and bandages that should help soothe your wound."

She gave her mother a brave smile. "I've heard about your skills as a healer. I'll benefit from them firsthand."

"You are strong, my daughter."

Nagora nodded. I'm trying to be.

# Branded
## *Masinâskisow*

As the riders came over the rise, high stone walls stretching out on each side of the tall, guarded gate came into view. To the left of the gate, the wall seemed to extend to the bluff of the headland they had seen when they exited the forest earlier in the day. To the right, the wall extended in a curve to a spot Nagora couldn't see.

As they approached the gate, hundreds of skulls lay strewn along each side of the road leading to the gate. Atop the gate, more skulls lined the top of the wall over which a dozen archers peered.

Gabe brought the riders to a halt and had them form up as planned.

For the first time, Nagora took a close look at Godomor's talisman, which granted them safe passage. It was bigger than the open palm of her hand. The circular silver medallion showed a human skull resting in a right palm, while the left palm covered the top of the skull. Did it symbolize King Godomor holding a skull in front of him? Rune-like symbols skirted the medallion's perimeter below the right palm and above the left.

What did the symbols say? Under his right hand, she guessed, "If you come in peace," and over his left, "you have my protection." I hope I'm right and I hope they can all see it.

The gate's huge wooden doors opened outward. Skulls nailed to the huge timbers covered each door, both outside and inside. The iron spikes, driven through the eye sockets of the sun-bleached skulls, gave them cold, dark, lifeless eyes to stare down on those who passed through the gate.

This medallion better work. Not exactly a welcoming sight. Even less so than when crossing the Blood River.

Would this give enemy invaders second thoughts? Whoever ordered the skulls to be nailed to the doors must've thought so.

Sagora spoke to Nagora's back as they passed through the gate. "Each skull has a story to tell. Like me, you'll never hear all of them, but you'll get to hear one or two before we leave this land."

Nagora looked at the two guards flanking her. I won't be leaving soon enough. She leaned her head back over her shoulder. "Whether I want to or not, I gather."

Sagora replied, "At a feast of Godomor's, for sure, you'd hear our bard tell at least one story a skull would tell, if it could. Listeners not too weak of heart usually regain their appetites the following day."

Nagora shook her head. "If there's a feast tonight, I doubt I'll be hungry. Hearing its telling won't bother me."

...

As they descended the road leading into the village of Skull Bay, Nagora found the answer to how far the wall curved. To the right, it turned toward a bluff in the distance that marked one side of the entrance to the waters of Skull Bay.

The guarded wall behind them was at the top edge of a tilted valley bowl, creating a smooth arc.

To the left, it bent into the sea onto a string of rocky bluffs until it reached the other side of the entrance to the bay.

The narrow breach allowed entry into the bay that provided a snug harbor for any boats anchoring during a storm.

A third of the bay's shore, not far from the town, was a sandy beach. The rest of the shore was rocky.

Boats, with sails furled, were tied to wharves of solid wood cribs packed with stones. Two boats had just sailed into the bay, most likely coming in to avoid the approaching bad weather the dark clouds promised.

"Nagora, see the large stone lodge, set back from the smaller ones below it?" asked Sagora. "That's Godomor's Grand Hall, where we're headed."

"In the distance to the left of the Grand Hall, there's a rectangular stone lodge with two big spruce trees at the back. That's our home, Nagora," called Tagnya.

"I see it." Our home—two simple words. They didn't connect with her, even if at the moment she saw it, she wanted to be there with her mother, Sagora, and her uncle. But she wasn't, so she took in the view.

The smaller lodges of the town were scattered along the rocky shore of the slope of Skull Bay's valley bowl.

Godomor's Grand Hall sat at the center, on the valley's biggest knoll at the base of a cliff. Fish nets hung to dry on sunbleached spruce polls planted in the sand above the summer-high water mark of the beach shore near the town. The tide was in. Nagora could smell the air freshening. Rain was on its way.

The imposing maze of a fishing weir stood three hundred strides from the beach. Opposite the weir and behind the poles that held the drying fish nets, racks of woven sticks held salted fish left to dry in the sun. Men, women, and children were busy stacking the pieces of fish and covering them with wooden gabled peaks upon which they piled flat slate stones.

Along each side of the road into the valley bowl, fences made of stones, cleared from the rocky soil, provided garden plots to grow vegetables and formed corrals for sheep, goats, cows, mules, and horses.

Every stone gets put to good use here.

The lodges of the town were built on the circular pattern of Godomor's hunting lodge. They were smaller than the hunting lodge, except for a few bigger ones. All their entrances looked onto the bay.

Godomor's Grand Hall was imposing with its high-peaked front. Its overlapping slate-stone roof sloped down to the back of the hall. The impression Godomor's Grand Hall gave, when viewed from the side, was it had somehow slipped off the knoll on which it had been built and come to rest at the base of the stone cliff towering above it.

Stone roofs are just about everywhere. An enemy will not waste fire arrows trying to set fire to this town. Stone walls and rammed earth walls are everywhere. Winter storm winds won't blow these lodges down.

...

As the group neared the town, people appeared at the doors of their lodges. Many seemed to have left for Godomor's Grand Hall, while others waited along the road, probably to get a better look at the approaching riders.

How many of these people still held to their beliefs about twins?

As Uncle would say, 'Keep a weather eye and ear.'

Her mother called to her again. "Nagora, I want to remind you. You two were born here of me, a woman from away, here under Godomor's protection. I bent to their beliefs and banished you, the second born, out of this land. Today, you return with Godomor's talisman, granting safe passage. I do not fear for your safety. I have, over time, earned a certain status among his people; so any harm coming to you would be like harming me. Nagora, do not be surprised by how some of the people will react."

"I won't, Mum. Two of Gabe's men thought I was evil itself when they learned that I was Sagora's twin. Surely, there are more like them in this land."

"Unfortunately."

"Why hadn't I ever heard of my sister's banishment from the Land of Skulls?" asked Sagora.

"It is their way. Banished from the eyes—not to be seen; banished from the ears—not to be heard nor heard spoken of; banished from the lips—not to be spoken of; banished from the hands—not to be touched; and the most difficult, banished from the mind—to be forgotten. Unless someone had more than a slip of the tongue in your presence, you wouldn't have known, understood, nor questioned what they'd said."

"You respected those five rules until recently?" said Sagora.

Tagnya nodded. "Except for the last one. Not a day has gone by without my thinking of Nagora. Had I told you as a young girl, you would've questioned everyone in the town for any piece of information about your sister. A child's mind is not always capable of understanding the whys of rules.

"When I received Raynhard's last missive telling of Nagora's possible arrival, only then did I plan on telling you. When Gabe's messenger confirmed she had arrived, I told you." Tagnya paused.

To their right a whole family, from the grandparents down to the grandchildren, stood before their lodge. An adult had pointed to the twins and started the ritual signing with her hands.

In rapid sequence, she covered her eyes, ears, and mouth; pulled her fists to her chest; brought the backs of her hands to her forehead; pushed her hands in front of her toward the twins; and then struck out twice with her fists crossed. She kept this up as she chanted the ritual formula to ward off the evil twin. Soon everyone in the family joined her.

"Eyes ahead girls. Try to ignore them. There'll be more."

Throughout all this Gabe and Nagora's two escorts kept their eyes on the road ahead.


"Tagnuska! Tagnuska!" called other people from the crowd as they waved. Nagora turned to confirm her guess. Her mother was waving back.

From behind, Sagora explained for her. "It's the name these people have given our mother. It's short for 'Tagnyoriva Nuska.' It means 'Tagnyoriva the Healing Woman.' Mum treated and healed those people, so they may call her by that name. It's their way of recognizing her healing powers."

"Sagnuska! Sagnuska!" A young boy, not yet ten, called and waved.

Nagora looked back at her sister. "You too?"

Sagora wore a proud smile. "Two winters ago he'd fallen while climbing a cliff. He dislocated a shoulder, broke a rib, and bit through his lip. Perchance, I was passing by and found him. I stopped the bleeding at his lip, reset his shoulder, and then set his broken rib. I cut poles from driftwood nearby to make a litter and dragged him back to his home the long way, back along the shore.

"When Mum checked on him, she said she couldn't have done any better and that he'd mend. Since then, when Mum is not available, people come to me for help. I do what I can, based on what I've learned from being with Mum and helping her care for sick and injured people."

"Tagnuska! Sagnuska!" A young woman, with an infant in her arms, called and waved, and waved her infant's hand.

"We brought her child into the world early this spring. It was a difficult birth. We feared for both their lives."

I'm proud of my mum and sister. "Mum, someday I too would like to learn those skills from you and Sagora."

"Yes, my daughter." Tagnya gave her a warm smile.

Some in the crowd became agitated as a murmur spread among the people. More people were performing the ritual signing. They were looking from Sagora, to Nagora, and then to her mother, and back to her as they pointed.

Yet many people waved and smiled as well. Nagora looked back. Her mother and Sagora kept smiling, returning the waves to those who called and waved. So she smiled as well.

Tagnya spoke. "Nagora, when we arrive at Godomor's Grand Hall, we'll stay mounted until he comes to greet us. Keep your eye on Gabe. He'll guide us. Either Sagora or I will translate for you, depending on who is closest."

"Understood."

As the riders approached Godomor's Grand Hall, the townspeople followed and gathered within viewing distance of the entrance. Godomor appeared at the top of the stairs leading to the entrance.

*Kihchi okimawiw.* "He is king." Aye, I know these words. I feel I know this king, this man. Why?

His personal guards flanked him on both sides, and the one she guessed to be his personal attendant stood to his left.

When they stopped at the bottom of the steps, Nagora gazed up at Godomor. He was pale. His eyes were sunken, framed by the long white hair that hung along each side of his face that wore an untrimmed beard. He squinted and his lips were barely visible beneath his mustache as he raised his left hand and spoke a feeble welcome.

The townspeople around greeted him with: "Long live Godomor!" His right hand grasped a plain wooden staff for support.

This king is ill.

*Piscipow.* "He is poisoned." *Mihkopiscipowin.* "Blood poison."

Does Mum know this? Hopefully the medicine we brought will help her cure him. How long does he have to live?

Godomor waved and acknowledged his subjects with a feeble smile. He coughed and waved again, bidding Gabe, "Bring our guests."

Nagora dismounted. I don't feel like a guest right now.

Gabe led her up the steps, flanked by his two men. She glanced back. Sagora, Tagnya, and Dangor followed. The landing before the entrance to Godomor's Grand Hall came into view.

The first thing Nagora caught site of, to the left of the hall entrance, was the burning brazier with its red-hot coals. A blacksmith pumped a two-chambered bellows that supplied a constant stream of air to the brazier's base, feeding the coals.

When she set foot on the landing, she saw an open wooden box on the slate stones at the smith's feet. It held three rows of brands, twenty-four in all with wooden handles.

They're not wasting time, are they?

She had seen such a box of rune brands at Geirador's forge. He used the brands to mark the leather sheaths he made for blades.

Tagnya joined Nagora and remained at her side.

Gabe embraced his father and stood at his side. Gabe spoke and Tagnya translated. "This is Nagora. She comes to our land wearing your talisman granting safe passage to her and to the one who travels with her, Dangor, her uncle."

Then Gabe motioned for Sagora to come forward. "Nagora is the twin sister of Sagora, the second-born twin daughter of Tagnyoriva. By our laws, Nagora was banished from our land on the day of her birth. Since then, Nagora has lived all her years with Dangor in the Land of the Danu. They come bearing messages and gifts from Geirador, who saved me from the attack of a bear.

"Today, as a returning twin to our land, Nagora has chosen to submit to our ways. She has chosen to be marked as the second-born twin with the Tiwaz so all who see her will know her as such and allow her to walk among us as an equal."

Godomor motioned for the twins to approach. He handed his staff to his attendant and spread his arms wide, inviting the girls to his sides.

As Nagora approached, she noticed four men standing at the wooden doors of the hall entrance. One of them kept repeating the ritual signing and chanting.

As soon as she was within reach, Godomor turned her, as he had Sagora, so they faced forward, looking at the crowd gathered below the steps of the Grand Hall. He looked from one to the other and smiled at them.

Sagora smiled back.

Nagora tried to, but couldn't.

Godomor looked over the crowd.

Nagora did also. She saw those still chanting and signing, and those waiting for silence to hear their king's words.

Godomor looked to the sky as he acknowledged the first drops of rain that fell from the ever-darkening sky. He was motionless as he looked skyward. His hand squeezed her shoulder.

Is he telling me to be strong?

The crowd grew silent.

Godomor seized the moment. From a voice deep inside him, he spoke as she could not imagine him capable. Tagnya translated. "Today, a twin daughter has come home to her land of birth. Nagora is a daughter of our land. Nagora is the daughter of Tagnyoriva. Nagora is the sister of Sagora. You see them, now, at this moment, as they are—twins, identical in appearance only, here before you, with no record of evil done to any of you here present, nor of any record of evil done to any absent here today. For those reasons, I welcome our daughter, Nagora, back to the Land of Skulls."

Godomor paused and squeezed her shoulder again, catching his breath before continuing. "Sagora will mark her so you also may welcome her back." Godomor let his hands fall to his sides and stepped back.

Gabe stepped forward.

The wind had picked up, the sky had darkened, and her sister had gone to fetch the brand. The downpour would soon be upon them. Gabe's voice was urgent. "Nagora, kneel here on the edge of the landing. Sagora will have the steps below to best position herself."

She obeyed. Tagnya stood on the steps below her with her medical scrip at the ready. "Child, do you want me to hold your head?"

"No, Mum, I'll be strong."

Tagnya moved aside.

Was Sagora about to return with the brand?

She looked into the wind over the bay below. Rain fell. The crowd was silent.

She looked at the crowd below as the rain fell harder. Many in the crowd were leaving.

Nagora caught sight of a tall, faceless, hooded figure standing on the road below flanked by two huge wolfhounds.

The crossguard of a long sword peeked over his left shoulder. No one stood near him. Was he staring at her? Surely.

Sagora stood before her. Her face almost touched hers.

"I am going to put one hand behind your head. When I do, close your eyes. I'll count to three."

"One, two … " A crack of thunder split the air above them so loud, all around her screamed. Orders were being yelled, and the rain came down in torrents pushed by the wind. Nagora opened her eyes. Sagora still held her head.

Next to Sagora's face, Tagnya's eyes concentrated on Nagora's forehead. The cool touch of salve, her sister and mother lifting her by the arms, and the rain striking her all happened in a sequence of time she could not count.

The crowd had dispersed. Only the faceless, hooded figure with his two hounds remained, oblivious to the downpour.

*Masinaskisow, nitisan, onakateyimowew.* "He is branded, my brother, my protector." Nagora had no time to reflect on these words as they came to her.

Tagnya was speaking fast as they pulled Nagora back. "We're going into Godomor's Hall. Godomor summoned us to attend his private council meeting. We'll remain at the back of the hall near the entrance until Godomor calls us forward."

Once inside, Tagnya continued in a hushed whisper. "Gabe and Dangor will meet with Godomor at his table at the front."

Tagnya wiped rain from Nagora's face with her sleeve. "Don't touch your face." Sagora opened the medical scrip to retrieve a roll of gauze. Tagnya accepted the gauze and unraveled the roll. "Look at me." She dabbed at Nagora's face to remove all the raindrops as she explained what would take place.

"Gabe will first give a report of his patrol and then introduce your uncle.

"Then Dangor will speak and offer greetings and news from Geirador."

Tagnya wrung out the gauze and wiped her own face.

"When Godomor calls us forward, I will speak to him and ask to introduce you, my daughters, to him. Sagora knows him well already. With your arrival, Nagora, this is a formality where I have to ask for a lift on your banishment. I foresee no problems in having my request granted."

Nagora touched Tagnya's arm. "Are you sure, Mum?"

Her mother gave a quick nod. "The only difficulty that could arise would be from one of the four counselors from the outer regions of the Land of Skulls. They represent the vassals of those regions. To date, they have proven to be loyal to Godomor. Though his failing health this last year could represent a turning point in that fealty, since Gabe has as yet to prove himself as a leader of men in battle."

Tagnya handed the gauze to Sagora.

"Let's just say he hasn't yet earned 'The Terrible' that his grandfather and father have worn with their names."

The brand on her forehead not only burned, but itched. Don't touch it. Don't touch it. I have to let the salve do its work.

"Nagora, Godomor is ill. Hopefully Geirador has found and sent the plants I asked for. They might give him some relief and perhaps heal him."

This doesn't sound so good. Geirador, I hope you found what Mum needs. What if Godomor dies before he consents to sending us his warriors?

Tagnya and Sagora guided Nagora to the last wooden bench with its attached narrow table at the back of the hall.

Nagora's eyes adjusted to the dim light of the tallow lamps. She held her fists clenched in her lap as she looked around to focus on anything else but the burning itch.

Huge supporting timbers rose from the stone floor to the ceiling. From them, the framing ribs, which supported the ceiling's wooden planks, curved upward and in to meet at the main center beam. It ran the length of the hall, like the keel beam of a huge drakkar turned upside-down.

Nagora's fists bounced on her knees as her toes lifted her heels from the floor in rapid succession.

The side walls had no openings. Now the outer walls of stacked stones made sense because they ran uninterrupted from the corners of the entrance wall to the face of the cliff, hiding the inside support timbers.

Nagora bumped her knees against one another as she pressed her fists to them.

The thunder outside seemed to linger at a distance above the hall. The pelting rain on the stone slates overhead told Nagora the storm raged outside, but it was the storm of her burning itch that she raged against with her clenching fists and knocking knees.

...

The stone floor, slanting down toward the cliff face, was almost all terraced, providing ample space for many to sit on the different levels to watch the proceedings below. Though today, they were the only ones in attendance at this private council meeting.

Godomor's simple wooden throne sat on a raised platform of carved stones. On the floor below the platform and to the right of the throne was a long wooden bench with a carved backrest. Four skulls sat along its top and it had a curved arm rest on each end. The four counselors were, at the moment, seating themselves on it.

*Tar piss! Finally! The salve is starting to do its work.*

Opposite the counselors, on the other side on the same level to the left of the throne, was a backless bench where Gabe and Dangor went to sit. Godomor did not sit on his throne; instead, his aid helped him to a chair at the edge of a table below the throne on the same level as the benches.

His attendant sat on a smaller chair to Godomor's right, and to his left, a scribe sat with books, sheets of vellum, ink, and a writing quill. Lit candles stood on the table and on stands nearby.

Godomor looked up at Tagnya and her daughters and motioned them to come forward.

They walked down to the front and sat on the bottom terraced ledge.

Nagora took a deep breath. *Good. It's starting.*

The attendant read the short order of the day's business.

Gabe's patrol report was first on the list. Nagora focused on Tagnya's running translation. The report was short.

Gabe got straight to the point of his meeting with her and Dangor at the hunting lodge. He had nothing else to report until the return of his men who would complete the patrol.

Next came Dangor with greetings from Geirador. Gabe translated Dangor's words. "Your Majesty, Geirador hopes the seasons are treating you well and your bees continue to provide you with a rich harvest to make many casks of mead.

"As agreed, Geirador sends arrowhead molds and a recipe for the iron alloy mix your smiths can use to make the molten metal for those arrowheads. He has also sent drawings and measurements of his own forge bellows that helps to attain the high temperatures necessary to heat this mix of alloys.

"Also, as agreed, Geirador has sent knife and sword templates, molds, and samples, along with alloy mixing recipes. He also sent instructions for the reheating and hammering steps to forge the hard sharp, burnished, edges like those on his samples.

"Finally, Geirador sends a cask of his latest batch of mead.

"Your Majesty, we will deliver the cask of mead on an occasion of your choosing. We'll also deliver the other items to your blacksmiths tomorrow."

Gabe and Dangor returned to their bench.

Wow! Geirador is ever full of surprises. The great relationship he seems to have maintained with Godomor surely can't hurt our quest for his help. Will we succeed?

Godomor looked at Nagora as he motioned them to come forward. She reached for Tagnya's hand. Her mother's grip was steady and strong as she led her and Sagora down from the bottom terraced ledge.

The eyes of the four counselors were on them, and one of them had a look Nagora did not like. His gaze seemed to bore into Tagnya. For a moment his eyes shot up to the ceiling. Nagora looked up and spotted an axe stuck in the beam above their heads. She hadn't noticed it from the back of the hall.

Is that axe connected to Mum? I'll ask Sagora.

When Godomor motioned Tagnya to come forward, she did.

Nagora reached for Sagora's hand as she translated.

"King Godomor, today is a most," Tagnya hesitated, "joyous day for me, for I am reunited with my daughters. It is another step in a long journey that brought me here to seek refuge and give birth to my two daughters. With respect for the ways of your people, I returned my second born, Nagora, to the Land of the Danu to be cared for by her uncle, Dangor.

"Nagora wears your talisman of safe passage. And now she is marked with Tiwaz, the symbol of her choosing, so all in your land will know her and allow her the same freedom of movement as her sister.

"On this day I take responsibility for her conduct and the conduct of Sagora, and I ask you to lift Nagora's banishment from the Land of Skulls. I promise at any sign of a problem, at your command, we will leave.

"Nagora has come here to be with her sister and me so we can plan the final steps in our journey back to the Land of the Danu. There, we will free the last dragon in the land and fight to give King Raynhard back his rightful crown."

Nagora's hand held by her sister had become damp. With her other hand, she wiped a tear from her eye as the pure sincerity of Tagnya's voice painted the reality of their enterprise and the weight of their shared responsibility.

The counselor, whose fuming stare had been boring into Tagnya, stood and spoke. "My lord. Why wait … "

Godomor raised his hand and his voice without looking at the counselor. "Counselor! I have not asked you to speak. Wait until I do so. You may continue, Tagnyoriva."

Tagnya locked her eyes on the counselor's and kept them on him until he sat down.

Only then did Tagnya return her gaze to Godomor. "My lord, I appeal to you to grant freedom of movement to my daughters and me while we are together in your land to do our planning.

"King Godomor, I am asking you again to consider my next request with care. I do not wish an answer today. I am ready to return in seven days at the next meeting of your council."

Tagnya took a deep breath. "To ensure the success of our attempt to free the dragon and to give back the crown to Raynhard, the rightful king of our land, we will need one hundred of your best warriors, led by your son, Gabyndor. Sixty archers armed with bows and arrows and forty mounted warriors armed with swords, spears and shields. These warriors would be used primarily for diversionary tactics. I cannot give you the details today because I have not yet received confirmation of the final plans, but I will soon, if you grant me this request."

"My lord … ," The counselor had risen again.

Again Godomor raised his hand, but this time looked at the counselor who sat down again.

Godomor turned to Tagnya and motioned she continue.

"My lord, I wish you to weigh the following when you consider my request for the help of one hundred of your best warriors.

"Since my arrival in your land I have mended ten times as many of your warriors so they live to fight another day.

"I have tended to the sick throughout your land and assisted in the birthing of many of your young subjects. This I have done while I have shared my knowledge and skills with your men and women who have asked to learn from me what I know of healing.

"My lord, I have done all of this because of the love I have for your people and because you and they welcomed me in my time of refuge." Tagnya stopped, bowed her head, and stepped back. She took her daughters' hands, and they returned to sit on the lower ledge.

Mum has spoken so well. Surely, Godomor cannot ignore her arguments. Yet I fear being the mum of twins just might outweigh her pleas.

Godomor seemed to be weighing Tagnya's words.

The counselor was obviously expecting to be asked to speak.

Godomor took a long breath. "Tagnyoriva, you and your daughters have safe passage here for as long as you wish. Old beliefs, perhaps once upon a time, had their reason to be. Your conduct these years in our land has been exemplary.

"As for your second request, to provide you with the hundred warriors you seek, I will lend my own warrior volunteers in equal numbers to match the number of volunteers my vassals agree to commit to your cause. I am sure they will take your request into serious consideration and, their counselors will return with the decisions and lists of volunteers."

Nagora raised her hand. "Pardon me, my lord, King Godomor, may I have permission to speak?"

Gabe stood and translated.

Her mother looked at her. As did her uncle. Both with frowns.

Godomor did not hesitate. "You may, Nagora."

"I wish to speak on behalf of King Raynhard who cannot be here today to greet you and plead for your support of his cause. I have chosen to fight for his cause. Through strange circumstances, I've become known as the warrior Edana. Raynhard asked me, as Edana, to offer you his most sincere apologies for not being here today. Urgent matters about the possible successful outcome of his cause need his attention and keep him away. Please accept King Raynhard's apologies. Thank you."

"Edana, your reputation preceded your arrival here. I accept King Raynhard's apologies. When the news of your double identity leaves this hall, I believe my people will see you in another light."

Godomor looked to his counselors. "Before any of the counselors of my vassals speak on these matters, I ask them to weigh their thoughts and their words, for hot and heavy words rarely, if ever, lead to worthwhile decisions."

All eyes turned to the counselor who was once again standing, waiting to speak. Godomor motioned him to speak.

Would this man heed Godomor's words?

"My lord, why wait until something evil happens? Maintain the banishment of this look-alike so you don't have to invoke it again when it will be too late. Is this not the way of our people as it has always been?"

Godomor raised a hand. "Time, knowledge, and understanding of the reasons behind beliefs that govern our people's way of acting in regards to look-alikes have taught us, at least me, that until further proof, there is no reason to put credence in these old beliefs. To continue to enforce such a way would be like outlawing all the mirrors in the land because they let my subjects to see doubles of themselves, look-alikes.

"Counselor, as you must know and remember, three years ago, we set a precedent to allow a twin to return on condition he be marked, with a brand of his choice, by his very own twin brother.

"And, Counselor, did not Tagnyoriva's daughter, Sagora, just a few moments ago, without argument, discussion, or debate from any member of her family or Nagora herself, apply a red hot brand to her twin sister's forehead?

"I ask you, Counselor, does this not show that Nagora, who has returned to her place of birth today as a twin, to be marked by her own twin, is someone who comes with great respect for the laws of our land?"

The counselor stood straight, his arms stiff at his sides, with his fists clenched. A clap of thunder resounded overhead. The man shook. "But my lord, Tagnyoriva is a witch!" He pointed up to the axe on the main ceiling beam.

How dare he call Mum a witch! Nagora was on her feet, intent to attack the idiot, but his words had also brought

Tagnya and Sagora to their feet. Tagnya held her back. Now three pairs of eyes were boring into him.

Godomor raised an eyebrow as he looked to the man. "Now Counselor, have you weighed that word? Does it carry such weight as to so easily fall off your tongue, or do you speak for my vassal Vorpinger? Answer me."

Thunder slammed the sky above the Grand Hall once again.

The counselor swallowed. His face was red and his lips trembled as he spoke. "Vorpinger has said as much." Again, he pointed to the axe in the center beam overhead. "My lord Vorpinger says: 'How else does one explain that? Only a witch could throw an axe like that.'"

*Kakwespaneyimew.* "He is afraid of her and thinks of her as dangerous." This Vorpinger is afraid of Mum and thinks she's dangerous. So skill can instill fear? She looked at her mother who was smiling as they sat down again. What'll Godomor say to that?

Godomor waved his arm. "After all these years, Lord Vorpinger is still fuming about being put to shame by Tagnyoriva's axe throw. We're still waiting for him to retrieve his axe and better Tagnyoriva's throw. Where, I ask you and my vassal, is there evil witchcraft in what she did? She hit a white winged moth resting on the beam. When the axe struck the moth, its wings fluttered to the floor here.

"Yes, we were all in awe at her throw. It was so quiet in here; we could've heard a mouse fart. Vorpinger agreed to Tagnyoriva's challenge and lost. Tagnyoriva is no witch. A better warrior than Vorpinger, yes, and he knows it, but is not man enough to admit it."

Nagora squeezed her mother's hand. I can't wait to hear you tell that story. You're a hero, Mum.

The counselor sputtered, "Twenty of Vorpinger's best men will not be forthcoming should the majority accord her request. I assure you, it will not be unanimous, and I beg my fellow counselors to recommend their vassals not lend their support in these matters."

The three other counselors rose from the bench.

Vorpinger's counselor strode back to the bench, grabbed the backrest, which rested on hinged armrests, and slammed it forward, turning the skulls that lined the top of the backrest upside-down. Then he sat on the bench with his back to Godomor and everyone else.

Godomor rolled his eyes to the ceiling. "I hope that's the last of the storm."

So this was how the counselors used the bench to show their decisions. If the four counselors sat with their backs against the backrest with the upside-down skulls, it would signify all the counselors were in disapproval. Though they would have to consult with their vassals first. Not this idiot.

Would the three standing counselors join the red faced counselor who sat alone on the bench? I doubt it.

One of the counselors smiled before he spoke. "My lord, I speak for your vassal, Charlengon. He, I am sure, will agree with a decision regarding safe passage of Tagnyoriva and her twin daughters, especially on the terms set out by Tagnyoriva herself. We have nothing but praise for the help she has brought to the people in our region. The women she has trained in her art are carrying on her good work. The continued, improving health of our people is testimony to her healing skill, which she has so generously shared. We see no witchery in her healing skills, nor in her skill with an axe.

"As to her second request, my lord, I will have to consult with Charlengon. Though, I am sure it will not be a problem finding twenty-five of his best men. I know there will be more than twenty-five who will volunteer. I will be back with a list of fifteen archers and ten mounted and armed warriors as requested. Knowing Charlengon, he will, most likely, volunteer his own services as well."

Tagnya squeezed Nagora's hand tighter. You're hopeful too, Mum.

The two other standing counselors looked at each other. They both nodded, and one spoke. "We as well concur, my lord, on both points, as will your vassals. We will go to them and return with lists of volunteers. Lord, if this be all the day's business, we will leave at once to return in time for the next meeting." The three standing counselors bowed to Godomor.

Godomor spoke. "Please, tell your lord vassals that all my own volunteers, archers and armed warriors, will have horses. Ask them to do the same for their volunteers. Counselors, if possible, let's next meet a day ahead of our scheduled meeting. Do you think you can manage that?"

The three of them looked from one to another before answering. "Yes, my lord."

"No further business. Good speed."

Tagnya did not let go of Nagora's hand. If I were her, I'd want to clap.

The lone counselor on the reversed bench stormed out behind the others as they were already halfway out of the hall. Godomor watched him leave and then motioned Gabe forward. He whispered something in Gabe's ear.

Gabe then went to his two men who had been on patrol with him. He huddled with them, giving animated instructions. Then his men left.

While this was going on, Godomor spoke to his scribe and his assistant. Then he stood and came around from behind the table. "Come Tagnyoriva, bring your daughters. Come Dangor."

Godomor was smiling. "Welcome to Skull Bay, Nagora and Dangor. All of you have my protection while you are here. It is my intention to honor your second request, Tagnyoriva. I'm confident so will three other vassals."

Godomor reached for Tagnya's hands. "My people and I are indebted to you for your selfless care of our wounded and sick, and for the generous sharing of your knowledge of healing. And we also want the rightful ruler to sit on the throne in the Land of the Danu so our border continues to be respected, and so we may better develop peaceful trade between our people."

Godomor turned to Dangor and offered his hand. "Dangor, I expect you to express my thanks and continued appreciation of the goods and knowledge that Geirador has so generously shared with us."

Godomor stepped back. "Tagnyoriva, I will leave you now so you can bask in the company of your daughters and Dangor. I am sure you have much to speak of. In due time, when all is ready and the warrior volunteers are here, we will feast your cause."

He reached out for Nagora's hand. "Nagora, I want you to know that from just having met you, I already feel my fondness for you will grow to equal that which I have for your sister and your mother."

Nagora smiled and believed Godomor's words.

Tagnya held her daughters' hands and had them bow. "Thank you, my lord." Dangor bowed as well.

Godomor turned to leave with his attendant. They disappeared beyond the curtain behind his throne. Two guards stood watch at the empty throne.

When they left the Grand Hall, the rain had passed.


Outside on the main landing, Tagnya pulled Nagora aside. "How does your burn feel?"

"I'm fine, Mum. The salve is doing its work. I have to concentrate to keep my hand from touching it. It's between a burning and an itching sensation."

"We'll put more salve on it when we get home."

"If I can keep myself busy and let the salve do its work, I should be fine.

"For a while, Mum, I worried in there. I wasn't sure how things would turn out. You must be happy."

Tagnya hugged her. "Aye, I am, Nagora. In so many ways."

They started down the steps to their horses. Three of Gabe's men were tending their animals. Tagnya and Sagora mounted and led the way. Nagora and Dangor followed, leading their mules.

# Promise
## *Asotamowin*

A stone-walled corral and stable for the horses and mules sat next to Tagnya's rectangular stone lodge.

Dangor must've done a quick calculation. "Tagnya, with our horses and mules, it'll be a tight fit in your stable."

"Aye, but we have a saddle room in our lodge so the animals will be comfortable."

Dangor seemed reassured. "Where will we put all this equipment we've packed on the mules?"

Tagnya pointed. "There should be plenty of space in the shelter over there where we stack our firewood. We haven't filled it for winter yet. The roof overhang will keep your equipment out of the rain. Sagora and I will help you unpack."

Nagora and her uncle did the unpacking. Sagora and Tagnya set the packs in the order Dangor wanted them under the shelter's roof.

Nagora helped her uncle carry a loaded packsaddle into the woodshed. "Did you bring something for Mum from Geirador?"

"I did."

"How about getting it for her right now? Sagora and I will finish up with the mules and horses."

Dangor held up his thumb. "Good idea. Geirador did say to give it to Tagnya as soon as we arrived." He went to retrieve a leather bound package from one of his saddlebags.

Sagora was petting Storm's neck. "You have a beautiful horse, Nagora."

Nagora smiled. "His name is Storm. Uncle bought him for me from Geirador. I've had him for almost a year now. I like the spotted coat on yours. What's his name?"

"That's my baby, Brith." Sagora smiled proud. "Had him since he was a colt, close to five years now."

"Brith obviously likes to be ridden by you. Which way to the saddle room?"

"Follow me, little sister."

Nagora smiled. Pare often calls me that. Now I'm hearing those words from my own sister. Right now they seem strange. They don't quite carry the same attachment as when Pare speaks them.


Nagora followed Sagora through the back entrance to the saddle room. "Wow!" Spears, swords, knives, axes, shields, bows and arrows. They all had their place on one wall. "This is a small armory."

Sagora laughed. "You'd think we're warriors instead of healers. Mum insists we keep our fighting skills sharp."


They returned to unsaddle Kimmo and Scout, Tagnya's horse.

Nagora unfastened her blades, bow, and quiver from the back of Dangor's saddle. After setting his saddle next to hers, she took a moment to examine her bow and a random arrow from her quiver.

Sagora had been watching. "Nagora, do you make your own bows and arrows?"

"Aye, I do, most of the time. No choice not learning how to do that with Uncle. I made this one to Geirador's design."

"Well, that's one skill I haven't learned."

"I'm sure Mum has taught you many skills I know nothing about."

Sagora looked at her forehead. "Is your brand bothering you?"

Nagora touched the side of her head. "I'll put it this way: I'm happy to keep busy. It won't leave my mind, at least not the feeling it's giving me now. How does it look?"

Sagora stepped closer. "Beneath the salve, from what I can see, it has blistered evenly. If you can keep from touching it and leave the scab fall by itself, it should leave a clean, neat, even scar. I must say I centered it on your forehead, despite the thunderclap."

Nagora had been watching her sister's eyes. "That's what big sisters do. They do it right for their little sisters."

Sagora smiled.

Then Nagora followed her sister back to the saddle room. Sagora picked up Dangor's saddlebags and said, "Bring yours. I'll show you where you sleep."

Nagora picked up her bags and followed her sister into the hall.

"Mum sleeps here." Sagora pointed to a room with a curtained doorway and went into the adjoining room. "And here is where we'll sleep, my room. Put your stuff on my bed. We'll go get you a cot from the sick room. I'll get you blankets as well."

Along the hall, a doorway opened onto the kitchen. Then Nagora and her sister came to the front entrance. To the right of the front door was the sick room. It had one window. Six cots lined each of the long sides of the room. Three narrow tables lined up in the middle of the room, and a shelf under each held blankets. A small stool rested beneath each shelf. Sagora placed Dangor's saddlebags on a table, pulled two blankets from the shelf, and set them on the far corner cot.

Sagora folded the cot near the doorway. "Will this do little sister?"

Nagora touched the back of her head. "All I need is a place to lay my head. Though, I might have to tie my hands to my waist tonight."

Sagora looked to her forehead, to her eyes, and away. "Worth considering."

As they left the sick room, they peeked into the room opposite where Tagnya was busy.

*Maskihkiwapohkew*. "She prepares medicine." Aye, she prepares medicine for Godomor.

Sagora held a finger to her lips.

On the table in front of Tagnya, something was simmering in a small container resting on a small tripod above a candle flame. Dangor had his hands on each side of an open leather package on the table.

*Maskihkiwiwat maskihkiwopakwa.* "A medicine bundle containing leaves and herbs with spirit powers." From Geirador, for his friend, Godomor. Godomor, may you heal.

It's not his time to go to the stars. I don't know him, but I'm attached to him in a way beyond the help he can give our cause. If there's a way I can help him, I will.

Smaller open packages rested on the piece of leather. Next to it was what appeared to be an open missive. Instructions perhaps?

As they watched from the doorway, Sagora whispered, "This is where Mum prepares medicines. She also keeps a written record of healing plants and herbs and roots of all kinds, edible and poisonous. And she keeps notes of her recipes and records who she treated, how, and with what. She spends a lot of time here, often writing into the night."

Mum is so disciplined and thorough in her work as a healer. If she's put as much effort in working for the Cause, we stand a chance her plan will work.

After setting up the cot in Sagora's room, they made their way to the kitchen.


"You must be hungry. Mum made soup, and I baked bread. We'll get something to hold us over until our evening meal."

"I can wait. Can I help you with something?"

Every time Nagora looked at her, Sagora's eyes were on her forehead and when she would bring her eyes to Nagora's, she would lower them or look elsewhere. How would I feel if I had branded my sister? How long will she avoid looking into my eyes? It's not her fault we were born here. To be marked must've been in my destiny. How many people will not look into my eyes when they see the mark?

"Come with me." Sagora had a pot in her hand. She walked to the wooden door at the far corner of the kitchen.

Sagora opened it. It was a food storage room, much like the cellar in Geirador's home. It smelled the same—damp, musty, and sweet all at the same time.

A small table with a knife and cutting board resting on its surface occupied the center of the room. Shelves with containers of all sizes lined the walls. They held various nuts, dried fruits, and grains. Below the shelves were bins where carrots, beets, and turnips lay in cool, damp sand. Apples rested in bins of straw, their smells sharp as they neared the end of their storage time.

The stone rim of a well rose on the other side of the table. Two ropes hung from two overhead pulleys fastened to a ceiling beam. Sagora placed the pot on the table and pulled on a rope. It brought up a bucket of fresh water. She filled the pot with water.

"Here, you pull up the wet box. Take out the butter and the pot of soup."

As Nagora pulled on the other rope, a box appeared, much like the one back home, made of wood with a double wall. The inner box had a cover flush to its walls' edges, which were higher and tighter than the walls of the outer box. In the well, the space between the two filled with water to keep the contents of the inner box cool.

On returning to the kitchen, Sagora lit the fire and pointed to the iron hook. "Hang the pot here. Put mugs and plates on the table for us. You'll find spoons in a mug. Within a few days, little sister, you'll have the run of the place. After all, this is your home too."

My home? It's not the image that comes to mind when I say that word. At least not yet. Will that change with time?

At the moment, it was Sagora who held her fascination. Nagora studied her every move and her face whenever she could see it. She was watching herself move as a magical mirror. Her movements were in another time. She could converse with herself and not know the exact words of her own reply.

Nagora looked for the differences. Her own skin was darker because of her time in the sun, and her hand and arm muscles were more pronounced and wiry from her work building curraghs with her uncle.

The replica of herself moved before her eyes. It was her, but by another name, Sagora, and yet she had questions.

When will she become Sagora to me, and carry with that name more meaning than being my twin sister, the one who marked me? Or Sagnuska, the healer? When will I feel a bond between us in my heart?

As Nagora set the table, Tagnya and Dangor came in.

Tagnya stood before her. "We're hungry also. Let me have a look at your forehead." The tips of her fingers were cool on each side of her face. "How does it feel?"

Nagora looked into Tagnya's examining eyes. "The same."

Her mother reached for a wisp of hair, pulled it from the salve, and repeated Sagora's earlier observations.

"She thinks maybe she'll have to tie her hands to her waist, so she doesn't touch it when she sleeps," said Sagora.

"Good idea." Tagnya stepped back and looked at Nagora. She seemed to be taking in all the features of her face, not just her brand. *Is she comparing me to my sister?*

Then Tagnya hugged her. "My Nagora. How I've longed to hold you like this. You were so young when I last fed you and that was at my breast with Sagora. It broke my heart to let you go. I knew the conditions for our cause would become right and we would be back together again. We're getting closer to the day we can fight for the return of Raynhard's crown."

*Why hasn't she mentioned Da yet?*

Tagnya's eye filled with tears when she let go of her and Nagora's own tears welled up. She didn't stop them.

"Mum, tell me about the axe-throwing incident with Vorpinger."

Tagnya smiled as she wiped at her tears. "Aye, I will. First, let me say he's the most likely threat to Godomor's rule in the Land of Skulls. He's been, by far, the most critical of Godomor and in recent years, he's been outright contesting Godomor's decisions for the sake of provocation."

Tagnya pulled back a chair and as she sat, she motioned for Nagora to do the same. "At the time of the axe incident, Vorpinger was a fearful, vicious warrior who relished a good fight.

"He had another problem. Although married, he kept making a play to climb into other women's beds, especially those women who were also warriors, be they married or not.

"He was a huge brute of a man, and any other man who'd taken him on in a contest had come out on the losing end, a few at the expense of their lives."

Dangor took a seat the table.

Tagnya smiled warmly at him and continued. "It was almost two years to the day since I'd arrived here. There was a feast to celebrate the defeat of an Outlander raiding party. I'd tended to the wounds of half a dozen men and eased one man's suffering who, in a matter of several counts, died of his wounds. At least he was without pain in his final moments."

Tagnya blinked and took a deep breath. "Godomor invited me to the victory celebration at his Grand Hall. I was still nursing Sagora, so I went to change my mind. I brought Sagora and sat with other women and their children. Ale and mead were flowing. Warriors were boasting of their deeds. Severed heads of the enemy were resting on the tips of spears planted around the fire pit outside where a pig was roasting on the coals of the fire.

"Inside, big Vorpinger was trying to convince two women warriors to wash enemy blood from his body. They weren't buying his invitation. Then he tried to engage other women around the hall."

I can see it coming.

"I'd just finished nursing Sagora when Vorpinger approached me. He said since I was not a warrior, he'd not invite me to wash his body. Instead he dared me to sweeten his mead with the milk of my breasts. He tried to grab one of my breasts."

Another pig. If ever you cross my path, I have something for you.

"I pushed his hand away and moved out of his reach. I held Sagora close. He turned on me. He was angry and drunk. I thought perhaps I should try to take control of the situation.

"I told him I was a warrior and where I came from, warriors held contests of skills wherein the challenger had to first best his opponent's counter challenge before proceeding. I said these contests dealt with the skill of axe-throwing. I chose this first because I knew I stood a good chance of beating him."

That's a weapon I haven't mastered. "You're an axe thrower, Mum?"

Tagnya smiled. "I learned from the best when I was much younger than you. That's not the only axe in a ceiling beam." She winked at Dangor who was smiling.

Another story I must ask about.

"Anyway, a huge grin broke out on Vorpinger's face. 'Bring it on, but you don't have an axe,' he said.

"'Mind if I use yours?' I asked, knowing that if he said yes, I could put him in a bind.

"He strode over to his table to get his axe, which he had been brandishing earlier on.

"In the meantime, I had handed Sagora over to one of my new friends at the table where I'd been sitting.

"Everyone was interested and watched what was about to happen. Vorpinger placed his cup of mead on his table and said, 'Are you sure you don't want to give me your milk now? If not now, it'll be later.'

"'First, beat my counter challenge,' I replied.

"'State it, then,' he said and handed me his axe.

"'I pick the target. All you have to do is throw like me and better my hit on the target. Agreed?'

"'Agreed,'" he answered.

"'So you can't say used a lucky charm, I'll strip my body of all I wear before I throw, like my fellow warriors back home.' I had a comb in my hair, a bracelet on my arm, a necklace, and the clothes on my back. In no time I was naked in front of all, holding Vorpinger's axe."

Sagora pointed at Dangor with the long wooden spoon in her hand. He was smiling and holding back a laugh as he nodded as if to say, "Why am I not surprised?"

Tagnya winked at him. "I looked for my target. It was still there up on the center beam, a moth with big white wings. 'I choose that moth above on the ridge beam.' Vorpinger laughed. I swung the axe with both hands between my spread legs, all the while focusing on the moth. Then, reaching back between my legs as far as possible on the swing back, I uncoiled my whole body and let the axe fly. A star spirit warrior must've guided it, for it was the best throw of my life.

"The axe blade struck just as Godomor said today. Everyone stared. Vorpinger's jaw dropped and before the moth's wings reached the floor, I'd dressed again. Vorpinger was trying to move his jaw to say something, but no sound came out. I pointed to his axe and said, 'There's your axe. It's your turn. Can you better my throw?'

Nagora clenched her fist. Yes! You truly put him in a bind!

"Vorpinger still couldn't speak. Most of the people in the hall were still looking at the axe. He looked around at them, as if to get confirmation that what he'd seen had taken place. Someone's voice from the back of the hall broke the silence with the words: 'Now there's a throw that's got Vorpinger by the balls.' The hall erupted with cheers, whistles, and pounding on the tables."

Dangor was grinning as he held both thumbs up.

Nagora did likewise. Mum, I'm so proud of you!

"Vorpinger didn't know which way to turn or what to say. After glaring at me, he stamped his feet and pushed his way out of the hall amid the din and calls of 'By the balls! By the balls! Vorpinger by the balls!'

"Vorpinger's cohorts followed as the calls and table pounding grew louder. Before I knew it warriors, men and women, surrounded me. They wanted to shake my hand in warrior fashion.

"All in the hall were chanting: 'Tagnyoriva! Tagnyoriva!' I was their hero of the moment. It's been sixteen years since. To my knowledge, since that day, Vorpinger has not set foot inside Godomor's Grand Hall. I think his axe'll stay there for a long time."

Dangor wore a grand smile. "Tagnya, I know a few people who'll love to hear this one."

"Mum! You're famous! Everyone in the Land of Skulls must know that story!" said Nagora.

Tagnya smiled. "I think Godomor is keeping a close eye on him. I'm sure he had the counselor followed today. Godomor must have an ear and an eye in Vorpinger's hold. Within a few days, Godomor will, most likely, know how Vorpinger has reacted to these latest developments."

"Soup's on the table," Sagora called.

Nagora touched Tagnya's arm. "Mum, have you been able to prepare a medication for Godomor?"

"Aye, Geirador sent the plants I'd asked for, and more. We still have two more boilings to do. When adding each ingredient, the medication has to be brought to a boil and then allowed to cool. Once cooled, the next ingredient can be added, mixed, and brought to a boil. The medicine should be ready by this evening."

Nagora's eyes were on Tagnya the whole time. Mum obviously trusts Geirador.

As Sagora sat next to Dangor, she asked Tagnya, "Will you get it to Godomor today?"

"That's my intention. I'll need your help. While Dangor helps me with the preparation, I want you to go find Gabe and instruct him that he has to have his father move in with him. I will get Umma to help me administer the medicine. Godomor'll need one of us at his side at all times.

"He also needs sunlight and fresh air. He's not getting those in his cave at the back of the Grand Hall. Otherwise, this medication won't be worth giving to him. His personal guards can just as well protect him at Gabe's."

Sagora held up her spoon. "He can be stubborn, Mum."

"I know. Just have Gabe tell him if he doesn't do what I ask, his days are numbered and he won't get the medicine. And also tell him I'm withholding Geirador's cask of mead until he gets better."

Tagnya's words made Nagora smile. I bet Godomor will listen to Mum's words of advice.

Tagnya continued. "With the medicine, if he follows my instructions, he should see a noticeable improvement in a short time, if we are not already too late. Because he was such a strong man before he fell ill, he stands a good chance of recovery."

"Do you think Gabe'll be at home?" asked Sagora.

"He should be there already, taking down names of volunteers. I'm sure Godomor had him get the word out. It won't surprise me if he has more names on the list than he expected."

"Nagora and I will go as soon as we finish eating."

Tagnya nodded. "It'll be an occasion for you to show Nagora Skull Bay's harbor."

"And it'll help take my mind off this." Nagora pointed to her forehead.

Nagora finished her soup, glad to be doing something that might get her mind off the itch of the brand. She stood up with Sagora. "I'll get my blades and then I'll be ready."

Tagnya frowned at her. "Your blades? Why would you need your blades?"

Nagora looked at Tagnya and paused before answering. "These days, I don't seem to have any say in what happens in my life. Pigs like Vorpinger caught me off guard once. I promised myself I won't be without my blades ever again. Upon stepping into this land, Gabe took them away from me. Now I wear this brand. It gives me freedom of movement here. If I cannot wear my blades to defend myself, then where is that freedom?"

"My daughter, I'm not trying to control you. It's about showing respect for the people here."

Nagora pointed to her forehead. "Here's my sign of respect. I'm sorry, Mum, but I don't trust that all the people here will respect me. That's why I'll wear my blades. Uncle, are there not sets of blades for Mum and Sagora in the packs we brought from Geirador?"

He nodded. "There are."

"Perhaps, if we were all to wear our blades, we'd be seen as warriors with a common cause because that is what we are. Is that not so?"

Dangor stood. "Tagnya, I believe your daughter has a point. I know how she feels, and I know she'll feel so much better wearing her blades. I'll go get the sets Geirador made for you."

As Nagora left the kitchen with her uncle, she glanced back at Tagnya and Sagora. Tagnya sat silent at the table, obviously in thought. Sagora had a hand on her mother's shoulder. I hope you don't think I was rude. I don't regret what I said. If I'm to be the warrior Edana, I'd better act like her.

When they returned, Nagora wore her blades and Dangor placed two more sets on the table. Nagora reached over her shoulder and pulled the big blade from its sheath. She held it up next to her face so Tagnya and Sagora could see the Tiwaz symbol etched on the blade near its crossguard. From the look in their eyes, they understood.

Then she turned to show them how to put the blade back in and lock it in place. "The brass loop latch allows for the sheath to be worn upside down so the handle is at the lower back."

She faced her mother and sister again, withdrew a small blade from its holster and in one swift motion, threw it at the cold room door where it stuck true.

Tagnya placed both hands on the table. "Very well, from now on when we step out of this house, we'll be armed warriors."

Nagora walked to the door to retrieve her small blade.

While Sagora put her blades on, Nagora slipped on her vest. She turned once more. "See? Barely visible."

Sagora went to get a vest and then they left to find Gabe.

# Brother
## *Nîtisân*

On their walk to Gabe's place, one person turned her back on the sisters and signed as she rushed away from them.

As they approached the lodge, the man with his two wolf-hounds was standing next to the entrance. His hounds sat to the left and right of him, their heads at the level of his waist. A chill settled on the back of Nagora's neck as she remembered Moreena's wolfhounds, Keng and Quinn. They resembled these two with their stringy, shaggy coats.

The coat of the hound on the right was rust red with strands of gold color running from under its chin down the belly and on to its legs. Like the runt of Quinn's litter.

Could the runt have grown this big?

The other's hound's coat was dark steel gray on its face, head, and back. It turned to light steel gray on its chin, belly, and legs.

Nagora touched her sister's arm. "That man, he watched me get branded. He didn't leave when everyone else did in the heavy rain and thunder."

"True, that he did. In a few moments you'll discover that he is, in a certain way, your twin. He has learned to speak our tongue with Gabe. They've been training together for the past three years."

Now the man's hood was down and so Nagora paid closer attention to his features. She guessed he was several years older than her. He wore his golden hair long. It fell just below his broad shoulders and almost reached his arms where they crossed on his chest. He was still as a statue, watching their approach, as were his hounds. What was his name? Sagora would most likely introduce him.

Tiwaz! We are twins of the same mark on our foreheads. How can this be? Do we share a common destiny? He must be the one who set the precedent.

Nagora's gaze went to the cross hilt of the long sword behind his left shoulder, and then to his blue eyes. They were the color of Tagnya's eyes. She had never seen a man with eyes like this. He too gazed into her eyes.

"Lars, I want you to meet my twin sister, Nagora."

Lars held Nagora's gaze and appeared to ignore Sagora's words. He remained still as a statue.

Nagora waited and tried to read his face, but it remained impassive as his eyes seemed to look inside of her.

The big red hound came forward and lay at her feet. Nagora's eyes escaped Lars's gaze. She let the hound smell and lick her hand. Then it rolled onto its side showing its belly. Like the runt had done almost a year ago in the wagon. Could it be the same dog? She bent to one knee, scratched it and patted it. Its size amazed her. Then she stood up and looked at Lars.

A grand smile spread across his face, causing his eyes to smile at the same time. He unfolded his big arms and reached out a hand.

Nagora could not help but smile at this giant of a man as she placed her hand in his. When she did, he placed his other hand over hers. A peaceful warmth radiated from his hands and touched her whole body. She knew she could put her complete trust in this man. When she looked to his hands, she found her other hand rested on top of his. His hound now sat at her side and was looking up at them.

That's when Lars spoke. "Today, I get to meet my sister, face-to-face."

She looked up into his face. "You speak our language?"

"Gabe taught me. It is the language we speak when we train together."

Nagora pointed to her forehead, and then to his.

Lars nodded. "Not my blood sister. My brand sister. I hope you bear no offense in my calling you 'my sister.'"

"No offense taken." Had her words come out loud enough for him to hear?

Lars let go of her hands, spread his arms open, and said, "Welcome home, my sister."

He spoke his words with true sincerity.

"I'm happy to meet you—my brother." Nagora stepped into his embrace. His strong arms held her to him. He would be, *onakateyimowew*, "her protector," just as the strange word had foretold earlier. She was sure of it, as sure as she had been branded.

Sagora cleared her throat. "Brother Lars, we've come to see Gabe. I imagine he's here."

Lars let his smile grow wide, almost from ear to ear. "That he is, sister Sagora," he replied. He let go of Nagora, reached back, knocked twice, and opened the door to wave them in.

Sagora gave Nagora a gentle push to get her going through the doorway.

Gabe stood up from the table near the window to greet them. "Looks like you've come to volunteer. I'll put your names down on the list with the forty-two who've come before you."

Sagora held up both her hands. "Forty-two already!"

"Word has spread fast. I don't think we'll have a problem finding one hundred volunteers."

Sagora was all smiles. "What do you think, Nagora?"

Sagora's question almost evaded her. She blinked. "Well, that's good news."

"You're damn right. Forgive my little sister. She just met her brand brother at the door. I think she may be a little taken by him."

Nagora lowered her gaze.

Sagora went over to Gabe, put her arms around him, and looked back at Nagora. "You know how it is Gabe. Tagnyoriva's girls are alike in lots of ways. Look at her. Her ears are red, and she doesn't know what to say."

Now Nagora's whole face burned and her heart beat faster. Why couldn't she control what was happening to her?

Gabe gave a quick peck on Sagora's forehead. "Well, what brings you girls here?"

Sagora explained why Tagnya had sent them.

"Well, my father won't have a choice. I won't give him one. I'll make sure he moves out of there today. It's something I've wanted for a long time. Now he'll have no excuse. Tell Tagnyoriva that when she comes by this evening, he'll be here waiting for her. And tell her to pay no mind to his complaints."

"We'll do that," said Sagora. "Before we go back, I'll take Nagora down to the dock."

Gabe looked from Sagora to Nagora. "Would you like Lars to go with you?"

Sagora looked to her sister for an answer.

Was she blushing even more?

Sagora gave her a nudge. "We'll take that as a yes."

Nagora reached out to slap her sister's arm, but Sagora moved away laughing.

Gabe smiled. "Tell Lars I give him leave for the time you visit the docks."

"Did Lars volunteer?" asked Sagora.

"Do you need to ask? He was number one."

"There you go, little sister. You have an official number-one friend. Don't you lose any time making friends with him."

Sagora was teasing her in the way Paruline often did. All you big sisters are the same.

She had to smile. "Aye, I'd like my big brother, Lars, to come with us."

"That's the spirit, girl." Sagora patted her on the back as they headed for the door.

Outside, Sagora waited a moment, looked at Nagora, and motioned with her arms and head toward Lars.

Nagora followed the unspoken instructions. "Lars, will you join us on our walk down to the dock? Gabe gives you leave for the time of our visit there."

"My pleasure, Nagora." He reached out and took her hand as they headed toward the harbor, each with a hound at their side.

Sagora talked all the way, pointing out this and that about Skull Bay, but Nagora missed most of it, even the people they passed along the way. She was at this man's side, her hand in his, lost in the moment with no cares about the past or what was to come. Being with him was all that mattered.

Only when they were standing at the end of the dock, facing into the cool breeze as they looked out over the bay, did her sister stop talking. Lars had an arm around Nagora, holding her to his side, out of the wind. She turned to look for Sagora. About twenty strides behind them, Sagora smiled and winked.

She pressed her cheek against Lars's arm and smiled back at Sagora.

Sagora approached and pointed out into the bay. "See the rock in the middle of the entrance? When seen from the beach over there," Sagora pointed to her left, "it looks like a skull. That's how Skull Bay got its name. Boats coming into our harbor leave the skull rock to their left. Otherwise, the rocks in the shallows on the other side will tear the boats apart."

Nagora looked out to the rock her sister had described. "The shallow side seems wider. Is there a warning marker for unsuspecting boats?"

Lars chuckled. "No, and that's the way Godomor likes it. Over the years, a few Outlander boats have gone aground there in their eagerness to come into our bay. Per chance, they seldom travel alone so the crews were able to get away on the boats that followed and could stop before running aground."

Nagora looked up into his eyes. He smiled and kept his eyes on hers. "Have you been to sea, Lars?"

"I have. For almost a dozen years, I sailed with the whalers from the Moroes Islands. When I learned where I was from, I wanted to make it home to find my family and at least see them, even if it meant I'd be put to death. Three years ago my Moroes Island friends brought me here. They said they wouldn't leave without me, dead or alive."

"I bet the people here didn't welcome you with open arms."

He lowered his gaze and pressed his lips together. "Welcomed with the news that my parents were dead, and that only my brother, Norbuls, remained. He was about to leave on a boat as crew member. I tried to bargain to be with Norbuls on that boat. There was no way any of the crew would hear of it. It was news to him that he had a brother. Had I not looked exactly like him and had Godomor not confirmed the fact to him, he would not have believed it."

"Why didn't you leave with your friends?"

Lars looked out into the bay and then back at his feet. Those past events must've caused him great deception, like her own had.

"When I saw him, I wanted to be with him. The boat and its crew were to return before winter. I figured if there was a way I could stay, Norbuls would come to his senses and want to be with me, his only brother. It was my idea that Norbuls brand me, to make me different from him. If he did, I would stay and wait for his return."

"How did you convince Godomor?"

Lars looked at her with unblinking eyes. "I didn't. Your mother, Tagnuska, did. I was lucky that she had been here at the dock tending to someone's injury when, perchance, Godomor asked her opinion on what I'd proposed. She didn't answer immediately. When she did, she spoke of the strength of blood ties and my honorable offer in the face of their long-standing tradition regarding twins."

Nagora caught the hint of tears in the corners of his eyes.

"Tagnuska's words moved Norbuls to come forward on his knees before Godomor and beg him to grant my wish so he could take the time of his days at sea to reflect on what it means to have a single surviving family member." Lars swallowed.

"Godomor replied that under the conditions I'd proposed, he had room in his heart and in his land for a returning son, and he hoped his people could see themselves in me and open their hearts as well. On that day, not one person voiced their opposition. 'Then let this be,' declared Godomor. Before my friends could leave on the next tide, my brother had branded me."

You set a precedent for returning twins. Our brands are linked. Your brave offer influenced my choice.

Nagora touched his arm. "Did you get to know Norbuls before his boat sailed?"

"I had three days with him. Not enough. When his boat did not return as planned, it was not long before some blamed me."

"There's been no news at all of the boat or its crew?" said Nagora.

Lars shook his head. "Not a word since."

She looked to Sagora. I'm lucky to have you, big sister. Poor Lars. How sad for him. She went over to her sister, put her arm around her, and brought her over to Lars. "Well, you're not alone anymore. You have two sisters." She pulled Sagora close with her to embrace Lars.

He put his big arms around them. "I do now."

"And based on what my mum said in your favor, I think you can also consider her your mum," said Sagora.

Lars smiled as he looked at them. "Needless to say, she holds a special place in my heart."

Sagora tugged on her sister's arm. "Little sister, it's time we head back."

Nagora bent and scratched both hounds' chests. "Oh! Aye, you shaggy lads are also part of the family. What are their names, Lars?" The hounds licked her hands.

"Aydan, the one that chose you. His name means 'born of fire.' This one is my Lyam. His name means 'protector.'"

"Aydan." She held his large red head in her hands. "Aydan, why did you choose me?" Aydan wagged his tail and whined. "Is that so? Well, I'm happy you did."

"He's yours, Nagora," said Lars.

"Oh! My! I wouldn't take Aydan from you. Lyam would miss him. I'd have to hunt every day just to feed him. Mum would have something to say about that."

"Tell you what. Here's a whistle." Lars handed her a tiny silver whistle pendant, which hung from a thin leather lace. It looked like the whistles she used to make from a willow branch when she was younger. The leather lace ends were tied together in the four-eights fashion. Hmm?

"Trust me. You can't hear it when you blow in it. Aydan can. Blow twice and he'll come to you if you are anywhere within Skull Bay's walls. I'll take care of feeding him. When he's gone, I'll know he's with you. To send him back, open a hand on your chest, then stretch your arm out from you and say: 'Go to Lars.'"

"Truly?" Nagora smiled at Lars in wonder.

Lars crossed his arms on his chest, smiled his grand smile, and nodded. "Take him with you. On the way home, Sagora will show you a few more commands. She's seen me with the hounds often enough to have picked up a few of the signals." He signaled and said, "Aydan, go to Nagora and Sagora."

"He'll obey both of us?" asked Nagora.

Lars nodded.

"Thank you, Lars." I feel happy, like a little girl who's been given a doll. She gave him a hug and hung the whistle pendant around her neck. Aydan was walking between them when they left.

Nagora stopped to turn around and watch Lars walk away.

Sagora touched her arm. "What are you looking at?"

"That's one big sword he's carrying."

"Sure. You're admiring his sword. Admit it. You're admiring the man. He is one big hunk of a man, isn't he? Those eyes, that hair, those broad shoulders, those strong arms ... "

"Stop right there. I thought you and Gabe were ... "

"We're not married yet. Look, many women have had their eye on Lars. Not just the unmarried ones. Though not a one would dare accept any advances from him. It's the stigma of being a twin."

Sagora wagged her finger. "Before this day is out, word about you two walking hand in hand will spread. Him holding you at the dock. You with your cheek on his arm. Those images and, believe me, plenty more will make their way around the village at least three times. Many women will go to bed tonight wishing they'd been branded instead of you."

"You think so?"

"Either they'll give you looks of admiration or intentionally sign to show their jealousy."

"Listen, Sagora. I can't explain what happened. I've never had that feeling with a man. I'm still trying to figure it out. Is it what people call love?" I can't speak what the strange words said. She wouldn't believe me. It has to be more than the brand we share. Are we destined for each other?

"No, Nagora. It's like a beginning, the pebble you throw into the pond, that first splash that creates that first ring. Love grows afterward, like all the other rings that grow out from that first splash, if you're lucky. Some people never even get the splash. My guess is you have. It remains to be seen if you'll see your love grow."

Did Mum speak those words to her? How many such ways of seeing things have I missed out on?

"Did you get the splash with Gabe?"

Sagora raised her eyebrows. "To be honest, no. Not at all. I hated him so much. He was always watching out for me as I grew up. For a while I couldn't do a thing on my own without him being there. Then somehow I grew to love him. I can't rightly say how that happened. Maybe because once he kept away from me, I began to miss him. But now, I know that I love him."

"And you can talk about Lars like that?"

"Little sister, Uncle Dangor raised you. You probably haven't had the chance to be around women, especially a group of women when no men are present. You can't imagine what and who they talk about. If only their men could hear them!

When I tell you that most of the women in this village would gladly jump in his bed if ever they had the chance, believe me, it's true. I've heard all the things they said they'd do to him and beg him to do to them. You cannot imagine."

"No, I can't."

Nagora bent down on one knee to pet Aydan, trying to escape all that Sagora was saying and find time to think about what was happening to her.

Is this truly happening? Did I die after swimming out of that cave? Am I living in a dream? Did I get branded today? And these feelings I have for this man, what are they? Is this person next to me truly my twin? And you, Aydan, are you for real? Everything is happening at once in my life. I don't have control over it. Did I ever have control? I need time by myself to think of all of this.

She stood up. "Well, I just talked to Aydan, and he said he's ready to listen to our commands. Show me what you know, Sagora."

"Follow me. Watch my hand and see if you can connect how I hold it to get Aydan to obey." Sagora walked ahead with Aydan following at her side.

Nagora followed behind them and watched for the hand signals. She was sure she had picked up the signals for: follow, stay by my side, sit by my side, lay at my side, rollover, and give me your paw.

"Let me try." Aydan followed, stayed at her side, sat, rolled over, and stood on his hind legs with his paws on her shoulders towering over her like his master. "Hold it, Aydan!" She couldn't help but try to wrap her arms around him as she nuzzled his chest. She let him down with a laugh. "Well, four out of five is not bad. Did you know that one?"

Sagora was still laughing. "No. Show me."

"Maybe I'll keep it to myself. Little sisters keep secrets from big sisters."

"Big sisters eventually find out." Sagora had her arms around her. "Or they make their little sisters tell." She squeezed her in a bear hug and lifted her off her feet.

Aydan barked. Sagora set her down. "Okay. We know who your master is." She reached over and scratched Aydan's head. "You know, Nagora, when I found out about you, I couldn't believe it. I had so many questions. Now you're here with me. Unbelievable circumstances have brought us together. I wonder if I'm living in a dream, if all this is true." She put her arm back around her waist. "When I touch you and hold you like this, you feel real. Almost like a part of me. Like we belong together. How do you feel?"

Nagora looked into her eyes. "My feelings are just like yours. My disbelief is still there. I also wonder if I'm living in a dream. I don't know what more to do to convince myself that this is happening. I'm just trying to accept it and see what happens next. One day at a time."

"What a day this has been."

They walked on in silence, Aydan at Nagora's side.

# Illusion
## *Mahtawinikewin*

"Mum. We're back. We have a new family member with us," called Sagora.

Tagnya looked up from the table where she prepared her medicines. She had been speaking with Dangor. When she saw Aydan standing with them in the entrance, she stood and approached.

"Well, look who's here. Aydan, you big, bad boy. Come to see Mummy."

Aydan's backside and tail just about wagged the rest of his body and his front paws stepped in place as he broke into a happy whine and spoke back to Tagnya in muffled barks and cries. It was obvious he was happy to see her and that they shared a special bond.

Tagnya had his big head in her hands and submitted to a thorough face licking.

"Mum helped save Aydan when Lars brought him here as a pup. He was the runt of the litter. Half the size of Lyam. Lars thought he might starve to death since he was not eating.

Mum showed Lars how to nurse Aydan back to health. She had Lars spend two days here, feeding and caring for Aydan, giving him back the will to live. It's taken him almost a year to catch up to Lyam in size."

Did Lars get his hounds from a trader?

Tagnya stood with a frown on her face. "You said something about a new family member."

"Aydan chose Nagora, so Lars gave him to her."

Her mother was weighing her words before speaking again, so Nagora spoke first. "Mum, don't worry, we won't have to feed him. Lars gave me a whistle to call Aydan when I want him, and I'm to send him back to Lars at the end of the day. He'll feed Aydan."

Tagnya's shoulders relaxed. "To be honest, Nagora, that arrangement suits me."

Sagora said, "And Lars is Nagora's brand brother, and so my brother. And since you're our mum and you spoke in favor of his offer to get himself branded and Godomor accepted, which set the precedent so Nagora could come back, that makes you, in a way, Lars's mum as well."

Tagnya shook her head and smiled. "Oh! That's how it works! Before the day is out, our family has more than doubled. We can't leave Lyam out of this, can we? If Norbuls ever comes back, we'll have to add him too. Dangor, could you make me a bigger table for the kitchen?" Now they were all smiling.

Tagnya reached for Nagora's hand. "Well, you've met your brand brother. What do you think of him?"

Nagora lowered her gaze, trying to think how she would answer.

Before she could, Sagora pointed at her and spoke. "Her crimson face doesn't tell the whole story, but I bet you can guess what happened. When you come back from Gabe's, stop by at a couple of neighbors and ask what they saw happen."

Nagora slapped at Sagora's hand. "According to her, I'm quite taken by Lars." She shook her head. "I'm still trying to figure out what's happening. I've never felt this way about a man before. Why my ears and face burn when you talk this way is beyond me."

Tagnya smiled. "For Lars to give you Aydan, I'm guessing the attraction is mutual. He wants you to be safe in Skull Bay, with Aydan at your side. I'd say he's looking out for you. If that's so, I'm happy for you, my daughter. I think it's a good sign, and that you share something very rare with that person. The uncertainty of your feelings at this time is normal, and exciting at the same time. Enjoy them while you have them and, with time, you'll come to a clearer understanding of the direction they'll take you."

Nagora had spoken more than she intended and wanted to change the topic. "I guess you're right. Mum, there's more."

Tagnya frowned.

Nagora looked from her mother to her uncle. "Good news. Lars was the first of forty-two to volunteer here in Skull Bay."

"That is good news!" Tagnya looked to Dangor, who was smiling as he held up his thumb.

Tagnya looked back at her. "How's your burn?"

"The feeling is at the back of my mind, like a slight itch nagging to be scratched. I'd like to look at it."

...

Tagnya went to a shelf along the wall. "Here's a mirror." She set a polished copper mirror in its pivoting wooden frame on the table. She pulled back a chair for Nagora to sit. "Have a look. I'll wash my hands and get more salve."

Nagora nodded as she took the mirror. Her mother went to a big bowl on the next table, where she washed her hands.

Nagora sat in the chair. Sagora stood behind her, silent, with her hands on her shoulders. She touched Sagora's left hand. "Move over to this side so I can get more light from the window." Sagora obeyed.

Nagora turned her face this way and that as she examined the three converging lines of the Tiwaz symbol. The blistering is even on all of them. I thought they'd be wider. Perhaps once they heal, they will be. The Tiwaz will be with me from now on, a small price to pay to reunite with Mum and Sagora.

Tagnya returned with a pot of salve and sat next to Nagora, watching her. When Nagora put the mirror down, her mother removed the lid from the pot. "I'll add more salve." Nagora turned to face Tagnya, her eyes on her mother's as she applied the salve. Mum's look is comforting. She deserves to be called Tagnuska, the healer.

As her mother put the lid back on the pot, she lowered her gaze. "Nagora, about your blades. I'm sorry. Dangor told me what you've been through. I think I have a better understanding of why you want to wear them. I would also, if I were you. I cried when I learned how close I came to losing you forever."

Sagora squeezed Nagora's shoulders.

She'll want to hear what Mum now knows. She patted Sagora's hand in unspoken reassurance that she also would be told.

"Mum, I cried too when I learned that you were alive and that I also had a sister. I'm so happy to be here with both of you. I can't wait for us to return to the Land of the Danu with the Hundred Best and help set things right."

Tagnya reached for Nagora's hands. "We've plenty of work to do yet to make that happen. I'm confident we'll get the hundred volunteers. Though, I'm still wary of Vorpinger. He's unpredictable, and he might try to interfere. You saw how his counselor acted. Vorpinger is Godomor's cousin. If Godomor were to die, Gabe is next in line, though not a battle proven leader. If Gabe was not there, and Godomor were to die, Vorpinger would be entitled to the throne."

Dangor said, "Do you think that would motivate Vorpinger to act in some way? Perhaps as justification to make a play for the throne? That opens up so many possible moves he could make. Thinking about them all and planning to counter them is enough to worry a man sick."

Something about what her uncle said bothered her. What was it? She wasn't making the connection.

Tagnya looked to Dangor. "I see what you're getting at, but I don't think that's the cause of Godomor's illness. He's a shrewd ruler. He knows who's loyal to him, and the forces at his disposition. Committing one hundred of his best is not something he'd do lightly if he felt there was palpable opposition."

Dangor uncrossed his hands and touched a finger to the tabletop. "Well, Tagnya, loyalties sometimes change overnight."

"True, but a leader has to be in the offing, not a bully like Vorpinger. Anyway, we have our own plans to consider. We'll do well to focus on those for now."

Tagnya turned to point to the pot on the other table. "Godomor's medicine is ready. I just have to pour it into jars to bring to Gabe's."

Tagnya turned back to the girls. "Sagora, I want you to go to Umma and ask her to meet me here after her evening meal. Tell her I want her to help me with Godomor. Tell her we'll be at Godomor's bedside for a few days. From Geirador's missive, chances are the first three days on this medicine will be hard on him. He'll have a fever unlike any he's ever had before, and his body'll empty itself from both ends. We'll have to keep him on a mix of honey water and dulse, at least a cup's worth per count. When he regains his appetite, it'll be a good sign.

"When you return, Dangor will meet with you and Nagora to brief you on your roles to help free the dragon."

Nagora reached for her sister's hand. "Take Aydan with you." She signaled and spoke the command: "Aydan, go with Sagora."

In the corral, Dangor led Nagora over to the woodshed to the packs with the poles, yokes, and other strange items he had said they would need.

"Uncle, Mum is a thinker and a planner. I'm impressed."

"She's always thinking. Likes to know where she's going. Wants to be in control as much as possible."

"We've got two of everything to make a set for each of you. We'll unpack all the pieces and sort them into two sets over there on the ground."

When they finished, Dangor pointed toward the door to the saddle room. "Let's go get our saddles. You'll saddle up Storm and we'll see if we can rig one of these sets on him."

By the time they had the rig adjusted on Storm, Sagora showed up. "You'll be meeting Umma later. Mum has been training her for years. She's confident Umma is ready to take over when we leave. She's become a close friend of ours. Her husband was the captain of the boat Lars's brother left on. Umma had begun training with Mum about five years before."

Sagora reached over to a pole hanging from Storm's saddle. "I see you have some kind of rig set up on Storm. What's it for?"

"To create the illusion of a horse running with hooves of fire," said Dangor. "We'll see if it moves as it's supposed to. If it does, tomorrow we'll practice with it."

Sagora took a step back. "Hold it! Aren't horses supposed to be afraid of fire?"

"True enough. Just the same, they can be trained to work around and with a certain amount of fire."

Sagora screwed up her face. "Will I have to train my horse to do this?"

"No. You'll use mine, for now. Geirador is supposed to have two almost identical mounts ready for you two to use for this illusion."

Sagora was scratching her head. "Why the illusion of a horse with hooves of fire?"

"I have the same question, Uncle. Why?" asked Nagora.

Dangor held up his hands. "Okay, lassies. All I can tell you for now is this: You two will take on the role of Edana, the

Dragon Warrior Princess, who comes to free the last dragon held captive deep inside the Isle of Smoke."

Sagora's jaw moved, but no words were coming out, so Nagora put her hand on her sister's shoulder. "I'll tell you what I know about the dragon and the Isle of Smoke later."

Dangor brought his hands together. "When I said 'illusion,' I not only meant the illusion of horses with hooves of fire. I meant this: Each of you will act as Edana and deliver the same messages at the same time, but in two different places."

He separated his hands, making them appear to jump to two different places.

"That way," he brought his hands back together, "when your appearances get reported to the authorities, they'll conclude that Edana was in two different places at the same time on the same night. I can't tell you more for now. Though, I can show you how these fire baskets will work to create the illusion that the horse Edana rides has burning hooves."

Nagora held up a finger. "So the burning hooves are because we'll be delivering our message at night. That would be something memorable and worth reporting."

Dangor pointed to her. "That's the idea, Nagora. Mount up."

As she put her foot in the stirrup, the left fire pole, which was pointing forward, swung out at an angle.

Dangor pointed. "See, Sagora, the yoke hangs just ahead of the saddle. Straps tie it around the chest and belly. A rope goes from the back end of the pole here, back through the ring at the bottom end of the hanging yoke and ties to the stirrup. Another rope goes from the middle of the pole here up to the ring near the top of the yoke. Same setup on the other side."

Sagora nodded.

Dangor pointed to her sister's foot. "Nagora's foot is relaxed in the stirrup. The weight of the fire basket on the end of the pole at the front holds the pole forward and along Storm's side. Push on your stirrup, Nagora."

She did.

"I see," said Sagora, "the pole swings the basket out to the side when she pushes forward. What goes in the basket?"

"Sheep's wool soaked in something Geirador concocted. I'll explain that another time. Get Kimmo and we'll saddle him up to see if you can set up the rig on him."

Sagora had her poles set up and working. Nagora helped her make a few minor adjustments to get them to work smoothly.

Just before they were to undo them, Tagnya came out into the corral.

Sagora saw her and said, "Look, Mum. We'll be practicing with these fire poles." They remounted and demonstrated their control of the poles.

Tagnya placed her hands on her hips and was nodding. "Looks good. Sagora, do you think you can find a place to practice tomorrow, away from prying eyes?"

Sagora nodded.

"Umma and I will be with Godomor for the next few days, so you'll be practicing with Dangor. Though, I want to see you in action at night on those horses.

"When you come in, we'll eat," said Tagnya.

Dangor clapped his hands once. "Good, lassies. Let's get these rigs put away. I'm hungry. We'll retie everything to the pack saddles, ready to set on the mules tomorrow."

...

After their meal, Tagnya came into the kitchen and made a show of putting on her blades and then threw a light brown woolen shawl over her shoulders. She had changed into a tunic the color of undyed wool with a keyhole neck and fitted sleeves that ended below her elbows.

Over her tunic, she wore a forest green linen apron that covered her bosom and fell just below her knees. "I'm an unlikely warrior dressed like this, but I know how much Godomor admires Geirador's work. These blades will give us something to talk about until the medicine knocks him out."

The word, *mihkopiscipowin,* "blood poison," came to mind, but she didn't dare speak it. Nagora would not be comfortable explaining how she knew. Would they even believe her? "Mum, good luck in this battle with whatever ails Godomor."

Tagnya smiled at her. "It's a battle we stand a chance of winning with the medicine Geirador sent. Oh! Nagora, I've put linen strips and a pot of salve on your cot. You might want to wear a bandana over your brand when you sleep."

"Thanks, Mum. That's a good idea, instead of tying my hands."

They heard a single deep bark from Aydan. Tagnya snapped her fingers. "That's Umma. I'll be back in a moment."

Tagnya returned with her medical scrip hanging from her shoulder and Umma on her other arm. "Umma, I want you to meet my daughter, Nagora, and her uncle, Dangor."

They rose to greet her. Umma's presence projected calm. Her every move was unhurried and made with assurance. Umma's grip on Nagora's hand was strong and warm. Perhaps because of her smile, framed in the red curls of hair on each side of her face, and how her blue eyes looked into hers, she trusted Umma completely. She must have an instant calming effect on the sick or injured she treats.

Dangor was obviously taken by this woman who was of Tagnya's age and build. Had another pebble just dropped into love's pond?

Her mother broke the spell. "Trust me. You'll have occasion to meet Umma again before we leave. We're off on urgent business. If I don't come home, don't worry. Umma is with me, and we'll be relieving each other as we care for and watch over Godomor."

"I am wish to meet you again, soon," said Umma, haltingly, before leaving with Tagnya.

Sagora looked over at her uncle. "Dangor, can you tell us the purpose of the nighttime appearances of the Dragon Warrior Princess?" His mind was truly elsewhere. "Uncle ... ?"

"Er ... yes, what, er ... ," he shook his head and placed his hands on the table and tilted his head. "What was your question, Sagora?"

Sagora smiled and repeated her question.

Dangor rubbed his eyes and took a deep breath before continuing. "Nagora, get your vest with the map on it."

Nagora had removed her vest and blades before supper and had left them in Sagora's room.

...

After Nagora returned with her blades on her back and set her vest on the table, Dangor started. "As I said earlier, whenever you appear, it will be at the same time, but in different places. We've planned six nighttime appearances, possibly more, if circumstances permit."

He rotated the vest to orient the map for them to see.

Sagora place a finger on the vest. "Nagora, why do you have a map on your vest?"

"I'll tell you all about it later, big sister. It's a long story."

For Sagora's benefit, Dangor pointed on the map where he and Nagora lived, the planned places for Edana's appearances, and the Isle of Smoke where Raganora held the dragon captive.

"Edana's nighttime appearance on a steed with flaming hooves at a given location and time to deliver a message was your mum's idea. Geirador and I figured out how to make it doable. Earlier today, I told Tagnya what we'd come up with—what she saw you demonstrate a while ago. She seems satisfied, but I can understand why she wants to see you work the fire poles at night before being completely satisfied.

"What we hope to do with the appearances of the Dragon Warrior Princess is to make real the legend of Edana coming to free the dragon. Since you'll both be identical in your Dragon Warrior Princess garb, weapons, shields, and the horses you ride, our hope is the reports of sighting you will be identical in those respects and in time of appearance, but not in place."

Dangor used his two pointer fingers to point to two different places at once on the map.

"As word spreads, it will become known that Edana has a magical power that allows her to be in two places at once. And every time she appears, she has the same message: 'All to the Isle of Smoke to free the dragon. Join me there on the Feast of Maxxa.'

Sagora held up her hand in the dragon chord salute. "That means the stories we've heard about Edana and what she did are true? You did all those things? I mean the promise she made—that she'd return, and that dragons would fly again."

"Sagora, it's a long story. I said Edana would return and that dragons would fly again over Windhaven. In doing so, I became identified as Edana. You'd have to tell me whatever else you heard about Edana's exploits because so many stories about her have popped up since then, I can't keep track of them. Later, when I explain about the map on my vest, I'll tell you what really happened."

Dangor held up a finger. "Sagora, we've built our plans on Edana's promises, the two you've just mentioned."

He gave Nagora a quick glance.

"To help set the stage for your appearances, peddlers and people traveling throughout the land, and who are loyal to our cause, have already begun spreading rumors about Edana's appearance on a horse with flaming hooves. They've been inquiring, in the places they visit, whether Edana has appeared at the village yet."

Nagora reached over and put a finger on the Isle of Smoke. "So if I understand, the reason of these appearances at night is to get people to go to the plain opposite the Isle of Smoke to help, or at least watch, Edana free the dragon on the Feast of Maxxa? That's the longest day of summer, isn't it?"

Dangor nodded. "Aye, that is our hope. We feel we are giving enough time for this message to spread throughout the land."

Sagora wore a frown on her face. "Will we actually do that? Free the dragon?"

Dangor placed a hand on Sagora's. "No. Because all the details of the plan have yet to be finalized. All I can tell you for now is that you will be creating a diversion for those who will free the dragon."

Sagora swallowed. "Still, in a way it's frightening just to think about what we'll be doing. I never imagined I'd be involved in something like this."

Dangor patted her hand. "I understand you, Sagora. You won't be on your own to do this. You'll be surrounded by warriors to protect you. Just take it one day at a time from now on."

Dangor folded the vest and pushed it over to Nagora.

She stood up and pulled her vest from the table. "I'm going out."

Aydan was up and stretching.

Sagora looked up at her. "Do you want me to go with you?"

She had wanted some time alone. She took a deep breath. "Sure."


Nagora and Aydan were already out the back door and well past the corral, walking on the path along the cliff wall in the early twilight, when Sagora caught up to them. She made no sign to acknowledge her sister's presence. Sagora kept just behind her.

She must be waiting for me to say something. "Does this path lead up to the top of the cliff?"

"It does, and at the top of the cliff, the path slopes down on the other side. Nagora, can I ask you a question?"

"Sure."

"Are you afraid of what we'll be doing?"

"No. I'm not afraid. I think I've already tasted fear greater than I could've ever imagined, up to now. I only fear being caught off guard again."

Sagora took Nagora to a stone ledge off the cliff path they had climbed. They sat with their backs against the cliff, giving them a view of the bay. Aydan lay at their feet.

Sagora gently tapped Nagora's knee. "Do you want to tell me about it? About what happened to you? About what Uncle told Mum?"

She told Sagora the version of her escape from the sea cave her uncle would have told her mother. That way, she kept many details to herself, as well as her sworn oath to the girls in the dungeon. It was best to do so until she could work out what information she could trust Sagora with and what she trusted herself to believe after Raynhard had rescued her.

She told Sagora about her hundred day banishment, visiting the smithies, and bringing back the chain. She told how she understood Edana came to be, but kept secret who Edana truly was. And she kept secret Moreena's gold dragon harp.

By the time they made it home, arm in arm, Sagora was still wiping away tears. It was dark, except for subdued light coming from the open windows and doors of the lodges visible from Tagnya's place. Nagora ordered Aydan home to Lars.

Inside, Dangor sat in front of the fire in the big kitchen. They said good night to him and went to Sagora's room.

"Are you still crying? Don't cry for me, Sagora."

"I'm not crying for you. I'm crying for what happened to you. I came so close to losing you."

Nagora held Sagora to her and waited for her to stop crying. When she did, Nagora handed her the pot of salve. "Put some on my brand. Then I'll tie on this bandana."

"Let me wash my hands first."

Sagora had regained her composure, but her eyes were still red, even in the light of the candle lantern. "Your touch is so gentle, Sagnuska. Thank you for caring for me."

Nagora tied on the bandana and kissed her sister's forehead. "Sleep well, big sister."

As she lay on her cot, she held the whistle Lars had given her in one hand and her amulet in the other. She brought the amulet to her lips as she looked out the window at the stars.

Mum, I used to speak to you as if you were up there with the stars. Now I have you. I can hardly believe it. It still feels like a dream to me.

Nagora closed her eyes and fell asleep to the sound of her sister's quiet weeping.

# Mother Dragon
## *Okâwîmâw Paskwaskisiw*

A cold, wet wind buffeted Nagora as she faced into it with her blade drawn. She had spread salve on her brand and wore a linen bandana over it. It had been days since she had practiced her ritual morning exercises, and today she vowed to return to them as Edana. She had left in the dim, early morning light with her rain cape.

Aydan had caught up with Nagora on the trail up to the cliff. Now he sat next to her rolled up cape. He was her silent guardian, observer of her hundred repeated and deliberate poses, attacking and fending off an invisible enemy.

When Sagora found her at the top of the cliff, Nagora was still in motion and covered in as much sweat as rain.

She paid no heed to her sister's arrival, content to reach for the goal she had set for herself this morning.

Sagora waited.

When Nagora finished wiping her blade and returning it to her sheath, Sagora spoke. "What are you doing? I was worried. Although Uncle guessed you were here."

"I'm trying to make myself whole again." She went over to Aydan, scratched his big red head, kissed him on the nose, and let him lick her chin. She picked up her cape and tucked it under her arm. "Have you eaten yet?"

"No, I wanted to find you." Her sister's face showed concern.

"I can take care of myself." Nagora stood, looking into the sky and letting the rain strike her face. "Doesn't look like we'll practice with the fire poles today. No fear, Uncle will have plenty of work for us inside. Lead the way. I'm right behind you."

They returned in silence.

At the back of Tagnya's lodge near the corral trough, Nagora stripped off her wet clothes and poured a bucket of water from the trough over her head. She gave her sweat and rain soaked clothes a quick rinse in the bucket and hung them under the roof overhang. Then she made her way into the saddle room where she had left a linen towel to dry herself off, a fresh change of clothes, and the pot of salve.

Nagora had predicted true. After a hot breakfast, the twins found themselves sitting at the table in the saddle room with a pile of more than a hundred arrows their uncle had set out for them to check. There would be six hundred in all, gifts destined to the volunteer archers. Dangor had told Nagora before they left for the Land of Skulls, "Archers always appreciate a gift of arrows. Besides, if we go into battle, ten extra arrows per archer just might make the difference. We've got a huge stockpile of fire arrows waiting for them when they come back with us."

Nagora showed Sagora how to examine the notches and the feathers. "Apply pressure with your thumb and finger to each side of the notch to make sure it's not cracked.

"Then stroke each feather with your thumb, applying light pressure first on one side and then the other. The feathers should spring back into shape.

"Between the feathers under the fine coat of hardened spruce gum, you can see the thread whippings that hold the split quills to the arrow shaft. Check that they're intact and the gum has not chipped off. Can you do that, Sagora?"

"Sure."

"Good. I'll check the shafts for straightness and the attachment of the arrowheads." Nagora did so before giving each point at least one pass on a whetstone to make sure both edges were sharp. They worked their way through the pile in silence.

Sagora set down the arrow she had just inspected and watched Nagora pick it up. "Little sister, you're not very talkative."

Without stopping to run the arrowhead across the whetstone, Nagora said, "Sorry about that. Old habits don't change overnight. I'm used to working alone or with Uncle. We can often go the whole day without speaking. It's no wonder I've earned nicknames from trainees in Cairnmase."

"Oh? What do they call you?"

"Loner, Stone, to name two." She stopped to look to Sagora.

"Well, I will not let you be a stone. We're sisters. You aren't alone and we have a lot to catch up on. Surely you must have questions."

Nagora's eyes roamed her sister's face. "I've thought about this situation a lot, wondering what questions would come to mind. What we would talk about. I wondered if questions would just come to mind. I guess I'll have to work at asking some.

"What do you know about dragons?"

Sagora looked surprised. "What do you want to know?"

"Whatever you know. Dragons are a forbidden topic back home, remember?"

Nagora almost wanted to retract that sentence. It was too late. She had said the words "back home." Those two words made her wonder where home was for her. Here at her mother's was not the image that came into her mind when she said the word "home."

Sagora touched her chin. "Well, I've just recently learned about the dragon at the Isle of Smoke, like you. I'm not sure what more I could tell you.

"Oh! There is one story I heard Mum tell Umma one stormy winter night by the fire in the kitchen. We'd set up our cots there because it was so cold. Mum wouldn't let Umma walk home in the storm with her young infant. Umma's daughter and infant son were in a cot next to mine. Mum thought we were asleep. Umma's kids were, but not me.

"I wish I could tell it the way Mum did that night."

Sagora paused to take another arrow. "Anyway, in the far past dragons would settle in places where people had not yet set foot. They lived and congregated in great numbers. They built nesting circles made of huge stone pillars planted like posts in circles, with other big pieces placed on the tops of the uprights to create a ring around which they would perch at nesting time.

"The dragons would come together at such rings to lay their eggs. Inside the big circles, there were other smaller circles of stone. The eggs with babies would be placed in the center circle and the ones without babies outside that circle."

Sagora's last statement made Nagora frown. "How would they know the difference?" This was more information than what she had learned from Grim last year in the Stone Stander council room.

"That's where the story gets interesting. Apparently, the egg shells of the ones without babies are blue with red veins on them. The ones with babies are also blue with red veins, but they also have veins of gold. Not just the color of gold, but of actual gold."

Nagora stared wide eyed at Sagora. "Gold? Real gold? Like the gold used to make gold coins?"

Sagora nodded. "Aye, according to the story."

"So what happens to the gold once the baby dragons hatch from their eggs?"

Her sister set the arrow on the table. "That's the thing. The closer the eggs get to hatch, the warmer and the hotter they become. Hot enough that the gold melts and disappears into the ground. Where the gold veins were around the eggs is where the cracks in the shells form, and the young dragons burst forth in a cloud of steam."

Nagora nodded and held up a finger. "I can see where this story is leading. Over time, people discovered the dragons and learned about the gold in the dragon egg shells. They began to hunt the dragons to get to the eggs before they hatched so they could take the gold."

Could that be the reason Raganora had the dragons hunted?

"That's right. According to the story, the hunters had tools, much like the fire baskets, but bigger, in which they placed the eggs to heat them over a fire so as to melt the gold, contain it, and capture the baby dragons at the same time, most often not completely formed.

"In the story, it was the hunters who ate baby dragons and drank their blood because they experienced unimaginable benefits when bedding their partners."

Nagora held up the tip of the arrow she had just checked. "So that's two good reasons to hunt the dragons. Though, the desire to scratch the itch between their legs blinded them to the possibility of learning how to work with the dragons to harvest the gold in some other ways."

"Aye, that's so. There are people that worked with the dragons, have always worked with them, and even helped them build their nesting circles. They are the ones who brought the dragons back to the Land of the Danu, to find peace and protection."

I know the Stone Standers built some of the dragon rings in the Land of the Danu. "So who were those people? You did say they 'brought the dragons back?'"

Sagora held up a finger. "I'll get to that. The people first. This is where you're going to laugh and say 'Okay, this is all stuff of legend.' For all I know it could be, or it's just a good tale invented by Mum to engage Umma on that winter night by the fire."

"So?"

Sagora looked her in the eye. "The Little People."

Could the Little People also be Stone Standers? "Okay. Sure. Why not?"

Sagora pointed at her. "You know about the Little People?"

"Sure."

"You've seen them?"

Nagora shrugged. "No. Geirador made the steel of my blade with a skystone he got from the Little People. If he says so, I believe him. How can I prove him wrong? Though, he has a big grin on his face whenever he mentions the Little People."

Sagora shook her head. "And you still believe him? Like a child?"

Nagora waved away her question. "What happens to the eggs without babies?"

"They're the first food of the hatchling dragons."

"Who are the people that let the Little People bring the dragons back to the Land of the Danu and why did the dragons leave in the first place?"

Sagora waved an arrow at her. "For someone who doesn't talk, you ask a lot of questions."

"I'm just asking what comes to mind."

Sagora touched the pointer finger of one hand to the palm of her other. "In the story, they're known as The People. They are the original people who were here from the very beginning."

"You say here. Do you mean in the Land of Skulls and the Land of the Danu?"

Sagora spread her arms apart. "I mean both because in the story, in the beginning, The People lived in what they called

The Land, one big island country made up of the Land of Skulls and the Land of the Danu today."

Again she touched her palm with her finger. "The story tells that the dragons were also originally from The Land, as were the Little People. They spoke the same language as The People, and that is the language spoken by the dragons as well."

Those strange words I hear and understand? "Why would the dragons have left in the first place?"

Still pointing to her palm, Sagora answered, "Winter came to The Land for a longer stay and covered it with snow and ice all year long. For many years, there was only winter. All the animals became white to survive, but the Little People left with the dragons. The snow was too deep for the Little People and the winter too cold for the dragons. The People and most animals, however, had adapted and survived in that long winter."

Sagora lifted another arrow from the pile. "Something happened to make winter leave. Before that happened, the great white owl and the great white bear led The People away over the snow and ice bridges to settle in a land far away."

Sagora waved the arrow once. "However, the sick, the old, and the very young stayed behind because they lacked the strength for that great journey. Though, the young were able to survive here and grow as The People again, as winter left. Then when winter left, the Little People and the dragons were welcomed back."

Nagora frowned. "The dragons spoke the same language as The People?"

"Aye. I remember Umma telling Mum she'd heard of elders here who speak a very different language, apparently the language of the first people, The People. They would be descendants of those people."

Nagora scratched her cheek. "Or of the Little People?"

Sagora smiled and stuck her tongue out a little bit. "There are all kinds of stories about the Little People here. Just like there must be in the Land of the Danu. Stories like the one Geirador told about the skystone. Here, just about everyone knows someone who knows someone who's seen them or captured one of them and has had a trick played on them."

Nagora pointed an arrow at her sister. "You think we could call on them to help with these arrows?"

Sagora laughed. "Now that would be something if we could. But would Uncle believe us?"

For the first time that day, she enjoyed her sister's presence. To see her mirror image smile and laugh made her happy. *How long has it been since I've laughed?* For a moment, she had nothing to worry about. She wanted it to last, but the arrow in her hand pointed to what was at the back of her mind.


In the afternoon, Dangor left with Sagora and a mule to deliver the weapon molds and templates to the blacksmith in Skull Bay. Sagora would translate to make sure the smiths understood the recipes and instructions.

The rain kept pouring as Nagora tended to the animals in Tagnya's crowded stable. The stable floor would become flooded if the rain kept up at that rate. She found a shovel to dig and scrape a shallow drainage ditch from the corral to the roadside ditch that was already filling with running water.

...

By the third day of rain the twins had checked all the arrows and tied them into bundles of ten.

They had checked and sharpened all their personal weapons and made them weather-ready with oils and waxes.

They had also inspected and prepped their saddles.

Then they had unpacked and repacked their personal scrips and saddlebags, keeping the essentials for their trip to the Land of the Danu.

Dangor had kept the sisters busy.

This day was no different, though most of it would be dedicated to preparing home-cooked fare to enjoy before they would leave. Being in the warm kitchen and working near the fire on this cold rainy day suited Nagora and, from what she could tell, Sagora as well. Signs of the downpour coming to an end didn't hold much promise. "I'll believe it when I see a change in the wind and you two stop battling with those spoons," Dangor told them.

They ignored him as they faced off across the table from one another, each armed with a long wooden spoon and a pot lid.

At the end of the afternoon, Aydan announced Tagnya's arrival with a happy bark. The rain had let up a short time before, and patches of sky appeared with the freshening wind. Tagnya looked tired, but happy as she removed her shawl and blades and pulled back her damp hair. "Umma and Gabe are with Godomor. He awoke at noon today. No more fever. He was hungry. We started to feed him solid foods with the honey water and dulse. He is weak, but if his appetite is an indication, he'll regain his strength soon. He lost even more weight these past days, but he'll start to gain some."

Sagora was at Tagnya's side. "We're happy for Godomor. You seem to have won the battle."

Tagnya put an arm around her waist and the other around Nagora's. "I hope so.

"What have you girls been up to?"

Nagora let her big sister list all the tasks Dangor had them work on, right up to and including what they had cooked. "If you're hungry, there's a good meal waiting for you."

"It smells delicious, and I'm hungry. Let me wash up. Then we'll eat."

After their meal, Sagora wanted to know the details of Godomor's treatment. Tagnya filled her in on how they had fought to control his fever and his thirst. "He was delirious much of the time and he often asked for Nagora. We figured it was because of your recent arrival. We considered sending for you, but decided against it since he wasn't conscious. Perhaps had he been agitated, hearing your voice might have helped calm him."

Why would he ask for me? "I could go visit him if you think that would help."

Tagnya gave her a smile. "It can't hurt. Perhaps tomorrow when we return from practicing with the fire poles. He'll have rested and regained some strength by then."

"I'll do that."

Tagnya rubbed the back of her neck. "I don't know about you people, but I'll be early to bed. I'm tired and a good night's sleep will do me good. Umma will stop by tomorrow morning at first light to report if all is well. If so, I'll ride out with you tomorrow. It'll be a good change." Tagnya stood. "Excuse me. I have a little bit of work to do before I go to bed." She left the kitchen.

After helping clean up in the kitchen, Nagora went to peek into the room where her mother was at work at her table putting notes to bound vellum pages.

Is she recording their treatment of Godomor?

Nagora watched in silence, studying her profile and her hands, willing herself to sear those images of Tagnya into her mind in that place where pictures of one's mother should always be. She waited until Tagnya closed the book and stood to place it on the shelf. Then Nagora stepped into the room.

"Nagora."

"Mum, will you hold me?"

Tagnya opened her arms and took her close.

Nagora held her tight, wanting to feel her mother's heartbeat to see if her own heart remembered it. She breathed in the smell of her mother's skin and the scent of her mother's hair on her neck, searching for the distant memory of those odors. From the lake of tears inside her, which she thought was empty, a flood came. She cried and Tagnya kept her arms around her until they both stopped crying.

# Practice
## *Sîsawewin*

The next morning, the twins returned from the cliff, with Aydan trailing behind Nagora. They each carried a spear. The sun had just risen over the horizon.

After eating and packing a lunch, they brought their saddles and those of their mother and uncle to the corral and saddled the horses.

Nagora held Storm's bridle and rubbed his nose. "*Tastapiw sohkapiskaw kaskitewastim*, today I'm happy we ride again. It's been four days."

Dangor joined them and helped set the pack saddle onto one of the mules. It held all they would need for the practices.

When Tagnya arrived in the corral, she looked to the sky. "This day will do us some good."

"I take it Godomor is doing well?" said Sagora.

"According to Umma, he is. She said when she left he was sitting at his table waiting for his morning meal, complaining it wasn't coming fast enough for his starvation stricken stomach. That's a very good sign. Umma will go back to check on him later today."

They mounted and left the corral. Nagora and Sagora took the lead. Aydan was just behind them. Tagnya and Dangor followed. The four riders and their pack mule got curious looks from the few that watched them ride by in silence on their way up to the wall.

The skull-covered gates opened before them, and the guards waved them through.

Sagora led them to a spot that was well away from the village wall and out of sight. They were in a hilly area covered in grass. She brought them over the rise of one of these hills to its gravel-covered side. It had a slight incline, and coarse gravel covered the ground for about eight hundred paces. At the bottom, the gravel became finer until it turned to sand.

The heavy rain of the previous days had left a sizable pond at the bottom, though now the ground had absorbed most of the water, leaving a muddied sand deposit.

Partway down the incline they stopped. The girls set up the yokes and fire poles under the watchful eyes of Dangor, Tagnya, and Aydan.

When the poles were in place and functioning to Dangor's satisfaction, he took out two leather-covered gourds. "These contain the combustible. I have five different-sized spigots for each gourd. We'll start with the middle-sized one. From there, we'll decide if we should use one with a bigger or smaller opening.

"The insides of the gourds are lined with a goat's stomach tied off at one end and tied to a wooden tube at the other. The spigot is placed inside the tube. It's a tight fit. The gourd's attached lanyard is tied around the neck of the spigot to add to the tightness of its fit in the tube and to keep it in place."

Dangor's fingers pointed to each item he described.

"Now lassies, untie the neck lanyards on the gourds and replace the spigots with these middle-sized ones. I suggest this be a two-person operation so as to avoid spilling any of the combustible. The two loops on each side of the gourd's seam help make it easier for you to remove or insert the spigot into the gourd's neck tube, and to hold the gourd when filling it.

"The small, wooden fid dangling there is to help you untie or pull tight the hitches around the gourd's neck."

Nagora worked the fid into the knots to loosen them. "Uncle, did you come up with this idea for the gourd?"

"No. The idea was your mum's. I designed the gourd for this purpose."

Tagnya had been watching. "We're lucky to have Dangor and Geirador build the things I dream up. He and Geirador have made my wildest ideas take shape."

Nagora looked over to Tagnya. "How'd you get the idea for Edana's appearances?"

"Soon after hearing about Edana, it came to me in a dream, like many good ideas. Though, it remains to be seen if it truly is a good one."

There has to be more to it than that. "All because you've been thinking of ways to free the dragon?"

Tagnya paused and looked across the valley. "Aye, all these years of planning, and now conditions seem right. If all goes well, we'll free the dragon and Raynhard will take back his crown and set things right in the land. At least that's my dream, my hope."

Mum hasn't seen the situation in the land with her own two eyes. Lots of work to be done.

Sagora nudged her sister's arm with her elbow. "From the way Nagora tells it, she wants to have that prince by his balls and make him pay for all his evil actions against those young women he holds in his fortress."

Tagnya's face grew somber. "And I want to make him pay for what he did to Nagora. Whether it be you or me or someone else who makes him pay, I too am with you, Nagora, in that desire. There will be justice."

Not soon enough. If I can get to him, he'll pay.

Nagora pulled the hitch knot tighter with the fid and clenched her teeth to hold her anger in.

They completed the spigot switch and attached the gourds to the poles. All that would be necessary was for someone to turn open the spigots so the combustible could spill onto the ground.

Sagora would go first.

Tagnya marked the starting line and, leading her horse, walked down the gravel incline one hundred strides to mark a circle with a spear like the one Sagora carried.

Then Tagnya mounted her horse and rode down the rest of the incline and up to the top of the next hill, where she turned in a slow circle. She was obviously surveying the horizon for any unwanted onlookers. She rode back down halfway, dismounted, sat on the ground, and waved. It was the agreed signal for the trial to begin.

Nagora and Dangor opened the spigots, and then Sagora trotted down the incline to the circle Tagnya had marked in the gravel.

That's when the problems started.

"Stop. Come back, Sagora," yelled Dangor.

Nagora touched his arm. "What's wrong, Uncle?"

"Hardly any combustible came out. You did replace the number one spigot?"

"I did, with the number three. I'm sure Sagora did too."

"We'll try bigger ones."

They were on their third try. The spigots that controlled the flow of the combustible did not work. Dangor waved Tagnya over to them.

"There goes one of my bright ideas," Tagnya said when she arrived.

Dangor waved one hand and scratched at his beard with the other. "They worked fine when I practiced with Geirador and Paruline. Bring the gourds and spigots here. I'll check them."

He removed the spigots. It turned out the stomach linings had been folding over onto the neck tube hole preventing the smooth flow of combustible. The stomach linings needed to be pulled out further from the gourds and re-tied at their necks. He instructed the twins on how to fix the gourds and watched them do it. "You'll have to check how well they pour before each appearance. Just to be safe. Now you know how to fix the problem."

Tagnya returned to her observation spot.

Sagora rode down the incline, turned in the circle with Kimmo and went back up to the starting point. Nagora and Dangor closed the spigots, removed the gourds, and installed the fire baskets on the poles.

Dangor had two smaller baskets with attached handles. He motioned Nagora to come next to him and take hers. He poured combustible into these small ones. Then he took out his flint and, with his dagger, he struck sparks to light the two Nagora held. He put away his flint and dagger, and then took one of the lit baskets from Nagora.

He patted his horse. "Easy, Kimmo. Remember. We practiced this with Geirador. Be careful, Nagora. He's a bit nervous. Sagora, stay calm."

They took their positions to the left and right of Sagora. "Give us the signal, Sagora, and we'll light your fire baskets, and then we'll set fire to the combustible on the ground," said Dangor.

"Okay," said Sagora. "On three, I'll raise my spear and you'll light the fires. One, two, three," Sagora raised her spear. They touched their fire baskets to hers and then to the wet combustible on the ground.

Sagora had already headed down the incline when the flames on the ground caught up with her. She moved along with them. In the circle she reared her steed and pushed back on the poles so they pivoted out to Kimmo's sides. When her horse's hooves came back down, she thrust her spear into the ground, relaxed her push on the poles, and then rode Kimmo back up the incline to the starting point, where Nagora and Dangor waited with capping thongs to put out and remove the fire baskets from the poles.

Tagnya remounted and rode over to them. "That is impressive. I have to see that in the dark. The spigots spread the right amount of combustible along the ground. Now they work fine. The flames all died out just as Sagora finished planting her spear. It would be ideal if we could get the flames in the fire baskets to die out at the same time as the rider returns from the circle. We have to figure out the right amount of combustible to use."

Dangor nodded. "That shouldn't be a problem. Do we come back here tonight?"

Tagnya patted him on the back. "We have a good wait until darkness. It won't have to be pitch black."

She turned to the girls. "Sagora, you know of an isolated beach on the coast not far from here. I bet you girls would like a swim, and perhaps we can catch a fish to cook on an open fire. What say you, lassies?"

They both smiled and nodded.

They removed the poles and yokes and helped Dangor tie them to the pack saddle along with the gourds and fire baskets.

When they finished, Sagora led them to the coast. She made a slight detour to a high hill that overlooked the sea. From there, she pointed down to the valley floor where a small stream wound its way down to a small inlet beach.

Did she want us to see the view? It's beautiful.

Sagora turned in her saddle to look back. "Uncle, the water in the stream is sweet. The horses'll be able to drink down near the beach. It comes from an underground spring. If you follow the stream back to its source, you'll find a large plot of reed grass in the softer ground."

Sagora pointed. "You see over there, Nagora?"

It had to be the circular patch, about ten strides across, further up on the hillside.

"It's the only spot like this around here. An ideal place to dig a well. Although I don't know if anyone would want to settle in this rather barren part of the land. As you can see, the land around here is rocky, especially on the other side of the valley. Not much grows in the way of grasses over there on that hill."

Nagora let her eyes roam over it. Slate rocks covered the hill as if some immense force had spread them about. "Compared to this side of the valley, the other side looks like a mess of scattered slate."

"You're right, little sister. Legend has it that a giant from the sea crawled up onto the land over there looking for a drink of fresh water. He pulled on that side of the valley to reveal the stream from which he drank, but in the process he flattened and destroyed whatever was over there.

"Another version of that legend tells that a witch lived there and had refused to allow the giant to drink from her well. Because of that, he destroyed her, her dwelling, and her well."

The words, *âkawâyihk wayipiyaw*, slipped into her mind, "hidden water hole." For some strange reason, that hill attracted her. Another secret she would keep for herself. Another mystery she would have to work out on her own. The answer was so close. Yet, did she want to believe it? What proof did she have that a water hole lay hidden on that hill?

"Have you ever been over there, Sagora?"

"No, I think it would be too risky to explore on horseback, even on foot. Imagine walking through that rubble."

...

Tagnya dismounted. "I want to look out to sea." She led Scout to a big, flat stone. Dangor followed her and sat next to her. They looked comfortable.

"Come on, little sister." Sagora helped her down from Storm, took her arm in hers, and led Nagora to another big stone about a hundred paces away. "We can sit here. Mum loves to look out at the sea. She doesn't do it often, but when she does, she does so for as long as she can. You do know that she loves the sea, don't you?"

"Aye. From what Uncle has told, she must. She's surely thinking of Da right now, and in her mind she's probably re-living one of those moments at sea with him."

"Could be. Have you ever sailed on the sea, Nagora?"

Strange, since I've been here, they haven't brought up Da yet. Do they no longer think of him, or are they keeping something from me? Do they know something I don't?

"No. But I've played in curraghs often, the ones Uncle and I make. I test them for leaks."

They sat in silence, gazing far out at sea. Nagora let her own questions drift away. She turned her face into the sea breeze and the sunshine like when taking a long walk on her beach.

Tagnya and Dangor approached. "Shall we go down to the beach, lassies?"

"Aye, Mum." Nagora savored the word "Mum," as it became more and more familiar and part of her. The word, "Mum," and the face of this woman she called "Mum" melted together in her mind and in her heart, filling the void.

Tagnya took Nagora in her arms and held her close as she gazed out to sea and then back into her eyes. Does she sense how I feel? Her mother's tears and her own pooled to fill their eyes, but they did not turn into the sobs of the night before.

"Sagora, you go on ahead with Dangor. Nagora and I will walk down."

Sagora took their mounts. She and Dangor headed down to the beach.

With an arm around her mother's waist, Nagora was happy as they walked down the grassy slope. Aydan was just a step behind them. They stopped.

Tagnya held her close. "Nagora, my daughter, I'm so sorry I abandoned you, and you had to live a lie all these years. I should've returned with both of you to take a chance at keeping you both together."

Nagora rested her cheek against Tagnya's. "It's okay. It was Da's wish too. He wanted your baby to survive. You didn't know you were carrying two. You didn't know the laws here. You did what you had to do. I didn't know I was living a lie. Now I have you, and a sister. A double gift. We have to look ahead from now on."

When they arrived at the beach, the horses were drinking at the stream and grazing on the marram grass that grew alongside it, above the beach's high water mark.

Sagora and Dangor were already hunting for flounder along the beach. They were up to their knees in the water, Dangor with the Edana spear and Sagora with her bow and arrow. They were at opposite sides of the cove's beach and working their way toward each other, with their weapons ready and their eyes fixed on the sandy bottom.

Nagora picked up a piece of dried dulse and bit off a little. The last time she had tasted it was in the soup Raynhard had made for her. Only now did she connect the charcoal heart on the egg to Raynhard.

"How did you and Da fall in love?"

Tagnya's smile was wistful. "Yogari and I were destined for each other. From the moment we met, it was as if we'd always known each other. We just fell into each other's arms. He was the man for me and I was the woman for him." She looked at Nagora. "Didn't Dangor tell you how we met?"

"No."

"Aiiiee!"


It was Sagora. She was holding her arrow by its feathers, trying to keep what she had shot from wiggling away. Dangor joined her with the spear to put an end to the wiggling. Together they lifted the flounder out of the water. Her uncle had one hand on the fish's tail and the other near the spear's tip while Sagora held both sides of the arrow that had pierced the fish

"Our meal!" yelled Sagora.

"A fish! Claimed by Edana's arrow!" called Dangor.

"Good shot!" Nagora yelled back as she and Tagnya went to see the fish.


Tagnya reached for Sagora's arrow. "A feast's worth with this one. Here, let me take it. You and Nagora go for a swim. Dangor and I will prepare to cook it. We'll call you when we put it on the fire."

The twins ran down the beach a ways to a pile of boulders and driftwood. Aydan followed at their heels. They stripped off their weapons and clothes, and in no time were swimming and playing in the gentle waves.

After a meal of succulent flounder, the four of them left the beach and made their way back up the valley as the sun started its descent in the sky.

Just before twilight, they arrived at their practice spot and set up the fire poles on Nagora's saddle. This time, they put half as much combustible in the fire baskets. After the practice, Tagnya rejoined them. "I couldn't ask for better. Whoever sees this at night will be impressed and frightened. Nagora, I like how loud you yelled Edana's message. You took your time and it was clear."

"That's because when Sagora did it this afternoon she was first, and I figured that if I were hearing it for the first time, I'd be more likely to report it if I'd heard it clearly. That's why I yelled louder and slower."

Sagora patted her on the back. "I like the way you did it. It was clear and it was more like a command. Also because you were a little slower, the fire baskets went out at the right time as you rode off into the darkness."

Pleased with their day's work, they packed up. Sagora led them back to Skull Bay.

Which star will guide us back to Skull Bay, Storm?

Sagora said, "Home, Brith."

You could do that too, Storm.

Sagora loosened her grip on the reins as Brith set an easy pace.

Aydan followed along behind them.

They rode back in silence. Are we all lost in our own thoughts?

Nagora's eyes and ears searched the surrounding darkness. When she gazed at the stars, she said the word "Mum." Tagnya's face appeared there among them. When she said the word "Da", her uncle's face appeared. Someday, Da, you'll sail home to me.

Once they arrived, Nagora sent Aydan home before helping the others unsaddle, unpack, groom, and feed the horses and mules.

They sat around the table lit by a lone candle. Tagnya prepared glasses of cider and a bowl of berries for them to eat before going to bed.

Since no one else mentioned it, Nagora did. "Who was the rider on the big dappled gray that followed us today?"

Sagora frowned. "What rider?"

Dangor spoke up. "He kept his distance. Didn't get too close. Tagged along all day. He must be hungry and filling his belly by now."

Tagnya looked at Sagora. "Who's the only one with a dappled gray in these parts?"

Sagora smiled and snapped her fingers. "Lars! Probably sent to keep an eye on us to make sure no harm would come to us, yet ordered to leave us to our business."

Nagora tapped Sagora's shoulder. "I thought it was him. Aydan picked up his scent and then ignored him."

Dangor raised an eyebrow. "Chances are he saw our practice with the fire poles tonight if he were in the right position. If I were him, I'd report to Gabe."

Tagnya didn't seem to be concerned. "If he does, I'll know soon enough."

"How come I didn't see him?" asked Sagora.

"Because, big sister, you weren't looking for him. You're familiar with these parts and feel safe here. Uncle has always taught me to be on the lookout and have a weather eye. We have a hand signal code. When I signaled I had spotted a rider, he signaled so had he and Mum and that we weren't to talk about it until back here."

"Nagora, you knew it was Lars. That's why you were so giddy when we came back from our swim. You knew he was watching us dance around the fire to dry off."

She gave Sagora her best imitation of a Lars grin and pose with her arms crossed and chest sticking out.

Sagora touched Tagnya's arm. "I hope you'll let me in on your signals. Are they like the ones we use when we travel from here to bring help or forage for plants?"

"Aye, they are, Sagora. There are only a few I've not taught you. Don't worry, you'll learn them soon. Besides, you were our guide today, focused on where you were taking us. We had your back." Tagnya patted her daughter's shoulder, and then turned to the others.

"What do you say we call it a day? We've accomplished much, and a good night's sleep will be welcome. Nagora, perhaps you can call on Godomor tomorrow morning."

"I will, Mum.

"Oh! You said I'd have to boil that big sea ear I found at the beach."

Tagnya pointed to the pot hanging in the fireplace. "You'll boil it in vinegar. Take a stiff brush to that shell first before putting it in the pot. After it's been boiled and has dried in the sun, it won't smell fishy. You said you were going to give it to Paruline as a gift?"

"Aye. Its iridescent colors are so beautiful and, with its seven holes, Pare'll be able to put it to good use in her kitchen like Sagora does with yours."

Tagnya smiled. "She'll be happy to have it to strain and serve vegetables. It makes rinsing berries so easy. Pour them in the shell. Immerse it in a pot of water. Twigs and leaves float to the surface. Skim those off. Lift the shell out. Water drains. Your berries are ready."

Sagora stood. "I'll take care of it for you tomorrow while you visit Godomor."

"Thanks. I left it outside, near the trough."

Tagnya put her arms around her daughters and walked them to their room.

# Story
## *Âcimowin*

The next morning after breakfast, Nagora set out for Gabe's place. Aydan walked at her side. As she approached, her wish came true. Lars was standing at his post. He watched her as she approached. What's he thinking? She waited for him to speak. Instead, he just stood there with his muscular arms crossed and his grin painted on his face. Today, he wore his hair in a single braid.

Maybe that's why his smile is so big. He's playing games with me.

"You must've been hungry by the time you made it back last night?"

"I thought I'd have to eat my horse to be able to walk home."

"I caught a glint from your sword hilt while swimming yesterday. Did you enjoy what you saw, Lars?"

"Kept me awake part of the night, Nagora." His grin grew even wider.

He's making me blush. "Were we in danger?"

That brought his grin back to normal. "Grumblings from Vorpinger's domain. Godomor and Gabe wanted me to keep an eye on you, just in case. We guarded your mum's lodge once you'd gone to bed, in the off chance an attacker made it past the wall."

"My uncle speculated as much at breakfast. Thank you, Lars."

"Just following orders." His wide grin was back.

Nagora took her time as she looked him up and down. She smiled her biggest smile as she let her eyes explore his face and settle on his eyes. "I'm glad to have seen you this morning, Lars." She held his gaze, winked, and caught him start to turn red. "I'm here to see King Godomor." She waited and then repeated the reason for her visit. His ears were almost crimson.

"Of course." He lost his grin and fumbled to knock on the door and open it to announce her arrival. He's a bashful little boy caught at his own game. I like that.

Gabe came to greet her as did Godomor who had been sitting by the fireplace. Gabe deferred to his father. Godomor held his arms open. "Nagora, I happy to see you. I glad you come. Gabe, I speak with Nagora. You busy somewhere, no?"

Gabe smiled at both of them. "Yes, Father, I have things to do elsewhere." He winked at Nagora. "Have Lars fetch me when you're done."

Godomor was up and walking without his staff to lean on. His beard and hair had been trimmed. He wasn't the feeble man she had met days before. His embrace was strong. "I'm so happy to see you, King Godomor. You are looking well and strong."

"Thanks to Tagnuska and Ummuska good care and medicine send by Geirador. I am young man again. I get more strong each day and very hungry. I eat many times in the day."

Gabe closed the door as he left.


Godomor took her hand. "*Ka Peyakot Mahihkan*, come sit with me by the fire. We will talk awhile." Godomor spoke all these words in that strange language she heard inside herself. That he called her Lone Wolf and spoke in that language surprised her. That she answered in that language did also, though, it seemed she had always spoken it.

"King Godomor. I will sit with you by the fire and we will talk awhile."

"Please, Lone Wolf, do not call me King Godomor. Call me *Ohtawimaw*, for I feel like a father to you because we speak the same tongue. If you call me 'Father,' I will call you *Mitanisimaw*."

"Father, I am honored you call me 'Daughter.' *Ohtawimaw*, please tell me how you know me as *Ka Peyakot Mahihkan*."

Godomor smiled as he showed her to a chair near the fireplace. "From your actions as Edana, Lone Wolf is the name that describes you best." That makes sense.

As he sat, his eyes as well were smiling. For some reason, she knew she must wait for him to speak, the way it must be. It was the way, the way of The People.

After long moments of looking into the fire, he brought his gaze back to her. "It is good to have you share my fire. Daughter, is there a story you wish me to tell by the fire?"

A story? Not a question, but a story? Nagora looked back into the fire for several moments before answering. The story she would ask for came to her.

"Father, tell me the story of what caused Winter to leave The Land."

He smiled back at her. He seemed pleased with her choice. Without losing his smile, he closed his eyes in thought. Was he watching it play out in his mind? "Daughter, you ask for a good story." His eyes opened. "I will tell it as my far-away great grandmother told it. The Land had been white for a long time, so long that all the animals in The Land were white. It was time for Winter to leave. How did Winter know that it was time to leave?"

She did not try to answer the question. It was the way. She waited.

"Winter knew because *Kisikawi-pisim* had given that task to *Miskinâhk*."

'Sun' gave the task to 'Turtle?'

Godomor raised a hand indicating the sun in the sky. "Sun had told Turtle when he was very young, before the long winter came, that when he would become very old and white and ready to die, it would be his task to remind Sun to ask Winter to leave. Sun had chosen Turtle because he was to be the last of his kind in The Land.

"All those long cold days of winter, Turtle lived in a hole at the bottom of Eagle's tree. He survived on scraps of the fish *Wâpikihew* had hunted in the sea. Crow, who lived on the ground below Eagle's tree, competed with Turtle for the fish scraps."

Turtle and Crow were lucky to have Eagle.

Godomor pulled his shirt collar closer around his neck and touched a finger to the side of his head. "All the long cold winter nights, Turtle tried to figure out how to remind Sun that it was time for Winter to leave. He realized he needed a bird strong enough to bring the message to Sun. Turtle knew he had what it took to give that bird the strength to fly to Sun.

"In the last days of his life, Turtle spoke to his friend, Eagle, of the task he had, and he asked Eagle if he would fly to Sun with the message." Godomor crossed his hands, palms up, hooked his thumbs together, and flapped his fingers like wings.

Nagora watched the bird fly.

"At first, Eagle did not think he had the strength to fly that far. Also there would be the risk of getting burnt by Sun's fire.

"Then Turtle explained how it would be possible. 'You must kill me so my flesh will not become frozen and uneatable. You must empty my shell of all my flesh. If you eat it all, you will have the strength to fly to Sun.'"

Godomor paused and drew his head back with eyes open wide. "'I cannot eat you, Turtle. You are my friend.'

'Eagle, all these years I have eaten scraps from your hunts because all my ponds and streams are frozen. Eat me before I die so you can fly somewhere you have never been and deliver an important message.'

'What if I burn up before I deliver the message?'"

Godomor made the motion of pulling a turtle shell over his head, then hooked a finger before each of his eyes. 'You will not because you will wear my shell on your head. Your beak will stick out where my head does now. You will see out of my leg holes. You will fill my shell with snow and ice to keep you from burning up.'

"Eagle considered Turtle's words. 'What is the message?'

'My shell is the message. Tell Sun that I send it as a gift. Sun will understand.'

'Turtle, my friend, I will do this for you, and to see Winter leave.'

'Sun will reward you.'

'I am not doing it for a reward. I am doing it for you, to help you, my old friend.'"

Godomor paused and raised a finger. "Now, all the while, Crow was hiding in the snow, listening to all of this. He told himself he was not going to miss out on this. There was a reward and he wanted part of it. He would watch and wait and follow Eagle, just as he always did to get the best scraps.

"When Turtle's time came, he called to Eagle, and Eagle did as promised." Again, Godomor made the motion of pulling a turtle shell over his head. "He put Turtle's shell over his head and filled it with snow and pieces of ice. It was heavy, but Eagle felt stronger than ever before. He spread his wings and flew toward Sun." Again, Godomor made the bird with his hands.

"Before long, Eagle heard *Kahkakow* behind him, complaining of the distance. Eagle ignored him." Godomor waved a hand over his shoulder in dismissal.

"Then he heard Crow complain of the increasing heat. Eagle continued to ignore him." Again, Godomor waved his hand.

"The melting snow and ice refreshed Eagle. Then Eagle felt Crow bite onto his tail." Godomor opened his eyes wide in surprise. "He tried to shake him off." Godomor shook his shoulders back and forth. "He threatened Crow, but in the end he ignored him, hoping the heat would burn Crow off."

Godomor cupped a hand next to his mouth. "Sun called out, 'Who comes my way?'"

Godomor cupped his other hand to the other side of his mouth. "Eagle answered, 'It is Eagle. I bring a gift from Turtle.'"

Godomor expanded his chest and made the come forward motion. "'Come closer,' Sun said. 'I will not harm you.'"

"Eagle flew closer. 'Sun, here is Turtle's gift, his shell.'" Godomor made the bird and brought his hands to the sides of his head.

"'I see. Turtle has not faltered in his duty. It is time. Winter will leave The Land. The People will decide what to do. I will reward Turtle. His brothers and sisters, wherever they be, will have shells with shapes and colors that will please all eyes. Eagle, as Turtle's messenger, I will reward you.'" Godomor pointed and made as if to look past someone. "'What is that on your tail?'

"At that moment Crow let go of Eagle's tail. 'It is I, Crow. I helped Eagle bring Turtle's message.'

"'Is that so, Eagle?'"

Godomor shook his head, no. "'Crow lies. He always follows me around for scraps. He surely wants part of the reward.'"

"'Well, if that is so, I will reward you, Crow. First, with my heat. Before you leave here there will not be a speck of white left on you. I will burn you black, and all your brothers and sisters as well, wherever they be. Second, with a song. From now on you and all your brothers and sisters will sing my nickname whenever you speak.'

"'Kaw. Kaw. Kaw,' was all Crow could manage, such was his dismay."

"'That will do, Crow. It will match your color and announce your arrival wherever you go.'

"'Eagle, for helping Turtle with his task, I give you and all your brothers and sisters, wherever they be, a beak of gold and talons of gold. In memory of Turtle's friendship with you, you may keep your head of white. Because Crow will continue to follow you around, I give you a tail of white to remind Crow of the color he once was. Return to The Land and let The People know that Winter will leave and return only once a year from now on. Eagle, you may decide to leave The Land to find other friends like Turtle, in some other land. It is your choice.'

"Eagle and Crow returned to The Land and when The People saw their new colors, they believed the message and made their choice." Godomor leaned back on his chair and looked at Nagora.

She looked back at him and smiled. "Father, the story you tell makes my heart happy. It is a good story to hear by the fire. I will remember it always. It is a precious gift. I will carry it in my heart."

Godomor stared into the fire for long moment before speaking. "What is on your mind, Daughter?"

"Are we speaking the tongue of the dragons?"

"Yes, we are. The dragons speak the tongue of The People."

"I am not one of The People. How is it, Father, I can speak the tongue of The People?"

"Daughter, you have been chosen, like Eagle was chosen."

One more piece of information revealed. What she hadn't dared believe, now she did. All the pieces pointed to it. Was it another secret kept from her? For what reason? Da, are you the Dragon Talker? Are you alive? I hope so. I will watch and wait to see how this plays out.

"Father, at times there are many voices that speak in me. They all speak of different paths. In those times, I do not know which voice to trust."

"Trust the one that speaks to your heart. It will be the one that speaks true. So must you speak, Daughter, from your heart, with truth, for truth is always the best path to follow."

"Father, you are wise. I will do my best to live by your words."

"Remember, Daughter, the best path is sometimes the most difficult to follow."

Nagora nodded and looked into the fire, searching among the embers below the flames, watching them blink from bright red to bright black, true to false, truth to lie, good to bad, do to don't, yes to no. They were the simple choices on the path, but the difficulty, at any moment, was in the choosing. Sometimes, the wrong choice could burn you. At other times, you had no say in the choice and you still got burned.

"Sometimes, Father, when the path is chosen for one, it is even more difficult to follow."

"It is the strong who get chosen, though they often do not know the strength they have. They find their strength on the path."

"Father, you give your daughter much to think upon. Someday, we will talk awhile by your fire once more. It will be my turn to tell a story of your choosing, and then we will talk of this again."

Godomor stood and held his arms open to her. "*Mitanisimaw*, today you have warmed my heart with your visit. May you find trust and strength on your path."

She stepped into Godomor's embrace. "Thank you, *Ohtawimaw*. I will carry your wisdom with me as I travel that path."

"*Ka Peyakot Mahihkan*, no matter what, you will always be welcome here."

Godomor's sincerity touched her heart and made her visit with him unique, a moment she, Lone Wolf, would only ever share with him.

Godomor walked Nagora to the door, opened it, and bid Lars to go fetch Gabe.

After Godomor had closed the door, Nagora stepped up to Lars, who was wearing his grand smile, looked him in the eye, and gave a quick look to the sky. As soon as his eyes followed, she gave him a quick jab in the stomach. His big arms unfolded. "I think you need a good night's sleep, getting caught off guard like that." She wagged her finger. "Come on, Aydan. Let's go. This man has duties to carry out if he can wake up."

She spun on her heel to leave and just as she did, Lars smacked her backside. "Sleep on that."

She skipped away laughing. Aydan yelped at her side, jumping and nipping at her arm.

# Preparation
## *Wawîyewin*

As Nagora entered Tagnya's kitchen, smiles from her mother, sister, and uncle greeted her.

"You're in a good mood. Did you see Lars, little sister?"

Nagora struck her Lars pose with matching grin.

Tagnya shook her head and Sagora smiled at her. "How's Godomor?" asked Tagnya.

"Mum, he's not the same man I met days ago. He's up, walking without his staff. His beard and hair have been trimmed. He says he's getting stronger. Feels like a young man again with an appetite to match. Your medicine has worked wonders."

Tagnya looked relieved. "I'm so glad to hear that. Was he happy to see you?"

"He was expecting me and pleased I stopped in to see him. I told him how well he looked. Then we had what I'd call a father-daughter kind of talk. It was good."

Tagnya was smiling. "I'm happy for both of you. That man has a good heart."

"I agree, Mum."

Tagnya pointed to Sagora and Dangor. "We've been discussing how Edana should dress for her appearances. Any suggestions?"

Nagora looked from her mother to Sagora and Dangor as she joined them at the table. "We'll be appearing at night. It could be cool or even cold. How about sheepskin vests, leggings, and boots? And our weapons, blades, bow and quiver. We could paint our faces. Though, given our short appearances at nightfall, I don't know how visible we'll be. Something simple. Distinctive, that can be easily remembered."

Sagora reached over to her. "I agree with you. Why bother wearing something different? The less we have to carry around with us, the better. We'll have enough dealing with the fire poles and stuff." She looked at Dangor.

He raised a finger. "You'll each have six flags and their spears. Maybe even more."

Sagora nodded, and then looked back at her sister. "How should we paint our faces?"

Nagora spread the four fingers of her right hand. "I want four red lines across my face like this." She closed her eyes and drew her fingers across her face, making clear where the lines would go—across her forehead; over her eyelids, from one cheek to the other across her nose; from below one ear to the other across her lips; and from one side of her jaw across her chin.

Dangor was staring at her. His nod was barely perceptible. Does he know Pug smeared my blood across my face?

Sagora looked to Tagnya. "Mum, can you make us some red paint?"

"Aye. I'll boil some beets, mix in some fat and honey and a bit of wax, and reduce it all to a pasty balm. I'll put it in small enough jars. There'll be one for each of you. Plenty for your needs. Unless you have another idea or another color?"

Sagora was nodding. "I like Nagora's idea. Four red stripes for us. Your Tiwaz will be healed by the time we make our first appearance. I could paint one on my forehead. You could paint over your scar. That way, we'd be identical."

"It'll be dark red, blood red," said Tagnya.

Nagora's promise to Pug surfaced. She clenched her jaw. "Perfect." My stripes will fuel the rage Edana carries in her heart. Her eyes caught her uncle's.

His nod was barely perceptible before he spoke. "Geirador will provide you with identical mounts. If I'm not mistaken, he's supposed to be working on something that will make them stand out."

Sagora smiled. "Sounds like everything will come together to make Edana stand out in people's minds. Those who see her will spread the word of her appearances."

Hmmm. She seems to have gained some confidence.

Aydan barked once, a low muffled bark at the knock on the door.


Sagora went to see who it was and came back with Gabe. "Look who I found." She placed one of Gabe's arms around her waist. "Says he's here on business." Then she frowned. "But I'm not his business today." She gave Gabe a quick hug and let go of him.

Tagnya gave him a warm smile. "Gabe, what brings you here?"

Gabe smiled and nodded to Tagnya. "Nagora had left Father before I returned, so I wasn't able to give her the message for you. Tagnyoriva, all the vassals have responded to your request for volunteers, except for Vorpinger, of course. We have no shortage of volunteers. In fact, the vassals want us to choose from the lists they've already tried to narrow down. That many warriors came forward."

Tagnya and Dangor were smiling.

"The three counselors seek a meeting today with you, Dangor, Father, and me, at our earliest convenience, to decide who'll make the final cut."

Tagnya's smile turned to worry. "Is your father up to this meeting?"

Gabe smiled and shook his head. "The only thing that'll keep him away is if there's no food on the table while we meet. I haven't seen him so well in over a year. The medicine you made with Geirador's ingredients and the good care you and Umma gave him have made him well again. Again, I thank you, Tagnuska."

Tagnya looked to Dangor, who nodded. "We're ready to meet now. We'll join you shortly. We meet at your place, I take it?"

"My place and, now, my father's." Gabe wore a smile.

"Tell your father and the counselors we're on our way."

"I will," said Gabe, and he left.

Sagora reached for Tagnya's arm. "Mum, anyone on those lists with knowledge of tending to wounds would be an asset. If our force ends up fighting, we'll need all the help we can get to deal with the wounded."

Tagnya bit the corner of her lower lip. "You're right, Sagora. I've been hoping we might get someone I've trained, someone with fighting skills."

"Like Mina or Vita," said Sagora.

"Exactly. I'd be happy with either one. They're archers, Dangor. They know how to make their arrows count.

"Sagora, while we're gone, how about you put together what we might need in our own medical scrips and set aside items for a third bag."

"I'll do that. Nagora will help."

Nagora nodded in agreement.

Tagnya held up the fingers of her hands as she thought out loud. "That would be three skilled in healing with Mina or Vita. We'll have Geirador helping us for sure. Four. He may have also enlisted help from someone else. Possibly five of us."

"He has, Tagnya," said Dangor. "That, I know for certain. He didn't mention Paruline in his missive?"

"Oh! Paruline! Of course! Why am I surprised? It only makes sense she'd grow up to learn from her da." Again Tagnya was biting her lip in thought. A sign of the mounting sense of urgency as her plan was coming together? Or was there something more?

Dangor stood and pointed to Nagora. "We'll need your vest with the map. It might come in handy at the meeting for certain explanations."

Nagora removed her vest and handed it to her uncle.

Tagnya pulled on her blades and swung her shawl over her shoulders as she joined Dangor. "Girls, we're off. I'm counting on you to make yourselves useful. I don't know how long this will take. The counselors will want to be heading back as soon as possible to inform the volunteers who made the pick."

In Tagnya's infirmary, Sagora set one of the medical scrips on the table. It was the box Tagnya had brought with her to Godomor's, the same one she had at the branding. It was made of stiff oiled leather that had been waxed and polished to resist wet weather. It was the length of two forearms, half as wide as a forearm, and a hand's length in depth. The bottom curved slightly along its length. It had rested on Scout's back, tied to the saddle.

Sagora slid the box's lid up along the adjustable leather carrying strap that was riveted to each end of the scrip. Two slots on each end of the cover allowed her to do this. Sagora deposited the lid next to the box. It became an open container for any needed items taken from the scrip and placed in the cover for easy access.

As Sagora unpacked the box, Nagora pointed to the back of the box. "A saw?"

"This is Mum's scrip. It contains her tools." She pointed to the various pockets as she emptied them all, one after the other, and placed most of the items in the cover. There were three sizes of knives, a small mallet, a chisel, pliers, tweezers, the saw, needles, skeins of thread, candles, a flint, and some milkweed silk fire starter. "Not exactly tools to build with. More often than not, to remove a limb or to patch someone up. Clean a wound and stop the bleeding as soon as possible is a healer's game in battle. There's mead in this flask to clean wounds. Believe me; you won't want to drink that kind. It's like drinking fire. The wounded say it's like pressing a hot coal to a wound."

Then Sagora pointed to the rest of the compartments. "Wound dressings and linen strips to bind wounds and make slings. All are cut to size, folded and tightly rolled up, then stood up to fit into the right compartment for quick access. No guessing. I'll show you where the strips are in the cupboard over there. You'll roll them up tight to fit their proper spaces. Pack each space tight, but not overly tight, so a rolled-up strip comes out easy enough.

"While you do that, I'll refill the vials with their solutions and the jars with their salves."

When the sisters completed Tagnya's kit, they worked on Sagora's.

On a neighboring table, they set aside an identical kit with a dozen different-sized partitions to hold the same implements, salves, and bandages.

When that one was finished, Sagora set out an older scrip, which they also set up. "It's bigger and not as well divided as these two. Still, it'll do. If either Mina or Vita has volunteered, she'll surely bring her own scrip. Or she can use this one. Or she can complete what's missing in hers from what we've set out in this one."

Nagora pointed to a small, covered leather box in one of the corner's of Tagnya's scrip. Whatever it held would fit in her hand. "What's in there?"

"I'm not supposed to tell, but you're my sister. Call it a 'healer's secret.'" Sagora reached for the box, lifted it out, and set it on the table. She placed an earthenware bowl on the table, picked up the box with great care, and unwound the fine leather lanyard wrapped around the bottom half of it. She lifted the cover up along the lanyard. It was designed like the medical scrips, but it only had one compartment. She set the box and its cover back on the table next to the bowl.

Sheep's wool seemed to fill the box. Sagora unpacked the wool with tweezers from Tagnya's kit. The wool made a nest around a small vial. Sagora found the string attached to the vial and, with the tweezers, lifted the vial out and placed it in the bowl. The vial was made of black glass shaped like a skull. The plug that sealed the contents was covered in wax all around the neck of the vial.

"Can you guess what it is?"

"A poison?"

Sagora nodded and took a deep breath. "If ever a warrior suffers too much from wounds Mum judges are fatal, she could give them a drop of this to allow them to fall asleep and go peacefully to the stars."

"You say 'could.' Has Mum not ever given a drop of this to someone?"

"No, but with all the suffering she'd witnessed, she decided to make this to never have to witness it again. Since making it, there's been no more such suffering to witness. She wonders about that."

"Would a drop kill a healthy person?"

"They would sleep for three days and perhaps never awake again. It was designed to ease the pain of the dying, not provide sleep to the living."

Nagora nodded as Sagora picked up the string with the tweezers to return the vial to its container and repack its nest. "Handle with extreme care. You do not want it to touch your skin. Anyway, it's for Mum to administer, no one else. She decides."

When Sagora finished, Nagora reached for her arm. "Will you treat enemy wounded?"

The front door opened. Tagnya and Dangor stepped in.

"I'll let Mum answer that."

"Answer what, Sagora?"

She repeated Nagora's question.

"We'll deal with our own wounded first. Enemy wounded will be dealt with if it's their desire and they promise to cooperate and not to raise a weapon against us ever again."

Nagora nodded.

The only wounded I plan to leave are the mortally wounded.

She looked from Tagnya to Dangor. "The meeting went well?"

Tagnya smiled. "It did. We'll fill you in."

Sagora waved to Tagnya. "Before you do, come and see what we did."

Tagnya did a quick inspection of the kits. She smiled at her girls. "Good work. I see you also prepared the old scrip."

"For Mina or Vita, should one of them volunteer."

"Mina has volunteered. Actually, so did Vita. They drew straws and Mina won. I sent word that she could stock her medical scrip here. She can take whatever she needs from the old one."

Sagora seemed delighted with the news. "Good! I can't wait to see Mina again."

"Have you girls eaten?"

"Not yet." They said it at the same time and laughed.

Tagnya put an arm around Nagora's waist as they made their way to the kitchen. She whispered in her ear. "You've won a spot in Godomor's heart."

She smiled. Her mother's words made her feel warm. She hugged Tagnya. "He won a spot in mine."

As soon as they sat around the table, Tagnya began to fill them in on the meeting. "Godomor had a feast spread on the table for us. He ate without stop all through the meeting. I can't believe how well he's recovered.

"For most of the volunteers, we stuck to the first-come lists unless there was a common agreement that a later volunteer would be better, which was the case with Mina. We wanted a third healer with us. And we had to justify why we bumped someone from a list so the volunteers would understand our decision.

"Gabe is pleased with the commanders who'll be under him. Since he's not battle proven, he wants it to be a joint command. Do what is best for our warriors and for our cause is what will guide his and our decisions and actions at all times. Stick to the agreed-upon plan.

"Dangor had to convince the counselors we'd be traveling as light as possible to move as fast as possible given the terrain we'd be covering. No wagons or extra followers. Trail rations and the game we hunt will be our fare. We'll carry grain for the horses and mules and allow them to graze when possible. All mounts and mules will be inspected before we leave here."

"When will the volunteers arrive?" asked Sagora.

"The first should be here before sunset tomorrow. They'll be setting up camp just inside the wall not far from the gates. Within three days they should all be here.

"Godomor has decided he wants his tent pitched near the wall also. Gabe will do the same, as shall we. Godomor suggests we four arrive on the morning of the third day. He wants us to show up as warriors on our horses leading our pack mules, to show the volunteers how we expect them to travel with us."

"Any news about what Vorpinger is up to?" asked Nagora.

Tagnya looked to Dangor.

He cleared his throat before answering. "Godomor reminded us of the words spoken by Vorpinger's counselor. He says they echo Vorpinger's. Vorpinger is not in Godomor's trust. Apparently he's been drinking an awful lot these days. In Godomor's words: 'A drunken Vorpinger is even less trustworthy—more unpredictable.' There's a rumor he's mounting a force to come oppose the departure of the hundred volunteers."

"Was there any confirmation of the rumors about how he's treated his wife?" asked Sagora.

Tagnya's smile became tight-lipped. "It's been confirmed that she left him over a year ago. Rumor has the reason being he raped his own daughter. Probably the last straw, since he's always been trying to bed any woman he gets near. Lately, several that have refused his advances have been taken into custody and raped. When, after being raped, the women refused to come back willingly, they were hanged."

"There must have been calls for Godomor to intercede?" said Sagora.

"None have yet arrived formally, as those who've disapproved of his behavior and voiced that they would do so have paid with their lives. That's why there are seven corpses hanging from the tree outside his gates." What Vorpinger might do obviously bothered Tagnya.

Sagora's face took on her mother's worried look. "His people must be living in fear. If he actually does mount a force to come against us, they'll not all be in full support of his actions, but join him out of fear. What'll we do?"

A slight smile crossed Tagnya's face. "Godomor says we'll have to teach Vorpinger and his gang a lesson, one they won't forget."

Nagora bit on a knuckle. Would it come to that? "So if all goes well, our force will leave Skull Bay in four, five days at the most."

Dangor nodded. "We've got two days left to finish preparing. Good thing we haven't wasted our time these past days."

For several moments no one spoke. We must all be thinking the same thing. Finally, there's a sense of moving forward toward our goal. After all these years of waiting, imagining, thinking, and planning, the plan is about to be set in motion.

Raynhard, will everything be in place so we can make this plan happen as soon as we arrive? You want your crown back and your country. You want Edana's help. She and Godomor's Hundred Best will be on their way soon.

Tagnya placed two hands on the table. "Godomor asked Gabe to set up two competition rings near the wall, one on each side of the gate."

Sagora looked to Tagnya. "Like was done two years ago? One for archery with moving targets, and the ring for one-on-one combat with training swords?"

"That's right. Godomor wants to keep the volunteers busy in friendly competition amongst themselves." Tagnya smiled.

"To that end, he has another possible activity lined up for them. The bridge we rode over on the way up to the wall got washed out when the heavy rains hit on the same day. The river turned into a raging torrent."

Sagora was wide-eyed. "Mum? He'd have us rebuild that bridge?"

Tagnya shrugged. "Gabe and the master builders will look into it tomorrow morning. The bridge near the charcoal mounds and saw frames, on the far side of the lumber yard, is intact. That means a detour that way for any coming and going from here. If there are sufficient beams and planks, there just might be a bridge-building party. Many hands make quick work of a job like that."

Dangor crossed his arms and leaned back in his chair. "Provided it's well planned and managed. If there's nothing for me to do tomorrow, I'd like to see the washed-out bridge and the other one, just to get a sense of what's involved."

Nagora slapped her hand on the table, louder than she'd intended. "So would I."

Tagnya stared at her and looked to Dangor.

He shrugged. "About the only thing we have left to do is pack our saddlebags, fill the grain sacks, and pack the mules. I can give our horses and mules a final inspection today. I know you're planning to meet with Umma."

"I'll stay with Mum and help make the red paste," said Sagora.

Tagnya smiled at Nagora. "Why not? You'll have to let Gabe know you'll be joining him."

"I'll go do that after we've eaten."

# Bridges
## *Âsokan*

Nagora and Dangor had left with Gabe and the builders at dawn the following day. Now they all sat on their horses surveying what remained of the bridge abutments. Even Aydan seemed to examine them. Nagora had trouble imagining the river had swelled so much as to dislodge the wooden bridge.

Then she learned, from what the master builders had said to Gabe, that the river had risen enough to undermine the abutment on the opposite shore to cause that end of the bridge to fall into the current, which, once it had taken hold of that end, had pulled the whole bridge away.

"Have you found any of the pieces of the bridge?" asked Dangor.

"Further downstream on this side, it's almost intact." Gabe translated what one of the master builders had said.

They rode along the bank until they found it. Its length would carry three carts with their mules hitched one behind the other, and its width would allow two carts to squeeze by side-by-side.

Dangor dismounted and climbed onto the end of the bridge that rested at an angle on one of its corners on the bank of the receded river. Each side of the bridge had a center post. From the top of that post, two trusses reached down to their attachment points at the opposite ends of the bridge's main floor beams, forming two joined triangles that spanned the length of the bridge. He bent on one knee to examine the base of each truss and their center post.

"Best kind of structure for the length of span. Plenty strong for anything crossing it. It's almost intact. A little work on the ends would make it almost new."

Gabe was nodding as Dangor spoke. "That's what the builders say. If we could haul it back upstream, fix it, and strengthen the abutments, we might be able to set it back in place."

Dangor jumped ashore and backed away from the bridge. "It'll have to be slid back in place on new beams spanning the river. Logs to roll it up onto the bank with the least incline. Ropes, horses, and warriors could do that."

Gabe spoke the builders then turned to Dangor. "We'll go see what we have in the way of timber to work with."

They made their way upstream along the river's shore to have another look at the abutments on the shoreline. Then they went on to the lumber yard.

Nagora had seen saw pits where one sawyer held one end of the saw below in the pit and another worked the end above, sometimes standing on the log being sawn.

Though here, on this stretch of bedrock land, builders had erected an open frame structure, much like the frame of Godomor's Grand Hall, but smaller. It had probably taken longer to chisel the holes for the upright frame posts than to dig a saw-pit hole in dirt, but there were obvious advantages.

Big logs could be rolled inside the sawyer's frame on smaller logs and then hoisted onto the big saw horses with a system of pulleys and hooks hung from the main center beam. At least both sawyers would be working above ground with this set-up.

Wisps of smoke from the charcoal mound beyond the lumber yard made their way to the sawyer's frame. In windless conditions, the smoke most likely settled like fog around the area.

Aydan barked once. Nagora looked around. The others had moved along to the lumber yard stacks. She followed. The builders walked around the stacks of planks and beams with their measuring sticks, pointing to and counting suitable beams.

Aydan barked again. From between the end of the row they were in, a dark figure on a black mule, followed by a black dog, appeared out of the haze of smoke. The silhouette appeared to drag smoke with it. A shout of words came from the dark rider, accompanied by the barking of his dog. The master builders and Gabe looked up, laughed, and waved. "Our watchman and his dog," Gabe called out to her. "They don't bite."

Gabe dismounted and led his horse over to Nagora.

The dark figure and his dog approached. As they got closer, she caught flashes of their white teeth and the whites of their eyes.

Gabe introduced the man and his dog in their language, "'Black' for the color of the charcoal he makes and 'Jack' for the way he builds his mound by using the strength of his legs and shoulders to jack logs into place. He's the King of Charcoal, the best charcoal maker in the land. That's his dog, Prince. You can tell how busy they are by the soot that covers them. Like his father and grandfather before him, he tends our charcoal mound and guards our lumber yard. Our smithies swear by his charcoal."

She dismounted Storm and offered her hand.

Black Jack reached out his, hesitated, looked at his hand, wiped it on his vest before thrusting it, blacker than it had been, into hers. This caused the others to laugh. Black Jack said something to her as he pointed to Storm.

Gabe translated. "He wants you to touch your horse with your clean hand and then show it to him."

She did.

Black Jack looked disappointed as he spoke. "His flanks are truly black. I was going to offer to buy him, but I'll never have enough to pay for such a beauty. Perhaps your dog? Mine is getting old."

Nagora smiled and shook her head, no.

Black Jack shrugged, smiled, and moved on to hassle the builders.

Gabe was smiling. "Everything he touches turns black. There's a saying in Skull Bay. If Black Jack touches a maiden's hand, and she does not wash it until the following day, it will bring her good luck in love for the remainder of the year."

She laughed. "Do they believe that?"

"Well, many a maiden has been spotted with a black hand."

"I can guess who started that saying, and why."

Gabe laughed.

Dangor and the builders approached, followed by Black Jack. Gabe spoke with the builders and relayed what they had told him. "They figure there's enough lumber for repairs and to make the required spans to slide the bridge back in place. Black Jack says there is a rock sled at his mound that he sometimes uses for big logs. He suggests we find bigger rocks for the base of the abutments, like those used on the bridge over here. We're going to have a look at it and then see if we can spot some nearby rocks."

Dangor had his arms crossed all the while he examined the bridge ends from the side of the river. "All quarried stone, set into places cut in the bedrock on both sides. The abutments here were not built by the same builder as the other bridge."

"True," said Gabe after consulting with the builders. "The same should be done for the repair."

Dangor scratched his beard. "We're looking at many days of work."

Gabe took a deep breath. "We'll do what we can before leaving. I'll recommend the warriors get the washed out bridge in position, ready to install, as well as the new span beams and rolling logs. The builders can find quarried rock even if some has to be cut. They can remove the remains of the present abutments and carve out proper seats in the bedrock. That way, all should be ready to install on our return from the Land of the Danu."

Dangor smiled. Nagora could tell he was happy with Gabe's decision. "Or your builders might be able to arrange to get it done before you return."

Nagora was happy too. "So we're looking at leaving with the Hundred Best as planned?"

Gabe gave her a smile. "As planned."

Gabe spoke to the builders. Now they appeared to be relieved, probably glad not to be pressured to get the job done on short order.

"Did you enjoy your time with Lars?" asked Sagora as Nagora walked into the kitchen.

"He didn't go with us. Too bad. I've fallen for someone else." Nagora held up her blackened hand.

Sagora laughed. "Ah! You've been smitten by Black Jack, have you? Lars will never live that down. Better you wash your hand. If Lars finds out, he'll be a jealous man."

"Showed him already. He dared me not to wash it off until tomorrow."

"Think you'll be the luckier for it?"

"No. I don't believe in that kind of luck."

"And the bridge?"

"It's repairable, but not before we leave. Most of what'll be needed will be set in place before we leave. Since the new abutment seats for the bridge will take some time to cut out of the rock, we'll be leaving as planned."

Sagora pointed to the two jars on the table. "See what we made. They've cooled."

Nagora looked into the open jars, poking the little finger of her clean hand into one. Its tip came out with the blood-red paste her mother had promised. She drew a line on the back of her other hand. "It smells of mint. This is perfect."

"That's what I think too. Mum says the mint oil and honey will keep the paste from turning sour." Sagora reached over to the two leather pouches and picked them up. "I made these to hold the jars. Cinch them closed tight over the beveled jar covers and there should be no spills."

"Nice work, big sister. I'll go wash up. Where's Mum?"

Sagora pointed in the direction of the infirmary. "With Umma, going over all she's leaving behind for her. I think we'd best give them the time it takes. Many years of her life are wrapped up in those notes and records of hers."

How does Mum feel about leaving all that behind?

Tagnya and Umma came into the kitchen and sat at the table. Nagora tried to read her mother's mood. "You're so distant, Mum, like you're lost in your thoughts."

Tagnya looked up at Nagora and her sister and then to Dangor. Nagora could tell she was thinking about what to say. Umma put a hand on Tagnya's shoulder. Umma most likely understood the language better than she spoke it. She had obviously grown close to Tagnya and must know very well what she was thinking.

Tagnya licked at her upper lip and blinked several times. "Today, it just donned on me that I've never been tied to the land for so long in my life. This is the place where I've spent the greatest part of my life. All of a sudden I realized how much I miss being on the sea. Soon, I'll be gone from here, and all this will just be a memory. I don't know if this is sadness I feel, or if it's fatigue."

Umma spoke slowly and clearly. "Tagnyoriva, you have done so much here. You will be remember by many for all you do for them. You will be miss by them and by many good friends you have. You will be sad in your heart when you leave here.

"You know you must leave for a long planned event and how it will end is not certain. That is the weight you carry now on you shoulders. You will leave Land of Skulls with one hundred finest warriors. When you arrive in Land of the Danu, more support wait for you. You not alone in this."

Tagnya smiled fondly at Umma. "I realize how lucky I've been in planning this enterprise all these years; and yet I worry. The volunteers could, for any number of reasons, change their minds. I'll believe it when I cross into the Land of the Danu with them. I know they'll be watching us and our every move up until we leave. We have to measure up to their expectations."

Dangor cleared his throat and placed a hand on Tagnya's. "You've won Godomor to your cause. He's doing so well now. The change is remarkable. His face has regained its color. He's alert and sharp. His appetite is truly back. Every day he grows stronger.

"Gabe is looking forward to leading the force. Godomor's Hundred Best will be gone for thirty days, perhaps forty at the most. In all likelihood, they'll be involved in one major battle, perhaps not even that."

Sagora reached for Tagnya's hand. "Mum, do you and Umma know what was ailing Godomor?"

I don't dare tell. They'd think I were crazy if I told them how I knew.

"To be truthful, we're not sure. We suspect it might be something from that hole in the cliff at the Grand Hall where he was living. Any damp place like that where the sun does not get in is not a good place to live. I suggested to Gabe he have a place built for Godomor with good exposure to the sun and a view onto the bay, so plenty of fresh air can circulate when he opens a window or door."

Nagora touched Tagnya's arm. "The counselors must've been surprised to see the change in Godomor at the meeting."

Her mother's smile came back. "They were surprised, and happy, except for Vorpinger's counselor. He, of course, had showed up empty handed. At the beginning of the meeting when the others placed their lists on the table, he couldn't sit still. He was obviously taken aback by the change he saw in his king. Godomor invited him to leave if he had nothing to contribute to the meeting. He did, on the spot, without a word. I'm sure he rushed back to tell of the change in Godomor's health. I wonder how Vorpinger'll take the news. I'm sure he'd been hoping Godomor would die of his illness.

"Anyway, after the meeting, one counselor told me of his fears of losing Godomor before the coming of winter. I imagine news of his good health is spreading."

Dangor placed a hand on Tagnya's shoulder. "What she hasn't told you is how Godomor, Gabe, and the counselors praised and thanked her for curing their king of his illness. And Geirador for sending the medicine."

Tagnya smiled and lowered her gaze.

Nagora was proud. "Mum, I'm sure the counselors, when they saw Godomor, felt even more convinced they'd made the right decision in recommending their lords' support our cause.

Everything is falling into place for us. You must look forward to get this campaign started."

Tagnya took a deep breath. "To be truthful, after all this planning, yes. A dragon's waiting to be freed and a king's waiting for his rightful crown. That won't happen overnight. There'll be a kingdom to rebuild. Much time will go by before it is back to its previous glory."

Tagnya looked at her daughters. "You girls are women now, capable of deciding on your own futures. You very well could have plans of your own. You just might decide to return here with your men." Tagnya pointed to Sagora. "Your Gabe could be a future king."

Nagora's mind tried to shape an image of herself with her king, Raynhard. What role would she have? Sister queens in sister countries? So far into the future. What would she choose? Did she even have a choice? For some reason she could not shape an image of herself as Raynhard's queen.

Tagnya pointed to Nagora. "Lars seems to be Gabe's constant companion. Nagora, your path might also bring you back here. Many things can happen between now and then. Do we know what the future brings?"

Mine has been told to me. I seem to be headed in that direction—Child, a dragon awaits you. The witch's words, after Hag read the rune tiles I chose. Will they prove true?

"Remember little sister, you washed your hand. That means no good luck in love coming your way for the rest of the year."

She smiled at Sagora. I've got that prediction beat already.

"Mum, if I come back with Gabe, I'll come to work with Umma. All your notes and records will be here," said Sagora.

Big sister, if I were a teller of good adventures, I'd say you're uncertain of your future. One little word, "if," tells me that. Have you just given me a glimpse into your future, a future you do not know? Why do I think such thoughts?

Umma, who had been listening to the conversation, joined in. "As you know, I copy your mother's notes and my daughter draw her plant samples. When finish, we have copies for us, we continue to grow with our own notes. You are most welcome to work with us, Sagora."

Sagora smiled at Umma. "Thank you, Umma."

"What about you, Nagora?" asked Tagnya.

"My destiny awaits me. I don't think I have a choice."

They all stared at her in silence.

# Warriors
## *Nôtinikêwiyiniw*

The morning was cold. Rain threatened. The sisters returned in a sweat from their exercises on the cliff. Aydan followed them. Dangor was in the corral giving the horses and mules a last thorough going over. The girls stopped to watch as he gave close attention to the underbellies, legs, knees, ankles, and hooves for any signs of sores or injuries. "Best we care well for these fine animals. They'll make our lives easier if we do and they should come out of this campaign no worse for wear."

"Do we pack the mules now?" asked Nagora.

"We'll eat first," said her uncle.

After their morning meal, Tagnya watched as Nagora and Sagora painted the blood-red lines on each other's face. "Girls, when we show up in camp, all eyes will be on us, watching and weighing our every move. These are the best warriors in the Land of Skulls. They'll fight their best if they feel they'll be fighting for the best and not only for our cause.

Many leave family behind. They're offering more than their weapons—they risk giving up their lives for our cause. From now on, we too must be warriors."

Nagora was the last to enter the corral with her saddle and saddlebags. Dangor had already set out the pack saddles for the mules. The fire baskets, yokes, and harnesses lay in a heap next to a stack of spears. The bundles of arrows and spare bows rested in a pile nearby. Pouches of grain for the animals were ready to be tied to the pack saddles. All the blades destined as gifts to the volunteers were stacked in a separate pile. "I see we can start packing."

"Aye. Set your saddle, bedroll, and bags next to our mounts over there. We'll saddle them after we get everything else tied away onto the mules. Your mum and sister are in the stable. I told them I'd send you for them when we were ready to pack the mules."

Nagora brought her mother and Sagora to hear Dangor's instructions.

He pointed to the supplies, weapons, and equipment. "We've got all of this out here in the open to make sure we've forgotten nothing. Once we're sure we have it all, we can start.

"I want us all to know what's been packed, where, and how to get to it, so we don't waste time looking for what we need.

"We must decide what can be tied on before the pack saddles go on the mules. No packed saddle should be heavier than two of you can lift. Think about accessibility. Tie each item so it alone can be reached without having to untie other items. With a little thought it can be done. Think about weight distribution for the mules that'll be burdened by this most of each day.

"In case we see action on the trail, we'd better try to distribute our weapons, rations, and supplies evenly among the mules in case we lose one of them. We don't want all our arrows on one animal.

"I'll take care of the mules with the gift blades and arrows for the volunteers and the cask of mead for Godomor."

Uncle is on top of things today. I better not let him down.

They all set to work. When they had finished, Dangor gave each pack saddle a once-over and checked their girth belts. "We'll stop to check the girth straps several times a day on the trail. We don't want to injure an animal or lose supplies because a saddle falls off. Good job. Now our mounts."

She and Dangor went to the other side of the corral while Tagnya and Sagora returned to the stable.

Nagora had tried to not let it show, but her uncle noticed. "You look preoccupied, Nagora."

"I am. I'm feeling uneasy inside about the campaign we're about to start. You've spent so much time training me and preparing me. I don't want to let you down."

"Nagora, the way you're feeling is a good sign. As we get closer to the thick of it, those feelings will increase. I'd be worried if you didn't feel that way. You won't let me down. You know what you're fighting for is right."

She cinched her saddle's belly strap. "Aye, but just the same, we'll be outnumbered."

"Those on the other side are not all convinced what they're fighting for is right. Even if they outnumber us, they don't all have a cause they truly believe in. They won't all have their hearts in it, and they won't put up the best fight. Many will turn and run."

"Do you think so?"

"You can only rule with fear and terror for so long. Raganora's mercenaries are in it for money. They don't have the leader they once had. Commander Setka's men have become lazy and undisciplined. They boss around the local conscripts and treat them as if they are servants at their beck and call. They've no respect for the local force."

"So I guess the local forces have little respect for the mercenaries. Thus, more reason to lack heart."

Dangor slipped Kimmo's bridle on. "That's right, Nagora. Plus Setka, apparently, has been clamoring for a raise for himself and the services of his mercenary force. This opens up interesting possibilities."

He rested an elbow on Kimmo's saddle. "One, he could use news of our impending attack to bargain for a higher mercenary wage. If he doesn't get it, he and his force could set sail. Their replacements are long overdue.

"Or two, they get their wage increase, take it, and set sail, leaving the local forces to fend for themselves."

A third finger joined his thumb and other finger. "Or three, they get their wage increase and stay around for the fight, if they think they stand a good chance of winning. We'll be doing our best to convince them that they don't."

"Does Mum know about this?"

Her uncle nodded. "Aye, she does. That's why we have to make our show of force look so impressive, to make the mercenaries think twice about sticking around for a fight."

"Whether they do or not, what if Raganora threatens to kill the dragon?"

"Aye, she could do that. To what advantage? There doesn't seem to be one at the moment. Raganora has kept the dragon alive as a guarantee that Hag help her son sire a male heir to the throne. Once the prince produces a male heir, Raganora will have the dragon killed to satisfy Hag. To what benefit? We do not know yet. We might never know. All we know is that once the dragon is dead, Hag will be gone. Raganora and her son must know how Hag will benefit. For Hag to wait all these years, there must be a worthwhile reason."

She's a witch. I'll find out somehow. Nagora was sure of the answer, but it hid somewhere in her mind. She couldn't bring it forward to see it. What was she missing?

Just then, Umma came into the corral carrying the two medical scrips the twins had put together. "Good morning, Dangor, Nagora."

Nagora returned her smile. "Good morning, Umma."

Dangor looked up in surprise. Umma smiled at him and before he could return her greeting, she said, "I see warriors are ready."

Dangor stepped around Kimmo. "Good morning, Umma. I wasn't expecting to see you here, now, today."

Nagora smiled. She had never seen her uncle react in such a way.

He brought his hands forward and then took them back. "Those must be for Tagnya and Sagora. I can bring it, them, to them."

"No hurry, Dangor. They come soon. Your saddle still need one strap to be tied. I wait here until they come."

"Yes, please, okay, do so." For once Dangor's skillful hands became clumsy mittens unable to find the so familiar saddle-strap buckle.

"Umma, did Mum say if she would return with Mina to fill her kit?"

"If she do not, Sagora will. We will see each other at the feast at Godomor Grand Hall before you leave Skull Bay. It will be time for good-byes."

"Yes. Mum will miss you, Umma."

"I will also. Oh! They come now."

Tagnya and Sagora led their horses over to where Umma stood.

Tagnya and Sagora took their kits from Umma and embraced her. Their mutual affection was genuine. Umma reminded Nagora of Moreena. Like Moreena, to meet this tall, blue-eyed, red-haired woman was to want to love her. One could not but be pulled into her calm warmth and strength. There seemed to be no middle ground. If there was, Dangor had not even come close to setting foot there.

"Well Umma, what do you think of my warrior daughters?"

"Tagnuska, your daughters will strike fear in Godomor's fierce warriors. They will think twice about fighting them. I am sure their skills match their looks."

"Thank you, Umma. Soon all our skills will be put to the test. I hope someday we can return here to tell you how we fared."

Tagnya and Sagora fastened their medical scrips to the back of their saddles.

"Tagnuska, you and Dangor must wear red stripes on your faces also?" Umma made the motion with a finger. "Down the face, not across?"

Sagora smiled. "Mum, Umma is right. You said we all had to be warriors from now on."

Nagora reached into her saddlebag and pulled out the leather pouch containing the jar of paste. She brought it to Umma. "It's your idea. Use a finger to paint the lines as you see them." Nagora unfastened the cinched leather laces, removed the lid, and held the jar out to Umma.

Tagnya stepped closer. "Please do it, Umma. I would be honored if you painted me."

Umma gave Tagnya three red lines. Each started on the forehead. Two went down over her eyelids and cheeks. The last down the middle over her nose, lips, and chin.

Umma turned to Dangor and studied his face. She gave him one down the middle of his forehead to the tip of his nose, and two like Tagnya, over his eyelids and cheeks. She held onto Dangor's hand and brought him to stand next to Tagnya so Nagora and Sagora could get a good look at them.

"Perfect!" said Sagora.

Umma smiled. Nagora put the jar back in its pouch and away in her saddlebag. Umma was still holding Dangor's hand when Nagora turned to face them. Umma smiled at Dangor and made like she had just realized she was holding his hand. Or was he holding onto her hand?

Tagnya motioned in an arc to the lodge and its outbuildings, "Umma, this is all yours now. I'm so happy to leave it in your capable hands. Skull Bay has a most capable healer. I'm sure you'll be treated with the greatest of respect." Tagnya held open her arms and embraced Umma.

"Good luck to all of you. I see you again at Godomor's feast."

The riders collected the lines of their mules and mounted their horses. Umma held the gate open for them as they rode through.

Tagnya led, followed by Sagora, Nagora, and Dangor who took up the rear. Aydan kept pace alongside Nagora. As they wound their way through the village to the encampment near the wall above the village, villagers stood by the road; some watching, some waving, and some with tears in their eyes. Two were signing.

Less than half a count later, they reached the top of the hill where the fortified wall came into view. Warriors from the different territories had set up camp.

The tent bearing Godomor's standard was visible. It surely had enough place for Gabe and his commanders to meet.

Most of the warriors had simple paired shelters, lean-tos held up by two spears at two of the corners, the saddles of their mounts placed under the lower edges of the tarps.

Tagnya led the way up to Godomor's tent as one warrior after another paused in silence to watch the four riders enter the camp. The silence that had settled over the encampment brought Godomor from his tent. He as well watched and waited as they approached.

As they drew closer, Godomor smiled.

He seems satisfied with the effect we've had.

Godomor raised both arms in greeting and motioned for the riders to set up next to his tent. Except for a helmet, he was dressed in body armor. He greeted each one of them with a hearty embrace. Sagora translated. "I bid you set up your shelters here. You have plenty of time. Before the evening meal, we will meet all the troops and speak to them. They should all be here by then. We will all meet in front of the main gate."

Then he spoke to Tagnya, "Did you meet with Umma?"

"Yes. All is well. The lodge is hers. She knows the routine for treating all manner of illness and ailments. Godomor, she will take good care of you and your people. I have no fear of leaving you in her capable hands."

"Yes, I can trust Umma. Tagnuska, again, I want to thank you for your care. I feel alive again."

Tagnya smiled and touched Godomor's arm.

Nagora got busy with her uncle. She unpacked four spears and two tarps to set up lean-tos. With rope and a few more spears, she made a temporary rack to set the saddle packs on. Sagora helped Dangor unload the mules. Once they had set up the lean-tos, they unsaddled their mounts. Sagora helped Nagora place their saddles and personal gear under the low ends of the tarps.

Finally, they brought their mounts and the mules over to the horse lines set up near the wall.

On the way back, Dangor spotted a pile of firewood. "Lassies, please bring back a few sticks for our fire." They each brought an arm full of various sizes, along with a few pieces of kindling. Slightly more than enough for the number of cooking fires they would make before leaving.

"Big sister, let's get stones for our fire pit. There are plenty strewn around here."

Dangor checked the lean-tos. "I like the way you overlapped the tarps at the back. Gives us a larger, protected sleeping area."


Tagnya arrived from Godomor's tent.

"We have time before we meet with the warriors. I suggest we go over to the training area and practice with our bows and the training swords. These warriors will want to know we can handle ourselves. Don't be surprised by challenges.

"Take them and do your best. These warriors are always out to best each other. Remember, there's no shame in losing a challenge. On any day, any one of them can best the other. They all know that and they expect to be challenged by the loser who, in most cases, comes back stronger. It's one way of keeping their skill levels up."

Dangor was already stringing his bow. "Your mum's right. Just be relaxed and go through your regular training exercises."

Sagora pointed. "Look, Mum. Here comes Mina."

Tagnya and Sagora waved to her. Mina waved back and picked up her pace as she approached.

"Mina, I want you to meet my sister, Nagora, and our uncle, Dangor."

Mina extended her hand in greeting to Nagora and Dangor and warmly embraced Tagnya and Sagora.

"You made an impression a few moments ago when you rode into camp." Sagora translated what Mina said.

"Well, none ran off to hide," said Sagora.

"They're just curious to see who they'll be fighting for."

"Mina, we've prepared the contents for a medical scrip for you. It's at the house. Do you want to go get it now?" asked Sagora.

"You've just unsaddled your horses."

"It won't be a problem. I will go with you," said Sagora.

Tagnya placed a hand on Sagora's arm. "Sagora, I'll go. I just remembered something important that I have to show to Umma." Tagnya turned to Mina. "It won't take me long to saddle up. My daughters and their uncle will practice with their bows. We'll join them when we get back."

Mina held Tagnya's arm. "Tagnya, I'm honored you've chosen me to be part of your campaign. I'm glad to be of service to you."

"I know I can count on your skills, as a healer and an archer. I'm so happy you volunteered. Vita did also, but you won the draw."


Two types of targets were set up at the range. Nagora was familiar with the stationary bull's eye targets with concentric circles painted on canvas stretched over a tight, thick mat of straw and held up on a tripod of sticks.

The second type was new to her. It was known as a "straw dog". Several such targets were attached to ropes and pulleys and they could be made to move from side to side and even bounce up and down. These had a human form, as they were made of old, ragged clothes tightly stuffed with straw. Then they were tightly bound and sewn together with twine.

As the three new archers approached, those practicing had already stopped and were making way for them, leaving six stationary targets free. They stayed to observe the shooting, and more warriors were gathering to watch.

Dangor wasted no time. He pulled the string of his bow several times to ensure it was ready, reached for an arrow from his quiver on his back, nocked it and, in one smooth motion, pulled it back, aimed, and loosed it. A bull's-eye, dead center.

No surprise there. That's my uncle, the best archer in the land.

Sagora loosed and hit the bull's-eye, just making it inside the lower edge.

Nagora hit a bull's-eye close to the center. Since Dangor had released first, it was his choice to challenge Sagora or allow her to challenge him. He deferred to Sagora.

Sagora called, "Straw dog moving, left leg."

Dangor replied, "Straw dog moving, right leg." And he upped the challenge. "Arrows in the quiver. First to hit the target called. Start on Nagora's signal."

"Agreed," Sagora replied.

The straw dog was in motion. Nagora called, "Release!"

Both arrows struck their targets as called and anyone present would be hard-pressed to say whose arrow struck first, for the straw dog did not pivot right or left when hit, but swung slowly back and forth.

All who were watching applauded.

Then it was Sagora's challenge since Dangor had upped her first call, and she had met his challenge. Sagora called, "Straw dog moving. Two arrows from the quiver. First arrow to the neck. Second arrow to the left leg. First to complete the hits wins. Start on Nagora's signal."

"Agreed," said Dangor.

Uncle, if anyone can win this challenge, you can.

The straw dog was in motion. Nagora called, "Release!"

Dangor's release matched Sagora's, arrow for arrow, and both arrows shot into the left leg had caused the straw dog to spin.

It was Dangor's call. "Two straw dogs moving. Two arrows from the quiver. One to the heart of either straw dog. The other arrow to the right leg of the other straw dog. Start on Nagora's signal."

"Agreed," said Sagora.

With two straw dogs in motion, Nagora called, "Release!"

Dangor held his bow horizontal, pulled two arrows from his quiver simultaneously, nocked one on each side of his bow's handle and pulled back overhand with the arrow feathers touching the inside of his index and little fingers. He aimed and, as Sagora's arrow had just caught the hand-sized red patch on the straw dog representing the heart, he released.

One arrow struck the heart dead center and, almost simultaneously, the other arrow struck the right leg. This caused Sagora to delay her release so that her arrow hit the right leg on the opposite side, canceling the straw dog's rotation.

Sagora looked at Dangor with her jaw dropped, trying to figure out how he had shot so quickly. She was not aware of exactly what he had done. The audience too was stunned. They finally broke into applause just as Nagora explained to her sister what her uncle had done.

Nagora stepped to Dangor's side, to hold his arm high. "You never showed me that shot."

"It's not worth learning. Not accurate. Requires too much strength. It was a one-in-one-hundred shot. Thought I'd chance it today. I was very lucky."

Nagora hugged him. "You're the best, Uncle. You've just proved it."

Soon Sagora was congratulating Dangor, and warriors and archers who had been watching the challenge were crowding around to shake Dangor's hand. None stepped forward to challenge Dangor.

Nagora went to Sagora. "Will you accept my challenge, big sister?"

"All right, but no trick shots like Uncle Dangor."

"He's never taught me that one."

"I challenge my sister! I challenge my sister!" Nagora called to get people's attention. Sagora translated. When the people backed away to give them room, she judged it was quiet enough and called her challenge, "Stationary target for each. Seven arrows from the quiver. Four in the bull's-eye. Three in the white circle surrounding the bull's-eye. Strike alternate in, then out. First to finish wins. Start on Dangor's signal. Dangor calls the winner."

"Agreed," said Sagora.

"Archers ready! On my word!" Dangor paused. "Release!"

On the fifth release she and Sagora were neck and neck. On the sixth release Sagora's arrow struck first, but then Nagora's sixth and seventh arrows hit, one right after the other before Sagora could release her seventh arrow. Dangor pointed to Nagora.

Sagora looked at Nagora in disbelief. "That was a trick shot."

Nagora shook her head. "I don't think so. It was a fair shot that met your challenge. You did say, 'strike alternately in then out.' I did release two arrows at the same time, a long one and a short one. If releasing at the same time, the longer arrow has to strike first."

Sagora translated for the audience and held up Nagora's hand. The audience applauded.

She opened her arms to hug Sagora. *That's a halfhearted hug big sister.*

"To me that's still a trick shot," whispered Sagora and she stepped back.

*She's not happy.* "Shall we go to the training swords next?"

"Yes. Let's do that. This time, I'll take you." Sagora's answer was almost a sneer with a hint of anger.

*She doesn't like to lose.*

"To the sword ring," announced Sagora.

As they moved on, the gathered crowd of warriors followed. A warrior was taking wagers. *Would the betting be close?*

When they reached the ring, the twins unstrung their bows, removed their quivers and blades and brought them to Dangor to hold.

"Lassies, this is no time to injure each other. Play it safe out there."

"Don't worry, Uncle." Nagora winked at him.

Sagora spit. "Well, I plan to get even, so she'd better be on guard."

*What's she trying to prove?*

Dangor must've detected Sagora's anger. He reached for her arm and held it. "Here's something to think about, lass. You can use your skills in the next few moments to the best of your ability and you'll stand a chance of winning or stand a chance of losing, with grace. Or you can go at your sister with all the fury in your heart, intent on getting even. I warn you, she'll use your fury against you and you'll lose face in front of all these warriors. Now think. Which do you want? To show off your best skills, or to show your uncontrolled fury?"

Sagora lowered her gaze and bit her lip.

Will Uncle's words carry any weight with her? Nagora made a point of taking her time to choose one of the wooden practice swords from the rack next to the ring. She found one to her liking. "Sagora, since you met my challenge with the bow, explain how the challenge with swords works."

Sagora swung her sword in a slashing motion and pointed to the center of the ring. "In the ring we'll each have a weighted dummy carcass representing a wounded friend on the battlefield, one we have to bring to safety." Then she pointed to the half dozen dummies leaning against the wall outside the ring.

The dummies were all made the same. A stone about the size of a human head was tied to a cage of sticks inside of which there was a fist-size stone. Near the head, two sticks were tied representing the arms. At the opposite end of the cage, a stone three times the size of the headstone was tied, and to it two longer sticks for the legs.

Sagora pointed with her wooden sword. "Killing an opponent's sleeping dog means breaking the cage to release the heart stone."

"I understand." Big sister, you look like you're going to put your heart into this challenge.

Sagora made her challenge: "Sleeping dogs, center of the ring, first out of the ring wins. Or first to kill the other's dog wins. Start on Dangor's signal."

"Agreed," said Nagora.

Good, now she'll have to think strategy and protect her dog. She won't be as likely to rip into me.

The warriors who attended the ring brought two sleeping dogs to the center of the ring, leaving just enough space between them for the opponents to stand facing each other with their swords crossed, ready to defend themselves and their sleeping dogs.

The sisters stepped into the space between the sleeping dogs, crossed their wooden blades, and braced themselves as they stared into each other's eyes waiting for Dangor to call the start.

A horn sounded instead.

# Trap
## *Wanihikan*

The horn brought commotion all around the ring as there was shouting from the sentries at the top of the wall. "It's a call to battle readiness," said Sagora. The main gates were opening. Gabe with six of his men rode in on horseback.

Lars was among them.

Sagora pointed. "See the one with the flag? That's what caused the sentry to blow the signal."

The main gates closed as Gabe and his men headed for Godomor's tent.

What on first glance seemed to be confusion was purposeful hustle by warriors returning to their sections of the camp to be ready to take orders. Those on foot headed for Godomor's command post had to be the commanders of the volunteer groups. More Skull Bay warriors and archers were taking to the wall.

Sagora took Nagora by the arm and they followed Dangor to Godomor's tent.

...

Godomor looked at them as they came in. "Where is Tagnuska?"

"Gone with Mina to get her medical supplies. They'll be back soon," said Sagora.

Godomor looked around the tent again. Obviously making sure everyone else who should be there, was. Then he asked Gabe to report.

Sagora translated.

"It's Vorpinger. This information is from our eyes at Vorpinger's hold. Vorpinger is on his way here to offer the services of his best warriors. Since he knows you'll decline his offer, he plans to rain arrows down on all those who volunteered to, in his words, ' ... aid the witch and her twin bitches in their quest.'"

Godomor raised his hand and made it into a fist. "Vorpinger's a fool. How many men is he leading, and when should we expect him to arrive?"

"He's leading a ragtag group of a hundred reluctant followers, many riding two per horse and carrying bows and arrows. At best, he could be here just before our evening meal, perhaps later, depending on how often he stops to piss. He has problems holding his urine. Sometimes he's so drunk he wets himself and doesn't realize he reeks of piss."

"You say 'reluctant followers.' Are there any of his best men among them?" Dangor said.

"A handful. Most of his best men at arms have refused to follow him," said Gabe.

"Is there someone waiting to take his place? Does he have an heir?" Dangor asked.

"His wife left with his daughter. Latest rumors say they are good as dead. Though, no bodies have turned up. His younger brother, Rhysonnger, has been back for over a year now, since having a big falling out with Vorpinger years ago. Rumors of his death away have proven false. Since coming back, he hasn't been trying to push Vorpinger out of the way. Rather, he's been advising him, but only when Vorpinger asks."

"Is he biding his time?" asked Dangor.

"Aye, most likely watching and waiting."

Dangor scratched his chin. "Were you and your father to die, Vorpinger and Rhysonnger, in that order, would have a claim to Godomor's throne?"

Gabe nodded. "A claim, yes. However, could Vorpinger defend it, should others contest it with force? He's not a leader. He's a bully. He doesn't have many friends in the Land of Skulls."

"Friends can be bought," said Dangor.

"True loyal friends, less so," said Gabe.


Tagnya arrived with Mina. Sagora filled her in on what Gabe had reported so far.

"Father, shall we go against him and get it over with?" asked Gabe.

Godomor seemed to be considering his son's question. Tagnya's breathing and fidgeting hands showed she wanted to speak.

Godomor let his eyes roam from one person to the next. When they fell on Tagnya, he spoke. "Tagnuska, what are your thoughts on this?"

Tagnya seemed to be holding back to collect her thoughts. Surely she already knows what she wants to say. It's probably just a question of how to say it.

"Godomor, deep down, Vorpinger wants to pick a fight with me. If we meet him before he gets within shooting range of these walls, I can probably deal with him easily without causing harm to his reluctant followers. They're looking for a reason to turn tail and run back home. They're with him out of fear of ending up hanging from his tree. If I can talk to him, I think I can get him to change his mind."

Godomor held Tagnya's gaze. "You think you can reason with a drunk Vorpinger, Tagnuska?"

"I can try."

Nagora touched Tagnya's arm. "Mum, I have an idea. If I could speak, you could explain it to them."

Tagnya gave her daughter an impatient look.

Godomor must have noticed. "Your daughter wishes to speak. Let her. We are looking for a solution. Let us consider what she has to say."

Tagnya bowed her head and turned to Nagora. "Godomor wishes you to speak."

Nagora's mind was racing. She had a plan. How much should she reveal, and how much should she keep for herself? She took a deep breath. To speak in front of so many had her heart beating. Could she find her breath to speak? Mum or Sagora will translate. That'll give me time to catch my breath and order my thoughts.

"Godomor, Mum is right. Vorpinger is looking to harm her. He lost face with her challenge many years ago. Today we have to give him a chance to gain face. We have to offer him a choice."

Tagnya gave her a strange look. "Daughter, how do you propose to do that?"

Nagora swallowed. "Two days ago, I saw the washed out bridge, then the lumber yard, and then the other bridge. Nearby is the sawyer's frame they use to cut felled trees into lumber and boards."

"What does that have to do with Vorpinger?" asked Sagora.

Nagora looked at her. She's still angry and still wants to get even.

She looked to her mother and then back to Godomor. "Here's what I propose. If this sounds crazy, I'm sorry I ever spoke in your presence today." She took another deep breath. "If we can meet Vorpinger at the bridge, before he crosses, we invite him and a handful of his warriors to cross and come to the frame structure. We'll need an axe that looks like his, not an exact match. We'll plant it in the center beam. Since there's no moth there, we'll put one there next to the planted axe. We'll make it out of vellum or something."

Sagora was making faces at her.

If you think there's something wrong with me, say so. Nagora paused for another breath. Why is she doing this? She knows everyone is watching.

"Two days ago there was a ladder there. The workers must use it to get up onto the logs set on the big saw horses and to adjust the pulleys and hooks on the main beam. We'll set the ladder near the axe planted into the main beam."

"Well, where's the choice?" asked Sagora.

Nagora glared at her sister, though she wished she hadn't.

"Here's what I propose. Mum says to Vorpinger: 'Many years ago when I counter-challenged you, I had a lucky throw.

Today, your axe is here. You can retrieve it, take up my counter challenge and whatever the outcome, my daughters and I will leave the Land of Skulls, never to return again.'"

Nagora turned to her sister. "Here comes the choice."

She turned to face Godomor once more. "Or, if even one of the Hundred Best from the Land of Skulls should die when away with me to support my cause, I shall return to face whatever new challenge you set before me, without counter-challenge. Godomor's son will hold me to my words. So, Vorpinger, retrieve your axe and tell me your choice and leave in peace with your warriors."

"Do you truly think Vorpinger will go for that?" asked Sagora.

This time Nagora did not acknowledge her sister's question, but spoke directly to Godomor. "The obvious third choice, though unspoken, will make him choose and appear to save face. Your mounted Hundred Best, with swords and bows drawn and arrows nocked, will leave no doubt that this could be his very last appearance before your warriors. His last day to be alive."

Godomor's full smile left no doubt in Nagora's mind he liked what he had heard. "What say you? Do any of you have something else to propose?"

She looked at the faces of the others in Godomor's tent. They were obviously reflecting on her plan or trying to come up with an alternate proposal. Surely they will. Sagora was staring at the ground. Her mother kept her eyes on Godomor. Gabe also looked at his father and waited. When Nagora's eyes reached Lars, he smiled at her.

Sagora stepped forward. "I don't like the choice you want Mum to offer Vorpinger. Chances are the Hundred will see battle, and we know what battle costs. It costs lives. That, every warrior knows. That means Gabe will be held to bring Mum back here to face a challenge from Vorpinger. One he will think up that will cost her life."

Nagora wanted to lay out the part of her plan she was keeping to herself. In her mind, it was justified, and yet it might not appear that way to Godomor and the commanders.

Rather, she offered what came to mind. "Instead, Mum can say if one of the Hundred Best dies, I, Nagora, her branded daughter, will come to face his challenge. That might please him even more, as it will offer him an opportunity to not only hurt Tagnyoriva, but to exact traditional punishment on a twin returning to the Land of Skulls."

Once Gabe had translated Nagora's words, the discussion among the commanders came alive. Gabe seemed to be taking their questions and dealing with them as best he could. Godomor followed with a certain detachment, whereas Tagnya did not seem to be pleased with the turn of events.

The familiar touch of her uncle's hand was on her shoulder. He spoke in a whisper. "Lass, there's more to your plan than you've told us here. Whatever it is, I hope you can make it work, because from what I can see, you've stirred the pot the wrong way. Old ideas about twins we thought were getting stuck to the bottom are starting to rise to the surface again."

She looked at Dangor. "I'm just trying to be of help. If they've got a better plan, let them speak."

"Perhaps what you said makes it so they can't see an alternative."

"What other alternatives are there? I think I've put them all out there. Let's face it. They want to be rid of Vorpinger. He's the fly on the horse's ass that should've been slapped a long time ago. All they have to do is like Gabe said, 'get it over with.' Why haven't they? Why won't they? From what you've heard, Uncle, I'm sure you'd side with Gabe."

"Aye, but Gabe is not king. Nor I. Godomor is, and he has his reasons. Whatever they are, he's not speaking them. Though, he does seem to like your plan. I think it might give him more time to figure out whatever it is he wants to know about Vorpinger."

That's two who side with me.

"Father." Gabe's call to Godomor brought the commanders' discussion to a close. "I made it clear to my commanders that this is to be a joint command. They agree with Tagnyoriva that going against Vorpinger to kill him could lead to the death of many of his followers. They just might be too foolish to not give up their arms and the fight.

"Also, they agree there could be possible injury and even death to some of the Hundred.

"And they agree with Nagora that Vorpinger be allowed to appear to save face, but with the second choice of her returning to face Vorpinger's challenge, instead of Tagnuska."

Godomor looked around the tent. "There are no other plans being offered?"

No one spoke up.

"Tagnuska, what do you have to say on this?"

Tagnya looked to Nagora and kept her eyes on her as she answered. "Godomor, I respect the decision of Gabe's commanders, if it is their consensus to go with what Nagora has proposed."

Nagora tried to read her mother's face.

Resignation or calculation?

Gabe placed a hand on the shoulder of one of his commanders. "The axe Vorpinger lent Tagnuska for his challenge was made by one of Tankar's warriors. Vorpinger had won it from him in a bet. For our purpose, it won't be a problem to get one that looks close enough to the one in the Grand Hall's main beam. Tankar says his warrior will even throw it so it holds well in the beam. Unless, Tagnuska wants to throw it."

Tagnya shook her head. "I haven't thrown an axe since then. I'm working on what to say to Vorpinger when we meet."

Nagora held up a hand to get Gabe's attention. "Since it's my idea, I'll take care of placing the ladder and making the moth."

Gabe raised his hands. "We'll have the bridge and nearby shores covered. Archers will hold forward positions. Mounted warriors will be at the ready to come forward from the flanks so archers can fall back to their mounts. Should Vorpinger go to the sawyer's frame, he'll do it with a limited escort and we'll follow along to keep him covered. When he sees we are ready for him, he won't try anything stupid. If he does, we'll cut him down and any who do not surrender."

"Good," said Godomor.

"We leave in two counts," said Gabe.

Should I tell Uncle of my plan? Only if I have to. Now I just need to get the tool.

Dangor put a hand on her back. "I'm going with you in case you need help. I'll get our mounts."

"I'll set the saddles out." She would have time to get the tool.

...

While her mother and sister were conferring with Gabe, Nagora headed for the lean-to. She wasted no time opening her mother's medical scrip and removing the saw. She slipped it into her quiver, down the side that rested against her back.

Then she set out the four saddles and replaced the target arrows with small, broad-tipped ones.

Nagora had vellum in her saddlebag. She unfolded a piece and from it and cut a smaller piece the size of her hand. She folded that in two and with a small knife, she quickly cut the rough outline of a moth with spread wings. Satisfied with her creation, she found a small spruce log from the firewood pile and pinched a blister of spruce gum to the middle of the vellum moth.

Just as Nagora placed the folded moth in her vest pocket, Tagnya and Sagora returned from Godomor's tent. They did not say a word, but readied their weapons as Nagora had.

*So I'm not the only one to keep my thoughts to myself when angry. A gift from you, my mum?*

Since many of the warriors had gone to the horse lines for their mounts at the same time, Nagora left her mother and sister to go lend a hand to her uncle. She found him waiting for some space to maneuver the four mounts before attempting to untie them.

"Glad you've come. It's busy here. I'll take Tagnya's."

Nagora untied Storm. "Thought you were going to have the day off here chatting up the girls?" She let Storm nuzzle her. "Well, we're on the road again. We won't let Sagora walk, will we? Or maybe we should." She untied Brith.

Most of the warriors around her were in their quiet place. Their time to reflect before the battle? Likely trying to focus on the things they can control, their tasks. Ready to follow orders.

Warriors were lined up at the latrines. I'll feel better if I take a turn there myself. I'll saddle Storm first.

"We're to follow Gabe," Dangor said, as Nagora prepared to mount Storm. Her mother and sister were mounted and continued to ignore her.

Gabe rode up with Lars and another warrior. All wore their embossed leather armor, helms, and had black dots painted on their eyelids. "Here's our axeman, Labrys," Sagora translated.

The axeman reached down next to his right knee and pulled the axe from its holder on his saddle.

It would be lethal in battle swung by this man's big arm. No doubt his throw would plant the axe head in the center beam of the sawyer's frame.

It remains to be seen if Vorpinger will climb the ladder to get it. Will he?

Gabe and his men took the lead. Nagora and the others followed as they made their way to the front of the four formations that waited.

As the warriors rode through the gate past the open, skull-covered doors, Godomor was sitting on his horse, in full battle dress. He watched in silence as the Hundred Best rode by.

Nagora glanced at him. Will he be joining us? I won't be the one to break the silence that stands like a wall of ice between me and my family.

Nagora focused on the road ahead. At least Aydan seems to be happy running at Lyam's side.

As the lumber yard and big sawyer's frame came into view, a rider approached and brought his mount alongside Gabe's. "No sign of Vorpinger yet."

Lars translated for Nagora and Dangor. She gave him a warm smile.

As they neared the sawyer's frame, Gabe pulled over to let Dangor and Nagora come alongside. "I'll leave you two with Labrys. We're going onto the bridge to set up there. If I don't come back before you're done, join us there."

The formations rode past.

As they dismounted, it was obvious Labrys had specific instructions. He wasted no time. With axe in hand, he walked into the frame structure. As he stood below the main beam at its center, he paused to look at Nagora. He pointed his axe up at the beam.

Nagora nodded. Labrys flexed his knees and brought the axe down so its head came alongside his ankle. He pointed with his left hand. His release was a blur followed by a loud thwack as the axe blade struck the beam. The handle of the axe was almost parallel to the beam, and it vibrated for a moment.

Labrys returned to his horse, mounted, waved, and left.

Dangor had his eye on the axe. "The man can throw. That axe will never fall of its own weight."

"Uncle, the hands on him! One moment it was in his hand, the next it was stuck in the beam. The sound it made. I thought he might've split the beam."

Dangor pointed. "The ladder?"

"Aye, let's move it."

Once it was in place, she rubbed her hands together and looked up at the axe. "I guess we can head to the bridge."

"Sure."

They mounted, and she looked back at the ladder. "Uncle, go on without me. I forgot to stick the vellum moth up there. At the same time, I'll make sure Vorpinger can easily reach the axe. If the ladder needs to be moved a bit, I can do it on my own."

Dangor gave her a nod. "See you at the bridge."

Before he was out of sight, Nagora had retrieved her mother's saw and was climbing the ladder. She pretended she was Vorpinger reaching for the axe handle. As she climbed higher to stick the vellum moth next to the axe, she judged his feet would be on the fourth rung from the top of the ladder, but he wouldn't have enough purchase to pull the axe free. It hadn't moved when she pulled on it.

She figured he would want to reach through the space between the first two rungs with his right hand to get two hands on it. That would put his right shoulder just under the first rung and his left arm over it. He would be putting most of his body weight against the second and third rungs.

So she cut into the top three rungs enough to at first hold Vorpinger's weight, but not enough to withstand the pressure he would add by pulling on the axe.

With that done, she cut into the fourth rung to weaken it, but still allow it to hold a man's weight.

When Nagora finished, she took care to hide the saw again.

Then she picked up some dirt and climbed the ladder to rub it into the thin spaces left by the saw's blade.

Before she mounted Storm, the wind had calmed and the smoky haze from Black Jack's charcoal mound began to settle over the plateau.

At the bridge, the archers were in place on both sides of the entrance along the shore. The mounted warriors flanked them. Nagora took her time approaching the bridge. The four on the bridge seemed to be in animated discussion. She was in no rush to join her mother and sister.

Dangor spotted her and rode over to her. "Vorpinger is on his way. Gabe wants your mum to carry a shield. She doesn't want to."

Nagora shrugged. "Don't think I could say something to get her to change her mind. The archers'll have her covered."

"That's what your mum says. Just as well you keep your distance. Soon as Vorpinger is visible, only Tagnya and Gabe will remain on the bridge."

"Do we stay here?"

"Aye. If Vorpinger decides to take his axe, we follow along. Keep away unless you're called for. Lars will be joining us. Is the ladder set to your liking?"

"It's ready. The moth's in place too."

Nagora stared at her mother on the bridge. Lars came into view with his dogs. Sagora joined him and they headed up the small hill toward Nagora.

...

When they arrived, Lars brought his mount next to Nagora's. He pointed to a spot on the horizon beyond the bridge. "See the slow-moving line?"

"Vorpinger and his followers?"

"Aaaaaaye."

He had said it with a drawn out sigh as if he had better things to do. She reached over and tapped his arm. "What's wrong? You think you'll not get your big blade wet today?"

"If only." He shook his head.

Nagora jumped down from Storm to spend time with the dogs. She looked up at her sister. Sagora opened her mouth, about to say something, but she turned her head away instead. Just as well. It won't take much to make me go and pull you out of your saddle and kick your ass. Even if you are my big sister.

Saying those words inside made her feel better. Actually doing it would make me feel a lot better. Instead, she settled for a good tussle with Lyam and Aydan. Soon they had her on the ground on her hands and knees. For a moment she could laugh with her playful companions. She finally struggled to her feet.

Lars and Dangor were smiling at her, and for a moment she was happy until her eyes caught the scowl on her sister's face. She gave a last hug to the dogs, told them to sit, and climbed back on Storm.

Nagora could now make out individual riders in the approaching line. The line would be visible to Gabe and Tagnya.

What's Mum thinking about right now? Perhaps I'll ask her someday.

The line came to a stop. She couldn't believe it, but it was true. At least twenty of the horses carried two riders. From where Vorpinger's followers were, they most likely had a good view of the bridge and the defensive positions taken up by the Hundred.

Gabe held a white flag on a spear. Four riders made their way to the bridge.

Nagora pointed. "Lars, the big one?"

His face was a scowl. "Who do you think?"

"Vorpinger?"

"That's him. If the wind were right, we could smell him."

"His counselor's there as well. Who are the other two?"

Lars turned to Sagora. "Sagora, do you recognize them? I think one is Vorpinger's brother."

"Yes, the one with the black hair is his brother. Rhysonnger's his name. I don't know the other one."

The four riders stopped, and then Vorpinger and his counselor continued onto the bridge.

If only I were closer to hear what's being said. Is that the counselor's voice? That useless toad. Mum's calm. She's sitting straight in her saddle. Hasn't moved her arms once. Probably staring him down.

The counselor was like a baby bird struggling to climb out of its nest until Vorpinger raised his hand in his direction. Only then did he stop flapping his arms.

Then Vorpinger waved him away.

Gabe waved the flag. Lars gently slapped the reins on his horse's neck. "Time for me to bring you forward, Nagora.

You're not to say a word unless Gabe orders you to. Understood?"

"Sure." She took a breath.

"Follow me."

Nagora followed. Lars stopped at the edge of the bridge. From there she locked eyes with Vorpinger. She had seen a few men with eyes like his, the whites awash in yellow, sunken in the dark rings that surrounded them. This man was sick and slowly dying.

When Vorpinger's eyes left hers, the counselor returned with the two others. Their horses clomped on the bridge's wooden floor.

Gabe motioned for Lars and Nagora to come forward.

In turn, Storm clomped into position.

Vorpinger spoke something she did not catch.

"Nagora, come here, between us," said Gabe.

Storm brought her forward.

Vorpinger came forward. He stared at her face.

She could almost feel his eyes on her brand. His foul breath reached her. Lars had spoken the truth. He also reeked of piss and stale ale.

Vorpinger coughed, turned his head, and spit blood onto a bridge floorboard. Then he seemed to fight for his breath as he licked at his lips and breathed in through his nose. He backed his horse away.

Just then Nagora glimpsed the face of Vorpinger's brother. It made the hair at the back of her head stand. A quick glance to his hand confirmed why.

Gabe ordered her back.

...

Did he recognize me? He didn't have a painted, armed warrior in front of him that day.

Lars waved. "Come, Nagora."

She followed. As soon as Nagora could, she pulled alongside him. "Lars, slow down. Listen to me."

"What's wrong?"

"You have to promise me something."

"What?"

"No matter what happens today, there's something you have to help me do. Promise, no matter what, you'll do it."

"Do what?"

"Promise! Damn you, Lars!"

"I promise." His face was a frown.

"Vorpinger's brother. The one with the bones on his hand. You have to help me bring him back to Godomor alive. If we could bring back the other two also, that would be even better."

Lars forced a silly smile onto his face. "While we're at it, why not Vorpinger as well? Just like that?"

"Lars, please. Follow my lead. Not a word to the others. I'm sorry I yelled at you." She rode on ahead of him.

"Arguing with Lars?" Sagora gibed.

"Shut up!" Nagora surprised even herself with the forcefulness of the command she had yelled at her sister. I can't believe she still wants to get even. Act your age, big sister.

Instead of saying so, Nagora took up the furthest position away from Sagora to watch what was happening on the bridge.

Gabe and Tagnya turned their mounts to leave the bridge. Vorpinger followed with his three companions.

A dozen archers found their mounts and followed along-side, followed by another dozen mounted warriors, carrying spears.

Lars spit. "Looks like he's going for the axe. We're to follow at a distance."

They let Vorpinger's group pass and slowly fell in about twenty horse lengths behind them.

At the sawyer's frame structure, a fine smoky haze snuck around the frame posts and crept along the ground.

Tagnya dismounted about a hundred strides from the structure and handed her reins to Gabe. She walked into the structure and stood near the ladder.

Vorpinger dismounted and made his way to the ladder. The archers had strung their bows and were holding them and an un-nocked arrow in one hand.

Tagnya was looking up at the axe.

Vorpinger had kept his eyes on the axe since dismounting. He tilted his head back completely as he stood next to the ladder, placed his left hand on a rung, and continued to stare up. After a long moment, he placed his right foot on the bottom rung and commenced a slow climb, one rung at a time.

He's actually going up there.

At the fifth rung from the top, Vorpinger stretched out his hand to reach for his axe. It was just out of his grasp.

The fourth rung. Will it hold?

Tagnya moved away from the ladder. She stood next to one of the side frame posts and kept her eyes on Vorpinger.

Vorpinger climbed up on the fourth rung. It held. He reached through the space between the first and second rungs for the axe handle.

It won't budge.

Vorpinger pulled on the handle with his right hand. It didn't move.

It's going to take some leverage.

He grasped the two ladder poles with his hands and repositioned his left foot on the fourth rung and brought his right foot up on to the third rung.

Then, once again, he reached through the space between the first and second rungs with his right hand to get a good hold on it. His left hand reached over the first rung.

As Vorpinger used the third rung to lever his pull, he caused it to snap. The weight of his body split the top two rungs, and then the fourth rung under his left foot snapped.

This left Vorpinger swinging from the axe handle. He was holding on and kicking out with his left foot, trying to hook one of the ladder poles.

Tar piss! The buried blade of the axe was holding, but not for long. The handle started to move to vertical.

For a moment, Vorpinger watched it move and then he tried to look down.

He's trying to judge the distance to the ground.

Vorpinger's companions watched, frozen in disbelief. The fate of their leader was suspended in time before them.

The axe handle almost reached vertical. Vorpinger let go and fell. He frantically tried to kick out with his legs. His full weight came down on his left leg, which buckled under him, throwing him backward so the back of his head smashed against the stone plateau. His impact pushed away the smoke on the ground where he fell.

The bastard's probably still alive.

His arms were splayed out on each side of him. Nagora saw movement from where her mother stood. Then, with the sound of the axe blade splitting Vorpinger's face in two, the movement stopped.

Tagnya turned away and reached for the frame post. She held on to it, pressing her face to its side.

At that moment, everyone seemed to come to their senses. Vorpinger's brother had turned his mount away and was riding off, followed by the two others. Gabe was yelling orders. Lars and Sagora were riding in Tagnya's direction. Nagora yelled, "Follow me. After him." She did not look behind to see what was happening.

By the time she made it to the bridge in pursuit of Vorpinger's brother, she saw she would have to deal with the mass of Vorpinger's confused followers as Rhysonnger raced past them. She rode around them and hoped she could outrun them if they chased her.

She looked behind to see if Lars was following. That was when she realized she was alone, and when Storm fell.

# Despair
## *Pomewin*

A distant voice spoke to Nagora. She heard her own voice also, yet it didn't seem to be part of her. "I remember. It's the smoke. The bones. The smoke. He touched me. The smoke. I remember. Hurts. My head. I remember, Lars. What happened? Hurts."

"Nagora. Nagora. Do you hear me?"

"I remember."

"Nagora, what do you remember?"

"The smoke. It's the smoke."

"Nagora, can you open your eyes?"

"My head hurts. What's wrong?"

"Open your eyes, Nagora. Do you recognize me?"

She wanted to say she did, but couldn't put a name on the distant voice.

"Thirsty. I remember."

"Here, drink."

Her lips had no sensation. They were too far away from her.

"Nagora, can you squeeze my hand? Good. Can you squeeze it again? Good. Do you want more water?"

Even if her lips weren't there, she was thirsty.

"Aye."

"Here, drink. Good."

"It stinks. It smells shit."

"I know. Nothing we can do about that for now."

"Uncle?" She connected a name to the distant voice.

"Aye, Nagora. I'm here. I'm with you. You said your head hurts. Do you hurt anywhere else?"

"My head hurts."

"Does your back hurt?"

"No."

"Do your legs hurt?"

"No."

"I'm touching your foot, squeezing it. Can you feel that?"

"Aye."

"Now I'm squeezing your other foot. Do you feel that?"

"Aye. Shit and piss. It stinks. Where am I?"

"You're with me, Nagora. We're at the wall that surrounds Skull Bay."

"I remember."

"What do you remember, Nagora?"

"It's the smoke."

"You remember the smoke?"

"Aye, I remember now."

"Nagora, can you open your eyes? Can you see me?"

"My eyes hurt."

"Nagora, please try to open your eyes, just for a moment."

"Uncle, I see you. It hurts. Why does it hurt?"

"Do you remember what you did today, Nagora?"

She tried to remember. How do I remember now?

"Today?"

"Aye, today. What do you remember about today? What's the first thing you did after waking up today?"

Did I wake up?

"I'm tired."

Nagora opened her eyes. It was dark. Her arms hurt. Her wrists were tied to something above her head. Her legs refused to move. Her ankles hurt. They too were tied. Her knees were slightly bent. When she tried to straighten up, the back of her heels rubbed against something. She pulled with her arms and one of her heels came to rest on something solid. She pulled again and pushed with her heel and brought the other onto the solid surface.

Her eyes adjusted to the darkness. A few stars peeked through the holes in the clouds.

She tried to straighten her knees. Doing so relieved some of the strain on her arms.

The stench that surrounded her seemed to cover her also. Shit and piss and something else foul and rotten. No matter how she tried to breathe, the putrid stink remained. I'm going to puke.

If only I can see where I am, I might be able to think of something else.

She strained her neck to the right as far as possible. Flexing her knees a bit allowed her to move her head further.

At least there was another stink. Horse shit. Sweeter than the other kind.

She strained further and her nose came to rest on it. It was wet. The odor was familiar. Wet leather.

She let her nose rest there and then moved it along the object to try to picture it in her mind.

It must be part of something. What? I can't move it.

She pulled with her right hand, and at the same time, the object moved against her nose.

When she pulled again, she tried to twist her other hand to feel something. Her breath came harder and quicker as an image began to form in her mind. She pulled with her left arm and twisted her right hand and touched as much of it as possible.

She strained her neck to move her head to the left as far as she could.

Again, the wet leather. No horse shit. Piss and something else.

She had smelled it before, even tasted it.

She brought her head forward and let it hang so her chin rested on her chest. She focused on what her back rested against, and then, one by one, the images in her mind joined, and she guessed where she was and how she had come to be there.

All the day's events played out before her eyes, right up until she had been pitched from Storm's back when he fell.

What she had wanted to tell Lars about the poison came back to her.

The questions her uncle had asked were now fresh in her mind. They no longer resided in that distant place.

I'm at the wall that surrounds Skull Bay. My wrists are tied to the knees of the man I killed today. We are tied to the ladder he climbed. It's leaning against the wall. What in tar piss have I done?

She started to cry, but no tears came, just the dry heaving empty sobs of self-deception. *Here I am—the evil twin on display, tied to the ladder with the victim of her crime. Here for all to see. But will they? What of Mum and Sagora?*

Then, in that strange language, the language of The People, the language of the dragons, Nagora began to scream with all her might. "Father! Godomor! Father! Godomor!" Over and over she screamed loud and long. "Father! Godomor! *Ohtawimaw!*"

The sound of the gate opening did not stop her screams. Only when the splash of cold water hit her did she stop.

Three people stood before her, Dangor, holding an empty bucket, a torchbearer, and Godomor the Terrible.

Godomor gave an order to the torchbearer. The warrior climbed the ladder by finding rung spaces where possible until she stuck the long taper into Vorpinger's belt so it pointed up and out at the side of the ladder.

With that done, Godomor motioned Dangor and the torchbearer away. Godomor and Nagora stared at each other. She tried to read his expression. *Was it disappointment or something else?* She wasn't sure.

*What do I say?*

She would do her best to keep it simple. She would speak what she believed to be the truth; however, all she had as proof was her word. She had to wait for Godomor to speak first.

Now he did, in the language of The People. "*Ka Peyakot Mahihkan*, my heart bleeds for you this day. Your actions show you wear your name well. Tagnuska and Sagnuska have returned to their lodge in Skull Bay. They say they can no longer face the Hundred Best who took up their weapons for King Raynhard's cause. They plan to leave after your execution tomorrow."

Nagora closed her eyes and let her head hang on her chest for a moment. She expected no less. She had no control over her fate. The only thing she had left was hope. At that moment, it appeared to be the slimmest of hopes. She held up her head and looked into Godomor's eyes.

"A warrior is missing. One I took in as a son. You, I took in as a daughter. Both of you twins.

"Above you hangs Vorpinger, tied to the ladder trap you set for him. These are truths.

"Will twins ever be allowed to return to the Land of Skulls again? Will second-born twins be banished from the Land of Skulls? Will second-born twins be killed at birth?

"Lone Wolf, you have gained fame today and you have sealed the fate of all future twins in the Land of Skulls."

Godomor had finished speaking. Nagora would get only one chance. "Father, I know that is not the story you will want to tell by your fire. Please, Father, listen to my story now. Perhaps it will become the story of Lone Wolf you will enjoy telling by your fire someday."

Nagora told the story of her capture by Prince Acindor's men, of waiting to be brought before the prince when she saw the man with the human hand-bone bracelet for the first time, Vorpinger's brother, and the last words he spoke to Prince Acindor that day. "The smoke of the candles works its magic, and soon there will be a throne at play. Then we'll meet another day."

Godomor's eyes widened ever so slightly when Nagora spoke those words.

Next she told of the rape, abuse, and murder of young women which she had witnessed while held prisoner in the dungeon sea cave. And she told of what she had learned of how Vorpinger treated women in his domain, and how he had tried to treat Tagnya. For those reasons, she had come to see Vorpinger to be as evil as Prince Acindor and his jailor, and deserving of punishment. They were her reasons for setting the trap.

Then Nagora told of seeing Vorpinger's brother and recognizing him, and how that made her want to capture him to bring him before Godomor, her father, for questioning.

Finally she told how she had gotten Lars to promise to help her do this for Godomor, their father.

"So, Father, someday, should the truth be found out, perhaps that will be the story of Lone Wolf you will tell by your fire."

Godomor held Nagora's eyes with his for several moments before looking up and speaking to a guard at the top of the wall.

Dangor and the torchbearer appeared. Godomor spoke to the torchbearer and left.

Her uncle spoke. "I can't do anything for you, lass. They've given me some time to talk to you. Did Godomor tell you?"

"He did. I'll let him tell you what I told him. Uncle, why are you even here? I see Mum and Sagora will have nothing to do with me. I wish I'd gotten to know them more. I've created quite a mess. Do you know what's happened to Lars?"

"Well, he disobeyed orders. It's not clear where he's gone to. You did yell: 'Follow me. After him.' People are guessing those words were meant for him."

"No sign of him?"

"None. Not his dogs, either. People are guessing he's high-tailed it out of the country. They won't see him ever again."

"Tar piss on these people. They don't know half the story and they're quick to condemn. There's no justice anywhere. Not here. Not back home. How am I to die?"

"You don't want to know that now, Nagora."

"I do. It might give me some comfort while I'm hanging here covered in Vorpinger's shit and piss and blood. He's probably peeking down at me from behind a star and having a good laugh. Even in death he pays back Tagnya and her daughter. Come on, tell me."

Dangor shook his head and then took a breath.

"They've got an old barge at the docks. They're going to build a frame on it. Surround it with firewood. Storm'll be tied inside it. They'll tie you on top of the frame and set it on fire tomorrow night."

Nagora swallowed as she took in the image of the scene, the flames reflecting on the water. It was the panic and pain Storm would feel that brought tears to her eyes. They know how to make this twin's punishment as painful as can be.

"They want me burned into their memories. Who's going to light the fire? Gabe? He'll finally earn the title of Terrible. Gabe the Terrible who burned the terrible twin because she sealed the fate of all future look-alikes in the land. Because she ruined the chances of freeing the dragon and putting a king on his rightful throne. Aye, I ruined it for everyone, including myself."

"Not Gabe."

"Who then?"

Dangor took another breath. "Your mum, your sister, and I are to shoot fire arrows at the barge. If we don't, we'll never leave here alive."

She started to laugh. Punish me and the ones I love too.

"It's not funny, lass."

"Maybe I'll escape and make matters even worse for everybody. I'm sorry, Uncle. I've deceived you. I regret that. I've learned so much from you. I don't know how you'll do it, but I know you'll free the dragon. Just as well I not be there. Best of luck to you, Mum, and my big sister."

Dangor hung his head.

The torchbearer must've finished her count. She touched Dangor's arm, climbed the ladder to retrieve the taper, and then led him away. He didn't look back.

"Goodbye, Uncle. Tell Mum I love her."

In a panic she yelled, "Uncle! Is there a chance I'll be eaten by wolves tonight?"

Dangor stopped and turned to face her. He raised a hand and shook his head. "No. The guards won't let it happen. Goodbye, Nagora." He turned away.

As the gate closed, she let her head fall to her chest to cry in silence.

Nagora's head jerked up. She must have fallen asleep. For how long, she didn't know, but her mouth was dry like when she awoke from a deep sleep. Then she heard it. Perhaps that was what had awoken her. She peered into the dark, trying to make her eyes ready to focus on the sound should it come again.

"Tar piss!" No sound, but this time she was sure her eyes had caught it. It was just a brief glint, but enough to tell her she had seen two eyes. She focused.

The sound of paws. Two eyes. "Tar piss! A wolf!" What if the guards are asleep like I was? What if they don't see it? What do I do?

The sound of the paws came closer. Where do I look? Her eyes had adjusted. A faint line on the horizon and shades of the shadows of nearby rocks appeared.

"AHHH!" Her heart stopped beating. The two big paws had landed on her breasts without warning. The next thing her face was being licked. "Aydan! Aydan! Ah! My dying star! You scared me." Her bowels had turned to water and emptied, leaving the back of her legs covered in wet shit.

"Aydan, where's Lars? If only I understood your happy dog talk. Lars sent you, right? That's what you're telling me, right? Oh! Aydan, I wish I could hold you right now. You'd take me to him, wouldn't you?"

The gate opened. Aydan dropped his front paws to the ground. The torchbearer approached with two warriors, one with a spear and the other with a bow and drawn arrow.

"Aydan. Stay. Sit Aydan. Lars's dog. Lars's dog. Don't shoot."

Aydan stayed at the foot of the ladder and growled as the three approached.

The warrior with the bow relaxed his pull and bent on one knee. He held out his right hand and called to Aydan.

Aydan approached. The bowman let Aydan lick his hand. He spoke, and the torchbearer moved the taper closer. The archer pointed with his bow. He pointed to blood on the hound's coat, and did his best to get a look at both sides of him. Aydan let the archer pet him. As he did, he was careful and looked for wounds.

Finally, the bowman stood. The warriors headed for the gate.

Aydan returned and lay at the foot of the ladder.

Nagora focused on where the road met the horizon. There was a hint of twilight there. Dawn was on its way, and hope began to rise in her again. The purple twilight turned into a sinking line of blood-red sky to let rise the orange glow that heralded a new day.

Aydan stood up, faced the horizon, barked a single low muffled bark, and then sat on his haunches without moving as he stared at the horizon.

Nagora's eyes picked up the specks on the horizon. To her, they looked like balls slowly bouncing back and forth, three small ones bouncing against a big one.

A lookout on the wall yelled. Many voices were talking at once.

She was crying. Her face was wet with tears of hope. Barely able to say his name through her tears, she kept repeating it until finally she said it aloud. "Lars. Lars. It's you! Lars! You kept your promise!"

Aydan whined once and gave another muffled bark.

She blinked away her tears and made out the tiny silhouette of a rider bent over his horse leading three men tied to a rope.

The gates opened. Gabe and four warriors rode out. They came over to Nagora.

He's not smiling.

"Your uncle will cut you free. Mina will tend to your wounds. Father wants you to go swim in the Bay to get thoroughly cleaned off. You go to your mother's. She'll also check your wounds. Eat something. You're to dress and wear your hair like the first time you saw Vorpinger's brother. Then come back to the wall with your mother and sister. Take your time." Before she could speak, Gabe had headed off in Lars's direction.

I'm fine, Gabe. Thank you for asking. I can understand that you didn't want to stick around. My stink isn't so inviting, is it? Having me cleaned up before sentencing me?

Her uncle arrived on horseback, leading Storm. Mina followed him. As they dismounted, two warriors approached carrying buckets of water.

Dangor cut the ropes and gave Nagora his own orders. "Strip out of those clothes. There's soap in a bucket over there to wash yourself. Once you're rinsed off, Mina will disinfect your wounds. After, wear my rain cape. Gabe told you the rest?"

Nagora nodded as she did her best to remove her soiled garments. Her arms were still sore and stiff. Have my arms ever felt this way before?

Finally, she was naked. She was grateful to hobble over to the buckets of water that waited; however, now she shivered and her stomach finally did what she had, so far, been able to will it not to do.

Nagora bent over and heaved until she puked her insides out. She coughed and spit as much as she could to rid her mouth of the aftertaste. All she wanted to do was rinse her mouth with water. First, she had to rinse off her hands.

Through teary eyes she plunged her hands into the first bucket and scrubbed her hands and forearms.

Then she went to her knees before the second bucket and scooped out handfuls of water, splashing it into her mouth and onto her face. She did a quick wash of the rest of her body.

Mina poured the last bucket of water over her head and pressed down on her shoulder to make her crouch. She wants to examine my head wound.

From the sounds Mina made, she obviously didn't like what she was seeing. She looked at Nagora and held a finger between her teeth as she held up the vial in her other hand. Mina was warning her it was going to hurt. She motioned for Mina to do it and clenched her teeth. It'll hurt more than the water she poured over me.

Mina placed Nagora's hands on her own hips and pressed them.

She wants me to hold on tight to her.

Nagora did, and was glad she had. It was a hundred times worse than her branding. The burning sensation left no doubt how long and jagged the cut in her scalp was. The intense burning sensation did not last. Thank the stars. Tar piss! That hurt!

Next came her wrists. The contents of the vial did the work as well as her clenched fists did theirs. The sting of the vial's contents told her it had cleaned out her wounds. Worse than tar piss!

Mina went to her open scrip and came back with a small pointed stick and a clean strip of bandage. She had Nagora crouch again as she wrapped the cloth around the tip of the stick. Nagora winced as Mina set to work on her head. She showed Nagora the tip of the cloth-wrapped stick.

She's picking out small stones and dirt.

Mina tapped Nagora's shoulder to let her know she was done. She motioned to Nagora, giving her instructions. Mina wanted her to dunk her head often when she went to swim in the bay. The saltwater would help cleanse her wound.

Now Nagora was shivering and her teeth were chattering. Her uncle placed his waxed woolen cape over her shoulders and lifted the hood over her head. She welcomed the wool against her skin.

"Here, chew on this." Dangor handed Nagora a strip of dried meat from his trail rations. He led her over to Storm, helped her up, and made sure the cape covered her.

Nagora rode Storm over to the ladder to have a look at Vorpinger. The axe was still in place. The handle pointed up above his head like a long feather. The blade had cut into his forehead from the hairline just off the centerline, through the nose bridge, down the left side of his nose, taking the nostril with it, two upper teeth, and one jaw tooth. His mouth was wide open.

He had probably wanted to scream.

His eyes were still open. They were crossed.

He had probably watched the axe fall.

At least I made you pay. You'll hurt others no more.

She turned Storm away and bit into the strip of meat. Venison. She patted Storm's neck. "Time for Edana to go for a swim. Take me to the beach."

...

The water in Skull Bay was cold. Nagora was cold. Still, she dove in. She wanted to flush Vorpinger's stench from her nostrils, her hair, and her body. She dove repeatedly, each time taking a mouthful of saltwater which she expelled through her nose as she surfaced. The water did its work, and for a few moments, she even felt warm.

As she made her way to the woolen cape Dangor held open for her, the early morning air wrapped itself around her, chilling her so her teeth chattered some more. She backed into the cape, pulling it tightly around her as she turned to her uncle. He pulled the hood over her head and held her tight until her chills subsided.

"I should've made a fire for you."

"No use. We'll be home soon. Does Mum know we're coming?"

"Aye, she will. Godomor sent word."

She breathed in the salt air and licked it from the drops on her lips as it mixed in with the odor of damp wool. She tried not to predict what events this day would bring. She tried not to think of Lars.

He was slumped over his mount. Wounded. For me. To keep a promise.

Nagora had wanted to go to him, but that was not in Gabe's orders. Instead she focused on her body. The chills were fading. The soreness was still there, but it was clean. In that moment, she was safe in the quiet strength of her uncle's arms.

She looked up to the stars. Am I headed there? Da, this might be as close as I ever get to having you hold me.

A single tear spilled onto the wool near her cheek. She took a deep breath. "Let's go."

A handsome fire in the kitchen greeted Nagora once Tagnya and Sagora released her from their embrace. They had prepared warm, fresh water to rinse her hair and washcloths to wipe the salt from her body. She welcomed the attention. She had been expecting accusations.

Once they had finished assisting her, Sagora helped her into a linen smock and put a woolen sweater on her shoulders. "I've laid out clothes for you on my bed. Should be something close to what you were wearing on that day."

"Thank you, big sister."

Sagora smiled. "When your hair is dry, I'll help you comb it. You'll have to do it up yourself, though."

Tagnya led Nagora to a chair. "Let me tend to the wound on your scalp. Then you can eat."

"Not a problem. I'm starved."

"I have to clean your wound and put in three stitches before you eat. Your hair will hide the scar."

"I might not be around long enough for it to scar."

Tagnya paused before she replied. "True. You'll know before nightfall. Don't give up hope. I did yesterday. I felt all was lost. Now I have hope again. I wish I knew why."

"You're right, Mum. We'll all know by nightfall. Hope is all we have."

# Confessions
## *Âcimisowin*

Skull Bay was awake. What news and rumors had traveled from one lodge to another, Nagora did not even try to imagine. Though as she, her sister, her mother, and her uncle made their way up to the encampment near the wall, people who were outside and had seen them coming ran inside, leaving shut doors to witness their passing.

The gate at the wall was closed. The top of the wall was crowded with guards, warriors, and people of all ages. Dangor led them to Godomor's tent. Nagora's heart raced when she saw Aydan and Lyam lying in front of the tent in the morning sun. Was Lars in the tent?

Dangor waved her off Storm. "Sagora and I'll take care of the horses."

The dogs went to her as soon as she dismounted. She was as happy to see them as they were to see her.

Tagnya had no choice but to do like Nagora and give the big dogs a good petting to their sides and a good scratching behind their ears. "You big, bad boys. What have you been up to?"

To hear her Tagnya speak the way she did to the dogs gave Nagora hope.

Mina must've heard Tagnya's voice. She appeared at the flap of Godomor's tent, called, "Tagnuska," and waved to her to come.

Nagora followed Tagnya into the tent. Lars lay on Godomor's table. He had a big arm behind his head, propping it up to watch his visitors come in. He was wearing his big smile and not much more than bandages around his hip, left thigh, and knee. A towel covered his manhood.

Tagnya put a hand on his knee. "Lars, you're in good hands."

"Mina just finished patching me up," he said for Nagora's benefit.

Tagnya pointed to his wounds. "Mina, he's taken a few hits. What's the worst?"

Lars translated for Nagora. "Arrow came through from the back of the hip, just caught the meat, might have nicked the bone. It stuck in his saddle. The arrow head is still in the saddle. He cut the arrow so it wouldn't tear his wound open. Good thinking."

Mina picked up the two pieces of the arrow, the section with feathers and the section she had pulled from his hip. "I put plenty of salve on it and a stitch on each hole. On the same side, here on the upper left thigh, a sword slice, not too deep, four stitches."

Lars grinned. "Got my blade good and wet on that one. Payback a thousandfold."

Mina pointed. "A stab wound here, just above the knee, three stitches. A little lower, it would have done more damage."

Lars made as if he were holding his sword. "He came down on my knee just as I ran him through."

Tagnya slapped his other knee. "Three wounds to the left side. You'll have to watch for infection, especially at the hip. Have your bandages changed at least twice a day for a few days."

Tagnya pointed to Nagora. "I put three stitches in her scalp. I hope they won't be wasted."

Tagnya made her way to the tent flap. "Good work, Mina. If you're done, we can leave these two alone for a moment."

Her mother had kept her hand on Lars's knee the whole time. Was it just to comfort him? She touched and looked at him with a certain familiarity. That's new. Am I jealous? It must be her way with those she cares for.

As soon as Mina left with her scrip, Nagora went to Lars.

"You kept your promise."

"I did. I brought them all back, alive." Lars gave her his best smile and held out his right hand to Nagora.

She took it.

He sat up and winced. His left hand went to his hip. He swung his legs over the side of the table. "I'll feel better when I stand." He stood and took Nagora in his arms. He held her tight and kissed her. She had never been kissed that way for that long.

Lars pulled his lips away and took a breath. "Will you help me get dressed? Godomor is waiting for us."

"I better do that. If I don't, we'll keep him waiting for a long time." She pushed herself away from Lars. His condition left no doubt he had the same desires she did. It took some playful tickling to get him into the clean clothes Gabe had brought for him earlier.

She pulled his shirt down to hide his proud-standing manhood. "Should I walk ahead of you?"

"Shit, no. Do that and you'll only make it worse. If I had my sword, I could carry it in front of me."

"They took your sword?"

"Yes. They took your blades?"

"We're weaponless twins this day, Lars. What will be our fate?"

Those words settled the matter of his too-proud member.

He pulled aside the tent flap. "Let's go find out. Follow me." They left the tent and made their way to the ladder nearest the gate.

All the warrior eyes were on Nagora and Lars. Tagnya, Sagora, and Dangor were already at the top of the wall above the gate. Godomor was nowhere in sight.

When they reached the top of the wall, Lars had Nagora stand next to Tagnya.

Nagora looked out at the scene everyone had been observing. They had most likely witnessed it being set up from the start.

The three captives were naked on their knees on the road a hundred strides away, facing the gate. Each of their heads stuck through the space between two rungs of a ladder.

The ladder I shared with Vorpinger last night.

A single rung space separated each captive's head. Vorpinger's brother was in the middle. Each arm was tied to one captive's arm. Their bound arms were tied to one of the ladder poles so it rested across their shoulders.

"Mum, who's the one to Rhysonnger's left?" asked Nagora.

"I don't know his name. I've been told he's a candlestick maker."

The middle of a long chain took a single turn around Rhysonnger's neck and from there, each half of the chain took a turn around the necks of the other two, and then to their free hands, which had not been tied to the ladder pole.

The remaining chain lengths lay on the ground and stretched behind the captives, thirty strides away to Vorpinger's body, which lay on the ground. The axe was still planted in his face. The ends of the chain were tied to Vorpinger's ankles.

On each side of the ladder, three warriors with spears stood guard ten strides away from the captives. Behind the spearmen, three mounted warriors, also with spears, looked on.

Below, Gabe sat on his horse. All watched and waited in silence.

A lookout blew a horn.

In the distance down the road, a lone figure approached on a galloping horse. The rider's cape flew behind him. He held a sword high in his right hand.

Godomor!

His horse jumped over Vorpinger's body, galloped on, and then jumped over the kneeling captives. Godomor reared his horse to a stop. Its hooves hovered for a moment above the dust near the captives. When his horse set its hooves down, all heard his command. Sagora translated, "Stand before me."

Many of the onlookers laughed at the three captives as they tried to coordinate their efforts to stand without choking each other. They looked so pathetic tied to the shit-covered ladder.

Nagora recognized the counselor to the right of Rhysonnger. He squawked the most until he could focus on the mounted rider before him. His jaw dropped.

He can't believe he's looking at Godomor.

Rhysonnger struggled to make his neck comfortable with the chain that bit into it.

Godomor dismounted with sword still in hand. He tapped the top of each captive's head once then swung his sword a hand's width above their heads.

They ducked. Their unplanned move sent the counselor's end of the ladder to the ground, and that toppled them on their backsides. The counselor shit himself.

Rhysonnger was choking.

Some onlookers clapped and laughed.

Godomor put away his sword, mounted his horse, and waited until the three could stand.

When they had, Godomor spoke. "I have a question. Which of you will tell me who had the idea to poison their king?" Godomor held his left hand high for a moment.

"That's our signal," said Lars. "He wants us to go down."

At the bottom of the ladder, Godomor's attendant waited. He held a black cloak on one arm and, in his other hand, he held a brass candle stand with six big candle stubs on it. He handed the cloak to Nagora. She looked to Lars. He nodded. She donned the cloak.

Then the attendant placed the candle holder in her hands. It was about the length of her arm in height, shaped like a tree with six branches. Each branch now held the stub remains of a candle.

So Godomor is going to have me set the evidence before the accused. And I will be his witness.

Lars looked at her as he raised the hood of her cloak. "You're to keep your face hidden. When Godomor signals to you, go place the candle holder on the road a few paces from Rhysonnger. I'll be standing near Gabe."

They passed through the gate. Nagora walked until she was next to Godomor's horse.

Godomor motioned to her.

Nagora walked forward and set the candle stand where she had been told, and then she returned to stand next to Godomor's horse, her face still hidden beneath the hood.

Godomor waited until all the onlookers had quieted down. In a loud, clear, paced voice, the king spoke. "A poisoned tribute. A gift from Vorpinger, brought to me by his counselor. The smoke from these candles almost brought me the gift of my death."

"That is not our doing," yelled the counselor. "You cannot lay the blame for your illness on us."

In the same voice, Godomor said, "I have a witness to your plan." He stared at them and waited.

He wants that to sink in. He wants them to start thinking.

Godomor continued, "Which of you recalls speaking these words? 'The smoke of the candles works its magic, and soon there will be a throne at play. Then we'll meet another day.'"

"Who would speak such words? To whom? They make no sense," yelled the counselor.

Godomor remained calm. "My witness will tell you."

Godomor held his right hand open at his side. Gabe rode forward. He took something from his scrip and placed it in Godomor's hand. Godomor held out his hand to Nagora.

Gabe spoke. "Take it, Nagora."

She did.

"You'll know what to say. I'll speak for you so all will understand."


Nagora stepped forward and stood before Rhysonnger. The candle stand was between them. She slipped the hood from her head, let the cape fall to the ground, and held up the human hand-bone bracelet. Rhysonnger's eyes flicked from the bracelet to her face. He swallowed and clenched his teeth.

The bastard knows. He remembers my face now, despite the brand.

"This man," Nagora paused, "who wore this bracelet," she paused again, "held my chin in his hand." She waited for Gabe to finish speaking. "He moved my chin this way and that, as he looked at me that day in Prince Acindor's fortress at Yhorgal Cliffs in the land Queen Raganora calls Innisfhail." Again she waited before pointing at Rhysonnger. "This man spoke those words to Prince Acindor that day."

The counselor turned to Rhysonnger with his mouth hanging open. Rhysonnger had been staring at Nagora. His eyes went to Godomor. He lowered his head and then looked sideways at the counselor.

The counselor spit at him and started to yell and kick at him.

The counselor's kicking fit, combined with Rhysonnger's attempts to protect himself made, the laddered captives topple once more. When they were on the ground, the third man reached over to pull on the chain at Rhysonnger's neck. He yelled to the counselor to do the same.

Nagora picked up the cape and the candle holder before making her way back to stand next to Gabe. Godomor's attendant came forward and took the cape and candle holder. He refused to take the bracelet. Nagora made to give it to Gabe. He shook his head. "No, it's yours now."

Godomor ordered the guards to stop the assault on Rhysonnger and to untie the counselor and the candlestick maker. The guards tied the wrists of the two behind their backs, led them past the mounted warriors, and forced them to kneel on the ground.

Then Godomor ordered Rhysonnger to stand. Vorpinger's brother struggled with the weight of the ladder until he was finally able to sit up with one end of the ladder resting on the ground. He fought to get on one knee, and then bring the other next to it. He rested a moment before dragging one foot in place to push his body up. When he stood, he bent over with the ladder balanced on his shoulders.

Godomor rode closer to him. "I will question your companions in turn, and then come to you with those same questions. Your answers had better match theirs."

Gabe dismounted. "Come, Nagora. We'll go stand with Lars near the gate."

Nagora followed Gabe, glad to be joining Lars, whose smile was now the widest she had ever seen it. He hugged her to him. "Well done. I think fate will smile on us this day." Lars pointed behind her. She turned to look.

Godomor dismounted. He led his horse over to the candle-stick maker, pulled his sword from its scabbard, and knelt on one knee before the man. He rested the blade of his sword on the man's shoulder and stared at the man for at least a hundred count before speaking to him. No one could hear their conversation.

Nagora did not want to be in that man's place.

When Godomor stood, he returned his sword to its scabbard and walked his horse across the road over to where the counselor knelt. He repeated the same ritual for his private conversation with the counselor. It took much longer than his previous conversation, but finally, Godomor stood before Rhysonnger.

Godomor pulled his sword and tapped Rhysonnger on the head. "Stand straight." Rhysonnger took his time straightening as he let the weight of the ladder shift from his shoulders to his arms and back. This caused him to grin in pain as the ladder pulled his arms back. Godomor walked around Rhysonnger until he stood behind him. He towered over the man by a head. "Look to the wall to those that witness your replies to your king. Speak your answers loud so all will hear. Whose idea was it to poison me?"

"Mine."

"Where did you learn of the poison?"

Lars took hold of Nagora's hand and continued to translate.

She squeezed his hand. Her palm was wet.

"Innisfhail."

"Who told you of the poison?"

"Innisfhail's Queen Raganora."

"Who provided you with the poison?"

"Hag, the queen's witch."

Nagora held on tighter.

"Where does Hag live?"

"At the fortress of Prince Acindor on Yhorgal Cliffs in Innisfhail."

"At what cost did you obtain the poison?"

"Gold, a promise of more gold, and an alliance once the throne was ours."

Godomor placed his blade's edge against Rhysonnger's neck. "An alliance to what end?"

Rhysonnger swallowed. "To help Queen Raganora root out the rebels in Innisfhail."

"Who's your messenger to the queen?"

"No one. I deal with her directly if I can. If not, with her son, Prince Acindor."

"What else did you pay?"

Rhysonnger hesitated and moved his neck away from the pressure of the blade's edge.

"A gift to Prince Acindor."

"Does this gift have a name?"

"Yes, Sellannye."

"Who is Sellannye?"

"My brother's daughter."

"How old is she?"

"She turned eleven on the day I gave her to the prince as a virgin bride-to-be."

"Was Sellannye, in fact, a virgin?"

"No."

"You knew this?"

Rhysonnger closed his eyes for a moment. "I suspected as much. Hag confirmed it."

"You say you suspected as much."

You're going to get cut.

Rhysonnger lifted his chin higher as he tried to stretch his neck away from sword's edge. "I knew. I knew it."

You bastard!

"How did you know?" Godomor relaxed the pressure of the blade on Rhysonnger's neck.

"Vorpinger told us he'd taken his daughter."

"Did he swear you to secrecy in this plot to kill me?"

"Yes."

"How did you seal that pact?"

Rhysonnger squeezed his eyes shut. "He made us rape her." He opened his eyes, pleading. "But she was no longer a virgin!"

You bastard! If Godomor doesn't kill you, I will.

Lars gave her hand a pat.

"Did someone witness Sellannye's rape?"

"Yes."

Godomor slapped the side of Rhysonnger's face with the flat of his blade.

Rhysonnger cried. "Sellannye's mother, Nausyka."

"Under what circumstances?"

"Nausyka had fled with Sellannye the year previous when she learned my brother had raped his own daughter. Vorpinger knew where she was hiding." Rhysonnger shook his head and tried to wet his lips with his tongue. "To seal our pact to kill you, Vorpinger wanted proof we would be loyal to him and follow through.

"He brought us to the cave near the sea cliffs where Nausyka hid. He had us strip his wife naked and bind her wrists and ankles, and then bring her to the edge of the cliff.

"Meanwhile, he stripped his daughter and tied a rope around her waist. We held his wife and forced her to watch as he raped Sellannye."

Rhysonnger was sobbing and shaking his head.

Godomor waited.

"Then Vorpinger held Nausyka and forced her to watch as we did the same as he'd just done to Sellannye." Rhysonnger sobbed even louder.

"When we finished, he told Sellannye to run to her mother or he would rape her again. We held the end of the rope. Sellannye ran to her mother to hold her. This caused Sellannye to push her mother over the cliff. The rope kept Sellannye from going over with her mother."

Nagora put her face into Lars's chest. Her tears wet his shirt.

Lars placed a hand on the back of her head. His breath settled just above her wound.

Godomor waited. "Is Sellannye alive today?"

"I've been told she is in Queen Raganora's care, being prepared to become the prince's bride."

Nagora pulled Lars closer so only he would hear. "He's a bloody liar, Lars. She's a prisoner in the prince's dungeon sea cave. He's abusing her. You can't imagine."

Godomor walked around Rhysonnger to stand before him. "Do you have anything else to say?"

Rhysonnger hung his head. "No."

"Go join your brother. Sit at his feet."

All present watched him turn to walk to his brother.

Godomor called six guards forward, took one of their spears, and drew a big X on the ground in the middle of the road where Rhysonnger had stood. He gave instructions. Two of the guards ran back through the gate.

Godomor turned to look up to those on the wall. He raised his sword and waved to them.

Cheers of, "Godomor! Godomor! Godomor!" broke out along the wall.

Tagnya and Sagora joined Nagora and Lars. Gabe motioned them to stand near his father. They did, and Godomor had them face the wall of cheering onlookers.

Godomor motioned for silence. He spoke a command. Nagora heard her name. "You're to go get the axe from Vorpinger's face," said Sagora.

"You're sure?"

Sagora nodded. "You can do it, little sister."

"Damn right I can." Nagora rushed along the road until she came alongside Vorpinger's body. She walked over and stood before the axe handle. It looked like it had sprouted from Vorpinger's face to stand above his head. She bent and pushed down on the handle as she grasped it, and then she pulled it up and forward to release it. A brief sucking sound spilled from the gash the axe blade left. She stared into Rhysonnger's eyes until he lowered his gaze. When he did, she left.

As she returned, she raised the axe. The warriors on the wall whistled. Dangor smiled and held both his thumbs up.

Godomor stepped between Nagora and Lars. He took Lars's wrist, raised it, and pointed with his sword, first to Rhysonnger, then to the candlestick maker, and to the counselor. The warriors chanted, "Lars! Lars! Lars!"

Then Godomor put his sword in its scabbard and unfastened it from his waist. He had Lars and Nagora hold onto the scabbard with their right hands, and then, holding onto the handle of his sword, Godomor raised their arms. Branded twins being cheered in this way was close to unbelievable, but Nagora was living it.

When Godomor lowered their arms, Tagnya and Sagora came forward to embrace her and Lars.

Godomor waited for the cheering to die down before he spoke. "Tonight we feast the departure of our Hundred Best. Tagnuska, your cause has become ours. We have won the first battle. You leave in two days. May you win all your battles."

The warriors took up their cheers again.

Tagnya thanked Godomor.

Godomor put a hand on Tagnya's shoulder and turned her to face Nagora. He wore a huge smile and Tagnya wore a face of tears as she opened her arms. "My Nagora." Tagnya held her close. "Please, don't ever do something like that again. I can't take it."

"Sorry, Mum. I shouldn't have taken justice into my own hands." But I'll never stand by and wait for justice to punish those who've wronged me and my family.

Most of the warriors that had assembled along the top of the wall dispersed. Nagora spotted the two Godomor had dispatched with instructions. They arrived with a mule cart. She could only guess at what the shovels and pickaxes could be used for. Her curiosity must have been obvious.

"Some of the guilty are going to be quite busy, little sister."

"You know what they'll be doing?"

Sagora raised an eyebrow and wore a flat smile. "The usual punishment for those found guilty of crimes against the throne. Do you want to know, or will you be able to wait and see?"

"I can wait. I'm becoming used to waiting to see justice done."

"You won't be disappointed. You might even be tempted to wager on the outcome if you have a coin to spare."

"Bet?"

"You said you could wait. I suggest you do before you put a coin down."

This is going to be good. I can't wait to see what'll happen to those three.

"Now what do we do?" asked Nagora.

"Go home. Eat something. You probably want to get out of those clothes to dress like a warrior. We'll get ready for the feast. Put on our war paint, weapons and all. It's not every day the Hundred Best leave the land. First ever in my memory. Plenty of food and drink, songs and toasts," said Sagora.

Nagora put an arm around her sister's waist. "A big celebration?"

Sagora nodded. "As is the custom here. Most will eat and drink and fall asleep right in the Grand Hall, hoping to wake by midday with something they consider to be their heads still on their shoulders."

Nagora smiled. "I've only heard of such parties. Never witnessed one."

"Witnessing one without drinking yourself under the table will make you want to be at the next one."

She gave Sagora a squeeze. "Big sister, have you ever ended up under the table?"

Sagora shook her head. "No. I like to know where my head is at all times, especially when it hurts."

"I'm with you on that." Nagora let go of Sagora's waist and brought both hands up to gingerly touched the top of her own head. Ouch! That's going to be sensitive to touching for a while.

As they followed Tagnya and Godomor past the skull-covered gates, Nagora glanced at the skulls. Would the next four skulls be given special places on the doors? Would such a courtesy even be considered? It was a question she let slip away.

At least one of those skulls will be instantly recognizable.

A hand came to rest on Nagora's shoulder. It shook her gently. Her uncle dropped his hand to her waist and pulled her closer without losing a step.

"Well, lass, I think this'll be a day you'll remember for a long time, aye? How do you feel?"

"Relieved and tired. Other than that, you know, Uncle, right now I don't think I have place in me for any other kind of feelings. I seem to have been through them all."

"It's the same for us, lass. I bet you're hungry now. I know I am."

"You're always hungry! So am I, and so tired. I'll have to eat before the feast. Otherwise, I won't make it there."

After the quiet meal at home, a tension of unspoken thoughts and emotions hung in the air around the table. No one seemed to have words to put on how they felt about all that had happened. Or if they did, they weren't sure how they would be taken if spoken aloud. Should I apologize for my actions? In light of the outcome, I see no need to. I have to get out of here, get some air.

"I'm going to the cliff. I'll have Aydan with me." Nagora put on her blades and left through the back door.

When Nagora arrived at the spot of her ritual morning practices, she climbed to the highest outcrop of the cliff's edge. She found a spot to sit with her knees pulled up to her chin and her amulet resting against her lips.

Despite the soreness in her arms and shoulders, she liked to sit this way as she looked out to sea, past Skull Rock at the bay's entrance.

Aydan rested his big muzzle on her feet. A single finger played in the curls on his head.

She let her mind wander to the horizon like she'd done so many times before back home at her spot on her cliff, looking for the sail that would bring her father home. Not a sail was in sight. What news of Father would Raynhard have for her, her mother, and her sister? No, I won't guess. I'll hope instead for the best.

The royal hunting dagger Raynhard had given her and the vest with the king's coat of arms—Did she aspire to what those objects symbolized? And what of how her king thought of her? Was what the amulet showed her for real? Could she trust what it had showed her? Did Raynhard truly see her as more than a duty-bound warrior?

Lars had kept his promise to her. Something he could so easily have ignored. Was that an expression of his love for her, or was it done out of loyalty to her because of the brand they shared? This morning, there was no mistaking his desire for her, and her own was just as strong. He truly had proven to be her protector, *onakateyimowew*, and her branded brother, *masinaskisow nitisan*.

The splash in the pond of her heart had spread its rings. They were definitely growing. Both Godomor and Raynhard had told her to trust her heart and her feelings when it came to following her path. I want to trust my heart. I want to trust I'm happy when I'm with Lars. I want him on my path with me.

I didn't feel that with Raynhard. Yes, I felt his strength, but not love in the way Lars expressed it. The weight of wearing the title of queen is a burden, not a boon.

Dangor, her father's brother, had raised her like she was his very own. He had been her ever, quiet, patient teacher, waiting for her questions, letting her draw her own conclusions, never judging her. He was there for her last night, the darkest, fear-filled night since her escape from the dungeon sea cave.

Godomor had welcomed her home, had taken her in as his own daughter, had listened to her calls of desperation and her story in the night, and he had given her hope.

Nagora pulled the sweater tighter around her as she let herself slide onto her side. In her mind, Lars held her in his arms and kissed her as he had done that morning. Sleep overtook her.

Aydan's wagging tail woke Nagora. He was sitting on his haunches looking in the direction they had come. "Who is it Aydan?" She rubbed her face. *How long have I slept?* She leaned on Aydan to see who was coming. Sagora reached the top of the cliff trail at that moment. Nagora waved. "Up here."

Sagora climbed to sit next to Nagora, but not without a happy face wash from Aydan.

"You're happy to see me, big boy. Great view from here."

"I've been enjoying it, lost in thought." She savored the sensation of waking from a long sleep.

Sagora looked in her eyes. "Mum sent me. She figured you might've fallen asleep."

"I did."

"We all had a nap." Sagora smiled. "These past two days have taken us through a lot."

Nagora took a long breath. "Much on account of me."

"Well, yes, but it's done, and things have turned out for the best." Her big sister patted her knee.

"Thanks to Lars and Godomor."

Sagora nodded. "Aye, well, for a while we didn't know what in the stars you were up to."

"Things happened kind of fast. I thought I'd have everything under control with Lars's help. Didn't turn out that way. I don't know why Storm fell." Nagora bit on her lower lip.

Sagora was smiling. "Uncle figures Storm landed on a big stone that flipped. He lost his footing, went down fast, and threw you."

Nagora pointed to her head. "I'll have a scar to remind me of that for a long time."

"You're lucky. The fall could've killed you."

"True. I could've died so many ways these past days. Guess my star hasn't come up."

Sagora reached out and patted her knee. "I'm glad it didn't. Let's go."

# Celebration
## *Môcikihtâwinihkewin*

Tagnya was smiling as the twins came in. "Look what Godomor sent for you two." Two of the kitchen chairs had new leather leggings and sheepskin vests draped over their backs. New boots rested on the chairs' seats. "Godomor had them made for you today. Nagora, he had the clothes you wore burnt."

"Look. He even had the map embroidered on the hide sides of both vests," said Sagora, as she handed one of the vests to Nagora.

"Dangor says everything is there, just like the one he'd drawn." Tagnya looked to Dangor who nodded. "Make sure you thank Godomor."

Nagora smiled. "Godomor's so thoughtful." It was a contradiction, not something someone wearing the name Terrible would do. He truly is like a father, *ohtawimaw*, to me.

"He also sends word that woolen shirts like the one you wore will be ready by tomorrow night. Knitters can only knit so fast."

Nagora couldn't help smiling as her eyes teared. "I love that man."

The twins each led a mule bearing gift sets of blades for all the volunteers. Tagnya and Dangor followed with a third mule that carried the remainder of the arrows for the archers and the cask of Geirador's mead for Godomor. Other feast-goers, who joined them along the way to the Grand Hall, greeted them with cheers.

How quickly one's fortune can change.

Nagora reached for her sister's hand. Sagora stopped and put her other hand on Nagora's neck to bring her closer in a warm embrace.

The music grew louder the closer they came to the Grand Hall. Musicians were standing on the steps with their flutes, lutes, and bodhrans.

As they walked the mules to the stable-side of the hall, they passed spits with roasting pigs, sheep, and calves. Cooks tended fires with cauldrons of boiling vegetables. Tables with piles of bread loaves waited next to others with big wooden platters ready to be filled. Nagora had never seen so much food in one place. As they tied up the mules, Lars showed up with four companions ready to give them a hand to bring their gifts inside.

Lars smiled at her. I know what I want. She smiled back.

For Nagora, most of the feast was a blur of images, sounds, voices, and tastes. Some were clear and present, others vague and confused. Perhaps it was the mead she had had to drink when she and Lars were toasted. She had handed out the sets of blades and taken each warrior's embrace in return. Each had wanted to shake her hand and to touch the axe Labrys had given her.

He had been the first in line to receive a set of blades. He spoke something to her which Lars translated. "In battle, if an enemy threatens you and I am within throwing distance, he'll taste my axe before he can get to you." His vow was sincere. Nagora had smiled at him and embraced him.

Nagora had been leaning next to Godomor at his table as he examined his set of blades. He was wearing his crown for the first time since her arrival. It was not the usual crown from the stories her uncle told. The thick band of black leather that surrounded his head supported a five-strand braid of fine gold chains. On that golden braid above Godomor's forehead rested a front-facing skull of gold, and on each side of the braid above his ears were two gold skulls, set in profile, faced forward.

Her memory of Vorpinger's split skull sent a momentary shiver through her. Which skull represented his domain? She would not ask.

Godomor had partially pulled the big blade from its sheath and pointed to the Tiwaz symbol. He spoke to Nagora in the Language of The People. "For a higher cause. It will inspire my best warriors to follow you, Lone Wolf."

Nagora pointed to her brand. "Father, I wear the Tiwaz. That does not make me their leader. Gabe will lead them."

"He will. You will lead their hearts."

"Father, I am not a leader."

Godomor placed his hand on hers. "Edana, they know your story. They have witnessed your actions. They have chosen to be part of your story."

Nagora held tight to Godomor's hand with both of hers. "Father, my wish tonight is that they return with a story that will make you proud of your daughter." For a moment she was lost in his smile, savoring the strength it gave her.

Once Nagora had emptied her plate, she made her move. She grabbed Lars by the wrist and then brought his head close so she could yell in his ear above the noise. "I want some hot meat. Let's go get some at the fires outside." She bit his ear.

Lars smiled as he licked his lips and wiped his mouth with the back of his hand.

As they pushed their way through the crowded passage that now snaked its way up to the back of the hall, they had to kindly refuse every toast offered to them; otherwise, they would have had to crawl out of the hall.

Just outside the door, Lars stopped. "Listen. The bard's going to sing about Tagnuska's challenge to Vorpinger. Hear that? They're chanting 'By the balls! By the balls!'"

"Do I have to grab yours to make you understand what I want?" She reached up, pulled his head down, put her face into his, and kissed him like he had kissed her in Godomor's tent. Satisfied with his reaction, she pulled her mouth from his. "I want you to finish what you started this morning. Come with me."

Once in the street, Nagora had him and his dogs almost running next to her. "Where are we going?"

"Somewhere we can be alone." She pulled him along.

As they approached the doorstep to Tagnya's place, Lars stopped and held Nagora back.

She was about to say something when he put his finger to her lips and pointed at the door latch handle. A scarf hung from it. "That's Umma's, if I'm not mistaken," Lars whispered. "And there's the candle lantern hanging next to the door."

"So?"

"It means she wants privacy. She has company."

"What do you mean she ... ," and then it hit her. "Umma was with my uncle at the feast. Now that I think of it, they weren't there when we left, were they?"

Lars nodded, and her smile grew bigger and bigger. "Well, I'll be ... " She had to hold a hand over her mouth to keep from giggling aloud as she led Lars through the corral to the back of the lodge. "Wait here. I'll be right back."

Nagora snuck into the saddle room and unfastened her sleeping roll from her saddle. She brought it and the rain cape it was wrapped in with her. On the way out the room, she took one of the round-bottomed lanterns from a hook and a skin for water.

"You have fire starter in your scrip?" she whispered.

Lars nodded. "Now, where to?"

"To the cliff path. I know just the spot. Aydan knows it too. We'll get some water on the way."

Nagora climbed to the top of the cliff's outcrop ledge and shined the lantern around so Lars could see that the ledge sloped back down at a slight angle. "Have your dogs stay down. We'll have plenty of room." She found a chink in the rock big enough for her to wedge the lantern in.

As Nagora unfastened the straps of her sleeping roll, Lars was behind her, removing her blades. He put them aside and removed his own.

She went to her knees and leaned forward to spread out her bedroll. Lars followed and pushed up her shirt and vest. He kissed her lower back first. His hands held her hips. His fingers play with the strings that held her leggings to her undergarments.

When they released, his hands moved from her hips, pushing her leggings down her thighs. Then his fingers went to the inside of her thighs. They slowly made their way up, just avoiding the spot where she wished they would linger.

Instead, they caressed her lower stomach. Lars kissed his way up her back as his hands pretended to reach for her breasts. He let his fingers play at the edge of their ripeness. He buried his face between her shoulder blades as his fingers finally caressed her nipples.

His warm breath reached Nagora's neck before his lips and tongue made their assault.

He was hot and hard between her thighs and against the linen shield of her undergarments.

Nagora reached down to take hold of him, but a hand stopped hers.

"Open the cape."

She did, and he gently brought her down with him onto his right side. His right arm was a pillow for her head. He blew kisses over her wound, and then brought his lips to her ear as he let her bite his thumb and fingers.

He kept her hands at bay so she ground back into him. "I want you, Lars."

"Have you ever been with a man?"

"A young bully tried to rape me. He spent before he could penetrate."

"This will be your first time?"

"Aye. Not for you, though. Many a woman here in Skull Bay, I'll wager."

"Not one of them. Last time I was with a woman was when I said my goodbyes to the Moroes-Island lasses."

Nagora smiled. "Many goodbyes, then?

"It's not what you think. Let's get undressed. Open your bedroll. We'll get under the cape."

When Nagora returned to his side, she was naked. So was Lars. He was on his back. She draped her right leg over his. He pulled her to him. The sensation of her skin against his as she inhaled the scent of him made her hungry for him. *Wrap me around you like this forever.*

Her fingers followed the line of his jaw. This time he let her sneak her other hand to him.

The heat and smoothness of his skin there surprised her. It pulsed and grew bigger and harder. She pressed her forearm down along its heat as her hand reached for his balls. The intake of his breath was sharp.

His hand caressed her hip and then moved to her buttock and squeezed it and pulled on it. Then his fingers reached down and under.

She pushed her unshielded mound to them, inviting them to explore. Explore they did, to her wet satisfaction.

He put both hands above her hips and pulled her on top of him. "You're in control now. Take me in and ride me. Careful of the wound on my hip. Take your time. Ease me in. I might hurt you."

Nagora kissed his chest as she lay straddled across his hips, savoring the hotness of him against her abdomen. She moved against his cock feeling her damp hair drag and pull away as her wet lips spread over its center ridge.

Back and forth, she slid against his shaft with more and more urgency. She reached down to hold him as she shifted her weight to her left knee and brought her right foot up alongside his hip. She raised herself a bit more and set the head of his cock at her entrance. She controlled her descent. She had the head in. Would more of it fit?

It would. The jailor had put his into smaller girls than her.

Now she was taking Lars into her, deeper, deeper, and then she backed off from the pain and resistance. She sucked in a breath, guided him back in, and brought herself to the edge of the pain, and then backed off a tiny bit.

Nagora brought her left kneed higher above his hip and pulled her right foot out so she could bring her right knee down. "Put your hands on my hips. Just keep them there."

He did.

She reached for his arms and began to rock back and forth, driving the head deeper each time. She kept it up until her excitement and desire forced her to push deeper, beyond the discomfort.

It was a flash of pain and the more she rocked his cock in and out of her, the more she soothed the painful spasm until it became only pleasure.

Nagora savored it as deep as she could take it, then she drew it out almost completely. She rode slow. She rode fast. He let go of her hips and caressed her back and her breasts. He wrapped his arms around her as she ground into him and moaned her pleasure repeatedly.

Nagora couldn't believe how her body shook with spasms of pleasure, how her legs had straightened and tensed and trembled on top of his. Had he not held her, she would've fallen off him with his cock still inside of her. If she would've fallen from the cliff to her death, it would've been a most welcome and happy death.

Lars held her there until her breathing slowed. When it did, he put his lips to her ear. "I beg you, ride me again."

She did, and when again she tensed and shook, he pulled her from him and placed her belly over him as he shot against her, covering their bellies. She convulsed and cried her joy uncontrollably.

He held her stuck to him in the juices of their lovemaking. When finally she had settled, he lay her back next to him, and then found his shirt to clean her off.

Sleep, come hold us in your arms.


Nagora opened her eyes. Fog hung thick in the morning air, hiding everything within its damp shroud. Lars still held her to him, pressed into her back.

She lifted her head. Lyam and Aydan lay at their feet. She smiled. She had fallen asleep in the arms of her protector on a rocky ledge, with two guardians to watch over them, under a starry sky, their stomachs full and their lust satisfied.

This must be what happiness feels like. What more is needed? What more can two people want?

She wanted more. She wanted her father to return someday. She wanted Lars's brother to return someday. Though
right now, at this very moment, she was satisfied, happy with
what she had.

Aydan crawled up to lay his big head a hand's width from
her face. One big eye watched her face. Nagora pretended to
sleep as she squinted at him. He turned his head away and
rolled back against her. Soon she would be baking under the
cape, but that did not bother her. Rather, she closed her eyes
to savor the moment.


When next Nagora opened her eyes, it was her bladder that
demanded attention. She nudged Aydan and pulled back the
cape to scramble down the side of the rock to relieve herself.

When she stood and stretched, a pleasant tangible ache and
tenderness radiated from her. No mistaking it, this was desire.
Now I know how to satisfy it.

Lyam and Aydan came down.

Lars must be awake.

She climbed back up and found him dressing. "I had to
pee."

"I heard. I did too. I hope no one's standing below this
cliff."

Nagora reached for him. "You men have this advantage."

"Is that why you women keep trying to take it from us?"

She put her chin against his chest as she looked up at him.
"For a moment last night, I thought I'd done so. Did I hurt
you?"

"A most pleasant hurt."

"It was for me too, Lars." She pulled him closer. "Looks
like you want me to hurt you again."

"You can try to take it from me again."

She pulled him down onto the bedroll.

Close to noonday, the sun had just finished burning off the fog when Nagora and Lars showed up at Tagnya's place. The smell of soup coming from the kitchen announced the ideal first meal of the day.

"Good morning, you two. Lars, have you taken good care of my youngest daughter?"

"Tagnuska, I've given your daughter only the best of care to satisfy her heart's desire."

"In that case, both of you must be hungry."

Nagora smiled at Tagnya. "Sleeping under the stars does that."

"Your uncle didn't sleep under the stars, and he was the only one up for breakfast bright and early this morning. Sagora just went to get him."

Nagora pointed to her ear. "Uncle was whistling. I've never heard him whistle a tune unless I played my flute."

Tagnya smiled. "Well, he's been whistling since he woke up. I sent him to the corral so I could get a bit more sleep."

Sagora walked in. "Good morning, big sister. Did you sleep well?"

"Probably as well as you."

Tagnya winked at Nagora. "She arrived just before you two."

Nagora was smiling and her smile grew even wider when her uncle came into the kitchen, whistling, with Umma's scarf wrapped around his neck.

"Morning, Nagora, Lars. Sagora says the soup's ready. I'm starved."

Nagora nudged Lars. "Aren't we all? Let's hope there's enough to go around."

Later that afternoon as the twins rode in, the warrior encampment was slowly coming to life. A knot of warriors at the foot of the ladder jostled with the man who was taking wagers.

Sagora pointed. "Let's go have a look at how the guilty are faring today. Then you might want to put down a coin on the outcome."

"Sagora, I've rarely had more than one coin in my scrip."

"You work for Uncle. Doesn't he pay you?"

"Aye, but I have no use for coins. He salts them away for me in some secret place for the day whenever I'll need them."

"A secret place? How will you find it?"

"There's a map. I know where that's hidden." In the secret pocket of my scrip where the chain once hid.

"I'll lend you some if you want to bet."

They climbed the ladder and found a spot on the wall not far from the gate where they could look down.

Two heads were on the road where Godomor had drawn a big X the day before. The dead eyes of one of the heads seemed to stare up at her, despite the bloody gap in the middle the face they occupied, Vorpinger's ugly face.

Nagora could only see the back of the other head and its right ear. That head moved. It was Rhysonnger's head. He and his brother were buried in a hole up to their necks in the dirt of the road, facing each other. Vorpinger's head was only a head's width from his brother's.

"The counselor and his friend dug the hole. Rhysonnger pulled his brother over to it, and the other two wrapped the chain around Rhysonnger and stood him in it. Some say Rhysonnger screamed when Vorpinger was lowered in with him. Finally, the candlestick maker and the counselor shoveled dirt back into the hole." Sagora seemed to relish explaining the details. Had Gabe given them to her?

"The counselor and the candlestick maker have to do their best to keep Rhysonnger alive. The longer he lives, the longer they live. See over there? They've dug their hole. It awaits them. Once they're in it, no one will give them food and drink." Could I have come up with a better punishment?

"So the bets are on how long Rhysonnger will live?"

"Aye, and then on which of the other two will die first, the counselor or the candlestick maker."

Nagora shook her head. "I have no desire to waste a coin on any of them."

# Departure
## *Sipwehtewin*

The next morning, King Godomor the Terrible stood on his wall above his gate with his back to the wind and intermittent sleet. He wore his crown. Today, a single raven's wing was attached to the left side of the crown. The wind bent it over the top of his head. His great, black, waxed, woolen cape was draped over his shoulders. In his left hand, he held a small shield with an embossed skull on it. In his right, he held his great sword.

Days ago I would not have believed him capable of standing there. He looked so frail. Mum's medicine has worked. Yes, I'll say it, almost like magic. Today, Godomor looks like his reputation.

He raised his sword in salute to the mounted Hundred. They were ready to ride out. Gabe was at the head of the double line with Tagnya and Sagora. Nagora, Dangor, and Lars brought up the rear. Counting the pack mules, there were a hundred and sixty animals in all.

A shout of "Long live King Godomor the Terrible!" resonated as all the warriors returned Godomor's salute with raised weapons.

Guards on the wall cranked open the huge-timbered doors. The enemy skulls that covered them glistened with rain.

Ahead of them, the heads of Rhysonnger and Vorpinger in the middle of the road would be framed by two ladder poles and their rungs. Would Rhysonnger survive being splashed with mud from the horses and mules that would ride past him today?

Gabe called, waved the signal, and the column advanced.

Godomor turned into the wind to watch their departure.

Despite the small trenches that had been dug to draw water away from each side of Rhysonnger's head, a mud-splattered, up-turned face spit dirt from its mouth and snorted muck from its nose, all the while gasping and coughing for air.

As soon as they had passed the ladder, Nagora stopped and turned Storm to face Godomor. Lars and Dangor did likewise. They waved to him. Godomor held the crossguard of his great sword to his heart, and then moved it to his shield hand so he could give them the dragon chord salute. Nagora splayed the fingers of her right hand over her heart and raised it.

*Ohtawimaw.* Father.

Before they turned to rejoin the column, Nagora cast a final glance at Rhysonnger.

How long will you survive?

To the left of the gates, a lean-to rested against the wall. Four guards were on duty keeping watch on the counselor and candlestick maker huddled under the tarp.

Nagora looked up at Godomor as she turned to leave. She caught his smile. She reached under her cape, found her dragon's tear amulet and held it tight. She kneed Storm.

Dragon, Edana is on her way.

Dear Reader,

Thank you for reading *BRANDED*. For the benefit of future readers and to help me as an author, you would truly warm my heart by leaving an honest review at:

www.hnhenry.com/testimonials

OR wherever you purchased this copy of *BRANDED*.

Sincerely,

H. N. Henry

P.S.: Here's a **SPECIAL OFFER** for you:

Get the first chapter of *BETRAYED* for **FREE**:

Find out how on the next page.

## First Chapter for FREE

*A dragon rules Nagora's future.*
*Her submission is total*
*... no matter the cost.*

Nagora leads a force of a hundred fierce fighters into the Land of the Danu against evil Queen Raganora's force of two thousand. Nagora and her warriors have pledged their lives to free the last dragon and return the crown to its rightful king, Raynhard.

News that Raynhard has for Nagora places a longtime wish within her grasp, and pushes her will to triumph beyond duty's call.

But Nagora's bloody acts of sworn vengeance against the witch, Hag, brand her as a rogue warrior in the mind of her king. He fears she will jeopardize the campaign and bans Nagora from the raid to free the dragon.

Even if her own life and the future of all the people in the land hang in the balance, Nagora will not ignore her dragon's plea, nor shirk from making her only wish come true.

Will lone-wolf warrior Nagora prevail? To find out... Come. Escape with Nagora into her dragon's world.

To learn more about the other books in this series, visit the author at: www.hnhenry.com

**BETRAYED** *The Dragon's Game*

Book III

H.N.Henry

ISBN 978-0-9958367-8-5

9 780995 836785

Go to the link below to get the FREE first chapter of
*BETRAYED* Book III of *The Dragon's Game*:

https://www.hnhenry.com/betrayedchapteronefree

## ABOUT THE AUTHOR

Other than writing, his passions include kayaking, baking bread, and trying to learn how to play guitar. He shares the profits of his work with a local community cause, *Point de Rue.* They help homeless people on the streets find meaning and passion in their lives. Learn more about it here: http://www.pointderue.com/point_de_rue.html

To learn more about the author and the other books in the series, please visit: http://www.hnhenry.com.

✝

Titles in **THE DRAGON'S GAME** series:

**BANISHED BOOK I**

**BRANDED BOOK II**

**BETRAYED BOOK III**

**BRED BOOK IV**

**BLAMED BOOK V**

H. N. Henry

## ACKNOWLEDGMENTS

*The Dragon's Game* books wouldn't have come about without the generous and invaluable support of these people throughout the creative process.

From the beginning, Staecy-Lee, my editor, gave my manuscripts tough, honest critiques. Her hard questions made me see my stories with fresh eyes for the benefit of my readers.

Randi, my proofreader, closely read the final formatted-for-publication texts, finding inconsistencies in details, descriptions needing clarification, and grammatical errors my own eyes could no longer see.

Staecy and Randi, avid readers of this genre, also offered truly valuable and insightful comments that have made me a better writer. Learning from them has been a pleasure and a privilege.

My passionate beta readers of the first original brick, in first name a-b-c order, Ann, Daniela, Danielle, Maria, Marie-Josée, Randi, and Staecy-Lee generously delivered invaluable feedback and constructive criticism that helped spawn *BANISHED*, Book I, and from the volume they read, give birth to Books II and III of the series. I am forever in their debt for their support and encouragement.

I am grateful to the stained glass window artist, Guido Nincheri (1885-1973), who over ten years (1924-1934) created the beautiful windows in the Cathedral of the Assumption in Trois-Rivières, QC, Canada. From the photographs of those windows that I took on February 27, 2006, I was able to digitally manipulate images from two of the panels to create the unique dragons that appear on the covers of the first edition of my books, a humble homage to Nincheri's masterful work.

Though not referenced as Cree in the context of my stories, I have used Cree, in Roman orthography form, for the chapter titles and chapter numbers throughout the books in the series. More importantly, it is the " ... strange yet familiar language ... " Nagora, the main character, a.k.a. *Ka Peyakot Mahihkan*—Cree for *Lone Wolf*, hears in her mind and eventually uses to communicate with her dragon and other characters. At those times, when used, Cree is referred to as the *Language of the People*, in reference to the *First People* of *The Land* where my story is set.

The *Language of the People*, or "dragonspeak" as some readers of The Dragon's Game books call it, in a way, reflects the status of the Cree language in our land today. Though Cree is the most widely spoken Native language still spoken in Canada, it has yet to be recognized as one of this country's official languages. Similarly, in the fictional setting of *The Dragon's Game* books, the *Language of the People* is now only spoken by a few in a divided and renamed land where two different languages (those of the invading Outlanders) have become dominant in use.

To the Online Cree Dictionary Team: *Kinanâskomitin. Thank you*, I am grateful to you for making this resource available to all. It has been indispensible in helping me lend realism to that second language in my stories. I hope my readers will have as much pleasure as I do in discovering the living Cree language.

In the end, what appears on the pages of my books is mine, and I take full responsibility for any errors that show up in the final versions.

www.ingramcontent.com/pod-product-compliance
Lightning Source LLC
Chambersburg PA
CBHW030645120726
47905CB00001B/64